'Did

Alice's forehead creased. 'I'm not sure.'

She took another turning and suddenly they were back in the Main Hall again, its oversized Christmas tree looming over the staircase. From beyond the next set of doors she could hear the dying chatter of people at the fundraiser, the last few guests still hanging on in there. But that wasn't the noise that had caught Liam's attention.

The sound rang out again, and this time there was no doubt in Liam's mind about what he was hearing. He knew the sound of a baby crying well enough. From the age of ten upwards it had seemed every foster home he'd gone to had had a new baby—one he'd been expected to help look after.

'Did someone bring their baby with them tonight?'

Except he couldn't see anyone nearby, and the cry had sounded very close.

As if it was in the room with them.

'I don't think...' Alice trailed off as the baby cried again. Then she stepped closer to the tree, taking slow, cautious steps in her long, shimmering dress, as if trying not to spook a wild animal.

Liam followed, instinctively staying quiet.

The crying was constant now, and there was no denying where it was coming from.

Alice hitched up her dress and knelt down on the flagstones, reaching under the spread of the pine needles, dislodging a couple of ornaments as she did so. Then she pulled out a basket—not a bassinet or anything, Liam realised. Just a wicker basket...the sort someone might use to store magazines or whatever.

A wicker basket with a baby lying in it.

NEWBORN UNDER THE CHRISTMAS TREE

BY
SOPHIE PEMBROKE

All rights reserved including the right of reproduction in whole or in part in any form. This edition is published by arrangement with Harlequin Books S.A.

This is a work of fiction. Names, characters, places, locations and incidents are purely fictional and bear no relationship to any real life individuals, living or dead, or to any actual places, business establishments, locations, events or incidents. Any resemblance is entirely coincidental.

This book is sold subject to the condition that it shall not, by way of trade or otherwise, be lent, resold, hired out or otherwise circulated without the prior consent of the publisher in any form of binding or cover other than that in which it is published and without a similar condition including this condition being imposed on the subsequent purchaser.

® and ™ are trademarks owned and used by the trademark owner and/or its licensee. Trademarks marked with ® are registered with the United Kingdom Patent Office and/or the Office for Harmonisation in the Internal Market and in other countries.

First Published in Great Britain 2017
By Mills & Boon, an imprint of HarperCollins*Publishers*
1 London Bridge Street, London, SE1 9GF

© 2017 Sophie Pembroke

ISBN: 978-0-263-92343-8

23-1117

Our policy is to use papers that are natural, renewable and recyclable products and made from wood grown in sustainable forests. The logging and manufacturing processes conform to the legal environmental regulations of the country of origin.

Printed and bound in Spain
by CPI, Barcelona

Sophie Pembroke has been reading and writing romance ever since she read her first Mills & Boon at university, so getting to write them for a living is a dream come true! Sophie lives in a little Hertfordshire market town in the UK, with her scientist husband and her incredibly imaginative six-year-old daughter. She writes stories about friends, family and falling in love—usually while drinking too much tea and eating homemade cakes. She also keeps a blog at www.sophiepembroke.com.

For Auntie Judy

CHAPTER ONE

LIAM JENKINS SQUINTED against the low winter sun as he looked up at Thornwood Castle in the distance and tried to imagine it as home.

He failed.

The dark grey of the stone walls, the rise and fall of the crenellations, the brooding shadow it set over the English countryside…none of them were exactly friendly. When he'd dared to dream about the idea of home over the years, he'd pictured himself somewhere warm and bright and welcoming. Somewhere near the beach and rolling surf of his country of birth, Australia. A house he'd designed and built himself, one that was purely his, with no bad memories attached.

Instead, he had a centuries-old British castle full of other people's history and furniture and baggage.

And it was starting to rain.

With a deep sigh, Liam leant back against his hire car and ignored the icy droplets dripping past his collar. Instead he wondered, not for the first time, what on earth his great-aunt Rose had been thinking. He hadn't seen her at all in the fifteen years before her death, and before their disastrous meeting in London he'd only ever visited Thornwood once. Two encounters in twenty-five years didn't make them family, not really. As far as he was concerned, she was just another in a long line of relatives who didn't have the time or the space in their lives or homes for him.

Even that first time he'd visited her, he'd known instantly that Thornwood Castle would never be where he belonged. Thornwood, with its buttresses and echoing stone walls, lined with rusting suits of armour, was a world away from the small home he'd lived in with his mother on the Gold Coast. Possibly a few hundred years away too. As a ten-year-old orphan, still grieving for the mother he'd thought was invincible until she wasn't, the prospect of staying at Thornwood had been terrifying. And that was before he'd even met Great-Aunt Rose in all her intimidating glory.

Thinking of it now, he shivered, remembering the chill of her presence. The way she'd loomed over him, steel-grey hair fixed in place, her dark blue eyes too like his for it to be a coincidence. He had the family eyes—no one had ever truly doubted whose son he was. Even if they didn't want to acknowledge the fact in public.

Liam shook off the memories and slipped back behind the steering wheel of his hire car.

Thornwood was his—a bequest he'd never expected, or wanted. The very idea of it filled him with a heavy apprehension. Thornwood Castle came with more than just history—it came with a legacy. An acceptance into a society that had cast him out before he was even born. People said that the class wars were over, that nobody cared about legitimacy or status of birth any more. Maybe that was true in some places, but Liam knew that those prejudices were still alive and well in Thornwood.

Or they had been when Rose was alive. Now she was gone…

Could Thornwood be a home? All he remembered of it

was cold, unwelcoming halls and the obvious disapproval of his great-aunt's butler as he'd met him at the door.

But then there was the letter. The spidery, wavering handwriting on thick creamy paper that had come with the lawyer who'd explained the bequest. The letter from Rose, written just days before she'd died, asking him to make Thornwood Castle his home, at last. To finally take on the family legacy.

You may find it rather different than you recall…

That was what she'd written. But from this distance it looked exactly like his memories of the place. Grey, forbidding, unwelcoming.

Liam was pretty sure that wasn't what home was supposed to look like.

Although, in fairness, he could be wrong. He could barely remember having a real home at all. Since his mother died, he'd ricocheted among his reluctant relatives—first his mother's, out in Australia, then later a brief trip over to the UK to be rejected by his long departed father's odd, unknown family—and foster care, never finding anywhere to settle for long. And since he'd been out in the world on his own he'd been far too busy building the life he'd craved for himself—one based on his own merits, not who he was related to—to worry about building that home of his own he'd dreamt of as a child.

He had the success he'd wanted. No one in his world knew him as the bastard son of the heir to an earldom, or even as Marie's poor little orphaned boy. These days he was known as his own man—a renowned and respected architect, owner of his own company, with turnover doubling every year. He was his own success story.

Maybe he could bring some of that success to Thornwood.

That was the plan, at least. The time for old-fashioned stately homes was over; nobody needed that much space any more. But that didn't mean he couldn't make Thornwood work for him. Tourists still had a fascination with the old British aristocracy—Liam's ex-girlfriend had watched enough period dramas for Liam to be sure of that. So if Thornwood was his it had to earn its keep—just like any other building he'd ever designed or renovated. Thornwood just had more potential than a lot of them.

And he couldn't help but smile out into the rain, just a little, at the thought of Great-Aunt Rose's face watching from above—or below, probably—seeing Thornwood turned into the sort of aristocratic theme park she'd always hated. He might not have known Rose well, but she'd made her feelings about the hoi polloi roaming around her ancestral grounds *very* clear. As clear as the fact she included him in that number, whoever his father was.

She'd hate everything he had planned. And that was pretty much reason enough to do it. Call it closure, maybe. Finally taking over the world that had rejected him as a child.

Then he could move on, find his *own* home instead of one that had been left to him because there was no one else. Preferably somewhere it didn't rain so damn much.

Liam stared up once more at the shadows of the crenellations in the grey and hazy light, the narrow windows and the aged stonework, and knew that he *would* stay, just as Rose had asked. But only long enough to close that chapter of his life for ever. To finally slam the door on the family who'd never wanted him.

Then he could return to his real life.

Liam started up the engine of the hire car again and, checking his mirrors, pulled back onto the road to drive the last half a mile up the long, winding driveway to the castle itself, smiling out through the windscreen at the rain as it started to fall in sheets.

He was nearly home, for now.

Alice Walters stared at the scene in front of her with dismay. 'What happened?' she asked as a couple of holly berries floated past on a stream that definitely didn't belong in the main hall of Thornwood Castle.

'Penelope was filling vases with water to add some of the greenery we collected from the woods,' Heather explained, arms folded tight across her chest. The frown that seemed to have taken up permanent residence on her forehead since Rose died looked even deeper than usual. 'Apparently she got distracted.'

'And forgot to turn off the tap.' It wasn't the first time that Penelope had got distracted. Alice supposed she should be used to it by now. 'Where's Danielle?'

'No idea,' Heather said, the words clipped. 'You know, for an assistant she doesn't seem to be very much help.'

Alice sighed. She'd noticed the same thing recently too. When she'd first hired the teenager to give her a hand with the admin and such at Thornwood, mostly to help her earn a part-time income after her mother died, Danielle had seemed bright and happy to be there. But over the last few months she'd barely even bothered showing up. 'Right, well, we'd better get the mops out. He'll be here any minute.'

'Our new lord and master,' Heather said, distaste obvious in her tone. 'I can't wait.'

'He might not be that bad.' Alice headed towards the nearest store cupboard and pulled out a mop and bucket. Given the number of leaks the castle roof had sprung over the last few years, they always tried to keep supplies close at hand. For a once grand house, the place leaked like a sieve and was impossible to keep warm. She wondered if the newest owner knew what he was letting himself in for. 'Rose wouldn't have left him the castle if he was.'

'Wouldn't she?' Heather took the mop from her and attempted to soak up some of the impromptu river, while Alice hunted for more rags and cloths to absorb the worst of it. 'He's the last of the line—illegitimate or not. It wouldn't matter *what* Rose thought about him. She'd leave him the castle because that's what tradition said she had to do. And you know how she felt about tradition—at least you should. You spent enough time arguing with her about it.'

'I did,' Alice said, sighing again. As if an indoor river wasn't bad enough, she had the prospect of spending her morning showing the new owner of Thornwood Castle around the wreck he'd inherited.

Rose might not have always been the easiest woman to get along with, but she'd been pragmatic, in the way that people who'd seen everything the world had to throw at them come and go, and leave them standing, often were. She might not have *liked* the suggestions that Alice put forward about how to keep the castle alive and running, but she'd been willing to grit her teeth and bear it, if it meant that her home, her family estate, would survive to be useful to another generation, as something more than a historical show-and-tell. More than anything, Alice was sure, Rose just hadn't wanted to be the one to let it go.

But what about her great-nephew? He was the unknown quantity. Would he care enough about Thornwood to work with them to keep it going? Or would he sell it to the first Russian oligarch who offered him seven figures for it?

Alice supposed she'd find out soon enough.

Not that it mattered to her. Not really. There was always work for a woman who could be organised, inventive, effective and productive—and Alice made sure that she was all those things. Rose had written her a glowing reference before she died, just in case she needed it. Alice would have no problem finding a new job—a new project to dive into and find a way to make it work. And it was getting time to move on—she'd already been at Thorn-wood longer than she'd planned. Normally she'd be look-ing forward to it. Except…

'Alice?' Penelope stuck her head around the door, her eyes huge and wide in her thin, pale face. Sixteen and al-ready so disillusioned by life, Penelope—and all the other girls and women like her—was the only reason Alice was reluctant to leave Thornwood. The castle might not be her home, but it was the only place some of the women she helped had—and it was the best shot Alice had at doing something that mattered. Sure, she could get a job organ-ising someone's office, or arranging meetings and sched-uling flights. But here at Thornwood she was making a difference. And that counted for a lot.

'What is it, Penelope?' Alice asked when the girl didn't say anything further.

Slipping into the hall, Penelope wrapped her oversized grey cardigan around herself, her arms crossing over her middle. 'There's a car just pulled up. A big black four-by-four.' Her eyes slid away from Alice's as she spoke.

Alice and Heather exchanged a quick glance.

'That'll be him, then,' Heather said with a nod. 'Penel-ope, grab those cloths from Alice and do your best to mop up this mess, yeah? God knows where Danielle has got to.'

Penelope did as she was told, just like she always did—without question, without complaint, without a word. One day, Alice hoped that she might just look up and say, 'No.' One day.

Hopefully not today, though, as they really did need to clear up the mini flood.

Alice wiped her damp hands on her jeans. 'Right then. I'd better…' She flapped a hand towards the entrance hall.

Heather nodded. 'You go. Go meet the beast.'

Alice rolled her eyes. 'He might be lovely!'

'You keep telling yourself that,' Heather said, turning away to help Penelope with the remaining puddles. 'Just because I've never met a man yet who was, doesn't mean that this Liam bloke might not be the one who broke the mould.'

'Exactly,' Alice said, hoping she sounded more certain than she felt. 'And, at the very least, we have to give him a chance.'

She just hoped that he gave her—and Heather, and Penelope, and all the others—a chance too.

Grabbing his bag from the back seat, Liam pressed the button to lock the car and turned to face Thornwood Castle in the flesh for the first time in twenty-five years.

'Yeah, still imposing as all hell,' he murmured, eyeing the arrow slits.

As far as he'd been able to tell from the notes his assistant had put together on the castle, it had never really been built for battle. In fact, it was constructed about two hundred years too late for the medieval sieges and warfare it looked like it was built to withstand. It was more or less a folly—one of those weird English quirks of history. Some ancestor of his—by blood if not name or marriage—had got it into his head that he wanted to live in a medieval castle, even if it was the seventeen-hundreds. So he'd designed one and had it built. And then that castle had been passed down through generations of family members until it reached him, in the twenty-first century, when all those arrow slits and murder holes were even less necessary than ever.

Well, hopefully. He hadn't been back to Britain in a couple of years. Who knew what might have changed…?

Normally, Liam would happily mock the folly as typical aristocratic ridiculous behaviour. But as his assistant, Daisy, had pointed out to him drily as she'd handed him his plane tickets, building follies and vanity projects was basically what he did for a living these days. And he supposed she had a point. How was designing and building a hotel in the shape of a lily out in the Middle East any different to a medieval castle in the seventeen-hundreds?

Except he didn't keep the buildings he designed, or force them on future generations. He did an outstanding job, basked in the praise, got paid and moved on.

Much simpler.

As he jogged up the stone steps to the imposing front door, Liam tried to find that desert warmth again inside himself, and the glow of a good job well done. He was renowned these days, and in great demand as an architect. He'd built structures others couldn't conceive of, ones that every other architect he knew said was impossible.

There was no reason at all that he should still feel this intimidated by a fake English castle.

Straightening his shoulders, he reached out for the door handle—only to have it disappear inwards as the door opened by itself.

No, not by itself.

Liam blinked into the shadows of the entrance hall and made out one, two, three—five women standing there, blinking back at him.

For a moment he wondered if this was his staff—all lining up to meet him, as the new master. Even if he couldn't inherit the title that would have been his father's, if he'd lived long enough, he had the estate now.

Then he realised that the women were all wearing jeans

and woolly jumpers—and that, somehow, inside the castle felt even colder than outside.

'You must be Liam!' the woman holding the door said, beaming. 'I mean, Mr Howlett.'

'Jenkins,' he corrected her automatically. 'Liam Jenkins. I use my mother's name.' No need to explain that he'd never been offered his father's.

From the colour that flooded her cheeks, the woman knew that. 'Of course. I'm so sorry. Mr *Jenkins*.'

She looked so distraught at the slip-up, Liam shrugged, falling back into his usual pattern of making others feel comfortable. 'Call me Liam.'

'Liam. Right. Thank you.' The pink started to fade, which was a shame. Without it, she looked pale and cautious, her honey-blonde hair made dull by the grey light and shadows of the castle. But for that brief moment she'd looked…alive. Vibrant, in a way Liam hadn't expected to find at Thornwood.

Which still told him nothing about who she was or why she was in his castle. 'And you are…?'

'Oh! I'm Alice Walters. Your great-aunt hired me to, well, to make Thornwood Castle *useful* again.'

'Useful?' Liam frowned. 'It's a medieval castle in the twenty-first century. How *useful* can it really be?' Interesting, he could understand. Profitable, even more so. He'd half expected to find a guided tour in progress when he arrived—all the people who'd been kept out for so long coming to gawk at everything Rose had left behind. Nothing compared to what he had planned for the place. He had so many ideas for what to do to Thornwood—things he knew Great-Aunt Rose never would have even considered—to make the place into a proper tourist attraction. One he didn't have to visit, but still paid him handsomely.

He'd considered all sorts of options since he'd first got the phone call telling him that Thornwood Castle was his.

He just hadn't considered *useful*, beyond his own financial purposes.

'Rose wanted to make sure that the castle fulfilled its traditional role in the community,' Alice said vaguely. 'She hired me to make that happen.'

'Its traditional role?' He was starting to sound like a bad echo. But really, Alice's explanations weren't explaining anything at all.

Perhaps it was time for some non-English bluntness. After all, he was more Aussie than English when it came down to it—whatever Rose's will said.

'Look,' he said, taking care to sound more bored than annoyed, 'I'll make this really easy for you. Just a simple answer to a very simple question. What the hell are you all doing in my home?'

CHAPTER TWO

OKAY, THIS WAS not going as well as she'd hoped it might. Even if she hadn't really hoped all that hard—her experiences were generally even worse than Heather's, after all.

Behind her, she heard Penelope let out a tiny gasp at Liam's words and realised it was time to move this conversation elsewhere, before he upset *all* their girls. He might sound so laid-back he was almost horizontal, but this was his house and he could still throw them all out on a moment's notice if she didn't do something fast.

'Mr Jenkins, how about you come with me into the estate office? I can explain everything there.' Plus there was a kettle. And biscuits. Maybe a nice cup of tea and a sit down would make them all friends.

'Works for me,' he said with a shrug.

She led him the long way round—partly to avoid any remaining flooding in the great hall, and partly to show off some of the parts of Thornwood that *weren't* underwater.

'Has it been many years since you were last at Thornwood?' she asked politely as they skirted around the edges of the library, avoiding the combination of mismatched tables pushed together in the middle of the room with abandoned wool and knitting needles strewn across them. Everyone had dropped what they were doing the moment Liam's car had pulled up. Understandable, given the impact he stood to have on their future. But still, Alice couldn't help but wish they'd paused to tidy up a bit first.

'Twenty-five,' Liam said, raising his eyebrows at a ball of neon orange wool that had rolled off the table and into his path.

Alice swept it up as she passed, and lobbed it back on to the nearest table once he wasn't looking. Really, for an Australian, it seemed he had the imperious English aristocrat thing down pat. The mixture of relaxed disapproval was most disconcerting.

'That's a long time,' she said, knowing it sounded inane. But really, what else was she supposed to say?

Your great-aunt was alone for the last fifteen years of her life, and you couldn't even spare an afternoon to visit?

Sure, he lived on the other side of the world. But Alice had been doing some reading up on Liam Jenkins, ever since she'd got wind of the details of the will, and she was willing to bet he'd been in London often enough over those twenty-five years. Looking at his résumé, he'd built at least a handful of buildings less than two hours' drive away. How hard would it have been to stop in and see a lonely old lady? Or even to check on his inheritance, if he was truly that heartless.

Alice frowned. So why hadn't he? Having met him, she could buy him not being bothered enough about Rose to visit. But he'd called Thornwood Castle his home. But how could it be home if he hadn't been there in two and a half decades? Maybe it was just a slip of the tongue. Or maybe not…

Suddenly, Alice got the feeling she was missing something in this story. It had the ring of the tales she'd heard from some of the women who stopped by the castle sometimes. Stories about slipping on the stairs, or losing their purse with the housekeeping money in it. No more believ-

able than walking into a door and getting a black eye, but
that was the point. Nobody expected those tales to be believed, not here. They didn't need to be. Thornwood was
a safe place.

But maybe Liam didn't know that yet.

Well, if he wanted to make it his home, he'd have to
learn. And hopefully he'd see the value of it, and let her
continue her work.

Otherwise, there were going to be a lot of local women
who didn't have a safe place any more.

With that dismal thought, they reached the estate office.
Alice reached past the suit of armour she'd named Rusty
and opened the door. 'Come on in.'

Inside, the office was as tidy as it ever got. Which, given
that it was essentially a store cupboard with a desk shoe-
horned in and covered in a mass of paperwork and Post-it
notes, wasn't very. Thornwood had plenty of rooms—far
more than one person could ever need. But when Alice had
arrived at the castle three years before, she'd known that
all those public spaces could be put to better use. Besides,
they were all far too big—echoing and full of draughts. At
least here in her little cupboard she was cosy. And hardly
anyone ever came looking for her there.

'Have a seat.' She motioned to the rickety wooden dining chair on the near side of the desk, and squeezed past
the filing cabinet to flip on the kettle. She didn't need to
look back to know he was staring dubiously at the seat—
she'd done the same. Rose had said it dated back over a
hundred years and hadn't collapsed yet. Alice thought it
might just be biding its time.

Maybe it had been waiting for Liam Jenkins…

She turned back but the chair was still standing, even
under Liam's weight. Which…well, he was a big man.
Lots of muscle. Objectively, she supposed he could even

be called well built, which was more than she'd have said for the chair before this point.

Maybe the chair was as scared of him as she was…

No. That was crazy—and not just because chairs didn't have emotions. She wasn't scared of Liam—he was too laconic to be scared of. She was…*apprehensive*, that was the word. And, even then, it was only because he could end everything that she'd built here in one fell swoop. It wasn't *personal*. He had no power to hurt her, not like other men had. He was her boss, and if he fired her she'd be fine and free to pursue other worthwhile projects elsewhere.

This wasn't like before. She had to remember that, even when he was scowling at her.

She wasn't that Alice any more, and she never would be again. That much she knew for sure. Life had changed her—not always for the better, but for ever.

'So,' Liam said as they waited for her ancient kettle to brew, 'what's the conversation we need to have that you couldn't have in front of all those women out there?'

'Not couldn't,' she corrected him. 'Chose not to.'

'Right.' He shrugged, obviously not seeing the difference. Alice sighed. Perhaps that was where she needed to start.

'Those women—they're part of the work I've been doing here,' she said, swilling hot water around the teapot to warm it. She might not have space for much in her utility cupboard office, but there was a sink, a kettle and a teapot with cups and saucers. Besides her laptop, there really wasn't much else that she needed.

'Yeah, your work. Making Thornwood *useful*, wasn't it?'

Did he really have to put such emphasis on the word? He made her sound like a small child trying to earn money for chores. 'How much do you know about the history of the English aristocracy, Mr Jenkins?'

'Not as much as you, I'd wager.' He watched her, curiosity in his gaze, as she measured out the tea leaves and added the boiling water, before leaving the tea to steep. 'I suppose you're going to educate me? Starting with the national drink?'

'I'm no expert myself,' Alice assured him. She placed the pretty floral cups and saucers on the tray beside the pot and the small milk jug, then swivelled round to place the whole thing on the desk. Settling into her own desk chair, she rested her forearms on the wood of the desk and eyed him over the steam drifting up from the spout of the teapot. 'But I know what that history meant to your great-aunt.'

'It meant she left me this place, for a start.'

'That's right.' However wrong a decision that might have been. Rose had been full of misgivings, Alice knew, about leaving Thornwood to someone she knew so little, who had shown no interest at all in his heritage or legacy before. But, when it came down to it, Liam Jenkins was the only family she had left. So blood had trumped legitimacy, and everything else that went with it. 'But I want to be sure you understand exactly the expectations that she was leaving with that. Thornwood is more than just a pile of stones and rusty armour, you know.'

'I know that,' Liam shot back, too fast to sound at all casual. 'It's home, right? My family pile, so to speak.'

There was that word again. Home. Obviously that mattered to him and, even if she never knew why, perhaps Alice could use it. Could appeal to his decency—didn't everyone deserve a home? Even those women out there whom he'd never met, who'd left hideously coloured wool all over the place and half flooded his castle?

It could work. Maybe.

Alice took a deep breath. She was going to have to try.

* * *

Liam eyed Alice over the desk and felt a small shiver of nerves at the back of his neck as she studied him back, then gave a tiny nod. She'd made a decision about something, that much was clear. He only wished he had the faintest clue what.

Alice, he was starting to realise, had plans for Thornwood—plans that were almost certainly at odds with his own. Which was why it was just as well *he* was the one who held the deeds to the castle, not her.

Maybe she was some sort of gold-digger. One who'd had his great-aunt wrapped around her little finger, taking advantage of her money and kindness—if the old bat really had any of either at the end—and expected to inherit. She must be furious to be done out of Thornwood, if that was the case. Good. He might not have deserved to inherit the place but, if she really was a gold-digger, she deserved it a thousand times less. And what was the deal with all those big-eyed women in cable knits?

'Rose believed, very strongly, that the privilege of owning a place like Thornwood, and the status in society that it conveyed, came with a very definite level of responsibility too,' Alice said, sounding so earnest that Liam almost put aside his gold-digger theory immediately. But only almost. After all, if she was good at it, of course she'd sound authentic. And, from what he remembered of Great-Aunt Rose, Alice would have had to be *very* good to fool her.

'A responsibility to the estate?' he guessed. Thornwood had been Rose's life—keeping it going would have been her highest priority. God, she must have shuddered as she'd signed the documents that meant it would come into his hands. But Alice's expression told him she meant more than that. So he kept guessing. 'Is this about the title? Or that seat in the House of Lords thing? Because I didn't inherit the title.' Even Rose wouldn't go so far as to convey that kind of status on the illegitimate son of her nephew. 'And besides, I heard that Britain finally moved with the times and stopped giving people power just because of who their parents were. Well, apart from that whole monarchy thing.'

Alice shook her head. 'It's not anything to do with the title, not really. Except that...' She sighed, as if the impossibility of making him understand her quaint British ways was beginning to dawn on her. 'In the past, the lord of the manor—or lady, in Rose's case—was responsible for the people who lived on their estate.'

'You mean feudalism,' Liam said with distaste. 'Just another word for slavery, really.' Just because he wasn't British didn't mean he wasn't educated. She looked slightly surprised to realise that.

'No! Not feudalism—at least, not for the last several hundred years. No, I just meant...the people who live on the estate have, traditionally, worked there too—usually as farmers. The local village is owned by the estate too, so it sets all the rents and has an obligation to take care of the tenants. They're more...extended family than just renters, if you see what I mean.'

'Yeah, I guess so.' It wasn't something he'd thought of before. He'd been so focused on the memory of Thornwood Castle's imposing walls, and the chilly reception the place had offered him, that he hadn't thought beyond the castle itself. He'd assumed that it would come with some gardens or whatever, but not a whole *village*. *That* was considerably more 'home' than Liam had bargained for, even if he didn't plan to stay. And how would they take the news that Thornwood Castle was about to become the county's biggest tourist attraction? He'd just have to spin it as good news—get them excited about the new jobs and tourist income before they realised how much disruption it would cause, or started getting nostalgic about the old days. Same as any other big project, really.

'So, what? They need me to open a village fete or something?' He'd seen the *Downton Abbey* Christmas special with his ex-girlfriend. That was practically a British documentary, right?

'Not exactly.' Alice looked uncomfortable but she pushed on regardless. Liam supposed he had to admire her determination to get her point across, whatever that point turned out to be. 'Times have changed around here. A lot of the farmland had to be sold off, and the village itself is pretty much autonomous these days. And Rose...well, as she got older, she couldn't get out and about so much. But she still wanted Thornwood Castle to be relevant. To be useful.'

There was that word again. 'And so she hired you. To do what, exactly?'

'To fundraise for and organise events that make the castle available to local women in need.' The words came out in a rush, and Liam blinked as he processed them over again, to make sure he'd heard her right.

'Like a refuge?' Because that was basically the last thing he'd expect from Great-Aunt Rose. After all, she hadn't even offered *him* a refuge when he'd needed one and he, whether she liked it or not, was her own flesh and blood.

Maybe Rose had changed over the years, but he doubted it. So what was he missing here? He guessed if anyone knew, it would be Alice. Which meant he needed to keep asking questions.

'Sort of,' she said, waggling her head from side to side. 'A lot of the girls and women we help, they don't feel they can spend a lot of time at home. So they come here instead.'

'They're abused?' Liam met her gaze head-on, looking for the truth behind her words. 'Then why don't you help them get out? Not just set them up with some knitting needles to make cardigans in some draughty castle?' He knew abuse; he'd seen it first-hand at some of the foster homes he'd been sent to. Suffered it too—both there and at home, with his mother's boyfriends.

But, more than that, he'd seen what it had done to *her*. It had broken his mother's spirit, if not her body. Somehow, he knew that it was the emotional and physical abuse that she'd suffered, the rejections and the hate, that had convinced her it wasn't worth fighting for life any longer. Medicine might not be able to prove it yet, but he knew in his bones that if she'd not felt so worthless she could have beaten the cancer that finally took her life when he was ten.

He could see it now—the fear behind the eyes of the women who'd met him at the door. He'd assumed it was just the uncertainty that came with his arrival, but he should have known better. Should have recognised what he saw. Had he been away from that world, safe in the land of money and prestige, for so long that he'd forgotten what fear looked like?

'We don't... Okay, yes, sometimes we hold classes and today's was knitting. But they don't knit their own cardigans.' She frowned. 'At least, not as far as I know. And that's not the point, anyway. You asked why we don't get them out of abusive situations. We do, if they're ready to go. We give them the support they need to make that decision, and put them in touch with the charities that can do it properly. But for some of them...' Alice sighed. 'The women and girls who come here, they all have their own stories, their own lives, their own individual situations. Some aren't abused; they just need something else in their lives. Some are still torn about what to do for the best—

for their kids, for themselves. And it's easy for us to say, "You need to get out, now." But sometimes it takes them a while to see that.'

'So you just set up craft classes to distract them from all the things that are wrong in their lives?' Fat lot of good that would do anyone.

Alice glared at him. 'So we provide educational opportunities—computer classes, job interview training, talks from the local college about what courses are available, that sort of thing. We help rewrite CVs, we run food banks for those local families struggling to make ends meet, or clothes swaps and donations to provide school uniforms or interview clothes, we help decipher benefits claims forms, we hold meditation groups, exercise classes, cooking classes, breastfeeding workshops for new mums, help with childcare…everything we can think of that will make everyday life easier or provide new opportunities for the women and families of this village. And if they need to get out of a situation, we help them do that too. And we do it all on donations, persuading people to volunteer their time, and by making do with what we have. So no, it's not just knitting.'

Her eyes were blazing now, her cheeks red and her pale hair had frizzed a little in the steam from the tea—or her anger. And Liam realised, with a sudden, sinking certainty, that Alice Walters wasn't a gold-digger. She was something much worse—for him, at least.

Alice Walters was a do-gooder. A determined, stubborn, dedicated doer of good. And while he might admire that kind of zeal in someone else, right now he was mentally cursing it. Not because he didn't want to help all those women—he did. That was the problem.

Because his vision for Thornwood Castle, his big middle finger to the society and family that had rejected him, sure as hell didn't include groups of troubled women and kids tramping around his personal space, while Alice harangued him to give more, help more, do more. He could see it now—a supplier meeting interrupted by a crying woman, or a visionary design lost to some child's scribbles.

They couldn't stay, that much was obvious. But he couldn't just throw them out either. It wasn't that she'd got to him or anything, with her speeches about safe places and refuge and need. But if Thornwood had become essential to the local community, he needed to convince the local community—and, more importantly, Alice—that their needs would be better served elsewhere, so he could get on with his own plans.

That, he suspected, might take time. Well, time he had—Thornwood had stood for this long waiting for him; it would last a little longer while he sorted all this out. The castle would be his, and only his, eventually. Liam Jenkins was renowned in business for always getting what he wanted—no matter how long it took.

But for now the only thing to do was to gauge exactly what he was up against. And whether he could buy his way out of it.

Reaching for a biscuit for the road, he said, 'You're right. I had no idea of the scope of your work here. Why don't you show me round the place while you tell me more about the work you do and the fundraising you've got going on?'

At least the surprise on her face was a small consolation for the work he had ahead of him.

CHAPTER THREE

THE MAN WAS *impossible* to read. Alice had always heard that Australians were open and honest, friendly but blunt. Clearly Liam had more of his father's side in him than his upbringing would suggest, because he was giving *nothing* away. Every relaxed shrug or bland stare hid his thoughts all too effectively.

He'd nodded politely as she'd shown him around the bedrooms, barely even acknowledging the King's room, where past monarchs had slept. She supposed that the history of the crown might not mean that much to him, but she'd expected at least a flicker of appreciation at the giant four-poster bed, or even just the place Thornwood held in the heart of the nation. Still, nothing.

'And do the women ever stay over here?' he asked as she shut another bedroom door.

'Sometimes,' Alice admitted. 'Not often, because even with this many bedrooms if we started setting up some sort of bed and breakfast we'd be swamped in days. We simply don't have the resources—and, to be honest, a lot of the bedrooms aren't really in a suitable condition for guests.'

'No beds?'

'No heating. Or insulation. Or glass in the windows, in some cases.' She shivered. 'Thornwood in winter is not a warm place.'

'Hence the cardigans.' What *was* his obsession with knitwear? Alice wondered, as Liam strode off down the hallway. He had a good stride, she couldn't help but notice. Strong, muscled legs under his trousers, a long step and a purposeful gait. He looked like a man who was there to get a job done.

Alice just wished she had some idea what the job at hand was, for him. Because *obviously* he had plans. A man like Liam Jenkins didn't just show up at Thornwood Castle with a vague dream of medieval re-enactments or something.

'So, which room is yours?' Liam called back, and Alice scurried to catch him up.

'Um, I have a box room on the ground floor.' Near the boiler, and close to the kitchens. It was the warmest place in the castle, and Alice loved it—even if it wasn't all that much bigger than her office. Small spaces were comforting. There was no space for anything—or anyone—to hide, there.

'Rose had the master suite, along here, though,' she added, taking a left turn in the corridor and leading him to a large oak door. 'We've cleared it out already, and it's made up fresh if you'd like to use it?' She hoped so. Rose's suite was one of the few bedrooms in a suitable condition for long-term accommodation. If he said no, Alice had a feeling it would somehow become her job to clear out and do up another room to suit him.

Somehow, a lot of things around Thornwood became Alice's job, mostly just because it was quicker and easier to take care of things herself than expect anyone else to do it.

Actually, not just around Thornwood. Alice's rule for living number two was: don't expect anyone to do anything for you. She figured if they did it was a pleasant surprise. And at least she was never disappointed when they inevitably didn't.

Technically, Rose had hired her as a fundraiser—to raise money to help keep Thornwood running, without having to open it up for tours. Alice had convinced her that the best way to keep the house open, useful and sort of private was to use it to help the local residents. Rose's sense of duty had been tickled, and now here they were. Alice raised money—through begging phone calls to donors, or fundraising activities on site—but she also organised the seminars and classes they held, as well as took care of the women. Her salary—small as it was—was paid from the money she raised, so she rarely took more than her room and board, and money for essentials. She was all too aware of the other uses that money could be put to.

Everyone else on site was a volunteer—except for Maud, the cook-slash-housekeeper, who'd been in Rose's service for decades. Even Heather, who practically ran the place when Alice was busy, did it for nothing. And she had quickly claimed responsibility for taking care of the women who came to them in real trouble, which Alice appreciated. They'd managed to put together a stockpile in the pantry, full of all the essentials women, children and babies might need—especially if they couldn't go home again. Some just needed enough food to see them through until payday. Others needed clothes, toiletries, nappies, a pay-as-you-go phone with a number no one had—and a way out. Alice was proud that their work meant they could help all of them—or at least get them to the best place for them to find real long-term help. She'd built up great connections with refuges and charities nationwide, and the work they did at Thornwood was well respected. Women came to them now from across the county, not just the local villages.

She just hoped Liam's sense of duty was as strong as his great-aunt's.

Opening the door to the suite of rooms, she let Liam walk in first, ignoring the slight pang in her chest she always felt when she saw Rose's space empty.

Alice couldn't honestly say that she and Rose had been friends, but she had certainly developed a great deal of respect for the old woman in the time she'd been working at Thornwood. Rose's beliefs and opinions might have been from a bygone age in lots of ways, but when it came down to the essentials she was practical and—to Alice's great surprise—compassionate.

Rose could have sold Thornwood for millions twice over, or she could have hired a company to make it into a tourist attraction. But instead she'd hired Alice, and told her to 'make Thornwood useful again'. Not in a large, flashy, lucrative way. In a way that served the community, and filled a gap in society. In a way that helped people— women just like Alice had been four years ago. Desperate.

Leaning against the heavy door, she watched Rose's great-nephew explore the room—running a hand over the antique dresser, sticking his head into the more modern bathroom. Then he crossed to the window and stared out at the gardens beyond.

'What do you think?' Alice asked when he didn't turn back. 'Will it suit?'

'Hmm?' Liam turned back, apparently startled out of his own thoughts. 'Oh, definitely. The space out there will be perfect for—' He cut himself off. 'You meant the rooms. Yeah, they'll be fine. I don't imagine I'll be spending much time in them, anyway.'

Which begged the question—where *was* he planning on spending his time? And doing what? Because he sure as hell hadn't been thinking about the bedroom when he'd been looking out of that window. He'd been making plans—plans he clearly had no intention of sharing with *her*.

And that made Alice very nervous indeed.

'Ready to show me downstairs?' Liam flashed her a smile, as if the last few moments hadn't happened at all.

Alice narrowed her eyes. He was hiding something, that much was clear. But what? And how much harm could it do to everything Alice had built up at Thornwood?

She supposed there was only one way to find out.

She took a deep breath and stretched her face into a bright and happy smile. 'Absolutely.'

Liam followed Alice back down endless, labyrinthine corridors, still thinking about the large expanse of forest he'd seen from Rose's window. It would be perfect for an outdoor pursuits centre. He could see go-karting and paintball, maybe a ropes course. Plenty to keep the kids entertained while the parents took high tea up at the castle, or whatever it was people wanted from a stately home. Regardless, there was plenty of potential there.

Once he'd dealt with the castle's *current* residents, of course.

After one last sharp turn in the corridor, they were suddenly spat out into a wide-open landing, leading to a grand double staircase, which joined halfway down to provide steps wider than he was tall. The dark wooden bannisters had been twined with glossy dark green leaves and bright red berries. Below stood an enormous Christmas tree, already strung with lights and glass baubles, the angel on top almost reaching the very top of the stairs. Liam couldn't imagine how they'd even got it in through the doors.

'Impressive tree,' he said, nodding towards it.

Alice gave him a small, tight smile. 'We like to celebrate life every way we can here. Now, after you?' She gestured towards the stairs.

Liam frowned. The staircase was clearly wide enough for both of them to descend at the same time, yet Alice hung back in a way she hadn't before. She was the one who knew her way around, so she'd led the way for most of the tour. What was different now? Was this some sort of prank?

He took the first step gingerly, relieved when it felt perfectly solid and ordinary under his foot.

Behind him, he heard Alice let out a long breath of relief, and knew that this was just another puzzle he'd need to figure out before he could leave Thornwood.

Safely at the bottom, Liam turned to admire the staircase. It would be a grand welcome for guests, a great way to make them feel they really had bought a piece of the English aristocracy experience. Then he blinked, and realised he wasn't looking at the staircase at all.

He was watching Alice.

She skipped down the stairs easily enough, one hand bouncing along the bannister in between the greenery. The tension he'd heard in her voice when she asked him to go first was gone, and instead she looked…what? Guarded, maybe? As if there was something here she was trying to hide—something more than leaky ceilings and missing windows. Something other than just Thornwood.

Something about *her*.

He frowned as she reached the ground floor and glided across to straighten an ornament on the tree. Why, exactly, had Alice Walters come to Thornwood in the first place? He'd assumed she'd just been an eccentric hire of Rose's, but now he was wondering. Obviously she had to be good at her job, and have great organisational skills, if she was keeping all the courses and sessions running that she claimed—even if her office was a bomb site. And Rose had never had any patience for slackers, so she must be a hard worker. Not to mention good at eliciting donations, to pay for everything.

Those sorts of skills could command a significant wage in the business world—far higher than he could imagine Rose paying her. So what kept her at Thornwood? Was it just the desire to do good—and, if it was, what had instilled that need in her?

Or, and this seemed like more of a possibility than he'd previously considered, was *Alice* one of the women who had needed the safe haven of Thornwood?

For some reason the idea filled him with horror—far more than the usual pity or anger he'd expect at a women being caught in such a situation. The idea of Alice—fired up, determined, intense Alice—being diminished by someone, a man, he assumed… That was unacceptable.

She turned to him, her bright smile firmly back in place and her honey-blonde hair bouncing around her shoulders. Suddenly, she didn't look like a victim to him any longer. She looked like a strong, capable woman—one he needed to negotiate with before he could move on with his plans.

He was here for business, not to save people. Besides, he'd never been any good at that, anyway. He hadn't been able to save his mother, had he? And for every fight he'd got in the middle of, how many of the people he'd protected had just gone back and got beaten up again the next day? Probably most of them.

Better to focus on what he *was* good at—designing buildings and making them a success. *That* he knew how to do—even if Thornwood was a little different to his usual projects.

And Alice was a lot different to his usual challenges.

* * *

Relief settled over Alice as she saw that the river from that morning had been thoroughly mopped up and the main hall was looking its usual impressive self again, ready for its new owner. The Christmas tree appeared perfectly festive, as did the garlands on the banisters. And hopefully Liam hadn't noticed anything odd about her behaviour by the stairs—although, given how observant he seemed about other things, she wouldn't like to place a bet on it. Still, even if he *had* noticed, why would he care? He wasn't likely to worry about it enough to ask questions and find out what her problem was.

People usually didn't, in Alice's experience. No one wanted the second-hand trauma and misery of another person when they were already dealing with their own.

'Right, well, let's start in the library,' she said, forcing a bright smile. Hopefully someone might have even tidied up the knitting stuff by now, since a new session had been due to start ten minutes ago.

The library was one of Alice's favourite spots in the whole castle. The walls were lined with books, as one might expect, but Alice had brought her own touches to the place since she'd arrived, with Rose's blessing. While three walls still boasted shelves laden with dusty, oversized hardback tomes on subjects no one had experienced a need to research in decades, possibly centuries, the fourth wall had been transformed over the last year and a half. The dark wood shelves were now stuffed full of more modern books—self-help classics, career advice books, parenting and childcare publications, not to mention shelf after shelf of fiction. Alice had made sure to collect a good range, mostly from second-hand bookshops on her fundraising travels, so they had romance, detective stories, fantasy and sci-fi, thrillers, as well as a good selection of the classics and award-winners. Something for everybody, Alice liked to think.

Today, now that the knitting class had finished, there was a group huddled around the central tables discussing interview techniques. Alice and Liam hung back at the door rather than interrupt, and listened to the questions the women were posing.

'But what do I say when they ask why I've been out of work for so long?' one woman asked, leaning across the table.

Melanie, the careers adviser Alice had persuaded to come in and run the session for free, leaned back slightly. 'Well, I think the best plan is to be honest. Explain what you've been doing instead.'

'What? Changing nappies and mopping up spit-up?' The woman laughed. 'Why would they care about that?'

'Because everything you do, every day, is what shapes you.' Alice startled as Liam spoke, and the whole room turned towards him. Men at Thornwood were a rarity these days, for obvious reasons. One or two of the women looked a little anxious. Several more looked appreciative—Alice decided not to speculate if that was because of his advice or his appearance.

Liam stepped forward into the room, placing his hands on the back of an empty chair as he spoke. 'Any company worth working for knows that previous experience isn't the most important thing for a potential employee to have.'

'Then why do they all ask for it?' Jess, one of the younger women, asked.

'Oh, they'd like it, sure,' Liam acknowledged. 'But what they really need is someone who can learn. Someone who can walk into an interview and show them that they're bright, they're willing and, most importantly, they're enthusiastic. If you can make them believe that you'll work well with their team, listen and learn what you need to know, then go on to make the most of every opportunity they give you—and benefit their company along the way— then they'd be fools not to hire you.'

'So…you're saying it's all about the right attitude?' Jess said, frowning. 'Not qualifications and stuff?'

'Ninety per cent of the time, yes.' Liam shrugged. 'Yes, there are some roles that require specific qualifications, but they're fewer than you might think. And a lot of companies will train you up and help you get those qualifications, if they like you, and if they believe you'll make the most of the opportunity.'

'Huh.' Jess's frown transformed into a wide smile that lit up her whole face. Alice didn't think she'd ever seen that expression on Jess's face before. She rather suspected that it might be hope.

Suddenly, she felt considerably warmer towards Liam Jenkins. Anyone who could put that expression on the face of someone who'd been through as much as Jess had, well, he had to be worth keeping around.

Melanie thanked Liam for his input, and Alice hoped her feathers weren't too ruffled. It was hard enough finding people willing to give up their free time to run the sessions at Thornwood, especially since she could rarely offer them more than lunch as payment.

'Shall we carry on?' Alice asked, and Liam nodded.

'I hope I didn't overstep my place there,' he said as they made their way down the echoing stone corridor.

Alice gave him a lopsided smile. 'The whole estate is sort of your place,' she pointed out. 'You'd have to step a long way to get over your boundaries.'

From the stunned look on his face, Alice guessed he hadn't thought of it like that before. Maybe Liam was going to find this adjustment as odd as the rest of them.

'Well, when you put it like that…' He shook his head. 'I guess it's still sinking in. I never expected to inherit Thornwood. Not in a million years. The idea that I own all this, that it's all *mine*, as far as you can see from those replica battlements… That's going to take some getting used to.'

'Rose never spoke to you about her will?' Alice asked, surprised.

Liam shrugged. 'I hadn't seen her in fifteen years. And I hadn't been near Thornwood for a decade before that. And when we did meet…let's just say there were other things to discuss.'

What other things? Alice was desperate to know, but the way Liam looked away, his expression closing up, she knew better than to ask. Not yet, anyway. Maybe when she got to know the new lord of the manor a little better she'd feel more confident about such questions.

Maybe she'd understand what it was about him that made her need to know the answers too.

Still, for him to not even know he stood to inherit Thornwood…that was strange. Rose had wanted everything settled in the last year or two of her life—that was one of the reasons she'd hired Alice when she did. Everything had been arranged for months before she died. So why wouldn't she have told him? And even before that…

'But you were her only living relative. You must have known that Thornwood would naturally come to you,' Alice said, knowing she was pushing but unable to stop herself.

'Why?' Liam's voice grew hard. 'She'd never given me anything else I was entitled to, so the idea of her starting with Thornwood was kind of ludicrous.'

Alice stumbled slightly as she processed his words and, fast as a shot, Liam's hand caught her arm, steadying her. 'Sorry,' she gasped, trying not to react to the sudden flare of heat that ran through her at his touch. She was absolutely *not* going to develop anything approaching a crush on this man. That way lay madness, frustration and probably a whole load of embarrassment.

'Uneven floor,' Liam said, peering down at the stone under their feet. 'I'll have to get that fixed before—' He broke off.

'Before?' Alice asked, curious. What exactly did he have planned for Thornwood, anyway? Whatever it was, she got the distinct impression it wouldn't involve knitting groups.

'Before someone hurts themselves more seriously.' Liam dropped his hand from her arm and kept walking.

Alice studied him as she followed, rubbing the spot where he'd held her arm. It was a neat enough cover, but Alice had plenty of experience with dishonest men.

And Liam Jenkins was most definitely hiding something.

'So, where's next?' Liam asked, changing the subject quickly.

'Um…the kitchens?'

'Sounds great.' Liam started walking. He wasn't entirely sure where the kitchens were, but the fantastic scents wafting towards him suggested he was going the right way. And at least if he kept moving Alice would hopefully be distracted enough not to notice his less than smooth cover-up.

Obviously he'd need to explain his plans to her, and everyone else, eventually—making a big splash and putting the English establishment up in arms was part of the reason he was doing it in the first place—the rest, of course, being money. But he wanted to do it in his own time, and in a way that would have maximum impact. Alice gossiping about it to the locals in the village was definitely not that.

He frowned as Alice caught him up and said, 'This way,' as she took a sharp left turn. She didn't seem like the gossipy sort, he had to admit. In fact, she seemed like the sort of woman who could keep others' secrets as well as her own—and, even on an hour or two's acquaintance, Liam was sure she had plenty of those. But then, so did he. And if he wasn't planning on sharing, there was no reason she should.

If he handled this right, Alice wouldn't be around long enough for him to worry about her secrets, anyway.

'Here we are.' Alice stopped in front of a giant wooden door, arched at the top, and reached for the huge iron ring that served as a doorknob. As she turned it and pushed open the door, the wonderful aromas Liam had been enjoying hit him at full strength, along with a heat that was sorely absent from the rest of the castle. Roasting meat and onions and deep savoury smells that made his stomach growl with hunger. He half expected to see a roast pig on a spit over a roaring fire.

But when he looked past Alice, instead of the rustic brick and wood kitchen he was expecting, Liam found a shining modern one, complete with range cooker and a very efficient-looking woman in an apron. In fact, it looked set up to cater for the masses.

'Liam, this is Maud,' Alice said, motioning towards the cook. 'She was Rose's cook and housekeeper for twenty years, and she's very kindly stayed on to help us keep the place up and running. Maud, this is the new owner of Thornwood, Liam Jenkins.'

Maud wiped her hand on her apron before holding it out for him to shake. 'Pleasure, I'm sure.' Something in her tone told him that she wasn't at all sure, actually, but he appreciated the attempt at civility all the same. She turned away again, back to the pot on her hob.

'This is an impressive kitchen,' he said appreciatively. It was always good to get in with the person who was in charge of the food, he'd found.

'It's functional,' Maud said without looking at him. 'But to be honest, I prefer the Old Kitchen.'

'Old Kitchen?' Liam asked. 'I know this place is huge, but how many kitchens does it really need? This one looks like it could cater for pretty much any function you wanted to hold here.'

Alice laughed, the sound high and bright—but nervous, somehow. 'The Old Kitchen is *really* old. Like a period piece. We use it when we do family days, to show the kids how they used to make different food and drinks here in the past. We've done medieval days, Victorian days, all sorts. It's much more atmospheric than using the new kitchen, but this is better for when we have lots of people to feed.'

'Which seems like most of the time,' he observed.

'The Old Kitchen wouldn't be any good for all those fiddly canapés and such you like for your fundraisers, any-way,' Maud grumbled as she placed two plates of food on the counter before them. 'I'm going to be wrapping Parma ham around asparagus for days, I know it, to be ready for next Thursday.'

Beside him, Liam saw Alice wince. 'Next Thursday?'

'I was…going to mention that. We had planned a fund-raiser for next week. It's been in everyone's diaries for months, long before we knew Rose wouldn't be here to host it. We have some great pledges of support already. It would be such a shame to cancel it now…'

The question she wasn't asking hung in the heavily scented air between them. Would the fundraiser still be able to go ahead, now he was in charge?

Liam considered. On the one hand, what was the point?

Things were going to change around here, and he might as well start now. On the other, for his first act as the new owner of Thornwood to be cancelling a fundraiser for local women and children in need… That didn't send a great message.

'Fine. You can have your fundraiser,' he said, and Alice clapped her hands and grinned.

'Fantastic! I just know you'll be a great host. You did bring your dinner jacket, right?'

Wait. What? Liam had a sinking feeling that he'd just signed up for far more than he'd intended to—and that getting Alice Walters out of his castle might not be as easy as he'd hoped.

CHAPTER FOUR

'OKAY, I THINK we need to move that table back across to the other side,' Alice said. The women she'd roped in to help her set up for the fundraiser glared at her. 'Last time, I promise.'

As the table got moved across the ballroom, Alice rubbed her forehead to try to fend off a headache, and ticked off another item on her clipboard. The checklist was almost done, at last. It had been a long few days of preparation—not entirely helped by Liam sticking his nose in every few hours to see exactly what she was doing.

Thornwood Castle's new owner had been in residence for almost a week now, and he was certainly making his presence felt. Alice had hoped, when he'd agreed to let them go ahead with the fundraiser, that it was a sign he was happy for Thornwood to carry on as it always had.

Apparently not.

Over the past week, Liam had shown up to observe various classes, taken lunch with the women and kids in the dining hall, climbed up into the attics to inspect the roof, been observed checking and annotating the castle blueprints, and spent a day exploring the woods on the edge of the estate. The rest of the time he'd spent working in the room he'd claimed as his office, between the library and the kitchens, making phone calls, typing on his lap-

top or just talking to himself as he paced. Reporting back
to Alice on what the new owner was up to had become a
full-time game for the kids who hung around the castle
after school. It was almost as if she had her own team of
spies—even if she didn't have a clue what to do with the
information they brought her.

Worst of all, whenever Alice had asked Liam if she
could assist him at all, he'd just shrugged and smiled and
said, 'Nah. It's all good. Just getting a feel for the place.'

It was making Alice very nervous.

'He's so infuriatingly laid-back,' she'd said to Heather,
after another one of his 'don't mind me' visits to a first
aid class she was giving.

Heather had laughed. 'Have you ever considered that
maybe you're just too tense?'

Alice had glared at her, and gone back to doing her job.
Mostly because she had no idea what else to do.

At least preparing for the fundraiser had given her
something else to focus on, besides whatever plans Liam
was hatching for Thornwood. If this was to be her last
big event at the castle, she wanted to make it a good one.

The guest list was solid, she knew—she had the mayor,
a couple of local councillors, a local celebrity chef and a
duke and duchess from the next county, along with the
usual bunch of lawyers, teachers, doctors and local busi-
nessmen and women. Maud had laid out a great spread,
and Alice had ordered in plenty of champagne so that the
bids in the silent auction should go high enough to make
the evening worthwhile. Spending so much on one event
always made her nervous, but she'd never failed yet to
make back at least four times what she spent in donations
and auction bids. She just had to keep reminding herself
that all the glitz, glamour and fuss were worthwhile.

Even if she did have to wear a stupid, shiny dress with a desperately uncomfortable strapless bra.

'How's it going?' Alice spun at the sound of Liam's voice and found him casually leaning against the giant double doors of the ballroom, his arms folded across that broad chest.

'Fine! All fine,' she said, forcing a wide smile. She glanced around the ballroom. The tables were set up with the best cloths, and her helpers were laying out the silver and glass flatware. There were candles in the candelabras that would illuminate the room, ready to be lit nearer the start time. The floor had been polished, and the string quartet was tuning up in the corner. All she had left to do was set up the stuff for the silent auction, and get herself ready to schmooze and smile for the night.

'Looks good.' Liam nodded, lazily pushing away from the door and crossing the ballroom towards her. 'Want to tell me what I'm expected to do tonight?'

Alice nodded. 'Of course. Um, mostly it's just about chatting to people. You're new, so *everyone* is going to want to talk to you. They're going to want to know your plans for Thornwood, for a start.'

'Are they, indeed? Well, they might be disappointed on that one.'

'Because you don't have any firm plans yet?' Alice said hopefully. If he wasn't set on one course of action, she still had time to sway him towards her point of view.

Liam gave her a wolfish smile. 'Because I never share my plans until they're finalised.'

Damn. 'Well, I'm sure you'll manage. Other than that… it would be great if you could do a welcome toast. Just a "Thanks for coming, it's a great cause, raising money for the work being done here at Thornwood"—that sort of thing.'

'Sure,' Liam said, shrugging. 'What's the name?'

'The name?'

'Your centre, refuge, whatever we're calling it. What's the name? So I can tell people exactly what they're donating to.'

'It... Well, it doesn't really have a name,' Alice admitted. It had never needed one. Word just got around that Thornwood was a safe place. Sometimes they advertised some of their classes at the local doctors' surgeries and schools and such. But other than that...a name would make it official. Permanent. And Alice wasn't ready to commit to that sort of permanence—especially now.

'You should give it a name. People like to know exactly what they're giving to.' Liam checked his watch. 'And now I guess I'd better go put that monkey suit on.'

Alice's eyes widened as she clocked the time. How had it got so late? 'And I'd better go get changed.' And check in on Maud, and the servers she'd hired and the quartet and the auction and...

Breathe, Alice.

She'd done this six times or more before. She knew what she was doing. Everything would be fine.

Liam flashed her another smile, looking as relaxed and unbothered as could be, and Alice resisted the urge to throttle him. Just once, she'd like to see him riled up about something.

Except that something would probably be throwing her out of the castle. So never mind.

'I'll see you at the shindig,' Liam said. 'Save me a drink.'

'Will do.' Alice gave him a weak smile and watched him go.

Then she grabbed her clipboard and raced towards her box room to get ready.

It was almost time for the schmoozing to begin.

* * *

Liam's bow tie was strangling him. Oh, he knew that the networking and the dressing-up were all part of doing business these days, but usually he was talking about his work, his buildings. Not some ancient castle that still didn't feel like his.

He'd spent the last week trying to familiarise himself with the estate he'd unexpectedly inherited. He'd explored the grounds, the house, checked blueprints and restrictions, talked to lawyers and contractors, and kept tabs on the day-to-day activities of the castle. And finally, after days of note-taking and brainstorming and thinking out loud, he thought he might have found a solution to what he'd taken to calling The Alice Problem.

He couldn't throw out women and children in need. But he couldn't let them stay either. It was a conundrum.

He smiled to himself. Luckily, he'd always liked puzzles.

Now, he just needed to get Alice alone to persuade her to go along with it.

But first he'd discharge all his duties at this fundraiser, show willing, and hopefully get her guard down. The woman had been tense as anything since the moment he'd arrived—he'd assumed it was to do with him initially, but now he was starting to think it might be her natural state of being. Perhaps a glass or two of champagne—and a few fat cheques from the partygoers—would help her loosen up.

Snatching another glass of his own from the tray of a passing waiter, Liam smiled pleasantly at an older woman obviously wanting to talk to him, then managed to side-step away before she reached him. He'd already spoken with enough people for one night, and that wasn't even counting his toast.

All he wanted to do now was get Alice alone and get

the deal done—and then kick all these people out of his castle so he could get some peace and quiet.

Making his way over to the secret auction table, he busied himself by pretending to study the offerings—which varied from afternoon tea with the Duke to a weekend on somebody's yacht. Nothing he was at all interested in. Instead, he took the opportunity to scan the room, looking for Alice.

She'd done a great job, he had to admit. The ballroom was transformed from the Thornwood he'd become familiar with over the last week—no knitwear and screaming children, for a start. Not that he had anything against the kids—they were a lot more fun than most of the stuffed shirts in attendance tonight.

Looking around him, he could almost believe he was in a period drama. The chandeliers glittered, rivalling the sparkle from the diamonds and gemstones on display on the women in the room. The string quartet played the same pieces musicians had been playing at these events for centuries, and the usual small talk and chatter rose up to the high ceilings, along with the clinking of glasses. Maud's canapés—so different to the hearty fare she'd been feeding him, and everyone else, for the past week—were gobbled down with delight by all the partygoers. Liam had to admit, they were delicious. But they weren't a patch on the roast they'd had for dinner the night before.

His stomach rumbled, and he doubled his search for Alice. He'd seen her earlier, draped in a golden dress that left her shoulders and arms bare, and clung to her slender curves before flaring out over her hips. He'd actually done a double take at the sight of her—that dress was a far cry from the jeans and jumpers he was more used to seeing her in.

Really, she should be impossible to miss, looking like that. So where the hell was she?

Ah! There—off to one side, deep in conversation with a couple who'd cornered him earlier and talked for twenty minutes about the local sewage system. Well, she'd worked very hard on tonight. The least he could do was rescue her from *that*.

Then maybe they could go and find some real food— and talk.

Alice couldn't quite decide whether to be thankful that Liam had saved her from the death by boredom that was conversation with Mr and Mrs Haywood, or annoyed that he'd dragged her away from the fundraiser she'd spent months organising.

'I really shouldn't stay away too long,' she said as she followed Liam down the corridor away from the ballroom. 'We need to announce the winners of the silent auction soon...'

'Heather's going to do it,' Liam said, not even glancing back. 'I spoke to her before we left.'

'Really?' She was about to ask what gave him the right to do that, before she realised that they were actually in *his* castle, and bit her tongue. 'And what do we need to do that's so much more important than my fundraiser?'

Liam flashed her a smile over his shoulder as they reached the kitchen doors. 'Find some real food.'

Well. She supposed she could get behind that, Alice decided, her stomach rumbling. Two and a half canapés did not make a dinner.

'Plus, I have some plans I want to run by you,' Liam added, and Alice's appetite faded. For a moment, anyway.

Since the New Kitchen had been taken over by canapés and serving staff, they edged cautiously around the outside, avoiding Maud's glare as she directed the hired waiters and loaded them up with trays.

'Where do you think she's hidden last night's leftovers?' Liam asked, his mouth close to Alice's ear to be heard over the din. Alice tried not to shiver at the sensation of his breath on her skin.

'Probably in the mini fridge next door, in the Old Kitchen.'

'Then let's go.' Grabbing her hand, Liam led her towards the second door that led through to the old-fashioned second kitchen space.

Alice pushed open the door between them and felt, as she always did, as if she'd stepped back in time. The scrubbed wooden table with low benches on either side, the open fire with cooking pots hanging beside it, the maids' aprons and caps behind the door…everything harked back to an earlier age. A previous incarnation of Thornwood Castle.

She crossed to the smaller, out of place fridge that Maud kept in there, and wondered if she was about to hear what the latest incarnation would be.

Liam grabbed a couple of the old stoneware plates from the large dresser that covered one wall and placed them on either side of the table. Alice pulled out dishes of leftovers and laid them out in the centre, before rooting around to find cutlery for them both.

Liam folded himself on to one of the long benches that sat on either side of the kitchen table. Alice followed suit, sweeping her golden dress under her as she sat facing him. She handed him a set of cutlery, gripping her own so tightly that her knuckles turned white.

'You don't need to look so tense,' Liam said, his Australian accent and mild tone making his words sound even more laid-back.

'Don't I?' Alice asked. 'I mean, you're about to tell me your plans for the future of this place, right?' She hoped so, anyway. Otherwise she'd read him totally wrong, and things were about to get worse, not better.

Oh, hell, what if he was just about to fire her on the spot, not discuss his plans? She hoped he'd let her finish her dinner first—even cold, Maud's roasts always tasted amazing.

Liam chuckled, as if he'd read her mind. 'Eat. We'll talk when we're both done. I never like to negotiate on an empty stomach.'

Negotiate. That sounded more positive than 'instantly fired'. But it did still sound as if she might be fighting an uphill battle. Alice was certain that Liam had considerably more negotiating practice than she did.

She'd never liked conflict, a legacy from her peacemaker mother, she'd always thought. Mum had been an expert at smoothing over any situation, defusing every fight, and Alice had picked the habit up from her. It had served her well with her friends in her teenage years, and her housemates at university and in her early twenties.

But in her marriage the skill had evolved into appeasement. Into making herself smaller so there was less to fight about. She'd given up on things she'd believed in, just to avoid an argument. Stopped having her own opinions, her own thoughts. Even stopped fighting her own corner.

Until the day the fights stopped being angry words and slammed doors, and became something more.

The minute she'd woken up in that hospital, her whole life changed for ever, she'd promised herself she'd never give in and play nice, just to avoid a fight, ever again.

So if Liam wanted to negotiate, she would damn well negotiate harder than any businessman he'd ever had to deal with. Because she was fighting for what mattered to her—the well-being of the women who called Thornwood

Castle their place. The castle might be Liam's home, but it was their refuge. Their safe haven.

And that mattered more to Alice than anything else had since that hospital bed.

That, she would fight for.

Placing her cutlery in the finished position, Alice pushed her empty plate away from her and rested her hands in her lap as she waited for Liam to finish eating too, watching him shovel food into his mouth, the action totally incongruous with his dinner jacket and bow tie. Consciously, she straightened her back, lowered her shoulders and practised the calming breathing that one of the courses from earlier in the year had taught her. Liam, apparently unaware that he'd just gained his fiercest opponent yet, continued eating.

Since he wasn't paying her any attention anyway, Alice allowed herself a moment to study him. He was more attractive than she'd expected, she admitted to herself. His photo on his website showed his face half in shadow—a professional headshot in black and white, with a sombre expression and a tie knotted tightly around his neck. In person, seeing him every day, he wasn't like that at all. He seemed relaxed, at home and untroubled by life—even in black tie.

Alice frowned as she realised how unlikely that was.

She didn't know the whole of Liam's story, but for him to be Rose's only living relative, well, that kind of hinted that there wasn't a lot of family in his life. In fact, she knew more than that—Rose had told her once that he'd been orphaned young. Add in the whole 'his father never acknowledged him before he died' thing, which *everyone* knew about, and, well... Untroubled by life and Liam Jenkins probably didn't go together in a sentence often, did they?

But she wouldn't have guessed that from looking at him.

Liam shoved his last forkful of Maud's leftover roast into his mouth, moaned appreciatively as he chewed, and closed his eyes as he swallowed.

'*That* is a hell of a lot better than those fiddly canapés.'

Alice allowed herself a small smile. He liked the food—that much had been clear from the way he hadn't missed a meal in the dining hall since he'd arrived. That in itself was a start—and not always a given with visitors from overseas. Maud had strong feelings about the sort of meals that should be served in a British castle. If a person wasn't into roasted meats, goose fat roast potatoes and a whole lot of gravy, there wasn't much for them in Maud's kitchen. But Liam had been vocally appreciative of her meals, which had definitely earned Maud's approval.

'I'm glad you enjoyed it,' Alice said.

Liam put down his cutlery and opened his eyes, his dark blue gaze meeting hers across the table. 'But now it's time to talk.'

'Apparently so.' Alice folded her hands in front of her and steeled herself. 'So, you've seen what we do here, I've talked about why it's so important, you've spoken with everyone here tonight about it too. I know you've spent the week getting to know the place. So, now it's your turn. What do you have planned for Thornwood?'

CHAPTER FIVE

LIAM TRIED TO shift mentally from taste bud bliss to business. For some reason, it was more difficult than usual—perhaps because of Alice's nervous gaze on the other side of the table. She was clenching her hands together so tightly that the knuckles were white, and the tension in her shoulders made her look as if she was wearing some sort of torture device to keep her upright—like those ridiculous corsets they all wore in the period dramas.

Liam frowned. Seriously, how many of those things had he watched that he remembered all the details? Apparently the universe had been preparing him to inherit Thornwood all along.

Even if nobody else had.

And, anyway, she wasn't wearing anything of the sort. She was wearing that slippery golden dress that moved with every breath she took, emphasising the cowl neckline that led down to the gentle curve of her cleavage…

Actually, maybe it was the dress that was distracting him. Or Alice in it.

But this wasn't the time for thoughts like that. It was time to lay it all out on the table, and see how Alice took the news.

Reaching up, he loosened his bow tie and left it hanging around his neck, popping open the top couple of buttons of his shirt.

'Okay, well, first off you have to understand that I've had no contact with Thornwood for years. I had no idea of the work you were doing here until I arrived last week, and all I know about it is what I've seen and what you've told me. Understood?'

Alice nodded.

'Good. Then you'll appreciate that when I first learned I'd be inheriting the castle I had my own ideas and plans for the place.'

'Plans that didn't involve helping local women, I'd guess,' Alice said.

'Exactly.'

'But now you've seen what we're doing here, how much good we're doing—'

Liam winced, and she cut herself off without him having to do it for her, which he appreciated. Someone who could read the conversational cues was always easier to reason with.

'My plans…they're already underway,' he admitted. 'I have investors interested, contractors coming out to look at the place next week…' He'd given himself a week to settle in before the first of the appointments his assistant had set up, but now that week was up.

'So finding us here has put a real spanner in the works.'

'You could say that.'

Alice bit her lower lip, and Liam hoped against hope that she wasn't about to start crying. He never knew what to do with crying women.

Well, he did. But those women weren't Alice Walters. They weren't his great-aunt's employee, or the woman he was about to turf out of her home. Liam was pretty sure his usual methods of cheering up women wouldn't work so well on Alice right now. Or ever, possibly.

'So. You're going to make us leave.' Alice's expression grew mulish and Liam knew that, even if that was what he'd planned, it wouldn't be as easy as the words suggested. He might own the castle, he might have all the money and the power in this situation, but Alice, doing what she believed in, was a force to be reckoned with.

In that sense, she almost reminded him of his great-aunt Rose.

'I didn't say that,' he pointed out.

'But that's what it comes down to, isn't it?' Alice snapped back. 'The women and families we're helping here aren't as important as whatever money-making scheme you've got ready to go.'

'Hey.' Liam put some edge in his voice, a sharpness clear enough to make Alice settle back down in her seat, at least. 'I understand your frustration—'

'Frustration!' Alice cried, and he gave her a look.

'But that doesn't mean I'm going to let you yell and rant at me before you've actually heard my proposal.'

'Let me? Ha. What on earth makes you think that a man like you *lets* me do anything?' Alice pushed her chair away from the table and stood, hands planted firmly on the wood between them. Liam waited patiently for her to catch on. 'Listen to me, mister. My life is entirely my own. Nothing you do, say or want can influence it without my say-so. This might be your castle, but that doesn't mean that I'm part of the property, okay? You don't *let me* do—' She broke off suddenly, and Liam knew her ears were catching up with her mouth at last. 'Your proposal?'

'Yes, my proposal.' Liam rolled his eyes. 'Why don't you take a seat and we can discuss it? Rationally. Without either of us trying to make the other do anything they don't want to do. Okay?'

Alice's eyes were cautious, but she lowered herself back into her chair all the same. 'I doubt we can manage that,' she said, most of the anger gone now. 'I mean, the very fact that you're calling it a proposal, and that you talked about negotiations before, suggests that your plan means that my plans will have to change. And I don't want that.'

'What if I could give you a better plan?'

'A better plan?' Alice scoffed. 'You've been here, what? A week? And you really think you know better than I do what we need here?'

'I think I can offer you something that you wouldn't have considered an option before.' He'd given this a lot of thought, while he'd been exploring the estate. Alice really was doing good work at Thornwood. And, given his own history, he couldn't just cast that aside. He just needed her to do it in a way that worked for him.

'Which is?' Alice asked, her tone sceptical.

'A dedicated building, for you to run the services you're already running here.'

Alice narrowed her eyes at him. 'What's the catch?'

'No catch,' Liam said with a shrug. 'I admire the work you're doing here. I think hiring you might have been Rose's last-ditch attempt to get into heaven, but that doesn't mean it was a bad idea. So I want you to continue.'

'Just not at Thornwood Castle.'

'Right.'

Alice leant back in her chair, still eyeing him suspiciously. 'So, let me check I've got this straight. You're going to turf us out of the castle into some other outbuilding on the estate, probably without heating or running water, and let us muddle through as best we can until we give up and leave you alone with your castle and your plans.'

Liam took a deep breath and tried to sound patient. 'No. I'm going to relocate you and your groups to a suitable building somewhere else on the estate. I'll also continue to pay your salary and give you an agreed amount of funding for your work every month.'

'There are no suitable buildings on the estate,' she said, wilfully ignoring his generous financial offer.

'I don't *have* to keep you here, you realise. There's nothing in the will about it.' At least, as far as he knew. He hadn't *actually* got all the final details yet. But if he could get Alice to agree to his terms he was pretty sure they wouldn't matter anyway.

'Then why are you?' Always so suspicious.

'Because you're right—you are doing good work here. And I respect that. I… My mother and I had to run to a women's refuge once. We left in the middle of the night, taking nothing with us. We had no money, no support, nothing—and they helped us. If we'd had somewhere like Thornwood, maybe we'd have been able to prepare better, or get out sooner, before it got so…bad. But regardless, I'm not about to kick all the women you help out into the street.'

'And that's very laudable,' Alice said, a hint of sarcasm in her voice. 'But it doesn't change the fact that there are no suitable buildings on the estate. So there's nowhere for you to move us to.'

'Nothing at all?' Liam raised his eyebrows. 'I find that hard to believe on an estate this size.' In fact, he knew different. He'd found at least six possible sites on just one afternoon's walk around the grounds.

Alice waved a hand, dismissing his objections. 'Just some broken-down old barns and the odd decrepit cottage.'

Liam settled back with a satisfied smile spreading on his lips. 'There you go, then.'

'You're going to throw these women out into draughty, falling-down buildings more suitable for housing animals?' The outrage on her face was almost comical. Liam resisted the urge to laugh at her, purely because he needed her on his side.

Which meant explaining. He hated explaining himself.

'Did you, at any point after you discovered that I would be inheriting Thornwood Castle, do any research into me and, say, my career?'

Alice blinked, the anger fading from her expression in the instant her eyes were closed. 'You plan to renovate a barn for us to use?'

Huh. Less explanation required than he'd expected. That was a good sign. Someone who could follow his train of thought without him having to sound out every single syllable was someone he might just be able to work with.

'If that turns out to be the best option, yes.' Pushing his chair away from the table, Liam got to his feet and paced the length of the table. He always thought better on his feet and, to be honest, he hadn't had the time to think the details of his idea all the way through just yet. 'I'm going to be having a lot of work done around the estate anyway, so adding one more building won't affect anything too much. I'm sure you have ideas about exactly what you require—' He glanced at Alice for agreement and she nodded firmly. 'So we take a look around together, find a suitable place, fix it up and move you in.'

'That easy, huh?' Alice still looked sceptical.

Liam shrugged. 'I don't see why not.' It wasn't as if he hadn't turned around bigger projects in record time. A building for a group of women to meet and knit and talk in…how hard could that be?

* * *

It couldn't be that easy. It never was, in Alice's experience.

'And what, exactly, are you expecting in return?' she asked.

Liam raised his eyebrows, gripping the back of his chair as he looked down at her, his bow tie hanging loose around his neck. He looked like a libertine from the twenties, ready for late-night cocktails, and it was incredibly distracting. Alice resisted the urge to stand up, to make them more equal again. This was a negotiation. She couldn't let him know he had her rattled, or that he'd gained the upper hand in any way. Even if it was just by being unfairly good-looking.

But the truth was, she'd been blindsided. She'd expected to fight for the survival of her women's groups. She'd expected to have to argue for the right to stay, to continue her work. And she'd certainly expected Liam to drive a hard bargain.

Instead, he seemed to be offering her exactly what she needed—a purpose-built building for her groups, perhaps even with proper heating. And so far he hadn't asked for anything in return.

No doubt about it, there had to be a catch.

'In return?' Liam asked. 'I get Thornwood Castle back. What more could I want?'

No, that definitely sounded too innocent. 'That's what I want to know.'

He flashed her a wolfish smile. 'So suspicious.'

'With good reason.' Reasons she didn't plan on sharing with him. 'So why don't you tell me *exactly* what you're planning here at Thornwood?'

'Okay, okay.' Throwing up his hands in defeat, Liam took his seat again. 'What do you want to know?'

'You mentioned building works. Are you planning on

knocking the whole place down and starting again?' It was a joke, mostly. But the more she thought about it, the more nervous the idea made her.

Liam laughed. 'No. Even I have more respect for the old place than that. But I do want to make some changes.'

'Like a roof that doesn't leak? Maybe even some working heating?' Those were the sort of changes Alice could get behind.

'Definitely those. But also some bigger changes to the grounds and accommodation here.'

'Like?'

Liam's expression turned serious again. 'I want to make Thornwood accessible to the wider world for the first time.'

'I'm not exactly keeping people out of here, you realise.' Thornwood had already thrown open its doors. It didn't need whatever grand gesture Liam had planned.

'Yeah. But your people...' He trailed off, and Alice made the leap to the obvious conclusion.

'The women and children I help aren't going to make you rich.' Of course it came down to money. Didn't it always with people like him?

'I want Thornwood to be self-sustaining,' Liam countered. 'And that means it needs to earn money from the people visiting it.'

He made it sound perfectly reasonable, but Alice knew what it meant. 'You mean you're going to turn Thornwood into the sort of tourist attraction your aunt would have hated,' she said bluntly.

'Basically.' Liam smiled unapologetically. 'I kind of imagine my ancestors rolling in their graves.'

'And you like that? That you're disrupting centuries of tradition here, going against what Rose would have wanted?'

Just like that, all of Liam's laid-back charm disappeared.

'Rose didn't want to leave me Thornwood in the first place, so don't pretend that she did. She said she wanted me to make it my home at last. Well, fine. This is what *I* want my home to be.'

'Really?' Somehow Alice found that hard to believe. 'Is that what home is to you? Complete strangers trampling through it all the time, gawking?'

'Isn't that what you've done? Opened my home to strangers?'

'It's different, and you know it,' Alice snapped. She frowned. Something in his words was niggling at the back of her mind, but she couldn't quite put her finger on it.

Liam sighed. 'Look, I'm offering you a good deal here. I'll even let you help choose the location—'

'So generous,' Alice murmured, still running his past sentences through her brain again.

'And we can have you set up somewhere else on the estate early in the spring, if things go well, and whatever renovations we decide on don't require planning permission.'

The spring. Alice looked up sharply. 'That long?'

'It's December, Alice. I'm good, but I'm not a miracle-worker. I'd say we're looking at February at the earliest, and that's only if we can agree on a location quickly—preferably one in decent condition.' He frowned. 'Is that a problem?'

'I just… I hadn't planned on staying that long.' She'd been putting off thinking about it, but she'd already stayed longer at Thornwood than anywhere since she'd left Robert. She'd sworn then that she wouldn't let herself get tied down like that again—wouldn't risk being trapped that way. Thornwood had always seemed a safe place, especially with Rose there, and she'd been doing good work. It had been easy to get sucked into that comfortable, secure feeling again.

But Alice knew that sort of security was only ever an illusion. Liam Jenkins's arrival had only made that clearer.

Maybe it was time to go.

'You hadn't… You're not staying?' Liam's eyebrows rose up in surprise. 'Then why am I working this hard to save a scheme you don't even care enough about to hang around and run?'

'It's not that I don't care,' Alice said, fast. 'I do. Very much. This…what I've set up here, it's important. It's one of the best things I've done in my life.'

'Then why go?'

'It's just…time.' She felt awkward just saying it, letting him see that it mattered to her.

But the way Liam surveyed her across the table, she got the feeling he might just possibly understand.

And then, finally, the words he'd spoken that had been stuck in the back of her mind made their way to the front.

'She said she wanted me to make it my home at last.'

At last.

Which made it sound as if he'd refused to make Thornwood home in the past, while Rose was alive. But why?

If she didn't stick around, she'd never know. And, more importantly, she'd lose any power she had to make sure that Liam continued the work she'd started the way he'd promised—with a new building and plenty of financial support. She couldn't leave until she was sure that the women she was leaving behind were safe.

She forced a smile. 'It's fine. I'm happy to stay—at least until everything here is settled.'

'So you'll move your group to whatever building I find for you?'

Nice try. 'No. So I'll stay and help you find the perfect place for my groups, somewhere even better than Thornwood Castle, and get them settled in. And then I'll leave.'

'The *perfect* place?'

'Well, of course.'

Liam sighed. 'In that case, we'd better get started. In my experience, perfection is pretty hard to come by.'

Alice didn't smile. She knew that better than most people.

She was leaving anyway. If he'd just held out, she might have agreed to leave without the promise of a new venue for her groups. And then he could have…what, exactly? Kicked a load of needy women and children out on the streets? Or, worse, back to abusive homes?

No, he couldn't have done that. He knew too well how it felt to have nowhere to go. Nowhere that felt safe. Nowhere to call home.

And now he had Thornwood. Which felt neither safe nor homely, but at least had the benefit of being potentially lucrative.

Once he'd turfed out the current inhabitants, of course.

Standing, he held a hand out across the table to Alice. 'So, we have a deal?'

She took it, her grip firmer than he expected from her pale face and slender form. 'We do.'

'Good.' He scanned her eyes, looking for any hint of emotion—doubt or fear or anything, but there was nothing there. Nothing at all.

He knew that expression. He'd practised it himself.

What was Alice Walters hiding? He suspected he might never know her full story, but he could guess a little of it right now. This wasn't just a job to Alice; this was personal.

Someone, some time, had put Alice in the same position as some of these women.

The thought made him irrationally angry, and his jaw clenched tight.

'Um, can I have my hand back now?' Alice tilted her head to the side as she asked, obviously surveying him the same way he had her.

He wondered what she saw. Then he decided he probably didn't want to know.

'Of course.' He dropped her hand and stepped back from the table. 'In that case, I'd better get back to work—unless you need my help ushering out the last of your guests? I'm figuring the main event must be over by now.'

Alice nodded. 'I think so. I'll go and check everything went okay with the silent auction, say any last goodbyes, and then I can finally get out of this damn dress and off to bed.'

The dress. Just the mention of it made Liam study it again, taking in those delicate straps, seemingly made out of thin golden rope, holding up the fabric that draped across her body, before widening into a fuller skirt. Something about it hinted at the idea that it might just fall to the floor at any moment.

Liam had to admit, he liked it a lot better than the woolly cardigans she normally hid herself behind.

'It's a great dress,' he told her with feeling. 'You look gorgeous in it.'

Alice's cheeks flushed a light pink. 'Thank you. Rose always said I had to look the part for these things, so she had someone send a few dresses over for me to choose from. This one was my favourite—not least because it has hidden pockets. Well, it *was* my favourite, before I realised how uncomfortable the bra I have to wear with it is.' Her blush turned darker as she said that, and Liam chuckled.

'Trust me, it's worth the discomfort.' Grinning, Liam started back towards the ballroom via the main hall. He was finally starting to get his bearings in the labyrinthine corridors of Thornwood Castle. Soon he wouldn't even need the sketched map he'd taken to keeping in his pocket, and glancing at only when he was sure no one was looking.

'I'm glad you think so,' Alice said, following him down the corridor. 'You don't scrub up half bad yourself, you know.'

'Aussie surfer dude turned English aristocrat, huh?'

Alice laughed. 'Something like that.'

'Glad to know I can pull it off.' Liam frowned as an unexpected noise echoed off the stone walls of the corridor they were walking down. 'Did you hear that?'

Alice's forehead creased too. 'I'm not sure.' She took another turning and suddenly they were back in the main hall again, its oversized Christmas tree looming over the staircase. From beyond the next set of doors, they could hear the dying chatter of the fundraiser, the last few guests still hanging on in there. But that wasn't the noise that had caught Liam's attention.

The sound rang out again and, this time, there was no doubt in Liam's mind what he was hearing. He knew the sound of a baby crying well enough—from the age of ten upwards, it had seemed every foster home he went to had a new baby—one he was expected to help look after. 'Did someone bring their baby with them tonight?'

Except he couldn't see anyone nearby, and the cry had sounded very close.

As if it was in the room with them.

'I don't think…' Alice trailed off as the baby cried again. Then she stepped closer to the tree, taking slow, cautious steps in her long shimmering dress, as if trying not to spook a wild animal.

Liam followed, instinctively staying quiet.

The crying was constant now, and there was no denying where it was coming from.

Alice hitched up her dress and knelt down on the flagstones, reaching under the spread of the pine needles, dislodging a couple of ornaments as she did so. Then she pulled out a basket—not a bassinet or anything, Liam realised. Just a wicker basket, of the sort someone might use to store magazines or whatever.

A wicker basket with a baby lying in it.

CHAPTER SIX

'WHOSE IS IT?' Liam whispered, as the baby gripped hold of Alice's finger and, just for a moment, stopped crying. She stared down into its unfocused eyes and felt her heart tighten in her chest. Gritting her teeth, she held her emotions in check. There was a reason she stayed away from babies.

And that reason meant she had to get this one back to its mum as soon as possible.

'I have no idea,' Alice murmured back. 'But it's very young. Newborn, even.'

She hadn't spent a great deal of time around babies before she came to Thornwood. But since then she'd met children of all ages—from a day old upwards. And this baby looked smaller, younger, fresher than any of them.

Who could have left it there? Who did she know who was even pregnant? Susie Hughes had given birth the week before, and Jessica Groves wasn't even six months yet. And neither of them would have left their child unattended under a Christmas tree, anyway.

Bracing herself, she lifted the baby out of the basket, taking care to keep the blanket tucked around it for warmth. Underneath, it was naked, except for a small cloth. Alice unwrapped it carefully, focusing on the clinical, hard facts—not the emotions coursing through her body as she held the baby close.

'It's a boy.' Not that it mattered. What mattered was the roughly cut and tied umbilical cord. 'Oh, God, Liam. I think he's just been born. Today, I mean.' Maybe even here at Thornwood. Alice swallowed at the thought of some desperate woman giving birth alone in a cold, dark corner of the castle, while they were all partying in the ballroom. And then leaving her son in the main hall, where he was sure to be found.

Who would be desperate enough to do such a thing?

'And abandoned.' Alice could hear the judgement in Liam's tone, but she didn't have time to argue with him. Later, she could explain the choices that some women had to face, and the reality of their world that could make such a dreadful decision necessary. Later, she could cry and hurt for all the feelings this moment had dredged up from where she'd tried to bury them.

For now, she just needed to get help for the baby.

'We need to call the doctor.' She eased herself to her feet, still clutching the baby close to her chest. Liam tucked a hand under her elbow to help her up.

'And the police,' he added, and Alice shook her head.

'No. Not yet. We need to see if we can fix this ourselves, first.' Getting the police involved would make everything official.

'Why? And besides, if you don't, surely the doctor will,' Liam argued.

'Not Dr Helene,' Alice disagreed. 'She's worked with us before.'

'This has happened before?' Liam's eyebrows shot up.

'No. Not this.' But plenty of other stuff. Enough for Alice to know instinctively that this was a desperate, last chance act for someone—not an act of cruelty. She wasn't about to punish a desperate woman—and certainly not before they'd tried to help her.

The baby started to squirm in her arms again, and Alice joggled him a little to try and calm him. Poor thing was probably starving, or in shock or both. Adjusting her grip, she felt in the hidden pocket in the folds of her dress for her phone and pulled it out. Reception at the castle was spotty, but if she could get hold of Heather at least she'd have some help. Someone she could hand the baby to and take a step back, regroup, recover her equilibrium.

'I need to make some calls,' she said again. 'But we can't... I don't want everyone to see him. Could you...?'

'You want me to get rid of the rest of the guests?' Liam guessed.

Alice nodded, relieved. 'I'll take him through to the library. I can call the doctor from there.' And Heather. She'd be able to get together some things to look after him. They'd need clothes, formula milk...everything. She started a mental list, knowing that Heather's well stocked store cupboard would be able to provide. Practicalities. That was what she needed to think about.

'Okay. I'll meet you there.' Liam turned to push the basket back under the tree before he went, then paused. 'Hey, there's something else in here.' Liam crouched over the basket and pulled out a scrap of paper—one of the leaflets that Alice had distributed around the shops and businesses of the local village, inviting women to Thornwood Castle whenever they needed support or aid.

Apparently someone had taken her up on the offer in a fairly major way.

'Is that writing on the back?' Alice squinted at the paper to try and make it out.

Liam flipped it over and started to read. '"*This is Jamie. He needs your help. I'm leaving him to Alice Walters and*

Liam Jenkins. Please take care of him and tell him I'm sorry and I love him." Well. That answers *all* our questions, then.'

'Jamie,' Alice murmured. 'It suits him.' Jamie had settled down into her arms now, perhaps having cried himself to exhaustion—or perhaps because he needed serious medical help. She needed to get the doctor there quickly... 'Wait. She left him to *me*?'

Oh, God, no. She couldn't take responsibility for a baby. Not now. She couldn't even *think* about this now, because if she did...

A paralysing sadness washed over her as the memories broke out of the cage she'd kept them locked in for the last few years. Since she'd woken up in that hospital bed and knew her life would be something new now. Gazing down at the sleeping baby, the depth of everything she'd lost yawned open inside her, a gaping hole at the centre of her being, one that could never be filled. Not now. That chance had been taken away from her.

Except she was holding a baby in her arms. Almost as if...

'To *us*,' Liam clarified, his voice harsh, and Alice blinked as the moment broke. She had to focus. This was an emergency—one she would deal with the same way she dealt with every other crisis that hit the women at Thornwood. With practicality, sensitivity and order.

Emotions she could deal with later. First, she needed to deal with the astonishing request in the note.

'She left him to me *and* you?' Her, she could understand—she'd been looking after the people of this community for over a year and a half, and Jamie's mother wouldn't necessarily know that she had no experience looking after babies. But why Liam?

'Apparently so.' Liam shoved the note in his jacket

pocket, shaking his head. 'God only knows what his mother was thinking—if she was thinking at all. Go on. You get to the library and make the calls. I'll meet you there once I've got rid of everyone else. We'll deal with what on earth this note means then.'

A plan. Good. That was exactly what she needed.

Alice nodded and, adjusting the baby in her arms, set off for the safety of the library as quickly as she could, given her long dress.

Maybe there would even be some books on childcare in there. God knew they were going to need them.

The library was thankfully empty. Alice sank into one of the battered leather wing chairs in the corner, her legs still shaking. She pulled out her phone again, scrolling through until she found Heather's number.

Heather answered on the third ring and, from the background noise, Alice was interrupting the servers and helpers finishing off the canapés in the kitchen. 'I need you in the library. Now. And grab one of the baby bags on your way.' Her voice stayed steady, which Alice was proud of. She could handle this. She had to—for Jamie.

Heather didn't question the order—she knew as well as Alice that sometimes when help was needed there wasn't time to debate. 'I'll be right there.'

Alice's second call was to Dr Helene, who promised to leave for Thornwood immediately too—although she required a little more information. 'I'll bring more supplies,' Helene promised, and Alice let out a tiny sigh of relief.

She needed professionals here. For all that she wanted to help Jamie's mother, she hadn't a clue what she was doing.

Alice took a shuddering breath and admitted the truth to herself—she was totally out of her depth. She'd protected herself from everything she knew she could never have—

could never be—by avoiding everything to do with babies, as far as that was possible in a place like Thornwood, always filled with mothers and children. She'd never learnt how to change a nappy, or how to soothe a child, or how to know a baby needed feeding.

If someone wanted a fundraiser organising, a seminar programme setting up, an escape route for an abused woman, she was their girl. She could fix the leaky toilets on the ground floor, and plug holes in the draughty windows of Thornwood. She could even manage the accounts and feed fifty women on a budget set for half that number.

But she couldn't look after a baby. That was knowledge she simply didn't have—knowledge she'd never sought or needed.

Until now.

The door to the library opened, and Alice tensed until she saw Liam slip through and shut it firmly behind him.

'The doctor is on her way,' she told him. 'And Heather. Both of them with supplies.'

'Good.' Liam eyed the baby with what Alice was sure was annoyance. But then he added, 'Poor little guy will freeze in this castle if we don't get him some warm clothes and some formula pretty soon.'

'They won't be long,' Alice promised, surprised that he cared at all. Perhaps Liam really did have a softer side— one that he'd kept very well hidden since his arrival at Thornwood.

But tonight wasn't a night for dwelling on the mysteries and annoyances of Liam Jenkins. Alice gazed down at Jamie, adjusting the blanket again to keep his tiny hands covered. Whatever deal she'd just struck with Liam, whatever promises she intended to hold him accountable to, she knew that her decision to stay at Thornwood for the time being had just been made a whole lot easier.

It wasn't just her women, her work or her legacy she needed to see settled before she left. She needed to make sure Jamie was safe and well cared for too—however much it broke her heart.

Until Jamie was reunited with his mother, Thornwood was home. Again.

'Could that phone call have been any more cryptic?' Heather burst into the library, a plastic bag dangling from one hand, the other placed firmly on her hip. 'What the hell is going on up here?'

Wasn't that the most appropriate question ever? Liam was still trying to figure that out, twenty minutes after he'd found that damn note.

Not the baby. Finding the baby was fine—a problem to be solved, a situation to be dealt with by passing it on to the appropriate authorities. The baby wasn't to blame for any of this.

But that note…

The moment he'd seen his name there, linked with Alice's, naming them as carers for Jamie, his whole body had frozen. And then, milliseconds later, the need to run had surged through him. Thornwood wasn't his home and he didn't need anything else tying him to it. This wasn't his place, Jamie wasn't his baby and this wasn't the sort of responsibility he had ever intended to sign up for.

Except he had a feeling that Rose might have made it his responsibility the minute she'd named him in her will.

Heather was still waiting for an answer, Liam realised, looking up at her as she stood in the doorway.

'Shut the door,' Liam commanded, and she obeyed before turning her attention to Alice.

Heather's eyes widened as she caught sight of the baby.

'This is Jamie,' Alice said, her voice soft now he was

sleeping. What was she making of all this? Liam couldn't tell. He'd thought he'd seen the same sort of panic he was feeling in her eyes when they'd found Jamie, but now she looked almost…content, holding him. 'We found him under the Christmas tree.'

'As far as I'm aware, Santa doesn't bring babies,' Heather commented. 'That's usually the stork's prerogative. Have you called the police? No, of course you haven't.' She answered her own question with a sigh. 'Well, at least I get why you needed this, now.' She held out the bag and Liam took it from her and peered inside.

'Nappies, clothes, pre-made formula bottles…you guys think of everything. This happen a lot round here, does it?' They were too well set up for this to be a one-off.

'Random babies being left as Christmas presents? No.' Heather glared at him. Liam wasn't sure if it was because he now owned Thornwood, or just because he was male. Probably both. 'But we do occasionally have women arrive with new babies who need our help. And sometimes they're not able to bring much with them.'

The words she wasn't saying echoed through Liam's head all the same, and his jaw tightened at the thought of them. Women who had to run, fast. Women who were terrified for their children, in fear for their own lives. Women who had nowhere to go except Thornwood. Women like his mother.

When he'd offered Alice his deal—a promise of a place to continue her work, outside of the castle—it had been for his own convenience as much as hers. He needed them out of the castle in a way that wouldn't enrage the local populace, and he hadn't been much inclined to rely on the misogynist tendencies of the occupants of Thornwood village to get away with just kicking them out. That kind of thing never played well in the papers—not to mention on the internet.

But now, watching as Alice carefully unwrapped Jamie—waking him and causing him to scream, of course—ready to put a nappy on him and dress him, he knew it wasn't just about convenience any more. He'd seen enough over the last week to convince him that Alice wasn't a gold-digger, she wasn't sent purely to try him. What she did mattered around here—and it mattered to her.

And for some reason that seemed to mean it mattered to him now too.

'You're doing it wrong,' he said, stepping forward without thinking as Alice tried to get the nappy on backwards. He'd thought those things were fairly idiot-proof these days, but he guessed if someone had never done it before it could take a moment to figure out.

Kneeling beside her, he turned the nappy the right way, so the tabs opened to be fastened at the front.

'I'd have got there in a second,' she grumbled.

'I'm sure you would have,' Liam said mildly. 'But since that would have meant another second of this kid wailing, I figured I'd help. What, never changed a nappy before?'

'She always gives them back at that point,' Heather said from behind them, where she was preparing a pre-made bottle. She sounded amused, which was more than Liam could manage. 'In fact, she gives them back when they cry too, normally. Or fuss. Or spit up. Or anything.'

'Yeah, well, I can't exactly give this one back right now, can I?' Alice snapped. Liam watched her as she struggled to get Jamie's tiny feet into a sleepsuit. Maybe she wasn't as calm as he'd thought. Especially if she had no experience of babies. She had to be freaking out as much as he was; she was just hiding it well.

'I can see why you never had kids,' he joked, trying to lighten the mood, but Alice didn't laugh. In fact, she paused, just for a moment, in dressing Jamie. And when she resumed the action, her hands were trembling.

Damn. He'd hit a nerve and he hadn't even been trying.

What was it with Alice and babies? She was clearly out of her depth here, but reluctant to accept his help. Liam suppressed a sigh. Well, she was just going to have to suck it up and let him help her. Not because *she* needed it, but because Jamie did.

As much as he'd wanted to run, fast and far away from Thornwood, the moment he'd seen his name on that note, he already knew he couldn't. Not now. He couldn't just walk away from an abandoned child, any more than Alice could.

His eyes narrowed as he watched Alice wrap Jamie back up in his blanket. Why was that, exactly? Liam knew why an abandoned baby hit his buttons, but which of Alice's was the situation pressing? Or, the thought occurred suddenly, was it something even simpler?

Alice had been so determined to hold on to Jamie until they found his mother, yet she apparently had no patience or interest in them normally. Did she know who the mother was, perhaps, and this was her way of protecting her? It seemed as likely as any other answer.

Which meant Liam would need to keep a very close eye on Alice, and see who she spoke to over the next day or so. He might have some sympathy for a woman in dire straits who felt she had no choice but to abandon her child—but that didn't mean he agreed with it. There were other options—there was *always* another option—and he intended to have strong words with Jamie's mum about them.

As soon as he found out who she was, anyway.

* * *

Of course, the minute she managed to get Jamie's tiny limbs safely enclosed within the sleepsuit Heather had found and rewrapped him in his blanket, Dr Helene came bustling in through the library door and they had to take everything off again for her to check him over.

Alice liked Dr Helene. She had the sort of no-nonsense approach that tended to calm people—including Alice, tonight. But at the same time she was caring, kind—and very understanding of the work they were doing at the castle. Helene had more than once been able to help out with women in dire straits, and she had great connections in the city too, which always came in helpful with relocations.

But tonight she hadn't come alone. Instead she'd brought a woman who Alice had spoken to many times in the course of trying to help the people of Thornwood.

'Hello, Iona,' Alice said before turning to Helene. 'You brought social services?'

'Iona's a friend,' Helene said. 'She can help us. Now, who does this little man belong to?' Helene frowned as she peeled off the blanket and pulled open the poppers on the sleepsuit.

'That's the million-dollar question,' Liam drawled. Helene glanced up at him, then apparently dismissed him as of no importance. Alice hid a smile; it would do his ego some good to be ignored, but she supposed she'd better perform introductions.

'Helene, this is Liam Jenkins—the new owner of Thornwood. And this—' she pointed at the baby '—is Jamie. We found him here, under the Christmas tree, just wrapped in a blanket with this note.' She nodded to Liam and he handed it over.

Helene scanned the note quickly, and her frown grew deeper. 'Well, he certainly looks like a newborn. And apparently the mother wanted him to be your responsibility. Have you fed him yet?'

Alice shook her head. 'We were about to try when you arrived. I was a little concerned about his umbilical cord...'

'It does look a little rough and ready. But actually it's been done safely, as far as I can tell. It does look like he was born very, very recently though.' She pulled her bag closer and took out the necessary supplies to sterilise the cord stump. 'To someone who knew how to cut the cord without the baby bleeding out, but had no idea what to do next.'

'Except abandon him.' Liam was sounding judgemental again. Alice ignored him. Their judgement didn't matter right now. What mattered was Jamie's well-being.

'I can't even think of any regulars here who it could have been,' Alice said.

'I've been making a list of pregnant women who've visited recently,' Heather put in. 'But I can't see it being any of them either.'

'We'll need to follow up with them, all the same,' Iona said, turning to Helene. 'Is there anyone who has been into the surgery recently who could be a candidate?'

Helene shrugged. 'No one obvious, but then you never know what might overtake someone. And, to be honest, if she chose to have the baby here rather than at the hospital, chances are she might not have had any prenatal care at all. She might not even have known that she was pregnant.'

'That really happens?' Liam asked, obviously sceptical. Alice didn't blame him; it sounded so unlikely. How could anyone not know that there was a life growing inside them? She'd known, within a few days. And when that life was gone...she'd known that too. The loss had almost swallowed her up.

'Not often,' Helene admitted. 'But probably more

often than you'd think.' She finished her examination and straightened up. 'Okay. Let's get this little man wrapped up, fed and asleep. Then we can all talk about what happens next.'

'He's okay?' Alice chewed her lip as she wriggled Jamie back into his clothes. He was so tiny, so helpless. The thought of what might have happened if she hadn't come through the main hall just then, if she'd stayed at the fundraiser and hadn't been back that way that evening... No. She couldn't think that way. Someone would always have found him.

It just felt weirdly like fate that it was her.

'Babies are surprisingly hardy,' Helene said. 'You must have found him very soon after he was left. He'd barely had a chance to get cold. And, lucky for him, it looks like the birth must have been straightforward—although I wish I could examine the mother and make sure she's okay too.'

'His mother.' Alice sighed. 'We have to find her.'

'We will,' Heather promised. 'I'm on it.'

'And in the meantime, I assume you don't want to alert the police just yet?' Helene said. Iona raised her eyebrows.

'Not yet.' Alice thought of some poor, desperate woman being led away in handcuffs for making the worst decision she'd ever have to make. 'Give us a chance to put this right first. Find the mother. Figure out what's best for her and for Jamie.'

Helene nodded. 'Okay. I'll come back tomorrow to check on him, but in the meantime...'

'I can take him,' Iona said. 'We have places we can look after him, until the mother comes forward.'

'And what if she doesn't?' Liam asked. 'If we involve the police, they can launch an appeal, right? Ask the mother to own up.'

'They could,' Iona allowed. 'But that's not always the best move.'

'How do you mean?' Alice asked, frowning. She hadn't thought about appeals. She'd just thought about Jamie, and how his mother had wanted her to look after him. About how she knew, deep inside her, that she *must* do that, however much it hurt, so that Jamie was safe.

'Sometimes those appeals can be counter-productive,' Iona explained. 'The mother knows the baby is safe then, and that makes it easier for her to stay hidden. She's more likely to come forward if she doesn't know what has happened to Jamie, so that she can make sure he's okay.'

That made sense, she supposed, although she hated the thought of some poor woman panicking alone, never knowing what happened to her child. How could anyone live like that?

'Which is why it might make sense for Iona to take him,' Helene said.

'No. His mother wanted me to look after Jamie. I'll take care of him.' Was that her voice? Her words? What was she thinking? She knew nothing about looking after babies. Heather was right—she didn't just pass back the crying babies or the vomiting ones. She handed them all back, the first chance she got. Not because she didn't like them, didn't love their new baby smell and their soft skin. But because…

Because it was just too hard. Being so close to something she knew she could never have, not any more.

So why was she putting herself right next to *this* baby, this helpless child who would hopefully be going home to his mother in the next twenty-four hours? This was the worst idea she'd ever had.

And yet she couldn't bring herself to let him go, to trust anyone else to care for Jamie.

'You?' Liam sounded incredulous. 'You couldn't put a nappy on without help.'

'I'll figure it out,' Alice snapped. 'Don't you think I can do it?'

'On your own?' He raised one eyebrow. 'Probably. But why would you want to?'

'Because he doesn't have anybody!' How could he not understand this? 'He needs help so I will help him. That's what I do. And Heather has her own kids to get home to, and everyone else here has enough on their plates, so it comes down to me, okay? So I will do it.'

'Of course you will. But why do you want to do it on your own?' Alice stopped and stared at him. He could not possibly be suggesting what it sounded like he was suggesting.

'Because that's how I do things,' she said slowly, realising as she spoke the words how true that was. And how sad, actually.

'Yeah, but this time I'm right here.' Liam shrugged. 'She left him to both of us to look after, remember? It's not like I can do much around Thornwood until I get our deal underway, so I might as well help you with this. With him.'

'Sounds like that's sorted, then.' Helene picked up her doctor's bag, and Iona nodded.

'I'll come back tomorrow with Helene to see how things are going,' Iona said. 'But in the meantime, try and keep him away from other people as much as you can, to try and draw the mother out.'

'And good luck!' Helene added.

'No, wait,' Alice started to say, but Iona and Helene were already preparing to leave.

'So we have a plan.' Liam flashed that too charming smile at the other women. 'Then, ladies, thank you for your help. But I think we can take it from here.'

CHAPTER SEVEN

OKAY, HE KNEW this was crazy. What was he thinking, offering to help Alice Walters look after a baby? Had he been thinking at all?

Probably not. But he couldn't forget the note in his jacket pocket—the one asking him to take care of Jamie. Given how many times he'd been turned away by people who should have cared for him, how could he do the same to a helpless baby?

Besides, he saw how the tension in Alice's shoulders had lessened, just slightly, and how the lines around her eyes looked less pronounced as she realised she wouldn't be doing this alone. She knew she needed him; that much was clear. She was still gripping the baby close to her chest, as if she was afraid someone might snatch him from her arms at any moment. But she didn't look quite so much as if she was about to bolt out of the door and run for the hills.

Liam understood the impulse—hadn't he thought of doing exactly the same thing? The only thing he still wasn't sure about was, if she'd run, would she have taken Jamie with her or not?

She obviously didn't have much experience with babies, and from what Heather had said she didn't seem particularly interested in them either—until now. Which brought him back to the nagging question at the back of his mind: what was it about Jamie that made her hold on so tight?

If it *was* that she knew who his mother was, staying close and helping her might enable him to find out too. And if not…well, they might not have got off to the best start but Alice clearly needed his help. He wasn't about to abandon her—or Jamie.

He knew how it felt to be abandoned. Unwanted. Cast out or turned away. He couldn't let this baby, born in Liam's own ancestral home, start his life that way.

Thornwood Castle might never have been a home or even a refuge to him, but Alice had made it one for others. And now it could be one for Jamie too.

'How come you know so much about babies, anyway?' Alice asked, sounding sulky as Jamie started to fuss again. 'Or was the nappy thing just a fluke?'

Liam reached out to take Jamie from her. Alice held on for a second, obviously reluctant to give the baby up to him, but finally released him. Supporting Jamie's neck with one hand, Liam held him against his chest, humming a little to help soothe him.

'Not a fluke,' Helene commented as she shrugged on her coat. Heather looked less impressed, Liam realised, but he doubted there was *anything* he could do to impress *her*.

'I had younger siblings,' he said by way of explanation.

Heather frowned. 'I thought you were Rose's *only* living relative.'

'Foster brothers and sisters,' he expanded. 'Various families, but no blood relatives.'

And that was what it all came down to in the end, for Rose. His blood. It might not be pure, but there was enough of her ancestors' DNA pumping through his body to be better than nothing.

'You were fostered?' Alice asked, her brow furrowed. 'But why—?' Jamie cut her off with a short cry.

'Do you have that bottle?' Liam asked, glad for the interruption. 'I think he's hungry.' Alice gave a quick nod and rooted through the bag, pulling out the sterile bottle, snapping off the lid and screwing on the teat before handing it to him.

Liam slipped the teat between Jamie's lips and waited for the tiny boy to suck. This, he could do. Taking care of a baby might prove easy compared to avoiding Alice's questions, longer term. He might not have known her long, but he was already sure that she was the sort of person who needed all the information, and didn't stop asking questions until she had it.

He knew what she'd been about to ask—why hadn't he come to live with Rose? Given how much respect she'd obviously had for his great-aunt, he suspected the real answer would disappoint her. In fact, she'd probably just assume that he'd refused or done something awful to make Rose reject him.

Which was fine by him. Better than having the world know the truth—that his own family had disowned him, just because his mother wasn't married to his father.

That was all in the past, now. Thornwood Castle was his, and there was no family still alive to look down on him.

Jamie spluttered and he removed the bottle, hardly even surprised when the baby spit up milk across the arm of his shirt.

He was his own man. And he wouldn't turn away a defenceless child the way his family had. Even one that had just thrown up all over his best dinner jacket.

'Well, since you have everything under control here, we'll see you all in the morning,' Helene said. 'And I'll do some digging tonight, see if I can find any leads to Jamie's mum.'

'Me too,' Iona added.

'Heather, are you okay locking up for the night?' Alice was normally responsible for clearing out all the rooms, making sure that doors were closed and locked, in a desperate attempt to keep what little heat the castle had inside. But tonight she had bigger priorities—and she wasn't leaving Jamie alone with Liam. Not because she didn't trust Liam with the baby—from the way he was cradling him as he fed him, she instinctively knew that Liam would take good care of him. But just because…

Did she have to have a reason? Because if she did, she didn't want to analyse it too closely.

'I'll be fine.' Heather shot her an unreadable look. 'Will you?'

Alice glanced away. She hadn't shared much of her past with her friend—or with anyone at Thornwood—but she'd obviously picked up on a few things. Heather might pretend to be brusque and uncaring, but underneath her tough exterior Alice knew she had more feelings than most people. She just hid them better—the result of a lifetime of protecting herself and her kids, Alice supposed.

'I'll be fine,' Alice lied as she took Jamie back from Liam's arms. 'Don't worry.'

She was worrying enough for both of them.

Heather watched her for a moment longer. And then she nodded.

'Okay. Helene? Iona? I'll show you out. Alice, there's a spare travel cot in the cupboard off the library, I think. I'm sure a famous architect will be able to figure out how to set it up.'

And then, with the swing of the door, she was alone with Jamie.

Well, Jamie and Liam.

'I don't need your help,' she told Liam over Jamie's sleeping head.

He smiled infuriatingly. 'Yes, you do.'

'I have books. And the Internet. I can figure this out.'

'Which brings me back to why would you want to? Trust me, babies are always easier when you can tag team. And, besides, you don't know how long it's going to take to find his mother.'

'No. I suppose.' She was out there somewhere, though. Alone, perhaps. And thinking about her son, she was almost certain.

'So we'll do it between us,' Liam said. 'It'll be good practice in working together.'

'Ready for kicking me out of Thornwood?'

'For finding your perfect place.'

Alice held Jamie closer against her chest as Liam picked up the bags of supplies. 'First we need to find that travel cot. And somewhere to put it up.' She hadn't thought that far ahead. There wasn't room in her tiny box bedroom for a travel cot—or any of the other junk babies seemed to come with, if the bags Heather and Helene had left were any indication.

Liam shrugged. 'That part's easy. We'll set it up in Rose's suite. There's plenty of room up there and we can both sleep near enough to hear his every movement, if that's what you're worried about.'

'Rose's suite. You mean your room.' His bedroom, where he slept every night, in his bed.

Alice knew what he was doing. He was taking control of this whole situation, because that was what he did. What he was used to. He'd marched into Thornwood Castle and taken over—holding court during her career sessions, sticking his nose in everywhere, deciding not just the future of the castle but *her* future, and the future of all the women she helped. He had taken charge of every single thing that happened at Thornwood since he'd arrived.

Well, not this time. Not Jamie.

'It's the bedroom that's best equipped to look after a baby in.' Liam gave her that look that suggested he thought she was infuriatingly slow. 'It has the best heating, and there's a daybed in the lounge area as well as the king-sized bed in the bedroom. There's even a mini fridge if we need it, and plenty of empty drawers for Jamie's stuff. It makes sense.'

It makes sense. How many times had she heard that from her husband? Every time she had a suggestion, or a request to do things differently—anything he didn't agree with—he'd put forward his argument instead, always finishing with 'it makes sense'. Dismissing her ideas, her dreams, with just those three words.

Frustration bubbled up inside her just hearing them again. And the very worst part was, this time, Liam was right. It *did* make sense. She just didn't want it to.

'I could set up a camp bed in the library,' she countered. 'It's close to the kitchens, and there's plenty of space.'

'And lots of reading material,' Liam drawled. 'But if there's only one camp bed, where am I going to sleep?'

'In your room. Alone,' she added, in case there was any confusion.

Jamie shifted in her arms, and she took the opportunity to change position. For such a tiny little thing he was getting kind of heavy.

'Then how will I help you?'

'As I said, I don't need your help.'

'You say that now. But at two in the morning, when he's been screaming for an hour or two, you'll be knocking on my door begging for help.'

'No. I won't.' She sounded like a stubborn toddler and

she didn't care. Jamie was her responsibility, whatever that note said, and she would take care of him. Somehow.

Liam sighed. 'No, you probably won't. And that's the problem.'

'Why is that a problem? I thought a self-described care-free, fun-loving bachelor would appreciate a full night's sleep. All the better to get on with his carefree, fun-loving ways.' Nobody in their right mind would describe Liam Jenkins as the responsible, paternal type. At least, no one who'd met him.

'I have *never* used those words to describe myself,' Liam said, sounding amused. 'And I want to because if you spend all night dealing with him then you'll be a wreck tomorrow. Share the load a little and you might be able to function in the morning. I don't imagine life at Thornwood Castle will halt just because you took in a waif and stray.'

Damn him, but he had a point. She had three classes planned tomorrow.

'Plus if the mother shows up, you want to be awake enough to talk with her,' he added, and Alice gave up the argument.

Well, part of it, anyway.

'Fine. We'll set the travel cot up in the lounge area, and I'll sleep on the daybed. You keep to your usual bed, and I'll be able to call you if I need you.'

For a moment Liam looked like he was about to argue, but in the end he gave a sharp nod. 'Fine. I'm a light sleeper. I'll leave the door open, so I'll hear him anyway.'

Alice shrugged. 'Your choice.'

'A compromise.' Liam's mouth twitched up into a lop-sided smile. 'Look at us. Finding a way to compromise. That bodes well for the future.'

'That or it's a sign of the apocalypse.' Alice nudged Jamie's head into a more comfortable position. 'Come on. Let's get this cot set up. This boy is getting heavy.'

The travel cot had been designed by a masochist, Liam decided. Who else would make it so damn difficult for sleep-deprived new parents to set up somewhere for their baby to sleep? He'd had a full eight hours last night, was only temporarily performing parental duties and had several advanced qualifications in architecture and engineering, and he still couldn't do it.

No. He *would* do it. It was just taking a little longer than he'd hoped.

'Are you still trying to get that thing set up?'

Of course, Alice's running commentary was *definitely* helping.

'Whoever designed this hates me,' he said, shoving one side down to try and get it to click into place. 'Like, they have a personal vendetta and they hate me passionately. It's the only explanation.'

Alice gave out a small squeak, and when he looked back over his shoulder he saw her lips were pressed together tightly as if she were trying not to laugh.

'Here, take Jamie.' She held the baby out to him. 'Let me have a go.'

'This is trickier than nappies, trust me,' Liam said, but he took Jamie all the same. Let her try. She was always so convinced that she could do everything herself, and better than anyone else—let her have a go.

Alice pulled a piece of paper from the bag the travel cot had been packed in, scanned it quickly, then did something he couldn't quite follow with one of the sides of the cot. Then she reached inside, pressed something, and stood back.

'All done. Where's the mattress?'

Liam nodded towards the pile of stuff Heather and Helene had left for them, amazed. Alice retrieved the mattress, settled it in place, then stretched a sheet across it.

'He'll probably refuse to sleep in it anyway. Don't you
have a bassinet or something around here?' It wasn't that
he was feeling emasculated or anything. Just annoyed that
he couldn't work the bloody thing.

And even more annoyed that she could.

'This is the best we have for now.' Alice went back to
rifling through the bags and pulled out a book from one
of the bags the doctor had left. 'I'll try and get hold of a
pram tomorrow. And, actually…' she reached deeper and
pulled out a large swathe of swirly purple and blue material '…Helene left us a sling. So at least we can try carrying him in that until then.'

'Are there instructions?' Liam squinted at the sling.
'Because that looks more confusing than the travel cot.'

Alice smiled across the room at him, then covered her
mouth as her smile turned into a yawn. 'We'll figure it
out tomorrow. It's late, and it's already been a long day.'

Liam suspected that the night would be even longer,
but it didn't seem worth reminding Alice of that right now.
Jamie had been as good as gold so far, only squawking
when he needed food or changing, but Liam had spent
enough nights trying to sleep through babies crying to
know that the chances were good it wouldn't last past their
heads hitting the pillow.

Although maybe that was just the babies his various
foster parents had taken in. The ones who had already
been abandoned, left with adults who were only looking
after them for the cash.

Liam knew there were good foster parents out there—
wonderful people who took children in to give them a better life, a better start. He'd met plenty of them since he'd

grown up, mostly through his charitable work with foster carers in the past decade. Once he'd found his feet, and his success, he'd wanted to give back—not to the system that had failed him, exactly, but to the other kids who ended up in his position. He wanted to make their chances a little better, their futures a little brighter.

So yeah, he knew there were great foster parents out there. He just hadn't had the good fortune to be fostered by any of them.

And now Jamie… He'd been abandoned too, left behind too. And all he had was Liam and Alice.

He hoped they could do a better job than the people who'd pretended to look after him over the years of his childhood.

'Are you okay with him for a few moments? Just while I go and get my overnight stuff?' Alice bit her lip as she waited for his answer, and she looked so uncertain, so concerned for Jamie, that for a moment Liam forgot to feel offended by her lack of confidence in him and just enjoyed knowing that this abandoned child, at least, would be loved.

He didn't know what Alice's issues were, what secrets she was hiding. But he knew that she loved Jamie already. He was barely half a day old, had no blood connection to Alice, and they didn't even *know* who his parents were, let alone care. But Alice loved that baby.

And that made her a good person. He could compromise for a good person. He could help her out.

Liam smiled and held Jamie a little closer. 'I'll be fine.'

'Okay, then.' Alice's blonde head disappeared through the door, and Liam let out a sigh of relief. He wasn't used to sharing space, yet here he was inviting a woman he barely knew and a baby he'd just met into his bedroom.

Well. He'd known that coming home to Thornwood would change his life.

Jamie wriggled in his arms and let out a small mewling cry.

'Shh… Shh…' Liam murmured, pressing a kiss to the top of the baby's head. 'It's all fine. Everything is fine. I'm here.'

Apparently Jamie didn't find that very reassuring, as his cries grew louder. Liam paced the room, jostling Jamie gently as he walked. Time to bring out the big guns.

Taking a deep breath, Liam began to hum, gratified as the music started to calm the baby. Growing in confidence, he opened his mouth and started to sing—snatches of lullabies and nursery rhymes he half remembered, interspersed with other songs from his childhood.

Jamie blinked up at him, silent again, and Liam couldn't help but smile down at his innocent face.

'It's all going to be fine, Jamie,' he whispered. 'I promise you. I'll make sure that everything is okay for you. I don't know how, but I will. You're never going to have to worry about being abandoned again.' He shouldn't promise anything, he knew. He wasn't staying at Thornwood. He had no power over Jamie's future. But, although the little boy didn't understand him, Liam couldn't bear the thought of Jamie feeling unwanted or lost for even a moment. 'You'll have a home. And a family. Somehow. I'll make it happen.'

Jamie would never grow up the way he had. He wouldn't allow it.

CHAPTER EIGHT

ALICE PAUSED IN the doorway, watching Liam pacing up and down the lounge area of the suite, Jamie nestled in his arms. He was talking to the baby, she realised, and strained closer to hear the words without being spotted.

'You'll have a home. And a family. Somehow. I'll make it happen.'

Her chest tightened at Liam's words. What had happened to make him so attached to a tiny baby on just a couple of hours' acquaintance? She knew it had to be connected with the baby being abandoned—his reaction to that had made his feelings very clear.

What she didn't know was what demons in Liam's past made him feel it so deeply. And what she didn't understand was why she cared.

Liam Jenkins had arrived at Thornwood ready to toss her out on her ear, along with all the other women she helped there. But instead he'd listened—maybe not immediately, but soon enough—and he'd changed his mind. He'd engaged with the work. He'd recognised its importance.

He might still be kicking her out, but at least he was making sure she had somewhere to go first. And now it looked as if he was doing the same for Jamie.

Liam looked up and caught sight of her in the doorway.

Holding up her overnight bag, Alice tried to make it look like she'd just arrived.

'How's he doing?' she asked.

'Just dozed off again. Might be a good time to try and put him down.'

Alice dumped her bag by the sofa and tried to remember what Helene's book had said. 'Don't we need to feed and change him first?'

Liam shrugged. 'He'll wake up when he's hungry or wet.'

'But won't he sleep longer if we do it now?' From the little she'd read and heard, maximising sleep was an important part of looking after babies. 'Plus, shouldn't we be trying to get him into a routine?'

She should be telling, not asking, she realised. She'd wanted to take control of this situation, but here she was, in his room, asking his advice.

On the other hand, he was the only one of them that had any idea about looking after babies. So maybe she was just being prudent.

'Stop overthinking it,' Liam advised. 'Chances are we'll find the mother tomorrow, get him home where he belongs—or find him a better place to be. But he won't—'

'He won't be here. Right.' Because he wasn't her son, this wasn't her life. Jamie would go to a new home, new parents, and they'd take care of getting him into a routine, and making sure he was taking the right amount of formula every few hours.

Someone else would be holding him, and putting him down to sleep. Which was just as it should be.

She really had to remember that.

'Put a blanket in the cot?' Liam asked. Alice blinked and jumped to do it, smoothing out the waffle blanket over the sheet.

Liam laid Jamie on top of the blanket, his head sticking out the top, then wrapped the blanket securely around his body.

'Swaddling?' Alice asked, surprised.

'Hardly,' Liam scoffed. 'Just keeping him warmly wrapped. My memory of childcare isn't good enough to remember the official way to do it.'

'He looks happy enough.'

Alice stood beside Liam and they gazed down at the sleeping baby.

It shouldn't feel so right, Alice knew. She shouldn't let herself feel so attached.

And yet she couldn't help it.

'You should take the bed,' Liam murmured. 'I'll be fine on the daybed.'

'A gentlemanly gesture?' Alice asked, surprised. 'Not likely. I want to be in here with Jamie.'

Liam sighed. 'Fine. It won't matter anyway. It's not like either of us are going to be getting much sleep.'

'Probably not,' Alice agreed. Normally, a bad night's sleep would bother her. But right then, looking down at Jamie sleeping peacefully…she didn't care at all.

She just wanted to see Jamie's blue eyes when he opened them again.

Sadly, Liam's words proved prophetic. No sooner had he managed to fall asleep—which wasn't as easy as it sounded—than he heard Jamie wake for the first time.

Resting an arm across his tired eyes, he waited to see if the baby might settle again. He'd already lain there awake for hours, listening to the small sounds from the next room. He wasn't used to sharing his space, and something about knowing Alice was just an open door away was distracting. Not to mention Jamie. Alice was the one lying beside the baby, listening for every breath, he was sure, but Liam couldn't help but try to do the same. What if something happened to him during the night? What if Alice didn't know how to deal with it?

God only knew how real parents coped with that kind of fear, night after night. It was driving him crazy and the baby was technically nothing to do with him.

Except for how it was living in his house. And sleeping next door. With his…employee? Lodger? Squatter? How exactly was he supposed to describe his relationship with Alice—especially now they appeared to be co-parenting a foundling child?

Jamie cried out again, and Liam decided to leave the ruminations for a more reasonable hour of the morning. Shoving the covers aside, he rolled out of bed, padding across the floor to the doorway.

Alice had turned on a small lamp in the corner of the lounge, and her hair glowed honey-gold in the soft light. She was bent over the crib, shushing Jamie as she stroked his head.

'Is he hungry?' Liam whispered, crossing to where she stood.

Alice shook her head. 'I don't think so. His eyes aren't even open; I'm not sure he's fully awake.'

Sure enough, after a few more moments, Jamie stilled again and his breathing evened out.

'You didn't have to get up,' Alice said, turning away.

'I know.' He could have waited, let Alice deal with it. But somehow he'd wanted to be there too.

Alice looked up at him, strangely vulnerable in the low light. For a moment, just a brief flash of a second, Liam could almost believe that this was real. That this was his life. His home, his family, his…Alice.

But it wasn't, not really.

He looked away. 'We should get some more sleep.'

Alice yawned in response.

Jamie woke a few more times in the night, usually settling again after milk or a nappy change. After the first couple, Liam left Alice to it—she only glared when he went in, anyway. But around three in the morning, Jamie started crying and didn't stop.

He gave it fifteen minutes, then went in to take over.

'My turn,' he said, holding his arms out for the baby.

Alice gave him the same glare he'd been getting all night, never stopping bouncing Jamie in her arms. 'I can do this.'

'You've *been* doing this all night. Now it's my turn.'

'Because you don't think I can do this.'

'Because you need a break.' He rolled his eyes. 'Just accept the help. Hand him over and go back to sleep.'

It took her thirty seconds or so to finally decide in his favour, and he could almost hear the argument she was having with herself in her brain. Then she yawned and handed him the baby.

'His bottles and nappies and everything are over there.' She waved a hand vaguely in the direction of the pile of stuff she'd piled up in the corner, and stumbled towards the daybed.

'Use my bed,' Liam said, and Alice paused. But obviously tiredness had begun to catch up with her, because she gave a small nod and changed her trajectory towards the bedroom.

Liam gave her a few seconds to reach the bed, then firmly shut the door behind her.

'Just you and me now, kid,' he told Jamie, who blinked in response.

How hard could this be?

* * *

Jamie's wails echoed off the lonely stone walls of Thornwood Castle. Liam kept pacing. He was far enough away on the ground floor that he was pretty sure Alice couldn't hear him, which was the most important thing. She needed her sleep—if only so he could go back to bed without guilt when she got up and took over again.

For all his assurances that he knew what he was doing, Liam was starting to doubt himself. He jostled Jamie against his shoulder again, as the baby seemed to prefer being upright to lying down, and rubbed his palm against his lower back. Jamie's cries snuffled and stopped, and Liam held his breath, not even wanting to look to see if his eyes were closed. Maybe, maybe…

Jamie let out another long, desolate cry, and Liam let out the breath he'd been holding.

'Not tired yet, huh?' he murmured.

Maybe he needed those childcare books Alice had been talking about, he thought, as his pacing led him towards the library. God knew he'd done everything he could think of.

Jamie had a dry nappy on, he'd drunk plenty of milk and declined the last bottle Liam had offered him, and he was warm and cosy—but not too hot. After that, Liam was out of ideas.

'Let's go see if we can find you a story,' Liam suggested without much hope. Obviously Jamie was far too young to understand books and stories, but maybe the sound of him reading to him would soothe him. It was worth a try, anyway.

Liam found a stack of picture books on a low shelf by the library door and picked a few at random, settling into a leather wingback chair with Jamie nestled in the crook of his arm. Once again, Jamie's cries lessened for a moment, but soon he was drowning out the words of the nursery rhyme book Liam had chosen.

Liam sighed. 'Be honest. Is this punishment for something I did in another life? Or are you just bored?'

Jamie's only response was to cry louder.

Exhausted, Liam let his head fall back against the chair and his eyes close. What on earth had he been thinking, agreeing to this—no, insisting on this? He wasn't meant to be playing happy families with a woman who didn't trust him and a baby that had landed unceremoniously underneath their Christmas tree. And he wasn't meant to be settling in at Thornwood either—he was supposed to be shaking things up and changing everything.

But instead he was spending all his energies on a tiny scrap of humanity who *would not stop crying.*

'I must have been mad,' he whispered. 'Actually crazy to even come back here.' Hadn't he known that Thornwood was the worst place for him to be? A place where he could never belong, and where he would always, always be found wanting?

Jamie was just bringing that home to him in a very vocal way. He couldn't do this, and he shouldn't even have wanted to try. This wasn't his life.

Jamie gave a tiny hiccup, mid cry, and the strange sensation seemed to be enough to quiet him for a moment. Liam opened his eyes and looked down into unblinking blue ones, and knew in an instant that none of it mattered.

Yes, he didn't belong here. Yes, he probably couldn't do this. And yes, this wasn't at all how he'd pictured his time at Thornwood going.

But he was going to do it anyway.

Because this tiny child, less than a day old, needed him. And that made him his responsibility, regardless of blood ties or his mother's request. Jamie *needed* him, and that was enough. More than enough.

Liam couldn't walk away now if he wanted to.

Jamie's little face started to screw up again, and Liam eased himself to his feet with a groan.

'Come on, little man. If you're going to be staying here, you need to get to know the place. Let's have a tour. We can start with Rusty—that's Alice's favourite suit of armour, you know.' He held Jamie a little closer, and breathed in the scent of him. 'You and me, we can get to know this place together. Okay?'

Because, however hard it got, Jamie was his responsibility now, for as long as the little boy needed him. And Liam wasn't going to let him down.

Where was she?

Alice sat bolt upright in a bed that definitely wasn't hers—it was far too comfortable. She blinked into the darkness for a few moments before the events of the previous night came flooding back.

She was in *Liam's* bed. Because they were looking after a baby together. And she'd spent half the night staring fixedly at the cot where Jamie was sleeping just in case he stopped breathing, until Liam had taken over and told her to get some sleep…

Jumping out of the bed, she raced for the door and yanked it open.

The lounge was empty.

Logically, she knew that Liam wouldn't have taken Jamie far—they were in his home, for heaven's sake—but that didn't make her heart pound any less. Pausing only to grab her slippers—the stone floors were freezing—she dashed out of Liam's suite and headed for the stairs, listening all the while for the sound of a baby's cries.

She heard nothing.

Nothing as she passed the Christmas tree where they'd found him, nothing as she ran past the library. Nothing at all…until she neared the kitchen.

The smell of bacon cooking was unmistakable, but it was far too early for Maud to have arrived. And Maud didn't sing songs from the musicals in a light tenor.

Alice slowed, smiling, as she took the steps down to the kitchen.

Inside, she saw Liam at the stove, turning bacon as he sang, while Jamie lay on a blanket, surrounded by cushions, on the floor a few feet away.

'Ready for breakfast?' he asked without turning, and she wondered how he knew she was there.

'You said you weren't going to take him anywhere.'

'You said,' Liam corrected her. 'And I didn't. We're still in the castle.'

'I meant stay in the suite.'

'He got bored, and I didn't want him to wake you up. So I took him on a little tour of the castle, introduced him to Rusty outside your office, and now we're raiding Maud's supplies to make you breakfast.'

'That's…kind of you.' She crossed to where Jamie was staring into the middle distance and knelt beside him to hide her confusion.

She wasn't sure what she'd expected when Liam had offered to help her out with Jamie, but breakfast hadn't really been part of it.

'He seems content,' she said, tucking Jamie's hands back under the blanket.

'He's a very happy baby, most of the time.' Liam flipped the bacon onto slices of bread already laid out on plates on the counter. 'Surprisingly.'

'Why surprising?' They'd taken good care of him so far. Why wouldn't he be happy?

Liam added the second slices of bread to the bacon sandwiches and handed her a plate. 'Well, considering the first thing that happened to him after his birth was being abandoned…'

'Since he can't focus his eyes properly or control his hands, I doubt that the significance of that event has hit him just yet,' Alice said drily.

'Maybe not. But it's only a matter of time.' Liam took a large bite of his sandwich, as if trying to stop himself talking.

Alice considered him across the table. This wasn't just idle talk. This was personal for him, somehow.

'Who abandoned you?' she asked softly.

Liam took another bite instead of answering.

'Ever since we found him… This is personal for you, isn't it? Because of your dad?'

'My father,' Liam corrected. 'I never knew him well enough to call him Dad.'

'Right.' Alice trawled through her sleep-deprived brain to try to remember what she knew about Liam's family. She knew that his father had never acknowledged that he was his son before he'd died. That had to impact on a person. And his mother… What had happened to his mother? 'What about your mum?'

'She died when I was ten.'

'Oh. I'm sorry.' Death wasn't abandonment, she knew, but it could feel like it. She frowned. 'Where did you go?' He'd mentioned foster parents the night before, but in the middle of everything it hadn't fully registered. And it didn't answer the obvious question: Why hadn't he gone to stay with Rose?

'Does it matter?' he said irritably, his usual cool evaporating for a moment.

'You don't have to—' she started, but he interrupted her with a heavy sigh.

'No. It's fine.' He shrugged. 'It was all a long time ago. I stayed with some of my mum's family for a while, over in Australia. But they couldn't cope with me.'

'You were a troublemaker?'

'I was a nightmare.'

She could imagine it easily enough. A guy didn't get as rich and successful as young as Liam had unless he was willing to take risks. And that kind of risk-taking didn't tend to manifest itself well in teenage boys, from her observations.

'So where did you go then?'

He looked down at Jamie. 'Foster homes, mostly. Like I told you last night. I bounced around between a few of them and the care homes.'

'Why didn't you come to Thornwood? I'm sure Rose would—'

'Yeah, well, maybe you didn't know Rose as well as you think,' he snapped, loud enough to draw a startled cry from Jamie.

Alice dropped her sandwich to her plate and went to pick the baby up, glad of the excuse to turn her back on Liam's anger. Even if it wasn't really directed at her, just the sound of it made her nervous, and she didn't need him seeing that.

Behind her, he sighed, loud enough for her to hear. 'Sorry. I didn't mean to upset Jamie.'

'He's fine.' And he was. Alice held him close against her body and remembered how special it had felt, every time he'd woken up in the night wanting her. She was sure it was the sort of feeling that wore off as the sleep deprivation increased, but for now it was magical. Especially since she wouldn't be doing it for long.

Sucking in a breath, she turned back to face him. 'What happened with Rose?'

CHAPTER NINE

LIAM TIPPED HIS chair back on two legs and stared at his hands. What had happened with Rose? That was a question he'd asked himself a million times over the years. What had he done at ten years old that meant he wasn't good enough for his great-aunt? And what had changed between then and now, to mean that she'd left him everything she held dear?

Looking up, he met Alice's eyes. She'd known Rose better than anyone at the end, he'd bet. Maybe she'd be able to explain it to him.

'I was ten,' he said, figuring it was easiest to just get it over with. She'd find out eventually. It might as well be him that told her. 'I'd been kicked out of my uncle's house in Brisbane, and the authorities were running out of places to put me. Someone figured out about my father's family over here in the UK and got in touch with Rose, who was more or less all that was left of it by then. She agreed to meet me.'

'You came to Thornwood?'

'Briefly.' Sighing, he let his chair drop back to all four legs again. 'I pitched up here, freezing cold and miserable, and this creepy old guy answered the door—the butler. He looked down his long nose at me and… I knew this wasn't the place for me.'

'What did you do?' From her tone, Liam knew she'd probably already guessed. Apparently he was getting predictable in his old age.

'I acted up. I was rude, objectionable and did everything I could to make sure Rose wouldn't take me in.'

'And she didn't.'

'No, she didn't.' What he didn't tell her, of course, was how much he'd wanted her to. How desperate he'd been for someone—even this old lady who was his only link to his father—to look past his act and see how much he needed her.

Of course, she hadn't.

'She sent you back?'

'Worse.' Liam tried to stop the pain in his chest at the memory. 'She looked down into my eyes, stared for a while, then stepped back and said, "Well, he's a Howlett all right. Can't mistake those eyes." That was the first time anyone from my father's family had ever officially acknowledged me.'

'What was so bad about that?'

'Because that got my hopes up.' Just remembering that hope, that brief shining moment when he'd imagined the possibility of family again, made acid burn in his throat even now. He shrugged the memory away. He didn't need that any more. 'But the next day I got the message—she couldn't take me in. So it was back to the foster system for me. It taught me a valuable lesson at least, I suppose.'

'What lesson?'

'That you can't rely on anyone—especially not family.'

He'd expected her to do as all his ex-girlfriends had when he'd expressed the sentiment—tell him he was a cynic, or try to convince him that he just hadn't met the right person yet. But instead Alice gave him a small smile and said, 'It took me twenty-four years to learn that one.'

'A man?'

'Yes.' One of the tiny pieces that made up the puzzle of Alice Walters fell into place. He wanted to know more, but before he could formulate the right question she said, 'That wasn't the last time you saw Rose, though, was it? You said it had been fifteen years...'

Of course she remembered that. Liam sighed. 'She asked to meet with me in London, when I was working on a project there. Turned out she'd followed my progress, my life, from a distance.'

'What did she want?' Alice asked, eyes wide. She was probably hoping for more signs of the Rose she'd known, he imagined.

'First, she wanted to offer me money,' Liam said.

'Nothing so bad about that.'

'And then she wanted me to sign away any claim to Thornwood, or the family title.' He could still feel the rage she'd awakened now. Sitting having polite conversation, sipping tea at the Ritz, and wanting nothing more than to tear down all that civility and history and privilege.

That he hadn't was a testament to the self-restraint he'd learned over the years. He made himself calm, relaxed, because he knew otherwise he'd hit out, hit back, cause trouble. And he wasn't that boy any more.

'What did you say?' Alice asked, her face troubled.

'I told her I didn't need her money, and I sure as hell didn't want her castle or her fancy title. And then I walked out.' And straight into the nearest pub.

Alice frowned. 'But I don't get it. Why did she leave you Thornwood in the end, then?'

'Because her other great-nephew—the legitimate one— died in a car accident seven years later.' Rose wasn't the only one who could keep track of family. 'Bet she was glad I hadn't taken her money then, when I was the only one left.'

'I think she changed, you know,' Alice said softly. 'The Rose I knew… I think she regretted the person she'd been in the past. She tried to make amends.'

'By opening Thornwood up to anyone who needed it.'

'By leaving you Thornwood.'

Liam looked away. He didn't want to think about that. Standing up, he began to clear the table. 'Dr Helene will be here soon,' he said. 'Along with an astounding number of random women, I imagine.'

'So we'd better get cleared up and ready for the day,' she agreed, handing him Jamie. 'Come on, then. Let's see how long it takes us to get him dressed today.'

'Well, you all seem to have survived the night well enough.' Was it Alice's imagination, or was Helene smirking as she said that? The last thing she needed was her friend getting any ideas about her and Liam.

'He wasn't too difficult in the night,' Alice said. Liam shot her an incredulous glance. She frowned. What exactly had he been doing with Jamie since he'd taken over, before he'd started breakfast? Whatever it was, it wasn't sleep, not if the bags under his eyes were anything to judge by. 'We took turns looking after him.'

'And you did a great job.' Helene looked up from her examination of Jamie. 'He seems to be thriving.'

'I take it the mother hasn't spontaneously come forward overnight. Any luck tracking her down?' Liam asked Iona, who was making her own notes.

'None yet, I'm afraid.' Iona shook her head sadly.

Helene handed Jamie back to him and began packing up. 'Basically, all the pregnant women who've been through my surgery lately are accounted for; I suspect she's either from out of town or she's been without prenatal care.'

'It's a miracle Jamie's as healthy as he is,' Alice murmured, watching Liam rock him gently.

'Women have been having babies for thousands of years without modern medicine,' Iona pointed out. 'But, yes, we were all lucky that it must have been a straightforward pregnancy and birth.'

'So now what do we do?' Alice asked, trying to ignore the way her heart beat a little faster. Just because they hadn't found Jamie's mother didn't change the fact that eventually he would have to go to a new family. However much she wanted to avoid thinking about that, she couldn't afford to. She had to keep that knowledge front and centre—and keep her heart safe.

'Give me another day or so,' Iona said. 'I want to check in with a few more places—colleagues, refuges. But if we haven't found her by the end of next week…'

'We're going to have to call the police,' Liam finished for her.

'And start putting the proper procedures into motion, before everything gets more difficult over the Christmas holidays,' Iona said.

'So he'll be taken into care.' Was it Alice's imagination, or did Liam hold Jamie a little closer as he said that?

She didn't blame him. Now she knew a little more about his background, and his own experiences of the foster system, she could understand him not wanting to put another child through that. He hadn't spoken explicitly about the foster carers he'd had, but the fact he'd been passed around more than a few families spoke volumes.

Liam had grown up unwanted, without a home. Of course he didn't want that for Jamie.

Alice wondered if he knew that, even if they protected

Jamie from it now, it was perfectly possible to lose a family, a home, a future, as an adult.

She'd been twenty-four before she'd realised how little others valued her as a human being. And twenty-eight before Rose had helped her find that value again.

Now, she knew, she made a difference. She mattered.

Just not in the way she'd always dreamt of. She'd never be a mother.

Except for right now. These brief few days, this Christmas miracle of motherhood. That was all she had.

And she intended to make the most of every second of it.

On cue, Jamie started to fuss.

'Let me take him,' she said, holding out her arms to Liam. 'He can feel your stress levels rising and it's upsetting him.'

Liam raised his eyebrows, but handed the baby over. Heather, meanwhile, scoffed. 'Stress levels? I don't think he has any. Didn't you say he was the most infuriatingly laid-back man you'd ever met?'

Alice blushed as her own words came back to haunt her. She didn't want to explain to Heather that she knew better now—knew *Liam* better. In fact, she was beginning to suspect that his casual, laid-back nature was actually a deliberate shield or disguise against the rest of the world.

If he didn't let on that he cared about anything, then he couldn't be hurt when no one cared about him.

Alice identified with that more than she'd like to admit.

'Well, since you're all busy playing Weirdly Happy Families here, I suppose I'd better get on with running the place for the day,' Heather said with a sigh. 'I assume you have your hands too full to help,' she said to Alice.

'Literally, right now,' Alice admitted. 'But I'll still be around; I can help out when he's napping or whatever.'

Heather snorted. 'Yeah, good luck with that. You focus on what you're doing. I'll take care of everything else.'

'Thank you,' Alice said, and meant it.

Thornwood Castle could manage without her for a couple of days. Right now, Jamie couldn't.

And it felt strangely wonderful to be needed again.

Initially, Alice seemed relieved to say goodbye to Dr Helene, Iona and Heather and retreat to his rooms with Jamie. But as spacious as Rose's suite was for one, for three it grew quite cramped quite quickly—especially when Jamie grew fussy after his feed and wouldn't settle to sleep.

'We should get out of here,' Liam said.

'Sure, where were you thinking?' Alice asked casually. 'Paris or Tokyo?'

'I was thinking a walk. You could show me the estate. I've done some exploring but I've barely scratched the surface of it this week.' Mostly because he'd been going through legal documents and figuring out how to get his castle back without actually being a monster. And getting to know the castle itself, of course. A building of such size could take years to know properly, and longer to find every hidden nook and cranny. 'Besides, I'd like to see it through your eyes.'

'What about Jamie? We still don't have a pram for him, and it's freezing out there.'

Liam glanced out of the window; she was right. Never mind Jamie, the way the frost still sat on the fields around them told him definitively that he wasn't in Oz any more.

'The good doctor left us this.' He reached into the bag Helene had handed him earlier and pulled out a tiny white snowsuit. It had a fluffy lining, integral gloves and feet, and ears on the top of its fur-lined hood. It was almost excruciatingly cute, and Liam was sure that almost every woman he'd ever met would have adored it.

Alice, meanwhile, looked pained at the sight of it. He was never going to understand her.

'Don't suppose she left a pram?' she asked.

'We have the baby carrier Heather found, remember?' The contraption looked like a rucksack that was missing its middle, but the illustration on the box suggested it would sit on his chest, with Jamie tucked against him. 'I'll carry him.'

'Then I guess I'm out of objections,' Alice said.

'Be honest—you were only objecting because it was my suggestion.' What was it about her that meant she just couldn't ever admit he was right, or that an idea he had might be worthwhile?

'Pretty much.' She flashed him a smile, and he forgave her. At least she admitted her prejudices. 'But it would be good to get some fresh air. And it might help Jamie drop off.'

'Exactly. And that almost sounded like you were agreeing with me for a moment there.'

Alice's face turned serious. 'I'll have to watch that. Bad habit to get into.'

It took a few minutes to get the three of them prepared to leave the castle. First, they all needed to get wrapped up warm enough to cope with the British winter. Then Jamie threw up his milk all over Alice's jumper and she had to get changed. But eventually they were ready. Jamie nestled against Liam's chest, his tiny face peeping out from under his hood with ears. Liam appreciated the extra warmth the minute they stepped outside.

'Jesus, this country of yours is cold.'

'It's yours now too, remember,' Alice commented as she strode off towards the fields at the back of the castle.

'So it is.' The thought was an astonishing one. That he belonged here—on this frozen, far-flung island. Not in the heat and the beaches of the country of his birth. The place he'd spent so long looking for home.

Instead, he'd apparently found it in the last place he'd expected.

No. Liam shook his head as he hurried to catch up with Alice. Thornwood Castle would never truly be home. How could it? It was an antiquated folly full of bad memories and family expectations. The castle wasn't home—it was a money-making scheme, at best.

But the land around it… Liam had to admit that the English countryside looked stunning, coated in a layer of frost that sparkled and shone in the winter sunlight. The air was cold but crisp, a sharp bitterness that woke up every cell in his body as he walked out into it. Overhead, the occasional bird chirped out from the bare trees and as they crested a small rise on the well-trodden path the village of Thornwood sprung into sight below them, all honey-coloured stone and the rising spire of the church. Picture perfect.

When he'd arrived, on that grey, rainy day, he'd decided that winter in Britain was unbearable—lifeless and miserable, depressing and dead. It had fitted perfectly with his memories of Rose and Thornwood.

Today, the world looked different. It looked alive— vibrant and full of possibility—from the wisps of smoke from a cottage chimney, to the warmth of Jamie's body tucked against his.

He hadn't expected life from this place. Hadn't for a moment thought he'd find anything that could entice him to stay any longer than he had to.

'It's beautiful, isn't it?' Alice said beside him.

'It is.' He glanced down at her, at her shining face, her hair like spun gold in the sunlight, and knew he wasn't just talking about the view. 'I'm starting to think you might not really want to leave.'

She didn't answer, but he didn't need her to. He could see the truth of it on her face.

Alice came alive in this place too. When they'd first met, he'd thought she was just another Thornwood relic—cold and unfeeling, miserable. But over the week or so that he'd been there she'd already shown him so many other parts of herself. Her passion for her mission, her love for the women she helped, and for Thornwood itself. But more than anything, the way she looked at Jamie.

Her face as she held that baby in her arms told him almost everything he needed to know about her.

But only almost.

It told him how brightly she could love, how fiercely. It told him what mattered to her—that every person had a place they could go that was safe, that could be called home.

But it didn't tell him what had caused the sadness behind her eyes as she looked at Jamie. And Liam knew he couldn't leave Thornwood until he'd found the answer to that question.

He blinked as she smiled up at him, and he felt something unfurl in his chest that he'd almost forgotten had ever been there.

He couldn't be falling for Alice Walters. Could he?

CHAPTER TEN

ALICE LOOKED AWAY from Liam's face, uneasy with what she saw there. Or, rather, how his expression made her feel.

He looked like a man who had found the promised land. Who had finally realised how much Thornwood Castle had to give him. He looked as if he'd come back to life—utterly unlike the laid-back, bored and uncaring man who'd arrived a week ago.

This Liam would want to jump into making changes immediately—which meant getting her out of there.

'Come on,' he said. 'Why don't we take a look around at some possible sites for your women? I think there were some barns over to the east of the castle…?'

She nodded. 'Of course.' He was already walking ahead but she didn't try to catch up, following a few steps behind instead, his earlier words echoing in her brain.

I'm starting to think you might not really want to leave,' he'd said.

But of course he was finding a way to get rid of her anyway.

The truth was, she *wasn't* sure she wanted to leave. But that feeling had nothing to do with the view, or the castle, or even the women she helped there. Well, maybe the women.

But the biggest reason for that feeling was snoozing happily, his little face resting against Liam's chest.

When she'd looked out over the village, she'd had a vision. A daydream, she supposed, but one so vivid it felt as if she could reach out and claim it for her own.

She'd imagined leaving a chocolate box cottage home and taking Jamie down to the village—as a baby, as a toddler, as a boy. Imagined walking down the path to the local school on a summer's morning, or the playground on a Saturday afternoon.

An entire life with Jamie had flashed before her eyes, as impossible as anything she'd ever wanted. As any of the dreams that had been stripped away from her four years ago.

Jamie wasn't her child, and he never would be. Daydreaming about a future with him could only bring her more misery.

And she wasn't even going to admit to herself the other part of that idle daydream—the man walking beside them, laughing and loving them both.

She hadn't seen his face, but even in her vision she'd known exactly who he was. And Liam Jenkins was an even more impossible part of her future than Jamie, for so many reasons.

No, she had to give up these thoughts. And she had to step up their efforts to find Jamie's real mother. If they couldn't find her, then she'd have to give Jamie up at the end of the week anyway, and who knew what would happen to him then? She was under no illusion that the care system in the UK was any better than the one that had let Liam down.

'What do you think?' Liam asked, and Alice realised, belatedly, that they'd reached the first of the barns he was considering as a possible location for her groups.

She blinked and tried to think objectively for an argument that sounded more impressive than *I don't like them*.

'I know they're not in great shape now,' he went on. 'But you have to ignore the state of them. I can fix all that, trust me. It's more about the location, and the possibility.'

'And the planning permission.' She was bursting his bubble, she knew, but she didn't care. She prided herself on being realistic. If Liam was pursuing flights of fancy with her future, she'd have to rein him in.

Just like she had to quash her own daydreams.

She turned and looked back over the path they'd walked, then spun slowly in a circle to take in the full surroundings. The location was what mattered, he'd said. And the location sucked.

'Won't work,' she said bluntly. 'What else have you got?'

'Hang on. I need more than that.' Liam's smile had faded slightly, along with his enthusiasm. '*Why* won't it work?'

'It's too far from the village. There's no easy road access—and that would be a nightmare to try and get permission for. And the path we just took isn't suitable for pushchairs. So, like I said, what else have you got?'

'Reasonable objections,' Liam admitted. 'But I'll find you your perfect location yet. Come on.'

They viewed three more sites before Jamie woke up hungry. Fortunately the last one—not big enough, and too close to the village this time—was a short walk from the Ring O' Bells, which served a tasty steak sandwich and chips and also had good baby facilities.

By the time they were all suitably replenished, the afternoon was wearing on.

'It's getting towards the shortest day,' Alice noted as

she shrugged on her coat again. 'It'll be dark in an hour and a half. We should head back to the castle.'

Liam nodded. 'Okay. There's one more site I wanted to show you, but it's on our way anyway.'

If it was on their way, Alice was pretty sure it wouldn't work as a venue for her women. They needed to be far enough away from the village that they couldn't be observed going in and out—otherwise a lot of them wouldn't come in the first place. Privacy and discretion were important.

But if it was on their way she couldn't reasonably refuse to view it either. She'd promised she'd be open-minded, so she strapped Jamie onto her front this time and trudged after Liam back up the hill towards the castle in the distance.

After about ten minutes, Liam veered off the path, up a small side track through a small copse of trees. 'I think it's up here.'

Curious, Alice followed. She'd never even noticed this path before, let alone taken it.

Ahead of her, Liam came to an abrupt stop. 'Yeah, no. This place is definitely too small, and I can't see me getting permission to expand as much as you'd need. Funny, it looked bigger on the plans.'

Alice frowned, leaning around him to try and get a glimpse of what he was looking at—and felt her heart stutter for a moment.

It was her cottage. The one from her vision on the hill. Oh, it looked different; it was half-falling-down, for a start. But underneath all that—under the overgrown ivy vines and the gaps where roof tiles were missing—it was her cottage.

Her impossible, dream life cottage.

Which was beyond absurd. She wasn't even staying, and if she was she wouldn't have Jamie with her.

She'd have no need for a family cottage like this one.

'No. You're right. Too small.' She turned her back on the cottage, and Liam. 'Let's go.'

Liam stared at the cottage a moment longer, then turned to see Alice already halfway back up the track to the main road. He frowned after her, trying to decipher what he'd heard in her voice as she'd dismissed the cottage as a possibility.

Of course it wasn't suitable—he'd told her that, for once. But there'd been something behind her words—something he hadn't heard at any of the other apparently also unsuitable sites. It had sounded like…longing? Like the way he'd felt sometimes as a child, wishing for something permanent, something real.

Something his.

Did she want the cottage? Or was the cottage just a symbol of all the things she didn't, couldn't or wouldn't let herself have?

He wanted to know.

He caught up with her easily, taking the path at a lazy jog.

'Shame, really. It's a great cottage. It would make someone a lovely family home, don't you think?' The track was too narrow for them to walk side by side so he couldn't see her face, but he was close enough that he could feel her shoulders stiffen at his question.

'It's very pretty,' she admitted without emotion.

'Did you ever want that?' he asked. 'The whole chocolate box cottage thing. Marriage, a family, not living in a creepy old castle.'

'I tried marriage once. It didn't suit.'

The words were throwaway, as if they didn't matter, but they hit Liam in the stomach all the same.

'You were married?' He tried to imagine it, and couldn't. The Alice he knew would never let any man that close.

Which, now he thought about it, was probably *because* of the aforementioned marriage.

Was this the missing piece of the Alice puzzle he'd been looking for? Part of it, maybe. But not all. There was still so much he didn't understand about her. And this admission was the first hint that she might be willing to give him some more clues.

'For a year and a half,' Alice said. 'It was a disaster, it's over, and I don't really like to talk about it.'

Yeah, he wasn't letting her off that easily. 'What happened?'

'Does it matter?'

'It might.' He couldn't say why, but it *did* matter to him. 'Did he cheat?'

'Probably.' She sighed. 'But not that I know of. Look, really, it was a long time ago.'

'You got married young, then?' She didn't answer so, as they turned from the track onto the main path, he nudged her shoulder as he walked beside her. 'It's still a decent walk back to the castle,' he pointed out. 'And I can keep hypothesising the whole way.'

She stalled to a halt. 'Why do you care?'

He shrugged. He didn't really want to analyse his reasons too deeply. He just knew he *did* care. 'We're working together, living together, looking after a child together... and I know next to nothing about you. I told you all about my shining childhood. Now it's your turn. It's only fair.'

She looked away and started walking again. Then she said, 'Fine. I'll give you three questions. What do you want to know?'

Three questions. So like her to put limits on his curiosity, to find a way to make him play by her rules again. He'd just have to choose carefully, then.

'Why did you split up?' That was an obvious one.

'He was abusive, so I left him.' Her words were almost robotic, as if she was distancing herself from the very memory as well as the events.

Liam clenched his jaw, a strange fury burning through him. He'd known, he realised. He'd already known that Alice had suffered—he'd read it in her eyes, in her words, in her very actions. He'd known all along—but it hadn't felt real until now. And the idea of anyone laying their hands on Alice made his fists clench and his mind rage.

'You have two more questions,' Alice pointed out, totally calm, and he realised he had to get a grip on himself.

'He was violent, I assume,' he mused. Keeping it abstract and factual helped. Looking at the particulars—and not the woman involved. Because if he thought too much about that he was going to lose it. 'And no, that's not my second question. How many times? Did you leave the first time he hit you or…' He trailed off, unable to even articulate the idea.

Alice looked away, her arms around Jamie's carrier on her front. 'The first time was just a push.'

'There's no such thing as "just" when it comes to this.' He'd seen it before. One of his mother's boyfriends who had 'just' slapped her, then 'just' pushed her and then she'd 'just' happened to fall down the stairs. The next time he'd 'just' broken her arm.

Liam had wanted to break his face. But he'd been eight years old and puny with it, and there hadn't been a damn thing he could do.

Just like he couldn't change the past for Alice.

'I know that now,' she snapped. 'But back then…'

'You stayed, then.'

'For a while.' She picked up speed as the castle came into sight. 'Look, we're nearly there.'

'I still have one more question.'

'Then ask it fast.' Alice didn't slow down at all. If anything, she walked more quickly.

Only one more question. It had to be a good one, then. And suddenly he knew what it had to be—the question he'd never been able to ask his mother.

'Why did you stay?'

She sighed. 'Because... Because I wanted the future he'd promised me. A family, a home, a place to belong. I'd built all my dreams on that marriage. I couldn't just give it up so easily. And...I honestly believed that I could change enough, be the person he loved enough that he wouldn't react that way again.'

Liam supposed that made a twisted sort of sense, although a future that involved being violently abused or being someone she wasn't didn't sound like much of one to him. And it should never have been up to her to change, to be anything else or less than what she was. The fault was with her husband, not Alice.

He opened his mouth to say as much, but she cut him off. 'And that was your third question, so we're done with this conversation. Understood?'

Liam nodded his agreement, even though he had an inkling they weren't anywhere near done with this topic. She'd answered everything he asked, given him the whole sorry story.

So why did he feel like he'd been asking the wrong questions all along?

It was almost too easy to settle into a routine over the next few days. Alice made sure to put all the focus on Jamie—

and not the exposure of her confessions—and in no time it started to feel as if this was the way things had always been. They still shared Liam's suite of rooms, taking turns between the daybed and the king-size, mostly, while Jamie slumbered in his travel cot. And if there had been one or two nights that had ended with all three of them sprawled out in the king-size, Jamie resting on Liam's chest as he sat up and held him, half-awake, and Alice curled up beside them, well, she wasn't considering them too closely. With a newborn, she'd learned quickly, you did whatever you had to do to make sure everyone got at least *some* sleep. That was all.

Even if it felt alarmingly like a family sometimes.

Keeping Jamie a total secret had proved impossible—the castle walls echoed with the baby's cries often enough that the regulars, at least, had figured out enough of what was going on to need properly filling in. But it was getting closer to Christmas now, and there was so much going on in the village, at the schools and at home, that the population of Thornwood Castle was of a different make up than usual anyway. There were fewer classes or seminars on careers and first aid at the moment, and more fun events for mothers to bring their children to after school or on the weekends. Maud was running a few Christmas baking classes that had drawn in a whole new audience too.

In the daytime, Liam kept Jamie with him in his study while she worked around the castle, running seminars or managing the lunch rush. She'd check in often enough to help out with feeding and changing him, but while he was still so small he mostly dozed in the pram Helene had found for him, or kicked on his mat. Once, she'd caught Liam with Jamie in his bouncy chair, practising a presentation as if the baby were an investor he was hoping to impress.

When Liam had calls or meetings, Alice took Jamie with her on her errands around the castle, securely tucked in his sling on her chest. There were always plenty of people around willing to take turns for a cuddle or a bottle when she needed to give something else her full attention and he was fussy. But mostly life in the castle went on contentedly, with only the shadow of the social worker's deadline looming over them to darken their happiness.

Until the day that Liam went out at first light for a day of meetings in the city, and left Alice alone with a screaming Jamie.

'I don't know what's wrong with him,' she fretted to Heather.

'He's a baby.' Heather shrugged. 'Sometimes they just need to cry. They don't have any other way of communicating with you, so they do this.'

'But what's he trying to *say*?' Alice tried rocking him again, but Jamie only wailed harder.

'That,' Heather said wisely, 'is the eternal question. Now, if you'll excuse me, I've got work to do and that racket is affecting my concentration.'

'It's affecting my sanity,' Alice muttered as Heather walked away. But what choice did she have but to listen to it?

The day dragged on unbearably. Alice tried everything—walks, milk, changes of scenery, singing—but nothing helped. Several of the women who stopped by during the day offered to take him for a while, but he only screamed louder in anyone else's arms so Alice always ended up taking him back.

'Is he really sick?' she asked Dr Helene, who'd popped by to run a quick clinic at the castle. She tried to hold one every month, for any women who couldn't or wouldn't visit their local GP. 'I thought he felt warm…'

Helene finished her examination and started dressing a red-faced, wailing Jamie again. Apparently he liked being poked and prodded by the doctor even less than he'd liked everything else today. Alice could feel the tension knots in her shoulders getting tighter with every second she waited for the doctor's answer.

'He's got a slight temperature, but that's all. Nothing to worry about,' Helene assured her. 'It's probably a touch of a viral bug—a cold, or what have you. There's not much you can do about it at this age, though. I'm afraid you're just going to have to wait it out.'

'Right.' Alice took Jamie back and tried to hold in a sigh.

'When's Liam due back?' Helene asked. 'I'd stay and help, but I've got more appointments this afternoon...'

Alice shook her head. 'Don't worry. We'll be fine, won't we, Jamie? And Liam said he'd be back this evening.'

What he'd actually said, now Alice thought about it, was that he'd be finished with his meetings by late afternoon, so to call him if she needed him to come back and help then. Otherwise he'd probably grab dinner in town with an old colleague and be back later.

She could call him, she supposed. But she knew she wouldn't.

Calling Liam would be admitting that she couldn't do this. That she wasn't cut out for the job of looking after Jamie. It was one thing to let him do his share when he was at Thornwood. But to call him back from the city because she couldn't cope? Not a chance.

Helene frowned with concern. 'Okay. Well, let the others here help while he's away, okay? Make sure you get some rest. And call me if his temperature goes up any more.'

'I will,' Alice promised. She might not like admitting

she needed help, but if Jamie's health was at risk she'd be on the phone in an instant.

But for now it looked like she should settle in for a very long afternoon with a very sad baby.

Liam tiptoed along the stone corridor outside the suite of rooms he shared with Alice and Jamie. He hadn't meant to be so late home from the city, but dinner had dragged on, and then there'd been problems with the trains... Hopefully, Jamie and Alice would both be asleep by now. Then he could grab a few hours and take over the baby duties from Alice. She must be exhausted, he realised, after a whole day and evening alone with Jamie. He felt more than a little guilty about that—certainly more than he'd expected to. But Alice hadn't called and asked him to come back early, so everything must have gone okay.

He listened against the door, smiling as he heard Alice's sweet voice singing soft lullabies. Maybe not both asleep quite yet, then. Perhaps there'd even be time for Alice to fill him in on Jamie's day—it wasn't as if he was *that* late back, after all.

Jamie let out a long wail, and the singing abruptly stopped. Liam frowned; catching up could wait. First they'd better get their boy to sleep.

Pushing open the door, Liam stepped through, smiling at the picture of Alice and Jamie curled up in the comfy armchair they'd moved up to the suite from one of the sitting rooms. 'Hey,' he said, over the sound of Jamie's cries. 'Everything okay?'

'Just fine. Can't you hear?' Alice snapped, and then she sighed. 'Sorry. He's been like this all day. Helene thinks he picked up a cold or something.'

Liam rushed forward, the need to hold Jamie in his arms, to be sure the little boy was okay, suddenly overwhelming. But as he reached for the baby, he noticed something else—the drying tears on Alice's cheeks, and the raw redness around her eyes.

All day, she'd said. He'd been like this all day. And she'd been alone with him.

And she still hadn't called him back to help.

The realisation stung, but he knew he couldn't deal with that right now. His first priority had to be Jamie—and Alice.

'Go lie down for a bit,' he suggested. 'Or take a bath. Whatever. Let me deal with our boy.'

He could see the exhaustion, relief and pride warring in her eyes, but eventually she nodded. Shifting Jamie into one arm, he held out his other hand to help her up, holding on for a moment too long, trying to convey the reassurance he needed her to feel.

Alice still believed she had to do everything alone. And it was going to be up to him to show her otherwise.

CHAPTER ELEVEN

ALICE STUMBLED THROUGH the bedroom to the en suite bathroom, feeling thoroughly zombie-like. Jamie was still crying but the sound was fainter now, muffled by the doors and walls between them.

Mechanically, she twisted the taps on, waiting for the usual groans and complaints of the plumbing as the water started to flow.

She'd made it. She'd survived a full day on her own with a sick baby. And, she knew, if Liam hadn't made it home when he had she would have survived the night too. Oh, she'd have sobbed, and been exhausted beyond limits she never knew she had, but she would have survived, alone.

Because that was what she did.

But Liam *had* come home. He'd returned and taken over and suddenly it wasn't all on her shoulders any more.

She wasn't alone.

And Alice wasn't entirely sure what to make of that feeling.

She tipped in a good measure of bubbles and climbed in, letting the bathtub fill up as far as it could without overflowing. Bubbles peaked high about the level of the bath, covering every inch of her as she sank into the wonderful warmth of the steamy water.

This was what she needed.

It took her a moment to realise that the crying outside hadn't just faded—it had stopped. Either Liam had some sort of magic touch or Jamie had simply exhausted himself completely and passed out asleep. Either way, Alice was grateful.

Until the light knock on the bathroom door startled her anyway.

'Are you decent?' Liam asked softly.

'I'm in the bath.' Alice omitted the 'you idiot', because he *was* still her boss. Then she looked down at herself and realised that there wasn't an inch of her skin showing under all the bubbles. That probably did count as decent, actually.

'I'll keep my eyes closed, then,' Liam said, and turned the handle. Alice sank down a little farther, just in case, but as he felt his way in and around the edge of the small room to perch on the edge of the closed toilet seat, she realised his eyes really were closed.

'Was there something you wanted?' she asked, confused.

Liam paused for a moment. Then he said, 'Why didn't you call me?'

'We were fine.' Alice didn't like to admit how close she'd come to phoning him for help several times through the day. But she'd made it through. She'd proved she didn't need him or anyone else. And that was important.

Even if, in her current exhausted state, she couldn't fully remember why.

'You weren't fine, Alice.' Liam shifted, and she looked away, not even wanting to meet his closed eyes. 'You were in tears. You *coped*, sure. But that's not the same thing.'

'I didn't need your help,' she ground out. Couldn't he see how well she'd done? She'd survived, alone. Surely someone should be cheering her on for that.

'Maybe you did and maybe you didn't,' Liam said. 'But

the point is, you wouldn't even let yourself ask, no matter how bad it had got. Would you?'

Alice lifted her gaze to his face and realised his eyes were no longer closed. He stared down at her, the understanding clear in his eyes. 'No,' she whispered.

'You don't have to wait until you can't cope alone, until things are truly desperate, to ask me for help, Alice.' Liam's voice was soft and warm, and the compassion in his gaze was mesmerising. Alice couldn't look away. 'We're in this together, remember? As long as Jamie is here, he's *our* responsibility, yours and mine. No matter how hard it gets, or how exhausted we both are. Neither one of us is supposed to do it alone. I'm here, and I want to help. So let me. Okay?'

'Okay,' Alice whispered.

Liam smiled. 'Good. Then I'll leave you to your bath. And maybe even nip down to the kitchens and put us together a late night snack. Okay?'

'That sounds good,' Alice admitted, and he nodded and left, closing the door gently behind him.

He'd meant it. He'd really, really meant it. This wasn't a 'Call me if you need me' with an underlying message of 'I really hope you don't, though'.

This was Liam, promising that she could rely on him. That he'd be there, for her and for Jamie, for as long as this strange situation went on.

And the weirdest part of all was she believed him. She *trusted* him, in a way she'd never imagined she'd be able to trust again.

She trusted Liam Jenkins.

Alice stared at the bubbles around her for a moment, then sank her head down under the water. She'd deal with all the emotions and thoughts that brought up when she'd had some sleep. For now, she was just going to enjoy the lifting of her burden, just for a little while.

Two days later, Jamie snoozed peacefully in the sling, his cold all better, as Alice helped Maud to run her Christmas pudding workshop in the Old Kitchen.

'The Christmas puddings we eat today originated in the Victorian period,' Maud said, handing out bowls while Alice passed around the tub full of wooden spoons. 'Before then, it was more of plum pudding, and before that more of a meaty porridge! But today we're going to make a pudding that everyone at your Christmas table will enjoy. Now, to start with, has everybody washed their hands?'

While Maud got everyone sorted with aprons and ingredients, Alice watched from the bench by the fire, rocking back and forth a little to soothe Jamie. When she'd arrived at Thornwood, Maud had been reluctant to let anyone— even Alice—into her kitchen. In fact, she'd resented having any outsiders in Thornwood Castle even more than Rose had. But over the last year and a half she'd watched the work Alice was doing and warmed to the idea. It had been her idea to start the basics cooking courses, ideal for girls going off to university, or starting their own families or setting up home. They'd proved so popular—and Maud's recipes so delicious—that they not only ran the basics course every month but also offered an intermediate one on occasion.

The Christmas pudding day had been Maud's idea too. 'If I'm making one Christmas pudding, we might as well make a dozen,' she'd said, so Heather had made up fliers, Alice had made enough calls to raise the money to hold it, and the course had been fully booked in no time at all.

The group around the large, battered wooden table chattered as they stirred their puddings. Strange to think that just over a week ago she'd sat at that table with Liam and they'd hammered out their deal. Since that first walk with Jamie, when they'd stumbled across the cottage, he'd found two more possible sites. Each time, she'd headed out with trepidation to view them, even though she couldn't put her finger on what was worrying her. That they'd be no good, that they'd never find a perfect location and Liam would just throw them out? Or that they'd be perfect, they'd get things set up and then it would be time for her to leave? Either way, she wouldn't be at Thornwood any more. She wouldn't have Jamie. And she definitely wouldn't have Liam.

She shook her head and hummed a snatch of 'O Little Town of Bethlehem' to Jamie. She couldn't think about that. Jamie wasn't hers; sooner or later he'd be going to his real, forever family. Either his mother would be found and he'd be taken home, or social services would find him a family to love and raise him. One with two parents, and maybe siblings to quarrel and play with.

Alice had done her research. She knew that she—a single woman of soon-to-be no fixed abode—didn't stand a chance at adopting Jamie, even with his mother's note. And while she could admit that having him in her life had made everything brighter, more worthwhile, how could she dream of taking responsibility for a vulnerable child when she didn't even know where she'd be, what she'd be doing next month? When she couldn't offer Jamie the home he deserved?

Liam could, though. He had Thornwood, and money and a future. He could give Jamie anything he wanted— everything that he'd never been given himself. Would he? Because Alice knew for certain that she couldn't stick around and watch that from the sidelines. See Jamie and Liam make their own family—watch Liam find the perfect mother for Jamie, even, perhaps. See the life that Alice could never have playing out in front of her, taunting her.

No. She'd lost everything once before. This time, she knew, she'd make sure to get out before everything she dreamed of was ripped away from her. It was the only way she'd survive a second time.

The door to the Old Kitchen clattered open, just as Jamie stirred and cried out.

'Looks like I timed that to perfection,' Liam commented from the doorway, holding out a bottle ready for him.

Alice forced a smile. 'You did.'

Liam descended the stairs and crossed the room to hand her the bottle, apparently unaware of the way all the other women in the room were whispering about him. Alice knew what they were saying; of course he looked as handsome as always, despite the same lack of sleep that had left her with giant suitcases under her eyes. And yes, it was adorable the way he knew baby Jamie's schedule so well.

But that wasn't all they were saying, she knew. They were speculating. Heather had taken great joy in telling her exactly how many conversations she'd overheard in the past week about whether Liam and Alice were a couple now.

'You told them all the truth, though, right?' Alice had asked. 'Explained that we're just sharing care of Jamie for the time being?'

Heather had just grinned even wider. It looked wrong on her usually sombre face, Alice decided, and told her so. Which only made her laugh.

Alice had given up at that point.

Easing Jamie out of the sling, she handed him to Liam, who settled onto the bench beside her and started feeding him.

'So,' he asked, giving her a friendly smile, 'what exactly are we doing here?'

And wasn't that just the million-dollar question?

Alice stared at him without answering, and Liam found himself reviewing his innocent question in his mind.

What are we doing here?

He'd meant in the kitchen, with all the spicy, fruity scent and the women, of course. But in an instant he saw his mistake. Because neither of them had ever clarified exactly what it was they *were* doing, beyond keeping Jamie healthy and safe. And occasionally having conversations while she was naked and covered in bubbles.

Not that he'd been thinking about what she might look like under those bubbles. Well, not much. Not at the time, anyway.

And since then…better not to think about it, he'd decided.

'I mean here,' Liam clarified, waving a hand to indicate the industrious baking going on around him.

'Oh! Obviously. Um, making Christmas puddings,' Alice explained, a slight pink blush on her pale cheeks.

'Right. Of course.'

He looked away, staring anywhere except at her. Because he knew exactly where her mind had gone—because his had done the same thing too.

It had been over a week now. Eight days since they'd found Jamie and offered to care for him, while the search for his mother went on behind the scenes. Even the social services lady was starting to look at them with that gleam in her eye that told Liam she was getting ideas.

But Alice wasn't, he knew that. She'd been very careful to maintain every boundary they'd put up—bubbles notwithstanding. She might be letting him help out more since that night, but that was all about Jamie. She wasn't letting him in on her feelings, her thoughts. She'd clammed up completely after her confession about her husband's abuse, and nothing he tried seemed to change that. He'd attempted to draw her out further on her marriage, tried to figure out what question he should have asked but hadn't, but she'd stonewalled him, or changed the conversation to Jamie's well-being. Her past relationships were clearly off limits, and the only things she was interested in discussing were Jamie and Thornwood. It was as if she wanted him to believe that she'd arrived here fresh-faced and with no past at all.

It only took one look at her for him to know that wasn't the case.

Oh, it wasn't as if she looked worn out by life, like his mother had at the end. On the contrary, despite the night feeds and the exhaustion of caring for a newborn, Alice looked bright and fresh and happier than she had when he'd arrived. It was almost as if Jamie had woken something within her, something that had brought her back to life.

If he was honest with himself, it was incredibly attractive, that kind of brightness. As if the way she looked at Jamie, the love she showed there, was enough to make him feel a tug on his heart.

He'd considered it, he had to admit.

He hadn't expected to fall for Jamie the way he had; all he'd intended to do was help out a clearly clueless Alice with the childcare, make sure that Jamie got a better start in life than most kids in his situation. He'd known that sooner or later—and probably sooner—Jamie would go back to his mother or be adopted by a real family, so he'd not even worried about becoming attached. If he'd never managed to fall in love with any of his beautiful ex-girlfriends in all the time he'd spent with them, he'd imagined it would take more than a few nights with a squalling newborn to win him over. Same with his foster siblings; he'd liked them well enough, loved one or two of them even, but it had never felt like it did with Jamie.

No, this all-encompassing love that made his heart feel too big for his chest every time he looked down at that tiny, trusting body…this wasn't what he'd expected at all.

And neither was Alice.

At first sight, he'd assumed she was a gold-digger, after Rose's fortune. Then he'd realised she was a do-gooder, and gone out of his way to annoy her. He'd had enough do-gooders try to interfere in his early life, and they'd always ended up making the situation worse, not better. He had no patience for them.

Except Alice was that rarity—someone who actually helped. Who did real good. Who made a difference in people's lives.

And, given the hell she'd been through, the fact she wanted to improve others' lots instead of just her own, well, that made him admire her. Just a bit.

The woman he'd got to know since they'd found Jamie wasn't at all what he'd expected, and he could understand now why Jamie's mother had left him for Alice to find— even if she did know nothing about babies.

Unbidden, an image from the night before rose up in his mind, like a film playing over and over. He'd walked into their rooms late in the evening, ready to help put Jamie to bed, and found Alice already dozing in the armchair, Jamie fast asleep on her chest. Their breathing seemed in perfect sync and they had matching expressions of peace and contentment on their faces. Alice's golden hair shone in the lamplight like a halo, and he'd thought instantly of those paintings on traditional Christmas cards—of angels, and Mary with the baby Jesus.

For a moment his chest had felt about to burst with emotions he'd thought he wasn't capable of feeling any more. And he'd known, without ever consciously deciding, that all of this—Jamie, Thornwood, even Alice—was no longer a reluctant responsibility for him, something he felt he had to do before he could move on.

It was where he wanted to be.

Alice's eyes had opened even as that realisation reverberated through him, and she'd met his gaze and smiled. And he'd been lost.

So yes, he'd definitely thought about Alice that way—more than he'd like to admit. He'd considered the possibility of keeping Jamie for himself and having Alice at his side to help. He knew that if Jamie's mother didn't come forward a new family would have to be found—and why shouldn't it be them? It might take some persuasion, but Jamie's mother had left him to the two of them. That had to count for something.

Except there wasn't really a 'them', was there? He and Alice weren't a couple, and the only thing that linked them was their love for Jamie.

But maybe that was enough?

He'd seen his mother fall for man after man, every time sure that he was the one—only to be let down time and again. From his father, who'd never even acknowledged their existence after discovering she was pregnant, to her last boyfriend, the one who'd led to their midnight flight to a local women's refuge, just before his mum got sick. He had no interest in that sort of love—something he regularly told his casual girlfriends. Company, conversation, sex, they were all good things. But you couldn't put your faith in them for more.

But Alice was different—not because he loved her, but because she wanted what was best for Jamie. She had no interest in love or forever either, not after her experiences. But maybe she'd be open to a deal—to sticking around long enough to persuade the authorities that they were a stable family for Jamie.

Liam didn't need love, marriage and all that. But he did need Jamie to have everything he'd missed out on. And Alice might just be the answer.

He just needed to find the right way to put his proposition to her.

'How do you feel about dinner tonight?' Liam asked, leaning casually back against the stone wall behind them as they watched the pudding-makers stir their mixtures.

Alice blinked. 'I was…definitely planning on eating some?'

'Great. Then it's settled. Who should we ask to babysit?'

Okay, she was definitely missing something here. 'Babysit? What are you talking about?'

He turned to her, the smile on his lips more charming than she'd ever seen from him before. 'You, me, dinner. Somewhere in the village, maybe. What's the name of that nice gastro pub?'

'The Fox and Hare?' Was he seriously suggesting the two of them go out for dinner? Together? Without Jamie?

Like a…date?

No. She was still missing something. There was an ulterior motive at work here; she just had to find it.

'That's the one. I'll call, make a reservation for what? Seven-thirty? I know you country types like to eat early.' He flashed another charming smile, presumably to show he was joking, but Alice didn't trust it one iota.

'I think you'll find that it has more to do with knowing I'll be spending half the night feeding and soothing a crying baby, so like to get to bed early.' Never mind that he took care of the other half. The man seemed to be able to function on no sleep at all, something Alice had never managed.

'Fine, I'll book it for six, then.'

Six. What was happening at six today? Alice frowned as she tried to visualise her diary. She smiled as it came to her.

'No can do,' she said. 'Tonight is the Christingle service at the village church, followed by the tree lighting on the green. I was planning to take Jamie.' By Christmas, Jamie would be with his real family. This might be her only chance to celebrate a little with him, even if he wouldn't have a clue what was going on.

'Even better,' Liam said, unfazed, pulling out his phone. 'We can go as a family. I'll go call the pub now.'

Alice started with a jolt at his words. A family? Was that what they were?

No, Alice knew that much for sure. She'd dreamed of what a family would feel like for too long not to recognise that this was as far away from it as she could imagine.

And she was more certain than ever that Liam was up to something.

Jamie finished his bottle and she took him back from Liam and brought the baby up to her shoulder for winding. 'Guess we'll find out tonight, huh, baby boy?' she whispered as she patted his back gently.

CHAPTER TWELVE

LIAM SAT BESIDE Alice on the uncomfortable church pew, Jamie snoozing in his arms, and tried to figure out how his plan had gone so off-track.

All he'd wanted to do was take Alice out somewhere private, away from the ears of Thornwood Castle's many, many female occupants, and put his suggestion to her—that they fake being a real family for a while so that he could keep Jamie safe at Thornwood. Easy.

Except the entire population of Thornwood village appeared to have turned out for the Christingle service, and every one of them had wanted to welcome him to town on the way in. Add in all the children racing up and down the aisles excited by their oranges with glow sticks in, and the sweets they'd get to chow down on later, and there hadn't been a moment's peace.

And then there was the other surprise.

Liam sneaked a glance beside him again, looking away quickly when Alice met his gaze. The last thing he needed was her thinking he was staring at her.

Except he was. Or he would be, if he wasn't being watched by an entire village.

He'd known objectively that Alice was an attractive woman. She had that willowy body that she hid under baggy jumpers to keep warm in the castle, but he'd imagined it had to be under there somewhere—hell, he'd seen it in that gold dress the night of the fundraiser. It just seemed to him now that he hadn't really been *looking*. And her features had always been pretty, her honey-blonde hair usually knotted up on top of her head and her face make-up free, but still obviously pretty.

He just hadn't ever thought about what she might look like if she made an effort. Not dressed-up-in-a-costume-to-con-money-out-of-people gold dress effort. Just an ordinary, everyday nice outfit and some make-up.

Church, apparently, was worthy of that sort of effort.

It wasn't as if she was even wearing anything fancy. But just the simple grey velvet skirt and black boots teamed with a bright red sweater transformed her body. He could see every curve, every dip, without having to imagine anything at all.

Except, maybe, what her skin felt like under all those layers...

No. He wasn't thinking about that. It didn't matter that her golden hair hung loose around her shoulders in waves, and he could smell the cinnamon shampoo he'd seen in the bathroom they now shared. The bathroom where she'd hidden that body under all those bubbles... No, definitely not thinking about that. And the fact she was wearing a little make-up, and her lips looked redder and more kissable than ever, didn't matter to him at all.

Not one bit.

Probably.

He had to stick to the plan—and that plan did not involve thinking about kissing Alice Walters. It involved a purely business-like arrangement where they took care of a child in need together—and that was more important than any lusty thoughts the evening might have brought out in him.

Liam focused on the service instead. He wasn't a churchgoer—church had never loomed large in his childhood—but apparently Thornwood Castle, and its owner, were patrons of the village church. The impression he'd got from the vicar was that he'd be expected to attend at least occasionally if he lived at Thornwood.

Which he wasn't planning to do, of course.

That was the other discomfiting side of his evening. From the conversations he'd had on arrival at the church, it was obvious that the village had very clear expectations of him. Expectations that he was going to fail, once he started moving on his plans for the future of Thornwood.

The children, all holding their Christingle oranges, paraded around the sides of the church, glow sticks held aloft as the lights went out. The organ started up with one last carol—'Silent Night'—and the whole church rang with song. The music reverberated in his chest and he looked down to see Jamie staring up at him, mesmerised by the sound.

If he adopted Jamie, he'd be heir to Thornwood, Liam realised. No direct bloodline descendant of the Howlett family, but the whole estate would be his, all the same. The castle, the village, the land—all of it in the hands of a boy whose parents weren't just unmarried—they were a mystery.

Liam smiled to himself. That seemed like a very fitting inheritance to pass on.

The music came to an end and, after a moment of silence, the lights of the church flicked back on.

'Come on,' Alice said, jumping to her feet. 'We need to get a move on if we want a good spot to see the tree-lighting from.'

Liam followed her, manoeuvring Jamie back into his snowsuit and tucking him into the pram they'd left at the back of the church. He couldn't imagine that the switching on of a few Christmas tree lights was really that spectacular, but Alice seemed so excited it was almost contagious.

That, or he wanted another look at how magnificent her legs looked in those long, shiny black boots.

Thornwood village green was situated just outside the church, and already it seemed to be full of people. In the centre stood a large pine tree, its base secured in a box made of logs and wrapped around with a bright red ribbon. The tree itself looked bare, though.

To one side of the green, the choir who had sung during the Christingle service filed out and took their places beside the tree. Then a group of schoolchildren, all in uniform under their thick coats, gloves and hats, were ushered into place by their teacher, until they stood neatly in rows in front of the choir.

Alice darted ahead of him and he hurried to keep up with her, pushing the pram through the crowd and hoping people moved out of the way before he crushed their feet. Finally she came to a halt, not too far from the tree and close enough to hear the kids' choir chattering excitedly.

'What's that for?' Liam pointed to an unexpected cherry picker beside the tree.

'How else did you expect them to light the lights?' Alice asked, eyes wide. The excitement sparkling in them made her more beautiful than any make-up or change of clothes had managed. Liam looked away in a hurry. He had a *plan*, damn it.

To be honest, he'd expected the lights to be lit by a remote—some local celebrity pushing a button that made the whole thing light up. Come to think about it, he'd half expected that local celebrity to be him, but no one had asked.

'Ladies, gentlemen, boys and girls!' A woman's voice rang out over the crowd, and Liam hunted to find the speaker. Then he realised her voice was coming from above. Up in the basket of the cherry picker, to be precise, which had now been raised to the same level as the top of the tree. In it stood a woman dressed all in white, with gossamer wings attached to her back and a shiny silver halo hovering somehow above her head.

Liam stared. 'And here I was thinking that you were the only angel of mercy in this village,' he murmured, and Alice's eyes widened even further. He flashed her a quick grin and turned his attention back to the angel.

'If she was a real angel, she'd be flying,' he heard one of the kids nearby mutter.

'But her wings would get tired,' another pointed out pragmatically. 'This is probably easier.'

'It is my great honour to start the Thornwood Christmas celebrations this year by lighting the village Christmas tree,' the angel said, and a cheer went up. 'Now, if you could all help me by counting down…'

'Ten! Nine!' the countdown started. Beside him, Alice reached into the pram and lifted Jamie out, holding him up to see the tree.

'You know he probably can't even see that far yet, right?' Liam asked, in between shouts of numbers.

Alice didn't answer him. She was too busy murmuring in Jamie's ear, holding him tight as the countdown continued.

'Two! One!'

At the top of the tree, the angel reached out and placed a silvery star on the tip and, as she did so, the whole tree burst into rivers of light—tiny sparkles and flashes cascading down the branches. It was, Liam had to admit, wholly magical.

On the ground, the choirs broke into song—the choristers and the children's voices mingling as they sang of peace on earth and other impossible things. And Liam looked around him and realised that this was unlike any Christmas he'd ever experienced or even dreamt of.

Then he turned to Alice, tucking Jamie back into his pram, her golden hair falling in front of her shining pale eyes, and realised it might just be the Christmas he wanted.

'What did you think?' Alice asked Liam, straightening up from the pram. Jamie hadn't seemed particularly thrilled by the whole event, but she hoped that Liam might have found it more affecting. It was her second Christmas at Thornwood, and she remembered how magical she'd found it the first year she'd been there.

She was glad she'd got to share that feeling with Liam and Jamie before she left.

She turned to hear Liam's answer.

'It was beautiful,' he said, but he wasn't looking at the tree.

He was looking at her.

Alice's next words caught in her throat as his gaze fixed on hers. There was something new in those dark blue eyes, something she'd never expected to see. A heat, perhaps. A wanting.

She stepped back but his hand caught hers and tugged her closer. 'This might just be the magic of the moment speaking, or possibly that angel has cast some sort of spell on me—'

'That's fairy, not angel,' Alice interjected, but he ignored her.

'—but I can't not do this. Just once.' And with that he dipped his head, bringing his lips to hers with the same decisiveness she'd come to expect from him in everything.

Except this time it didn't annoy her. It set her whole body alight like the Christmas tree behind her.

For a shining moment Alice forgot that the whole village would be watching, forgot that Liam was still trying to find a way to get her out of Thornwood Castle. Forgot, even, all those incredibly good reasons she had for never getting involved with another man again.

Instead, she let Liam's kiss wash over her like a cascade of stars in the darkness, bringing the night to life around her.

And then he pulled away and reality came crashing down.

She stumbled backwards and this time he let her go. 'We shouldn't have done that.'

'Oh, I don't know,' Liam said, looking far less flustered by the kiss than she felt. 'Seemed like a good idea to me.'

A good idea? It was possibly the worst idea in the history of terrible ideas. She couldn't get involved with the man who basically had the power to throw her out of her home and force her to abandon her vocation. And she really couldn't risk a relationship with the man who was helping her take care of Jamie—if only because when she had to say goodbye to both of them it might break her all over again.

But Liam didn't seem to understand either of those concerns.

'Come on,' he said. 'Let's get to the Fox and Hare before they give our table away to someone else.'

Alice was freaking out.

Oh, she was keeping it very quiet and civilised, but Liam could tell her brain was going crazy with all the reasons why it was a mistake to have dinner with him. Well, and to have kissed him. He imagined that might be preoccupying her a bit too.

A day ago he'd have agreed with most of her arguments,

he decided, as he queued at the bar in the Fox and Hare. Over at their table, Alice was fussing with Jamie and refusing to meet his gaze.

The thing was, a day ago he hadn't had his brainwave. He was known in his company for flashes of genius—for the one second, game-changing idea. He'd thought he'd had one yesterday, when he'd decided to ask Alice about faking a family so he could keep Jamie. But now he realised that was only the start.

He knew, better than anyone, that family could tear you apart, that love counted for nothing when things went wrong. But that was the beauty of it—Alice knew that too and, crucially, they weren't in love. But he'd come to respect and like her over the past couple of weeks—and he hoped she felt the same about him.

And from the way she'd kissed him back...there was no doubt in his mind that the physical attraction was mutual too, no matter how much she might try to deny it.

Which left them with an unprecedented situation in his life. One he intended to take full advantage of.

Liam took the bottle of beer and the wine glass from the bartender in exchange for the payment he handed over and headed back to the table, already running counterarguments through his brain.

Alice immediately started rooting through Jamie's change bag the moment he sat down.

'What're you looking for?' he asked casually.

She stopped fiddling with the bag and sighed. 'Honestly? I have no idea.'

Chuckling, he nudged the wine glass across the table to her. 'Calm down. Have a drink. This is just dinner, remember?'

Alice looked up at that. 'Just dinner? We kissed, Liam. Well, you kissed me.'

'I might have started it, but you have to admit to being an enthusiastic participant.' He could still feel the touch of her lips against his, the fire they'd sent streaming through his veins. That was no ordinary kiss. And it was *definitely* something they should do again.

Alice flushed, her cheeks as red as her sweater. 'Fine. I might have joined in. A bit.'

'A lot.'

'But it was your idea. So you need to tell me exactly what you're expecting from this.' She looked up and met his gaze head-on, her eyes no longer confused or cautious but demanding and stubborn.

And for once Liam felt strangely compelled to tell her everything. To give her the truth.

'What I'm expecting?' Liam shook his head. 'That's the wrong question.'

'Then what's the right one?' Alice asked, frustration leaking out in her voice. The man was beyond infuriating.

'You want to know what I'm proposing.'

'I think I got a pretty good handle on that,' Alice said drily. After all, that kiss had not been subtle, and they'd been pressed very close together. She could well imagine *exactly* what he'd been proposing. Too well, really, since it probably shouldn't happen. Probably.

Liam gave her a lopsided smile. 'You think this is about sex.'

'Isn't it?'

He shook his head. 'It's about Jamie.'

Alice's blood ran cold, and she resisted the impulse to wake Jamie in his pram and hold him close, just to be sure he was still there. 'What do you mean?'

'I mean, Jamie needs a family.'

'Yes, he does.' Oh, she really didn't like the way that

this was going. 'But there's still been no luck tracing his mother. So social services will probably want to take him soon.' Something she was trying very hard not to think about.

'Except Jamie's mother left him for us to care for, right?'

'I'm not sure that note would stand up in court. And we're hardly the ideal carers for him, are we? You're going to be flying back to Australia as soon as you've got things set up here, and I'll be moving on as soon as we find a new location for the groups and we get everything up and running.' Something *else* she'd been avoiding dwelling on.

Somehow, it seemed her whole life had turned around until she was entirely focused on where she was, and not where she could run to next, for the first time since she'd left her marriage behind in a pool of blood.

'What if we didn't?' Liam asked. Alice stared at him and he went on. 'We both know that family and blood and love and all that don't guarantee you a damn thing.'

'Right.' But she wanted it for Jamie, anyway. Wanted his experience to be different to hers, to Liam's.

'We're both too damaged to even try for that fairy tale, I reckon,' he added, looking to her for agreement. She nodded. 'But we could give it to Jamie.'

Her heart stopped. He was offering her exactly what she needed. 'How?'

'By convincing the courts that we are a stable, loving home for him. That together we can raise him as heir to Thornwood.'

'You mean we fake being a couple?'

The look he gave her was heated. 'It doesn't have to be entirely fake.'

Alice bit her lip. 'I don't understand.' His words didn't seem to make any sense in her brain, and she reached for her wine glass. Maybe there'd be some truth in there.

'It's simple. Stay here, with me. In my suite—in my bed—wherever you want. You know what I want.' He smirked, and she felt the heat flooding to her cheeks again as she remembered how clearly she'd felt what he wanted. 'But that side of things is up to you. All I want from you is a promise that you'll stay at Thornwood with me and Jamie until I'm allowed to legally adopt him.'

'Wait. Until *you're* allowed to adopt him?' Of course, it couldn't be that perfect, could it? Sooner or later, he'd push her out.

Liam shrugged. 'Or us. If you decide you want to stay. And I hope you will. But if you do…that's it. You're in it for life. No running away to the next thing the moment you think you've stayed too long.'

'I don't—'

'Don't you?'

Alice looked away. Of course she did. Every time. The one time she'd stayed—in her marriage—she'd had everything ripped away from her. Her love, her future—and any possibility of having children.

'Why?' he asked softly. 'Why run so much?'

Could she tell him?

She'd have to, she realised, if she wanted what he was offering. It might not be love and fairy tales, but it would be a life together. A family. And he might have…expectations. Ones that she could never meet.

It was only fair to tell him *exactly* what he'd be signing up for.

'We'd be a proper family?' she asked, her voice small.

'You, me and Jamie.' Liam nodded, sure and certain. But then his expression changed, and she could actually *see* the moment the other possibilities came to him. 'And maybe more kids one day, if you wanted.'

He wanted. She could tell by the smile on his face. And

that small, wistful smile was exactly why she knew this could never work.

And yet…

She wanted it. So badly. It was everything she'd ever dreamt of—the vision from that day on the hill—everything she'd thought she had to give up for ever.

Alice was a practical woman. She didn't need true love, not the sort that films and books talked about. She needed an everyday affection, fondness from a partner—someone she could work as a team with.

And hadn't Liam shown her he could give her that already?

Over the past two weeks Jamie had fulfilled every dream she had of being a mother, and many she'd never even imagined.

Between the two of them, they could make Alice happier than she'd ever imagined being.

If Liam still wanted to, after he knew the truth.

'That…the more kids thing. That can never happen.' The words came out staccato and sharp, and they felt like glass in her throat as she spoke them.

Liam's eyebrows furrowed. 'You don't want more kids? Really? Because the way you are with Jamie—'

'It doesn't matter what I *want*,' Alice interrupted. 'I can't have them. Ever.'

'Why?' he demanded, obviously confused.

Alice reached for her wine again and took a long gulp. 'You asked me what happened with my husband. And why I run so much. Well, it's the same answer to both.'

'Tell me.' Liam's tone was no longer demanding. Instead, it was entreating. Begging her to trust him enough to bare her soul and tell him everything.

Could she? Alice knew she had to try.

So she took a deep breath and began.

CHAPTER THIRTEEN

LIAM KNEW FROM the moment she opened her mouth that he wouldn't like this story.

He'd thought he needed to know about her past, her secrets—needed to understand what had brought her to Thornwood, and what would make her run again when the time came. But, in truth, they were her secrets and she had every right to keep them. And now it was time to hear them out loud…he'd give anything not to have to listen. For it never to have happened. For Alice's life to have been blissfully happy and untroubled.

Except, if it had been, she wouldn't be there with him and Jamie.

So he listened.

'My husband… I told you he was a violent man. And I hoped he would change, or that I could, and that we could be happy again. You asked me why I stayed, but the better question is…'

'Why did you leave?' Liam whispered when her voice trailed off.

Of course it was. *That* was the question he should have asked on their walk that day. If she'd stayed so long, what had changed to force her to leave?

'I was pregnant,' Alice whispered, so soft that he had to lean across the table to hear her. His heart clenched at the misery in her voice, the lost expression on her face. He reached out and took her hand, and she squeezed it gratefully.

Whatever had happened to her, just remembering it was enough for her to accept his support. That alone told him how bad this was going to be.

'I was six months gone, and those six months had been so different. He'd been supportive and thoughtful—all the things I thought he was when I married him. I was honestly starting to believe that *this* was what we'd needed to make us happy. That the baby would make him a different person—a father, a loving husband.'

She wasn't the first woman to hope that, Liam knew. He suspected his own mother had believed that, once presented with the evidence of a child, his father would have suddenly welcomed them both into his privileged existence.

He hadn't, of course. And he already knew that Alice's husband hadn't changed either.

'One night, just before Christmas, he came home drunk and furious. I didn't understand, because nothing had happened, nothing was different. But whatever it was that had upset him—and I don't think I ever even knew—he blamed me. He yelled, he glared, and he reached out to push my shoulder. I stumbled back and hit the table and I realised, in that split second, that nothing would ever change. That I could not bring up a child in that house. So I grabbed my bag and started shoving things in it.'

'What did he do?' Liam asked quietly, his stomach already sinking at where the story must be going.

'He followed me around the flat as I packed, screaming abuse at me. But I couldn't hear him any more. I was lost in my moment of clarity, knowing that from this moment my life would be different. It would be me and my child against the world, and I would never let anyone make me feel the way my husband had, ever again. I was so fired up with the possibilities in front of me I didn't even consider the problems. Or what he might do to try and make me stay.

'As I walked out the front door of the flat, into the stairwell of the building, I turned to him and I told him I was never coming back. And then I spat in his face.' Alice looked away, her fingers toying with the beer mat on the table before her. Her gaze darted to Jamie, then away, then back again. Liam didn't push her; he just waited silently.

Finally, she spoke again. 'That was what did it, really. His face turned bright red, almost purple. And he grabbed my arm, yanking me around on the landing outside the flat. And then he flung me down the stairs.'

Liam had known what was coming more or less since the story started. But nothing prepared him for the white-hot rage that surged through him as Alice spoke. He knew that violence wouldn't help the situation, or endear him to Alice, but he couldn't help the primal response that rose up inside him.

He supposed the only thing that made him different from Alice's ex-husband was that he conquered it. Swallowed it down and held Alice's hand tighter instead. He needed her to know he was there. That she could trust him, even if she never trusted any other person again.

'I woke up in hospital two days later, on Christmas Eve.' Alice looked up, and Liam lost his fury in the wide, sad pools of her blue eyes. 'I lost the baby, of course. But there were other complications. Along with the broken bones and concussion, they had to operate to save my life as I miscarried. They did their best, of course. But in the end they told me—' She broke off with a sob, her gaze dropping down to the table.

'You could never have children,' Liam finished for her. 'God, Alice, I'm so sorry. I'm so, so sorry.'

So many things that had puzzled him fell into place as she finished her story. Why she'd kept such a distance from babies—but fallen so completely for Jamie. Why she never let herself believe she could have that happy ever after that everyone else seemed to want. Why she always, always ran. Because if she kept moving she could never care enough about anything for it to matter when it was ripped away from her.

It was as if he'd stripped away a suit of armour from her, and when she met his eyes again he could see the whole of her for the first time since they'd met.

He knew who Alice Walters was now. And he only loved her more for it.

No. Not love. That wasn't what she wanted, or what he needed. He admired her. Liked her. Wanted her in his life very badly.

But that wasn't the same thing at all. It couldn't be.

Could it?

Liam shook his head. This wasn't the time to be worrying about such abstract things as love. He needed to focus on what mattered most—convincing Alice to stay at Thornwood and help him give Jamie the life he deserved.

And maybe, just maybe, he and Alice would find the life they dreamt of in the process.

Alice watched the flood of emotions playing over Liam's face, and knew he'd say no now. That she had to leave. That she couldn't give him what he was looking for.

She was damaged goods. Literally.

'I can't imagine how devastated you must have been,' Liam said slowly. 'But I think I understand now. You, I mean. I think I understand you.'

Alice shrugged. Maybe he did. 'So you see why I can't agree to your plan, then?'

'No. That part still baffles me, actually.'

'I can't give you what you want.' Did he really need her to spell this out? 'I can't give you more kids. Jamie would be it. And if we weren't allowed to keep him…' Then she'd lose everything again. Her baby and the man she'd hoped to build her life with. The man she…

No. She couldn't think that.

But she knew the risks. If she stayed with Liam, if they were together…he'd already taught her to trust again. To hope.

What if he taught her how to love once more?

How could she ever recover from that?

'They're going to let us keep him,' Liam said, with far more confidence than she felt. 'They have to. Trust me.'

She wanted to. Oh, how she wanted to. 'But if they don't?'

What if they take him, and I've already fallen in love with you?

'Then we'll deal with that if it happens. But we'll deal with it together. As a team. A family.' Liam's fingers traced up her arm, rubbing her skin reassuringly. 'Just say you'll give us a chance. Me and Jamie. Please.'

She sighed. 'Let me check I've got this straight. We work together to give Jamie a real family. You, me, him. No promises of love, or anything like that. Just a practical arrangement for Jamie.'

'Exactly.' Liam's expression was so earnest, so hopeful. 'I can't promise you love, not now, not after just two weeks. But I can promise I won't do anything to hurt Jamie, or you, ever. And I'll do everything I can to make us all happy. Our little family.'

He was right; it was crazy to worry about love so soon.

And if they were to lose Jamie, it would be soon too. Iona, the social worker, had said the end of this week. That was only a few days away now. She didn't have to worry about losing her heart to Liam in that time. Right?

And she'd already lost it to Jamie. So why not enjoy these last few days as a family, if that was all she ever got?

Alice stared at Liam's face, at the openness there. This was her chance. Could she take it? Could she stay? For Jamie?

Could she take the risk?

She didn't know. She couldn't promise for ever, just like he couldn't promise love.

But she could offer for now.

Leaning across the table, she placed a hand against his cheek and kissed him softly on the lips.

'Is that a yes?' he asked against her mouth.

'It's a yes for now,' she said, unwilling to commit any further. 'Until we know what the social worker says at the end of the week. If she says we have a chance…'

'We'll take it,' Liam said, and kissed her again.

He'd wanted to leave the Fox and Hare right then, and drag Alice home to Thornwood and to bed, but naturally Jamie chose that moment to wake up, ready for his evening bottle.

'We'll get back to this,' he murmured as he broke away to find the milk they'd brought with them. Alice fell back into her chair on the other side of the table, a pensive look on her face.

He hoped to God she didn't start overthinking this now.

Yes, there were issues to be ironed out. And yes, the chances were maybe fifty-fifty that the plan would even work. But one thing Liam knew for certain—Alice wasn't sleeping on the daybed tonight.

Part of it was lust, he admitted. But another part—a big-

ger part, even—was the story she'd told him. After hearing
that, he couldn't bear her to be out of his sight, not even
for a moment. He needed her close and safe. Somewhere
he could look after her.

Tucked up warm in his arms, for preference.

The waitress brought their food shortly after and they
took turns eating, swapping Jamie between them as he fed,
was winded, and fussed. It was, Liam decided, by far the
weirdest first date he'd ever had—and not just because it
had started in a church, hit terrible lows, practically involved a marriage proposal, and still wasn't guaranteed
to end with sex. On the other hand, it had sort of been
blessed by an angel, so he let himself be a little optimistic
about the outcome.

Eventually, Alice finished her wine and they wrapped
Jamie back up into his snowsuit, ready for the walk home.
Liam knew logically that Thornwood Castle was only a
fifteen-minute walk from the village, but somehow tonight
it seemed to take for ever. Finally they reached its ancient
wooden doors and Alice eased them open carefully, trying not to wake the sleeping baby.

'Bedtime?' Liam asked as he lifted Jamie from the pram
and rested him against his shoulder.

Alice bit her lip, making him think thoughts he really
shouldn't be thinking while holding a child, and nodded.

Upstairs, they went through Jamie's usual bedtime routine, minus his nightly bath given how much later than
usual it was. Finally he was swaddled in his blanket, asleep
in his cot. Liam stared down at him and wondered when
he'd become the sort of man who could picture himself
as a father.

Hell. A father. Him.

He hadn't thought of it like that before, and for a moment every muscle in his body screamed at him to run.

He'd never wanted kids, never imagined being ready to take on the responsibility. He had no male role models—save perfect examples of what not to do.

But maybe that was enough. He reached down to smooth a curl of fluffy baby hair away from Jamie's forehead and smiled to himself.

Maybe knowing what not to do was all that he needed. Just do the opposite of what every man and family member in his life had done to him, and everything any guy had ever done to Alice, and they'd all be fine.

He hoped.

Turning away from the cot, he saw Alice watching him from the bedroom door, her head resting against the wood as she studied him. In the low light, her hair glowed golden and she'd already removed those incredibly sexy boots. But somehow, seeing her in her stockinged feet seemed even sexier. He'd shared this suite with her every night for over a week, but tonight the air felt thicker, more full of promise.

'Shall we go to bed?' Alice asked, her voice low and husky.

Liam smiled. 'Sounds like a plan.'

Yeah. This was all going to work out just fine.

Alice blinked into the darkness as her exhausted body tried to process what she'd heard.

Jamie. Crying. Of course.

She checked the time on her phone—time for his next feed. It didn't matter to him that his pseudo parents had barely drifted off after what Alice had to admit had been some pretty phenomenal lovemaking.

On autopilot, she made up his bottle, shushing and changing him as she waited for it to reach the right temperature. But even the familiar, everyday actions couldn't clear her mind of the memories of the last few hours—of how Liam's body had felt against hers, or the relief that had flooded through her body as he'd taken her.

She hadn't known how much she'd wanted him, needed that, until he'd kissed her that evening. Now she couldn't imagine not having it again.

And, as much as she hated to admit it, she knew it had only been so good because all the secrets were gone. Because she'd told him everything, left her soul bare, and he'd wanted her anyway.

Not just wanted her. He wanted her to *stay*.

He'd called them a family. The one thing she'd never thought she could have again.

She swallowed hard, her eyes wet just at the thought.

'He okay?' Liam slurred from the doorway, his eyes barely open. He had to be every bit as exhausted as her—possibly more, actually—and he'd still dragged himself out of bed to check on them.

'He's fine,' she assured him. 'Go back to bed.'

But Liam shook his head and slumped onto the end of the daybed, watching her as she settled Jamie in her arms ready for his feed.

'You're good with him, you know,' he said as she sat beside him and reached for the bottle.

'I guess it's one of those things learnt best on the job,' she replied.

They sat together in silence for a minute or two, the only noises in the room the ticking clock on the mantel and the gentle snuffling sounds of a feeding baby.

'Are you okay?' Liam asked eventually. 'About tonight, I mean. About us.'

Alice considered, taking stock of her exhausted but oh-so-satisfied body. 'I'm just great,' she assured him with a smile.

Liam let out a long breath. 'Good. I mean, I know you

enjoyed it…' He flashed her a smug grin and she rolled her eyes.

'As much as you did,' she observed.

'God, yes. But anyway, the physical stuff aside. What we're doing here…'

'It's not the normal way to go about things,' she finished for him, and he nodded.

'Exactly. And after everything you told me tonight… I know you know that it…it might not work.'

Alice swallowed again, her throat suddenly thick with emotion. 'I know.' She cradled Jamie closer. How many more times would she get to do this? To hold his body to hers as he fed or slept?

How would her heart survive if she had to give him back? How would Liam's?

She didn't even bother thinking about what would happen to them. The only tie they had was Jamie. If he was taken from them, what would there be left to fight for? Some incredible sex and joint heartbreak? It wasn't enough.

She wasn't fooling herself. This wasn't love. It was lust, maybe, and convenience. But it wasn't a white cottage with roses around the door, and family lunches and bedtime stories with a sleepy little boy.

What she had was a broken man, a broken heart, and the most perfect baby she could imagine. One out of three was plenty for her—as long as she got to keep that all-important one.

'But I promise you I'll fight for him. For us. For our family,' Liam said, his voice so sure and determined she almost cried. 'I'll do everything I can to give us the future we need.'

'I know,' Alice said, her voice breaking.

Liam reached an arm around her shoulder, holding her

head against his upper arm, enfolding them both in his embrace. The three of them. A family.

It was almost too perfect for her to believe in.

'Do you think his mother misses him?' Alice asked, her voice so soft she wasn't sure Liam even heard her.

Until he replied, his voice rough, 'If she does, then she should never have abandoned him in the first place.'

'No. I suppose not.' Jamie had finished feeding and Alice winded him gently against her shoulder before placing him back in his cot and wrapping him up again. 'Come on,' she said. 'Let's get back to bed.'

If all of this could be taken from her again, then she had better enjoy it while she had it.

CHAPTER FOURTEEN

IT WAS NEARLY CHRISTMAS, Liam realised one morning a few days later, as Jamie slumbered in his bouncy chair beside the desk in the room Liam had taken for his office. When he'd arrived, it had barely been December. Now, downstairs there was a horde of children awaiting the arrival of Father Christmas for some sort of festive afternoon tea with presents. Alice had explained it that morning as she'd been dressing, but he'd been rather more interested in the sight of her in her underwear than the topic of conversation.

Alice. She'd sneaked up on him even more than Christmas had.

How had she gone from an irritation to get rid of to someone he couldn't quite bring himself to imagine his days without?

He shook his head and went back to his list of possible sites for Alice's groups and seminars. It was just familiarity, that was all. Familiarity and fantastic sex. Nothing more.

He'd scoured every inch of the Thornwood estate over the past three weeks—sometimes alone, sometimes with Alice, sometimes with another local who wanted to make him understand the history of the place, and often with Jamie strapped to his chest. The lands were vast, with plenty of outbuildings and sites ripe for conversion—and not one of them suitable for Alice's women.

He sighed, thinking again of the cottage he and Alice had found on that first day. It wasn't at all suitable for the seminars and groups that Alice ran—too small, too close to the village, no potential to extend. But for some reason he kept coming back to it. He'd visited it twice more on his excursions, and the last time he'd even snapped some photos. Pulling out his phone, he scrolled through them again, taking in the whitewashed walls, the tiled roof, the broken windows and the curve of the front door. It needed a lot of care and attention if anyone was ever to live there again.

It wasn't at all what he was looking for. But he knew it would make a perfect home for Jamie.

Liam shut down his phone. He couldn't be thinking about such things. Jamie wasn't his yet—and there was a very real chance he'd never be. The social worker was due back this afternoon to discuss options, now it seemed clear that the mother would not be coming forward. Liam was apprehensive and excited all at once.

But if they were allowed to keep Jamie, maybe he *could* stay at Thornwood. It wasn't something he and Alice had discussed—where they'd live long-term. In fact, they hadn't really hammered out any of the details of their arrangement beyond keeping Jamie. Everything else seemed on hold, until they knew that they had a chance to be his parents.

As a result, he'd never seriously considered Thornwood as a for ever option before. But the more time he spent there...

He flicked his phone on to stare at the photo of the cottage again and remembered Alice's face as she'd looked at it. She'd wanted it, he knew, even if she wouldn't admit it to herself. Just like she'd wanted him but hadn't given a single sign until he'd pushed. Just like she wanted Jamie, even though she wouldn't let herself believe it was a possibility.

He'd worked so hard to convince Alice that things could change. That she could trust him with her secrets. That they could be a family—an unconventional one, for sure, but a family. What was one more step?

Thornwood *could* be home, he knew now. If Alice was there with him.

The very thought made him smile. And, as he looked down, he saw that Jamie was awake again, staring up at him with open, trusting eyes.

Closing down his laptop, Liam unfastened the buckles on the bouncy chair and picked Jamie up.

Time to take his son down to meet Father Christmas. And if he was very lucky, perhaps he'd get a chance to make a Christmas wish of his own.

'Don't you want to go and see Father Christmas?' Alice crouched before the little girl hiding in the corner of the main hall behind the Christmas tree. The girl shook her head. 'Why not? Are you scared?'

The girl nodded, making her blonde plaits bob. What was her name? Alice tried to picture her mother and remember what she'd called her. Bethany, she thought.

Alice wanted to tell her that there was nothing to be scared of. That Christmas was the season of goodwill to all men and nothing bad could happen.

But she knew herself how untrue that was.

'What are you scared of, Bethany?' she asked instead.

'I've been a bad girl,' Bethany whispered. 'My stepdad said so. Santa won't come for me this year.'

Alice's heart ached for her. She was so young to already believe that she was beyond redemption. 'Why don't we ask Santa that?' she said. 'Even if he can't come on Christmas Eve, I definitely spotted a present for you in his sack today. Shall we go find out what it is?'

Bethany's face lit up as Alice led her over to the grotto they'd set up beside the main stairs.

'Your child skills have definitely improved since Jamie arrived,' Heather commented from her position as Santa's elf. 'I'm starting to think you might even like the little monsters.'

'Of course I do,' Alice said, but Heather still looked sceptical. She supposed she couldn't blame her. Until Jamie, she'd kept her distance from the children and babies who came to Thornwood Castle, as much as she could. It just hurt too much to see and hold what she could never have. But now she had Jamie it was as if her heart had opened up again, ready to welcome in all the love she'd been holding at bay.

'And it's not just your love of children that seems to have grown.' Heather nodded towards the stairs, where Liam was descending with Jamie in his arms. Alice held her breath until they safely reached the bottom. She'd got over her fear of stairs to some degree, but she'd never be fully comfortable with them again after her accident.

'Now I know you're definitely talking rubbish,' Alice said absently, smiling as Liam held Jamie up to see Father Christmas.

'Am I?' Heather raised an eyebrow. 'Be honest. You're besotted with the pair of them.'

Was she? Maybe. But Alice was enough of a realist to know there was still a chance it wouldn't last—even if the bubble of hope in her chest reminded her how much she wished it could.

Liam turned and spotted her at last, smiling that lazy, slow smile that melted her insides every time.

'In fairness, they both seem pretty besotted with you too,' Heather observed, before wandering off to help with the next child waiting to see the man in red.

Alice stared after her, computing her words. Besotted? That sounded a little too close to another emotion—one she and Liam had been very clear didn't enter into their arrangement. Which was how it had to stay. Wasn't it? She'd promised herself she wouldn't let herself fall in love with Liam. Especially not before they knew if they could keep Jamie, if they were in this for the long haul. Falling in love now would be a disaster.

Because if it was love that was causing this feeling in her chest, then how would she cope if she lost it again?

'Alice?'

At the sound of her name she spun to see Iona, the social worker, Dr Helene and another pale teenager standing behind her. Not just any teenager. Danielle—her missing assistant. And in that moment her bubble of hope burst.

She knew what this meant. There was only ever one way this fairy tale she was living was going to end—and now apparently that ending was here, at Thornwood.

Her legs wobbling, Alice walked forward to join them— even though all she wanted to do was grab Jamie and run far, far away. Somewhere where all the misery to come couldn't touch them.

But there was no place that could save her from this.

'Hello, Danielle,' she said. 'You must be Jamie's mother.'

Liam watched as Father Christmas—the vicar in a fake beard and red suit, apparently—handed out a gift to a small girl in plaits, who held it close to her body as if it was hidden treasure. It was hard not to smile, not to imagine Jamie, a couple of years from now, excited to meet Santa.

He turned to share another smile with Alice, doing refreshment duty over by the Christmas tree, only to find that she'd gone. He scanned the room and finally spotted her in the archway that led through to the library, talking with the social worker and Dr Helene—and someone else. Someone he didn't recognise.

Frowning, he shifted Jamie in his arms and crossed towards them, trying to ignore the heavy, hard feeling growing in his chest.

'Alice?' he asked as he grew nearer. 'Everything okay?'

She spun and looked at him, then at Jamie, her mouth pressed into a tight line and her arms wrapped around her middle. She looked as if her whole world had fallen apart, and any hope that this wasn't what he thought it was faded. He wanted to take her in his arms, to hold her and Jamie close and never let them go.

God, never. Never let *either* of them go.

The realisation of what that meant hit him straight in the chest and he almost stumbled backwards at the impact.

He didn't want Alice to leave. Not because of Jamie, but because *he* needed her in his life.

Because he loved her. Every bit as much as he loved the tiny boy in his arms.

How had he gone from having no family, no love, to feeling as if his heart and his home were overflowing with them?

And how would he cope with losing them?

'Alice…' He started to move towards her—to touch her, to comfort her, anything. But she shook her head.

'I'm sorry. I can't…' And with that, she dashed away, up the stairs, out of his reach.

'Liam?' Dr Helene brought his attention back to the pale, thin teenager standing with the social worker. 'Is there somewhere private we could talk?'

Dazed, Liam nodded. 'The library. I'll…I'll send for some coffee. Or tea.' He was growing more British by the day. Australia might not even *want* him back at this point.

Especially as he suddenly didn't want to go.

He spoke briefly with Heather, who was hovering nearby looking concerned, then led the small group through to the library. The large table in the centre of the

room was clear for once, and he moved to take a seat—
only to stop when the young girl approached, her gaze
fixed on Jamie.

'You're his mother, I take it.' His words came out hard,
but Liam didn't care. Yes, she was young—hardly more
than a child herself. But she'd left his boy alone when he
was only a few hours old. How could he forgive that?

The girl nodded and raised a finger to touch Jamie's
face, stopping just a few centimetres away before she
pulled back. 'I'm sorry. I—I—'

Tears were streaming down her face, Liam realised.
She looked so, so young, so lost, he could almost feel the
ice of his anger cracking.

'Liam, this is Danielle,' the social worker said, putting
an arm around the girl. 'Danielle, why don't we take a seat
and you can explain everything to Mr Jenkins? Just the
way you told it to me.'

The girl nodded and let herself be led to a seat. Liam
followed suit and prepared to listen. Maybe not to understand, but he could at least hear her out, he supposed.

It was more than Alice had managed.

The thought tore at his heart, but he pushed it aside.
He'd deal with Alice after. First, he needed to fix whatever was trying to tear apart his family from the outside.

'Tell me,' he said. And she did.

It took a while, the story punctuated by sobs and out-
bursts and the tea tray arriving. But it didn't take long for
Liam to get the pertinent points.

Danielle was fifteen. She'd been fourteen when she got
pregnant at a party. She didn't even know who the father
was, let alone how to contact him.

The party had been one month after her mother died,
leaving her alone with her uncaring, emotionally abusive

father. She'd gone out to try and have fun, to drink away her pain and her grief.

And instead she'd ended up pregnant.

'My mother was a midwife,' Danielle said. 'I'd seen home births before, even helped at one, so I knew what to do. But I was so scared…'

'Why did you leave him here?' Liam asked.

Danielle wiped at her eyes with another tissue. 'My mum…she used to bring me here sometimes, before she got sick. When she died, Alice hired me after school sometimes to help her out. I think she knew I needed the money. So I knew Alice was a good person. I mean, I didn't know her very well, but everyone could see that. I knew my baby would be safe with her.'

'But you didn't know me at all,' Liam pointed out. 'Why put my name on that note too?' Nobody in their right mind would leave him in charge of a child. But Danielle had been desperate. Maybe that was all it was.

She looked up and met his gaze. 'Thornwood Castle is yours. And Mum always said the lord at Thornwood took care of us, down in the village. She used to tell me stories about her grandma and granddad. They worked at the castle, you see. They were butler and housekeeper. When they got married, the old Lady at Thornwood gave them the cottage in the woods, and that's where they lived until they died. I know things are different these days, and I'm not expecting anything from you, I promise. I just… I hoped that you would feel that too. That you'd look after Jamie, and give him the life I couldn't.'

The butler. The same butler who'd looked down on him so many years ago? Maybe. It didn't matter now, Liam realised. None of it did.

Danielle had wanted what was best for her baby, and she'd trusted them to give it to him. It was a stupid, crazy move—one that had to be born out of desperation rather than logic.

And, in the weirdest of ways, she'd been right.

'But now you've come back for him,' Liam replied. That was the part that stung the most.

Danielle shook her head. 'I can't look after him. My dad… I won't bring him up there in that house. I won't let him go through what me and Mum went through.'

'We've found a place for Danielle,' the social worker put in. 'We're working to help her get herself back on her feet, away from her father's influence. But Jamie…'

'He'll go up for adoption,' Liam guessed, and the social worker nodded.

Suddenly, everything was clear. Crystal clarity, with all doubt swept away. No fear, no uncertainty.

Liam knew exactly what he needed to do. It was no longer a pipe dream, a scheme with no plan behind it. It was his future. His and Alice's and Jamie's.

It was meant to be.

'Let me adopt him. I'll make him my heir. Thornwood will be his one day. And he will be my son, I swear to you, in every way that matters. He'll be loved, he'll have a home and he'll have a family.' Everything Liam had never had, he would give to Jamie. And he'd do it with Alice by his side, showing both of them every day just how much he loved and cherished them.

Liam knew it would be the best thing he ever did in this world.

Alice grabbed another handful of clothes from the drawers by the daybed and shoved them into her suitcase. How had so much of her stuff ended up in Liam's room, anyway? This had only ever been temporary, but from her packing it looked as if she'd moved in.

And now she was moving out again. Out of his rooms, out of Thornwood, out of his life. Out of Jamie's life.

It was for the best, she reminded herself. Jamie would be back with his mother, Liam could get on with his plans for Thornwood, and Heather was more than capable of taking over Alice's work. It was time for her to move on, to find a new start somewhere else.

This had only ever been an impossible dream, and she'd known that from the start.

So why did her heart ache so much?

'Alice!' Liam burst into the suite, his eyes alight and his smile broad—until he saw her suitcase. 'What are you doing?'

'Packing.' She didn't look at him. She couldn't.

It was time to move on.

'You're leaving.' It wasn't a question. 'You're running again, aren't you? Even now. Why?'

'Jamie is going back to his mother. You've got your work to get on with. It's time for me to look for something new too.' She kept her voice steady. She was rather proud of that.

'Danielle is giving him up. I've asked to be considered to adopt him, and Danielle has agreed. The social worker thinks we have a strong case. Alice—' He reached out and pulled her clothes from her hands. 'Stop it. I'm telling you it's going to be okay.'

It's going to be okay. It's different this time. It won't happen again.

How many times had she heard those words? How many times had she believed them?

And yes, this was different. And yes, that small bubble of hope was growing again.

But Alice stamped it down. She knew too well how many ways things could go wrong. The only way to avoid being hurt when everything you loved was torn away was by not loving in the first place.

She'd made a mistake with Jamie; she'd got too close, too fast. And she'd run the risk of the same with Liam. But if she left now, right now, she thought she might survive.

If she stayed, if she fell any deeper…she didn't know if she could make it through losing everything a second time.

'You can't know that,' she said softly. 'You can't know it'll be okay.'

'I can promise I'll do everything in my power to make it okay.' Liam held on to her hands and tried to tug her away from the suitcase, but she resisted. She couldn't let him get to her now. She'd made her decision. 'Alice, please. Trust me.'

She shook her head. 'I'm sorry. I have to go.'

'Why?' She didn't answer. 'Because you're a coward? You're too scared to stay? Too scared to be happy for once in your miserable life?'

That was better. Anger she knew how to deal with. Bitterness and frustration were her old friends—and far more familiar to her than love and kindness. And they made it so much easier for her to go.

'So what if I am?' she spat back. 'You've got no idea what you're getting yourself into, have you? So we looked after a baby for a couple of weeks. That's not parenting. That's babysitting. You're signing up for a lifetime job—and you can't build a family or a home just like one of those buildings you design. It's just a fantasy for you—trying to create everything you never had. It's not as simple as all that, Liam.'

'Isn't it? I think you're the one making it hard. You're so scared to trust in something good you're going to throw everything away.'

'I'd rather throw it than have it taken! You say the

mother wants you to have Jamie. What if she changes her mind? What if the courts say no? What if the father comes forward? There are so many things that can go wrong, Liam. And then what will you do?'

'I thought I'd at least still have you,' he said quietly. 'But apparently I was wrong about that.'

'Me? What use would you have for me then?' Because the idea of it being just the two of them, without Jamie there, with no prospect of giving Liam a child of their own... They'd never be able to adopt another child if the state wouldn't even let them have Jamie. So Liam would grow to hate her, she knew. And she couldn't live like that again. Couldn't see hate where she'd once hoped for love.

No, not hoped for. She didn't need love. Love led to disappointment and pain when it was torn away.

Why would she want that?

'What use would I have for you? Alice, I lo—'

'Don't you say it!' She cut him off, her voice shrill. 'Don't you dare say it. We agreed. We don't do that. We're too broken for that.'

'Well, maybe you mended me. You and Jamie. You made me the man I never even hoped I could be. And if we just stick together—'

'No. You want me to believe in the power of home, and family and even love? Well, I can't. That was taken from me four years ago by someone else who said they loved me. And I won't stay here, waiting for the other shoe to drop. Falling deeper into a life that can be ripped away from me at any minute. I won't do it, Liam. Not even for Jamie. Not even for you.'

And with that, she threw her bag over her shoulder and walked out.

She'd burned the last of her bridges with Thornwood. It was time to start over. Again.

CHAPTER FIFTEEN

'YOU LOOK EXHAUSTED,' Heather said, eyeing Liam up and down. 'Do you want me to take Jamie for a bit so you can go lie down?'

Liam shook his head. 'He's no bother. And anyway, I need to work.'

'You've been doing nothing but working and caring for Jamie since—' Heather broke off, but Liam knew what she wasn't saying.

Since Alice left.

Nobody mentioned it around the castle—although he was sure they were gossiping about it in the village. How the lord of the manor had been abandoned, left holding the baby—literally.

It had been a full week since she'd left. Long enough for Liam to be sure she had no intention of coming back.

He knew why she'd run, of course. Understood her fear, her desperate need not to be hurt again. But he'd hoped he'd shown her, in the time they'd spent together with Jamie, that she didn't *have* to be afraid of that any more. That she could trust him—not just with her secrets, her body, or their child—but with her heart.

But apparently her faith in him didn't run as deep as his faith in them, in their little family.

That was her choice. Just because she was too scared

to live, and to love, that didn't mean he had to be. And anyway, he had Jamie to think of. He'd give Jamie the perfect home and family he'd promised, no matter how much work it took.

'There's a lot that needs doing,' he said. 'Plans to be made. Contractors to hire. Planning permission to sort.' A lot of what he wanted to do was just improving what was already standing at Thornwood, but some jobs would take longer, and need official permission before he could begin. Fortunately there was plenty of other stuff to be getting on with.

'It's two days before Christmas,' Heather pointed out. 'Everyone you need to speak to is probably off at their office Christmas do, having sex on a photocopier or whatever people who don't work in castles do.'

He smiled at her. 'Regretting accepting that promotion?' With Alice gone, he'd needed someone to oversee all his new plans, and Heather had been the obvious choice. So far it seemed to be working well. Thornwood Castle was now officially known as Thornwood Haven. There wouldn't be an aristocratic theme park, or go-karting in the woods. And it would never make him any money—but he'd always been good enough at doing that himself anyway.

No, Thornwood Haven would help women and children and families, not just for a while but for good. And that felt right.

'Never.' Heather paused in the doorway. 'You're doing a good thing here, you know. Rose would be proud of you.'

Liam smiled awkwardly as she turned and left. He hadn't done it for Rose. He'd done it for Danielle, and for Jamie. And for Alice.

Even if she wasn't there to see it.

Even if it broke his heart afresh every time he thought of her.

He looked down at Jamie, contentedly watching from his bouncy chair.

'It's just you and me now, kid,' he said. 'So I guess we'd better get on with it.'

Alice looked up as the door to the café she was sitting in opened and jumped to her feet as Helene entered. Christmas music blared out of the speakers and the baristas were all wearing festive headbands and Santa hats.

It was Christmas Eve morning, and Alice had never felt less festive—not since the Christmas she'd spent in hospital.

Hard to imagine it was four years ago today that she'd woken up to learn that her world had changed. And once again she was spending Christmas Eve reflecting on everything she had lost—except the list was even longer this year.

'How are they?' she asked as the doctor approached her table.

Helene gave a low chuckle. 'Not missing them at all, then? Let me grab a coffee and I'll tell you everything.'

Alice dropped back down to her seat, stirring her already cold hot chocolate, and waited. Impatiently.

She'd thought it would be easy to leave everything behind. She'd done it so many times before, after all. What was so different about this time?

Of course, she already knew the answer to that—even if she didn't want to say the words out loud. That would make it real. That would mean she'd walked out on the only life she'd ever wanted.

And she couldn't be that stupid. Could she?

'So, how're things in the big city?' Helene asked, slipping into the seat opposite her. 'Pining for the country yet?'

'Not the country,' Alice muttered. 'Look, just tell me. What's happening back at Thornwood?'

Helene sighed. 'You could come home and find out for yourself, you realise.'

Alice shook her head. 'No, I can't. Trust me. That bridge is well and truly burned.'

'Is it?' Helene raised her eyebrows. 'Seems to me that there are two boys with a row boat that would be more than happy to help you get back across your hypothetical river.'

Her boys. Liam and Jamie. She hadn't even let herself think of them as truly hers until after she'd left. But now that was the only way she could see them. 'How are they?' she asked again.

'They're fine, on the outside,' Helene said. 'I can't speak for their hearts, though. They miss you—anyone can see that. Liam is working a lot on Haven—'

'Haven?' Alice asked, frowning.

'Didn't he talk to you about it?' Helene looked surprised. 'I thought you must have talked him into it. He's turning Thornwood into a proper centre for the women, children and families of the area. He's doing up the place to make it work better—a proper canteen and better facilities in the rooms, that sort of thing. And he's looking at setting up some activities and stuff for summer camps and the like in the grounds.'

He'd said she needed a name for it, for the services and refuge she provided. And now she'd left he'd given it one.

Haven.

It was perfect.

'But not… He's not going to be charging tourists to visit?'

'Apparently not. And he's planning on staying at Thornwood too, it seems. Heather was telling me about all the furniture he's been ordering for Jamie's room.'

Alice stared down at her half-empty mug, trying to process everything she'd heard. Liam was staying. He was building a life, a family at Thornwood, with Jamie. And he was carrying on what she'd started there, helping people.

And he was doing it all without her.

'I should be there,' she whispered.

'Yes, you should,' Helene said bluntly. 'So why aren't you?'

You're a coward, Liam had said. And he'd been right.

If she was honest with herself, she'd known it the moment she'd left. Known how much she was leaving behind, and how much it would hurt. But she'd hoped by enduring that pain now, she could avoid worse pain in the future.

Except there wasn't only pain in the future she was giving up, was there? There were happy moments, and love and family, and everything else she'd ever wanted.

She'd been a coward to run. But how much more of one would she be to stay away?

She was letting her terror of loss rule her life. Letting her past ruin her chance of a happy future.

And if she didn't face up to that fear now, she never would.

But could she really do it?

There was only one way to find out.

'Helene. Can I get a lift?'

'I'm not sure he likes the Santa hat.' Liam eyed Jamie, who stared balefully back at him from Heather's arms. He'd known asking her to watch him for the morning was a mistake.

'It's Christmas Eve, and he looks adorable,' Heather replied. 'Don't deny it.'

'Fine. But he'll have to take it off to get his snowsuit on.'

'You're going out?' Heather asked. 'Where?'

'Just for a walk,' Liam said vaguely. Heather didn't need to know he was taking Jamie on the same walk they'd taken every day since Alice left. This was private—a pilgrimage for him and his boy.

Liam wrestled Jamie into his snowsuit, forcing a knitted hat onto his head in place of the Santa one, and making sure his gloves were firmly in place. Then he tucked him into his pram, blanket on top, and waved goodbye to Heather as they headed out through the front door.

Outside, the air was crisp and cold and Liam breathed in deeply, feeling it chill his lungs. For someone who'd grown up with Christmases on the beach, and Christmas dinner on the barbie, he had to admit an English Christmas was growing on him.

'Come on, then. Let's go.' The quicker they got there, the sooner they'd be back and in the warm again.

Liam pushed the pram along the driveway, towards the main road, frowning when he saw a car approaching. Was that Helene? Wasn't she supposed to be in the city visiting her sister?

Then the passenger door opened and Alice stepped out, wearing the same red coat she'd worn to the tree-lighting ceremony, her golden hair almost translucent in the winter sun.

Liam's heart thudded against his breastbone as she approached, her movements cautious, obviously uncertain about the reception she was likely to get.

She didn't need to worry, he realised suddenly. He'd thought that he'd been abandoned by people he loved too many times before, that anyone who did that to another person wasn't worthy of his time.

But what he realised now was, it didn't matter how far they went. Only that they came back when they were ready.

'You came home,' he said. Because Thornwood *was*

home now, however unlikely that had seemed a mere month ago.

Alice nodded. 'I…I hope so. I figured some stuff out. Will you listen?'

Liam paused. There was so much he wanted to ask, so many questions he'd imagined demanding answers to, if she ever returned. But now, he realised, he had to let Alice talk. Later, he could ask the only question that really mattered any more.

'Why don't you walk with us?' he suggested. 'We talk best when we're walking.'

'Okay. But first, can I…?' She gestured to the pram and, when he nodded, reached in to lift Jamie into her arms, holding him close as she murmured soft words in his ear.

Liam had never doubted Alice's love for Jamie, but seeing it again, so raw and open, he knew that the love she felt for him was for ever.

He just hoped that the fact she'd come back meant that maybe her love for him could be too.

Alice placed Jamie back in the pram and tucked the blanket around him. 'Okay. I'm ready.'

They walked in silence until they reached the road then, as they turned to follow it down towards the village, Alice started to speak.

'When I told you what happened to me… I've never told that story before, you know. Heather doesn't know… Rose didn't know. Nobody.'

'So why did you tell me?' Liam asked.

'Because…you were offering me the life I wanted. One I didn't believe I could have. And I couldn't accept if you didn't know the truth. Didn't understand that I was damaged, that I could never give you what you wanted.' Did she really think of herself that way? Damaged and broken?

'All I wanted was you,' Liam murmured. 'And I never

saw you as damaged. To me, you were strong. Magnificent. You still are.'

She flashed him a small, uncertain smile. 'The thing is, I realised, when I was away, that I wasn't just thinking about what I couldn't give you. I didn't believe I deserved any of this—to be happy, to have love, a child. Not after what happened.'

'You can't believe that what happened to you was your fault.' Liam stared at her, stunned.

Alice shook her head, just slightly. 'I should have left sooner. I shouldn't have provoked him by spitting in his face. I should…' She sighed. 'There are so many things I should have done. But no. I know it was his fault.'

'Good. So why did you run?'

'The Christmas I ended up in hospital…I lost everything. Not just the husband I thought had loved me, or the child I wanted so badly. But my whole future. How could I trust anyone who said they loved me after that? How could I risk having a family of any sort, when I knew how easily it could be snatched away? I was so scared that it would happen again…that's why I kept running. Why I even ran from you and Jamie, when the two of you were the only things I've wanted for so, so long. To be loved by you. To be a family with you. That's…that's the future I never dreamt I could have. And I ran because I was so damn scared of losing it.'

'You realise that makes no sense at all,' Liam said, reaching out to take her hand, holding it with his on the pram handle.

'I know,' Alice sniffed. 'But in my head…it was the only way I had to protect myself. But when I was gone, I realised something else. I wasn't only protecting myself from pain, I was keeping myself from ever being happy again.'

He sighed, wishing he didn't understand so well—but

he did. Wasn't that why he'd planned to leave Thornwood as soon as possible? So that his past couldn't come back and hurt him again?

'I can't lie,' he told her. 'Even though I knew why you'd gone, I hated that Jamie and I weren't enough for you. That you didn't trust me to make it work—even if we weren't allowed to keep Jamie.'

'I couldn't believe that I'd be enough for you,' Alice said, shaking her head. 'And I was so damn scared of falling in love with you...'

'Scared?'

'Terrified,' Alice admitted with a watery laugh. 'I thought I could run and not get hurt. But the two of you were already too deep inside my heart. I already loved you both too much.'

Love. She loved him. Liam had hoped she might, but he'd never imagined she'd come home and say it, just like that.

But she still hadn't said the most important thing, the one thing he really needed to hear.

She still hadn't promised that she'd stay.

'I realised that you were right,' she said after a moment. 'Not just when you said that I could trust you, but that I needed to. Being with you, loving you...that makes me stronger. And running away from it can only make me weaker again.'

They'd reached their turning. Liam paused and turned to look at her. 'So what happens now?' Because that was all that mattered now. The past was gone. All he was interested in was the future. Hopefully, their future.

'I don't want to live in fear any more,' she said, looking up at him with clear, pale eyes. 'I'm done being scared. I can risk any pain, any loss—as long as I get the happiness that comes along the way, and as long as I have you by my side. I'm ready to make my own future—with you and Jamie. If you'll have me.'

Liam smiled as all the pieces fell into place in his heart. 'In that case, we have something to show you.'

Alice followed Liam and Jamie down the track, her heart buoyant and lighter than it had been in years. Jamie was still there—something that had amazed her at first, but she realised now that it shouldn't. Liam was the right parent for him—and maybe she could be too. She wanted to be, and would strive to be. Maybe that was the most anyone could ask.

But what she didn't know was—where were they going? It looked like the same path they'd taken that day when—

Oh.

Alice stumbled to a stop as the cottage came into view—the one from her vision. Her dream of a happy ever after made solid with bricks and mortar. But instead of the overgrown, unloved wreck she remembered, this cottage had clearly been shown a little TLC.

Outside the front door stood a Christmas tree in a pot, strung with tiny white lights that blinked in the afternoon shadows. Over the cottage door hung more lights—brightly coloured lanterns that made the place look warm and welcoming.

Had someone moved in? When? Who?

'Whose home is it?' she asked, not wanting to step closer if they were trespassing. Not daring to speak the hope that was in her heart.

'Ours,' Liam said. 'Yours and mine and Jamie's, if you want it. Because we both love you too. Me especially—more than I ever imagined I could love. And if you can trust me I'll spend every day showing you both just how much. All you have to do is say you'll stay.'

Alice turned to him, the hope inside her overflowing until all the fear that had clung on was washed away. 'For ever?' she asked.

Liam gave her a lopsided smile. 'Longer, if you'd like.'

Wrapping her arms around his neck, Alice reached up and kissed him, long and deep. 'I'm so sorry I ran. I'm so sorry I was scared,' she murmured against his lips.

'All that matters is that you came back,' he replied. 'We missed you so much.'

'I missed you too. My boys.' She glanced down at Jamie, snoozing in his pram. 'And I promise I'll never leave you again.'

'Thank God for that,' Liam said, and kissed her once more. 'Our family isn't complete without you.'

'I couldn't find home anywhere you weren't,' Alice said, filled with the warmth and happiness that came from knowing that she was home at last.

And that none of them would ever be lonely again.

* * * * *

If you enjoyed this story, check out these
other great reads from Sophie Pembroke

PROPOSAL FOR THE WEDDING PLANNER
SLOW DANCE WITH THE BEST MAN
THE UNEXPECTED HOLIDAY GIFT
A PROPOSAL WORTH MILLIONS

All available now!

Praise for *New York Times* and *USA TODAY* bestselling author RaeAnne Thayne

"Romance, vivid characters and a wonderful story; really, who could ask for more?"

—Debbie Macomber, No.1 *New York Times* bestselling author, on *Blackberry Summer*

"Entertaining, heart-wrenching, and totally involving, this multithreaded story overflows with characters readers will adore." —*Library Journal*

"This holiday-steeped romance overflows with family and wintry small-town appeal."
—*Library Journal* on *Snowfall on Haven Point*

"A sometimes heartbreaking tale of love and relationships in a small Colorado town.... Poignant and sweet."
—*Publishers Weekly* on *Christmas in Snowflake Canyon*

"This quirky, funny, warmhearted romance will draw readers in and keep them enthralled to the last romantic page." —*Library Journal* on *Christmas in Snowflake Canyon*

"RaeAnne Thayne is quickly becoming one of my favorite authors.... Once you start reading, you aren't going to be able to stop." —*Fresh Fiction*

"RaeAnne has a knack for capturing those emotions that come from the heart." —*RT Book Reviews*

"Her engaging storytelling...will draw readers in from the very first page." —*RT Book Reviews* on *Riverbend Road*

THE RANCHER'S
CHRISTMAS SONG

BY
RAEANNE THAYNE

All rights reserved including the right of reproduction in whole or in part in any form. This edition is published by arrangement with Harlequin Books S.A.

This is a work of fiction. Names, characters, places, locations and incidents are purely fictional and bear no relationship to any real life individuals, living or dead, or to any actual places, business establishments, locations, events or incidents. Any resemblance is entirely coincidental.

This book is sold subject to the condition that it shall not, by way of trade or otherwise, be lent, resold, hired out or otherwise circulated without the prior consent of the publisher in any form of binding or cover other than that in which it is published and without a similar condition including this condition being imposed on the subsequent purchaser.

® and ™ are trademarks owned and used by the trademark owner and/or its licensee. Trademarks marked with ® are registered with the United Kingdom Patent Office and/or the Office for Harmonisation in the Internal Market and in other countries.

First Published in Great Britain 2017
By Mills & Boon, an imprint of HarperCollins*Publishers*
1 London Bridge Street, London, SE1 9GF

© 2017 RaeAnne Thayne

ISBN: 978-0-263-92343-8

23-1117

Our policy is to use papers that are natural, renewable and recyclable products and made from wood grown in sustainable forests. The logging and manufacturing processes conform to the legal environmental regulations of the country of origin.

Printed and bound in Spain
by CPI, Barcelona

RaeAnne Thayne finds inspiration in the beautiful northern-Utah mountains, where the *New York Times* and *USA TODAY* bestselling author lives with her husband and three children. Her books have won numerous honors, including RITA® Award nominations from Romance Writers of America and a Career Achievement Award from RT Book Reviews. RaeAnne loves to hear from readers and can be contacted through her website, www.raeannethayne.com.

To my dad, Elden Robinson,
who loved Westerns and cowboy music and
who made the best popcorn west of the Mississippi.
I miss you more than words can say.

THE WRANGLER'S CHRISTMAS SONG

Chapter One

The twin terrors were at it again.

Ella Baker watched two seven-year-old tornadoes, otherwise known as Trevor and Colter McKinley, chase each other behind the stage curtains at the Pine Gulch Community Center.

In the half hour since they arrived at the community center with their father, they had spilled a water pitcher, knocked down a life-size cardboard Santa and broken three ornaments on the big Christmas tree in the corner.

Now they were racing around on the stage where to-night's featured act was set to perform within the next half hour.

She would have to do something. As organizer and general show-runner of this fund-raising event for the school's underfinanced music program, it was her responsibility to make sure everyone had a good time.

People's wallets tended to open a little wider when they were happy, comfortable and well fed. A gang of half-pint miscreants had the potential to ruin the evening for everyone.

She had tried to talk to them. As usual, the twins had offered her their angelic, gap-toothed smiles and had promised to behave, then moments later she saw them converge with four other boys to start playing this impromptu game of tag on the stage.

In order to tame these particular wild beasts, she was going to have to talk to someone in authority. She gave a last-ditch, desperate look around. As she had suspected, neither their uncle nor their great uncle was in sight. That left only one person who might have any chance of corralling these two little dynamos.

Their father.

Ella's stomach quivered. She did *not* enjoy talking to Beck McKinley and avoided it as much as possible.

The man made her so ridiculously nervous. He always treated her with careful politeness, but she could never read the expression on his features. Every time she spoke with him—which was more often than she liked, considering his ranch was next door to her father's—she always felt like she came out of the encounter sounding like a babbling fool.

Okay, yes. She was attracted to him, and had been since she moved back to Pine Gulch. What woman wouldn't be? Big, tough, gorgeous, with a slow smile that could charm even the most hardened heart.

She didn't *want* to be so drawn to him, especially when he hadn't once shown a glimmer of interest in return. He made her feel like she was an awkward teenager back in private school in Boston, holding up the wall at her first coed dance.

She wasn't. She was a twenty-seven-year-old professional in charge of generating funds for a cause she cared about. Sexy or not, Beck had to corral his sons before they ruined the entire evening.

Time to just suck it up and take care of business. She was a grown-up and could handle talking to anyone, even big, tough, stern-faced ranchers who made her feel like she didn't belong in Pine Gulch.

It wasn't hard to find Beck McKinley. He towered about four inches taller than the crowd of ranchers he stood among.

She sucked in a steadying breath and made her way toward the group, trying to figure out a polite way to tell him his sons were causing trouble again.

She wasn't completely surprised to find her father was part of the group around Beck. They were not only copresidents of the local cattle growers association this year, but her father also idolized the man. As far as Curt Baker was concerned, Beck McKinley was all three wise men rolled into one. Her father still relied heavily on Beck for help—more so in the last few years, as his Parkinson's disease grew more pronounced and his limitations more frustrating.

At least her father was sitting down, leaning slightly forward with his trembling hands crossed in front of him atop the cane she had insisted he bring.

He barely looked at her, too engrossed in the conversation about cattle prices and feed shortages.

She waited until the conversation lagged before stepping into the group. She was unwilling to call out the rancher over his troublemaking twins in front of all the others.

"Beckett. May I have a brief word?"

His eyebrows rose and he blinked in surprise a few times. "Sure. Excuse me, gentlemen."

Aware of curious gazes following them, Ella led Beck a short distance from his peers.

"Is there a problem?" he asked.

She pointed toward the pack of wild boys on the stage, who were chasing each other between the curtains. "Your sons are at it again."

His gaze followed her gesture and he grimaced. "I see half a dozen boys up there. Last I checked, only two of those are mine."

"Colter and Trevor are the ringleaders. You know they are. They're always the ones who come up with the mischief and convince the others to go along."

"They're natural leaders. Are you suggesting I try to put the brakes on that?"

His boys were adorable, she had to admit, but they were the bane of her existence as the music teacher at Pine Gulch Elementary School. They couldn't sit still for more than a few minutes at a time and were constantly talking to each other as well as the rest of the students in their class.

"You could try to channel it into more positive ways."

This wasn't the first time she had made this suggestion to him and she was fairly certain she wasn't the only educator to have done so. Trevor and Colter had been causing problems at Pine Gulch Elementary School since kindergarten.

"They're boys. They've got energy. It comes with the package."

She completely agreed. That was one of the reasons she incorporated movement in her music lessons with all of her students this age. All children—but especially boys, she had noticed—couldn't sit still for long hours at a time and it was cruel to expect it of them.

She was a trained educator and understood that, but she also expected that excess energy to be contained when necessary and redirected into proper behavior.

"Our performers will be taking the stage soon. Please, can you do something with the boys? I can just picture them accidentally ripping down the curtains or messing with the lights before we can even begin."

Beck glanced at his boys, then back down at her. His strong jaw tightened, and in his eyes, she saw a flash of something she couldn't read.

She didn't need to interpret it. She was fairly certain she knew what he thought of her. Like her father, Beck thought she was a soft, useless city girl.

Both of them were wrong about her, but nothing she did seemed to convince them otherwise. As far as her father was concerned, she belonged in Boston or New York, where she could attend the symphony, the ballet, art gallery openings.

Since the moment she'd arrived here with her suitcases a little more than a year ago, Curt had been trying relentlessly to convince her to go back to Boston with her mother and stepfather and the cultured life they had.

Beck seemed to share her father's views. He never seemed to want to give her the time of day and always seemed in a big hurry to escape her presence.

Whatever his true opinion, he always treated her with stiff courtesy. She would give him that. Beck McKinley was never rude to anybody—probably one of the reasons all the other ranchers seemed to cluster around the man in public. Everybody seemed to respect his opinion and want to know what he had to say about things.

The only thing she wanted from him right now was to keep his boys from ruining the night.

"I'll talk to the parents of the other boys, too. I'm just asking if you'll please try to round up Colter and Trevor and have them take their seats. I'll be introducing our performers in a moment and I would like people to focus on what they came for, instead of how many straws Colter can stick up his nose."

He unbent enough to offer that rare, delicious smile. It appeared for only a moment. His cheeks creased and his eyes sparkled and his entire face looked even more gorgeous. "Good point, I suppose. The answer is five, in case you wanted to know. I'll grab them. Sorry they caused a ruckus."

"Thank you," she said, then walked away before she was tempted to make another joke, if only to see if he would offer up that smile again.

Better to quit while she was ahead, especially since her brain was now struggling to put together any words at all.

Beck watched Ella Baker walk away, her skirt swishing and her boot heels clicking on the old wooden floor of the community center.

He had the same reaction to her that he always did—sheer, wild hunger.

Something about that sleek blond hair and her almond-shaped eyes and the soft, kissable mouth did it to him. Every. Single. Time.

What was the *matter* with him? Why did he have to

be drawn to the one woman in town who was totally wrong for him?

Ella wore tailored skirts and suede boots that probably cost as much as a hand-tooled saddle. She was always perfectly put together, from the top of her sleek blond hair to the sexy but completely impractical shoes she always wore.

When he was around her, he always felt exactly like what he was—a rough-edged cowboy.

Can you at least pretend you have a little culture? Do you have any idea how hard it is to be married to someone who doesn't know Manet from Monet?

Though it had been four years since she died—and five since she had lived with him and the twins—Stephanie's words and others she had uttered like them seemed to echo through his memory. They had lost their sting over the years, but, boy, had they burned at the time.

He sighed. Though the two had similar blue-blood backgrounds and educations, Ella Baker looked nothing like his late wife. Stephanie had been tall, statuesque, with red hair she had passed on to their sons. Ella was slim, petite and looked like an exotic blonde fairy.

Neither of them fit in here, though he had to admit Ella tried a hell of a lot harder than Stephanie ever had. She had organized this event, hadn't she?

He should probably stop staring at her. He would. Any moment now.

Why did she have to be so damn beautiful, bright and cheerful and smiling? Every time he saw her, it was like looking into the sun.

He finally forced himself to look away so he could do as she asked, quite justifiably. He should have been keeping a better eye on the boys from the beginning, but he'd been sucked into a conversation about a new ranching technique his friend Justin Hartford was trying and lost track of them.

As he made his way through the crowd, smiling at neighbors and friends, he was aware of how alone he was. He had been bringing the boys to these community things by himself for nearly five years now. He could hardly believe it.

He was ready to get out there and date again. The boys had somehow turned seven, though he had no idea how that happened.

The truth was, he was lonely. He missed having someone special in his life. He was tired of only having his uncle and his brothers to talk to.

Heaven knows, he was really tired of sleeping alone.

When he did jump back into that whole dating arena, though, he was fairly sure it wouldn't be with a soft, delicate music teacher who didn't know a mecate from a bosal.

It might be easier to remember that if the woman wasn't so darned pretty.

In short order, he found the boys on the stage and convinced all of them it was time to find their parents and take their seats, then led his own twins out of trouble.

"Hey, Dad. Guess what Thomas said?" Colter asked, as they were making their way through the crowd.

"What's that, son?" He couldn't begin to guess what another seven-year-old might pass along—and was a little afraid to ask.

"His dog is gonna have puppies right before Christmas. Can we get one? Can we?"

He did his best not to roll his eyes at the idea. "Thomas and his family have a miniature Yorkie that's no bigger than my hand. I'm not sure a little dog like that would like living on a big ranch like ours with all our horses and cattle. Besides, we've already got three dogs. And one of those is going to have her own puppies any day now."

"Yeah, but they're *your* dogs. And you always tell us they're not pets, they're working dogs," Trevor said.

"And you told us we probably can't keep any of Sal's puppies," Colter added. "We want a puppy of our very own."

Like they didn't have enough going right now. He was not only running his horse and cattle ranch, the Broken Arrow, but also helping out Curt Baker at his place as much as possible. He had help from his brother and uncle, yeah—on the ranch and with the boys. He still missed his longtime housekeeper and nanny, Judy Miller, who was having double–knee replacement and would be out for six months.

Adding a little indoor puppy into the chaos of their life right now was completely unthinkable.

"I don't think that's going to happen," he said firmly but gently.

"Maybe Santa Claus will bring us one," Colter said, nudging his brother.

At seven, the boys were pretty close to understanding the truth about Santa Claus, though they had never come right out and told them. Every once in a while he thought they might know, but were just trying to hang on to the magic as long as possible. He was okay with that. Life would be full of enough disappointments.

He was saved from having to answer them by the sight of beautiful Ella Baker approaching the microphone.

"Hey! There's Miss Baker," Trevor said, loudly enough that she heard and looked in their direction.

Though families had been encouraged to attend the event and it was far from a formal concert, Beck was still embarrassed by the outburst.

"Shh," he said to the boys. "This is a time to listen, not talk."

"Like church?" Colter asked, with some measure of distrust.

"Sort of." *But more fun*, he thought, though of course he couldn't say to impressionable boys.

Trevor and Colter settled into their seats and Beck watched as Ella took the microphone. He figured he could watch her here without guilt, since everyone else's eyes were on her, too.

"Welcome, everyone, to this fund-raiser for the music program at the elementary and middle schools. By your presence here, it's clear you feel strongly about supporting the continued success of music education in our schools. As you know, programs like ours are constantly under the budget knife. Through your generous donations, we can continue the effort to teach music to the children of Pine Gulch. At this time, it's my great pleasure to introduce our special guests, all the way from northern Montana. Please join me in welcoming J. D. Wyatt and his Warbling Wranglers."

The introduction was met with a huge round of applause for the cowboy singers. Beck settled into his chair and prepared to savor the entertainment—and prayed it could keep his wild boys' attention.

He shouldn't have worried. An hour later, the band wrapped up with a crowd-pleasing, toe-tapping version of "Jingle Bell Rock" that had people getting up to dance in the aisle and in front of the small stage.

His twins had been utterly enthralled, from the first notes to the final chord.

"That was awesome!" Colter exclaimed.

"Yeah!" His twin glowed, as well. "Hey, Dad! Can we take fiddle lessons?"

Over the summer, they had wanted to learn to play the guitar. Now they wanted to learn the violin. Tomorrow, who knows, they might be asking for accordion lessons.

"I don't know. We'll have to see," he said.

Before the twins could press him, Ella Baker returned to the mic stand.

"Thank you all again for your support. Please remember all proceeds from ticket sales for tonight's performance, as well as our silent auction, will go toward funding music in the schools. Also, please don't forget tomorrow will be the first rehearsal for the Christmas show and dinner put on by the children of our community for our beloved senior citizens at The Christmas Ranch in Cold Creek Canyon. This isn't connected to the school and is completely voluntary. Any students ages four to sixteen are encouraged to join us."

"Hey. That's us!" Trevor said.

"Can we do it, Dad?" Colter asked, with the same pleading look on his face he wore when asking for a second scoop of ice cream. "We wanted to last year, remember? Only you said we couldn't because we were going to visit our Grandma Martin."

That had been a short-lived visit with Stephanie's mother in Connecticut, who had thought she would enjoy taking the boys into the city over the holidays and showing off her grandsons to her friends. After three days, she had called him to pick up the boys ahead of schedule, sounding ages older than she had days earlier. She hadn't called again this year.

"Can we?" Trevor persisted.

Beck didn't know how to answer as items on his massive to-do list seemed to circle around him like buzzards on a carcass. He had so much to do this time of year and didn't know how he could run the boys to and from the rehearsals at The Christmas Ranch, which was a good fifteen minutes away.

On the other hand, Ella Baker lived just next door. Maybe he could work something out with her to give the boys a ride.

Of course, that meant he would have to talk to her again, though. He did his best to avoid situations that put them into closer proximity, where he might be tempted to do something stupid.

Like ask her out.

"Please," Colter begged.

This was a good cause, a chance to reinforce to them the importance of helping others. The holiday show had become a high point to many of the senior citizens in town, and they looked forward to it all year. If the twins wanted to do it, how could he possibly refuse?

"We'll see," he hedged, not quite ready to commit.

"You always say that," Trevor said. "How come we never really *see* anything after you say we will?"

"Good question. Maybe someday, I'll answer it. We'll have to see."

The boys laughed, as he hoped, and were distracted by their friend Thomas—he, of the tiny puppies—who came over to talk to them.

"Are you gonna do the Christmas show? My mom said I could, if I wanted."

"We want to," Trevor said, with another cajoling look at Beck.

"Maybe we can have a band," Thomas said. "I'll be J.D. and you can be the Warbling Wranglers."

As they squabbled good-naturedly about which of them would make the better lead singer, Beck listened to them with a sense of resignation. If they really wanted to be in the Christmas program, he would have to figure out a way to make it happen—even if it meant talking to Ella Baker again.

The thought filled him with far more anticipation than he knew was good for him.

Chapter Two

"What a fantastic event!" Faith Brannon squeezed Ella's hand. "I haven't enjoyed a concert so much in a long time."

"Maybe that's because you never go out," Faith's younger sister, Celeste, said with a laugh.

"Newlyweds. What are you going to do?" Hope, the third Nichols sister, winked at their group of friends.

Ella had to laugh, even as she was aware of a little pang. Faith had married her neighbor, Chase Brannon, about four months earlier, in a lovely wedding in the big reception hall of The Christmas Ranch.

It had been lovely and understated, since it was a second marriage for both, but there hadn't been a dry eye in the hall. They seemed so in love and so deserving of happiness.

Ella had managed to smile all evening long. She considered that quite an accomplishment, considering once upon a time, she had completely made a fool of herself over the groom. When she first moved to Pine Gulch, she'd had a gigantic crush on Chase and had all but thrown herself at him, with no clue that he had adored Faith forever and had just been biding his time until she came to terms with her husband's premature death.

Ella had almost gotten over her embarrassment about events of the previous Christmas. It might have been easier to avoid the happy couple altogether except the Nichols sisters—all married now and with different surnames but still "the Nichols sisters" to just about everyone in town—had become some of her dearest friends.

They were warm and kind and always went out of their way to include her in activities.

"You did a great job of organizing," Hope said now. "I couldn't believe all the people who showed up. I met a couple earlier who drove all the way up from Utah because they love J.D. and his Wranglers. I hope you raked in the dough."

"Everyone has been generous," she said. "We should have enough to purchase the new piano we need in the elementary school with plenty left over for sheet music at the middle school."

She still didn't think it was right that the art and music programs had to struggle so much to make ends meet in this rural school system. Judging by tonight, though, many members of the community seemed to agree with her that it should be a priority and had donated accordingly.

"It was a great community event. What a great turnout!"

"Just think." Hope grinned. "We get to turn around

and do this again in a few weeks at The Christmas Ranch."

Faith made a face. "You wouldn't believe how many people have brought up that Christmas program to me tonight, and I'm not even involved in the show!"

"You're a Nichols, though, which makes you one of the co-queens of Christmas, like it or not," Ella said.

The Nichols family had been running The Christmas Ranch—a holiday-themed attraction filled with sleigh rides, a life-size Christmas village and even their own herd of reindeer—for many years. It was enormously successful and attracted visitors from around the region.

The popularity of the venue had grown exponentially in the last few years because of the hard work of the sisters.

A few years earlier, they had come up with the idea of providing a free catered dinner and holiday-themed show presented by area children as a gift to the local senior citizens and the event had become legendary in the community.

"We are so lucky that you've agreed to help us again this year," Celeste said now to Ella.

"Are you kidding? I've been looking forward to it all year."

The event—more like an old-fashioned variety show—wasn't professionally staged, by any means. Rehearsals didn't even start until a few weeks before the performance and there were no auditions and few soloists, but the children had fun doing it and the attendees enjoyed every moment.

The previous year's performance had been a wonderful growing experience for Ella, serving as an icebreaker of sorts to help her get to know the local children better.

She hoped this year would only build on that success.

"Wait until you see some of the songs we have planned. It's going to knock your socks off," she said.

"How can you be so excited about wrestling seventy schoolchildren already on a Christmas sugar high?" Faith shook her head. "You must be crazy."

"The very best kind of crazy," Celeste said with a smile.

"You fit right in with the rest of us," Hope assured her, then changed the subject. "Hey, did you see that good-looking guy who came in with Nate and Emery Cavazos? His name is Jess Saddler and he's temporarily staying at their cabins. Em said he's single and looking to move in and open a sporting goods store in town. He's cute, isn't he?"

She followed the direction of Hope's gaze and discovered a man she didn't know speaking with Nate and Emery, as well as Caroline and Wade Dalton. Hope was right, he was great-looking, with an outdoorsy tan and well-styled, sun-streaked hair that looked as if it had never seen a Stetson.

He also had that overchiseled look of people who earned their strength at the gym instead of through hard, productive manual labor.

"I suppose."

"You should go introduce yourself," Hope suggested, ignoring the sudden frown from both of her sisters.

"Why?" Ella asked, suspicious.

Hope's innocent shrug didn't fool her. "He's single. You're single. Em said he seems like a great guy and, I don't know, I thought maybe the two of you would hit it off."

"Are you matchmaking for me?"

"Do you want me to?" Hope asked eagerly.

Did she? She wasn't sure how to answer. Yes, she was lonely. It was tough to be a single woman in this family-oriented community, where everyone seemed paired up. There weren't very many eligible men to even date and she often felt isolated and alone.

She wasn't sure how she felt about being the latest pity project of her friends. Did she seem desperate to them?

That was an uncomfortable thought.

"I don't need a matchmaker. I'm fine," she told Hope. "Even if I met the right guy today, I'm not sure I would have time for him, between working at two schools, doing music therapy at the senior citizen center and taking my dad to doctor appointments."

"When you care about a man, you make time," Celeste said.

"I don't think the guy is going anywhere. After Christmas, you should think about it," Hope added.

"Maybe." She could only hope a bland nonanswer would be enough for them.

Hope looked disappointed but was distracted when another neighbor came up and asked her a question about a private company party scheduled the following week at The Christmas Ranch.

While she was occupied, Faith turned to Ella with a frown on her soft, pretty features.

"It sounds like you have too much on your plate," Faith said. "Now I feel guilty we roped you into doing the Christmas show again."

"You didn't rope me into anything," she assured her. "I meant what I said. I've been looking forward to it."

"When will you have time to breathe?"

She didn't mind being busy and loved teaching music.

It had been her passion through her teen years and pursuing a career in music therapy was a natural fit. She had loved her job before she came here, working at a school for students with developmental disabilities, but there was nothing like that here in this small corner of southeastern Idaho. Teaching music in the schools was the next best thing. She had to do something with her time, especially considering her father continued being completely stubborn and unreasonable about letting her take over the ranch.

She was busy. She just wasn't *that* busy.

"If you want the truth," she admitted, "I may have slightly exaggerated my overloaded schedule to keep Hope from making me her next project."

Faith looked amused. "Very wise move on your part."

"Don't get me wrong. It's sweet of her and everything. It's just…"

"You don't have to explain to me. I totally get it."

"I'm just not looking for a male right now."

"Too bad. Looks like a couple of cute ones are headed this way."

She followed Faith's gaze to find the twin terrors barreling straight toward her at full speed. To her relief, they managed to stop inches from knocking her and Faith over like bowling pins.

"Hey, Miss Baker. Miss Baker! Guess what?"

The boys' faces were both covered in chocolate, a fairly solid clue that they'd been raiding the refreshments table. How many cookies had they consumed between the pair of them? Not her problem, she supposed. Their father could deal with their upset stomachs and sugar overload.

"What's that, Trevor?" She directed her question to the one who had spoken.

He hid a grin behind his hand. "I'm not Trevor. I'm Colter."

"Are you sure?" She raised an eyebrow.

He giggled. "How come we can never fool you? You're right. I'm Trevor."

The boys were the most identical twins Ella had ever seen and they delighted in playing those kind of switch-up games with the faculty and staff at the elementary school. From the first time they met, though, Ella had never struggled to tell them apart. Colter had a slightly deeper cleft in his chin and Trevor had a few more freckles.

"Guess what?" Colter finished his brother's sentence. "We're gonna be in your Christmas show."

Beside her, Faith gave a small but audible groan that completely mirrored Ella's sudden panic.

On the heels of that initial reaction, she felt suddenly protective of the boys, defensive on their behalf. It really wasn't their fault they misbehaved. None of it was malicious. They were high-spirited in the first place and had a father who seemed more interested in taking over her father's ranch than teaching his two boys to behave like little gentlemen.

But then, she might be a tad biased against the man. Every time she offered to do something to help Curtis, her father was quick to tell her Beck would take care of it.

"Is that right?" she asked. The show was open to any children who wanted to participate, with no auditions and guaranteed parts for all. They wouldn't win any talent competitions, but she considered the flaws and scenery mishaps all part of the charm.

"Our dad said *we'll see*," Colter informed her. "Some-times that means no, but then I heard him asking your dad if he thought you might be able to give us a ride to and from practice on the days no one from the ranch could do it."

Her jaw tightened. The nerve of the arrogant rancher, to go to her father instead of asking her directly, as if Curt had any control over the matter.

"And what did my father say?"

"We didn't hear," Trevor confessed. "But can you?"

Their ranch was right next door to the Baker's Dozen. It would be no great hardship for her to accommodate the McKinleys and transport the twins if they wanted to participate, but it would be nice if Beck could be bothered asking her himself.

"I'll have to talk to your father first," she hedged.

The boys seemed to take her equivocation as the next best thing to a done deal.

"This will be fun," Colter said, showing off his gap-toothed grin. "We're gonna be the best singers you ever saw."

To reinforce the point, Trevor launched into a loud version of "Rudolph the Red-Nosed Reindeer" and his brother joined in. They actually had surprisingly good singing voices. She'd noticed that before during music class at school—though it was hard to confirm that now when they were singing at the tops of their lungs.

They were drawing attention, she saw. The cute guy with Em and Nate was looking this way and so was Beck McKinley.

Ella flushed, envisioning the nightmare of trying to keep the boys from trying to ride the reindeer at The Christmas Ranch, or from knocking down the gigantic sixteen-foot-tall tree inside the St. Nicholas Lodge.

"You can be in the show on one condition," she said, using her best teacher's voice.

"What's that?" Colter asked warily.

"Children of all ages will be participating, even some kindergarten students and first graders. They're going to need someone to set a good example about how to listen and pay attention. They'll be watching you. Can you show them the correct way to behave?"

"Yeah!" Trevor exclaimed. "We can be quiet as dead mice."

That was pretty darn quiet—and she would believe *that* when she saw it.

"We can be the goodest kids in the whole place," Colter said. "You'll see, Miss Baker. You won't even know we're there, except when we're singing."

"Yeah. You'll see," Trevor said. "Thanks, Miss Baker. Come on, Colt. Let's go tell Thomas." In a blink, the two of them raced off as quickly as they had appeared by her side.

"Those boys are quite a pair, aren't they?" Faith said, watching after them with a rather bemused look on her features.

Ella was again aware of that protective impulse, the urge to defend them. Yes, they could be exhausting but she secretly admired their take-no-prisoners enthusiasm for life.

"They're good boys. Just a little energetic."

"You can say that again. They're a handful. I suppose it's only to be expected, though." Faith paused, her expression pensive. "You know, I thought for sure Beck would send them off to live with family after their mother left. I mean, here was this tough, macho rancher trying to run his place while also dealing with a couple of boys still in diapers. The twins couldn't have been more than two."

"So young? How could a mother leave her babies?"

"Yeah. I wanted to chase after her and smack her hard for leaving a good man like Beck, but he would never let anybody say a bad word about her. The only thing he ever said to me was that Stephanie was struggling with some mental health issues and needed a little time to get her head on straight. I think she had some postpartum depression and it probably didn't help that she didn't have a lot of friends here. We tried, but she wasn't really very approachable."

Faith made a face. "That sounds harsh, doesn't it? That's not what I mean. She was just not from around here."

"Neither am I," Ella pointed out.

"Yes, but you don't constantly remind us of how much better things were back east."

Because they weren't. Oh, she missed plenty of things about her life there, mostly friends and neighbors and really good clam chowder, but she had always felt as if she had a foothold in two places—her mother's upper-crust Beacon Hill society and her father's rough-and-rugged Idaho ranch.

"Anyway, she left to get her head on straight when the boys were about two and I can't imagine how hard it must have been for Beck on his own. A year later, Stephanie died of a drug overdose back east."

"Oh, how sad. Those poor boys."

"I know. Heartbreaking. Her parents are high-powered doctors. They fought for custody of the boys and I think it got pretty ugly for a while, but Beck wouldn't hear of it. He's a good dad. Why would any judge take the boys away from father and the only home they've ever known and give them to a couple of strangers?"

"He strikes me as a man who holds on to what he considers his."

"That might have been part of it. But the truth is, Beckett adores his boys. You should have seen him, driving to cattle sales and the feed store with two toddlers strapped in their car seats in the crew cab of his pickup truck."

Her heart seemed to sigh at the picture. She could see it entirely too clearly, the big, tough rancher and his adorable carbon-copy twins.

"He's a good man," Faith said. "A woman could do far worse than Beckett McKinley. If you're ever crazy enough to let Hope fix you up, you shouldn't discount Beck on account of those wild boys of his."

That wouldn't be the only reason she could never look seriously at Beck, if she was in the market for a man—which she so totally wasn't. For one thing, she became nervous and tongue-tied around him and couldn't seem to string together two coherent thoughts. For another, the man clearly didn't like her. He treated her with a cool politeness made all the more striking when she saw his warm, friendly demeanor around others. And, finally, she was more than a little jealous of his close relationship with her father. Curt treated his neighboring rancher like the son he'd never had, trusting him with far more responsibility than he would ever consider giving his own daughter. How could she ever get past that?

She was saved from having to answer when Faith's husband, Chase, came over with Faith's daughter and son in tow.

Chase smiled at Ella and she tried to ignore the awkwardness as she greeted him. This was all she wanted. A nice man who didn't make her nervous. Was that too much to ask?

"Mom, can we go?" Louisa said. "I still have math homework to finish."

"We're probably the only parents here whose kids are begging to leave so they can get back to homework," Chase said with a grin.

"Thanks again for the great show, Ella," Faith said. "We'll see you tomorrow. Now that we've been warned the McKinley twins are coming, we'll make sure you have reinforcements at practice tomorrow."

She could handle the twins. Their father was another story.

As much as he enjoyed hanging out with other ranchers, shooting the, er, shinola, as his dad used to call it, Beck decided it was time to head out. It was past the boys' bedtime and their bus would be coming early.

"Gentlemen, it's been a pleasure but I need to call it a night," he said.

There were more than a few good-hearted groans of disappointment.

He loved the supportive ranching community here in Pine Gulch. Friends and neighbors came through for each other in times of need. He couldn't count the number of guys who had stepped in to help him after his father died. When Stephanie left, he had needed help again until he could find a good nanny and more than one neighbor had come over without being asked to lend a hand on the ranch.

The Broken Arrow would have gone under without their aid and he knew he could never repay them. The only thing he could do now was help out himself where he could.

As Beck waved goodbye and headed away from the group, he saw Curt Baker climb to his feet with the aid of his cane and follow after him. Beck slowed his steps so the older man could catch up.

"Thanks again for stepping in today and helping Manny unload the feed shipment."

"Glad I could help," he answered.

It was true. He admired Curt and owed the man. After Beckett's father died, Curt had been the first neighbor to step in and help him figure out what he was doing on the ranch. Now the tables were turned. Curt's Parkinson's disease limited his ability to care for his own holdings. He had reduced his herd significantly and brought in more help, but still struggled to take care of the day-to-day tasks involved in running a cattle ranch.

He had actually talked Curt into running with him to be copresidents of the local cattle growers association. It wasn't a tough job and gave Curt something else to focus on besides his health issues.

"Have you thought more on what we talked about over lunch?"

As if he could think about anything else. As much as he enjoyed cowboy folk songs, he'd had a hard time focusing on anything but Curt's stunning proposal that afternoon.

"You love the Baker's Dozen," he said. "There's no rush to sell it now, is there?"

Curt was quiet. "I'm not getting better. We both know that. There's only one direction this damn disease will go and that's south."

Parkinson's really sucked.

"I'm not in a hurry to sell. So far Manny and the other ranch hands are keeping things going—with help from you and Jax, of course—but you and I both know it's only a matter of time before I'll have to sell. I want to make sure I have things lined up ahead of time. Just wanted to plant the seed."

That little seed had certainly taken root. Hell, it was spreading like snakeweed.

The Broken Arrow was doing better than Beck ever dreamed, especially since he and his brother, Jax, had shifted so many of their resources to breeding exceptional cattle horses. They still ran about 500 cow-calf pair, but right now half the ranch's revenue was coming from the equine side of the business.

He would love the chance to expand his operation into the Baker's Dozen acreage, which had prime water rights along with it. He wasn't trying to build an empire here, but he had two boys to consider, as well as Jax. Though his brother seemed happy to play the field, someday that might change and he might want to settle down and become a family man.

Beck needed to make sure the Broken Arrow could support him, if that time came. It made perfect sense to grow his own operation into the adjacent property. It would be a big financial reach, but after several record-breaking years, he had the reserves to handle it.

"How does Ella feel about this?" he asked.

Curt shrugged. "What's not to like? You take over the work and we have money in the bank. She'll be fine. She could go back to Boston and not have to worry about me."

He wasn't sure he agreed with Curt's assessment of the Ella factor. Yeah, she didn't know anything about ranching and had only lived here with her father for a little longer than a year, but Ella was stubborn. She adored her father and had moved here to help him, though Curt seemed reluctant to lean on her too much.

"Anyway, we can worry about that later," Curt said. "My priority is to make sure I sell the land to someone who's actually going to ranch it, not turn it into condominiums. I've seen what you've done with the Broken Arrow since your father died and I have no doubt you'd give the same care to the Baker's Dozen."

"I appreciate that."

"No need to decide anything right now. We have plenty of time."

"You've given me a lot to chew on."

"That was my intent," Curt said. "Still need me to talk to Ella about taking your boys to the music thingy tomorrow?"

He winced, embarrassed that he'd even brought it up earlier. He was a grown man. He could talk to her himself, even if the woman did make him feel like he'd just been kicked by a horse, breathless and stupid and slow.

"I'll do it," he said. "I actually have a few things in town so should be able to take them tomorrow. When I get the chance, I'll try to talk to her then about future rehearsals."

He wasn't sure why his boys were so set on being in this Christmas program, but they were funny kids, with their own independent minds. He had always had the philosophy that he would try to support them in anything they tried. Basketball, soccer, after-school science clubs. Whatever.

Even when it meant he had to talk to Ella Baker.

Chapter Three

"Trevor. Colter. That's the last time I'm going to ask you. Please stop making silly noises. If you keep interrupting, we won't make it through all the songs we need to practice."

The twins gave Ella matching guilty looks. "Sorry, Miss Baker," Colter said.

"We'll be good. We promise," his brother added.

Somehow she was having a hard time believing that, especially given their track record in general and this practice in particular. After a full day of school, they were having a tough time sitting still and staying focused for the rehearsals, as she had fully expected.

She felt totally inadequate to deal with them on a December afternoon when they wanted to be running around outside, throwing snowballs and building snow forts.

Would it distract everyone too much if she had them

stand up and do jumping jacks for a minute? She decided it was worth a try. Sometimes a little burst of energy could do wonders for focus.

"Okay, speed workout. Everyone. How many elf jumping jacks can you do in one minute? Count to yourself. Go."

She timed them on her phone and by the end the children were all laughing and trying to outdo each other.

"Excellent. Okay, now close your eyes and we'll do one more moment of deep breathing. That's it. Perfect."

That seemed to refocus everyone and they made it through nearly every number without further incident, until the last one, "Away in a Manger."

The song sounded lovely, with all the children singing in tune and even enunciating the words—until the last line of the third verse, when Trevor started making noises like a certain explosive bodily function, which made the entire back row dissolve into laughter.

By the time they finished the ninety-minute rehearsal, though, she felt as wrung out as a dirty mitten left in the snow.

As soon as parents started arriving for their children, Hope popped in from the office of The Christmas Ranch with a mug of hot chocolate, which she thrust out to Ella.

"Here you go. Extra snowflake marshmallows. You deserve it. You survived the first rehearsal. It's all uphill from here."

"I hope so," she muttered. "Today was a bit of a disaster."

"I saw Beck's boys giving you a rough time," Hope said, her voice sympathetic.

"You could say that. It must be tough on them, coming straight from school to here."

Eight rehearsals. That's all they had. She could handle that, couldn't she?

"Do you need me to find more people to help you?"

She considered, then shook her head. "I think we should be okay with the two teenagers who volunteered. Everyone is so busy this time of year. I hate to add one more thing to someone else's plate."

"Because your schedule is so free and easy over the next few weeks, right?"

Hope had a point. Between the Christmas show, the care center where she volunteered and the two schools where she worked, Ella had concerts or rehearsals every single day between now and Christmas.

"At least I'm not a bestselling illustrator who also happens to be in charge of the number-one holiday attraction for hundreds of miles around."

"Lucky you," Hope said with a grin. "Want to trade?"

"Not a chance."

Hope wouldn't trade her life, either, Ella knew. She loved creating the Sparkle the Reindeer books, which had become a worldwide sensation over the last few years. She also adored running the ranch with her husband, Rafe, and raising their beautiful son.

"Let me know if you change your mind about needing more help," Hope said.

"I will."

After Hope headed away, Ella started cleaning up the mess of paper wrappers and leftover sheet music the children had left behind. She was gathering up her own things when a couple of boys trotted out of the gift shop.

Colter and Trevor. Was she supposed to be giving them a ride? Beck hadn't called her. He hadn't said a word to her about it. Had he just assumed she would do it without being asked?

That didn't really seem like something Beck would do. More likely, there was a miscommunication.

"Do you need me to call your dad to let him know we're done with rehearsal?"

Colter gave an exasperated sigh. "We told him and told him about it last night and this morning at breakfast. We took a note to school so we could ride a different bus here, then our dad was supposed to come get us when practice was done. I don't know where he is."

"Maybe we'll have to sleep here tonight," Trevor said. "I call under the Christmas tree!"

"You're not sleeping here tonight. I can give you a ride, but I need to talk to your dad first to make sure he's not on his way and just running late. I wouldn't want us to cross paths."

At least he hadn't just assumed she could take care of it. Slightly mollified, she pulled her phone out of her pocket. "Do you know his number?"

The boys each recited a different number, argued for a few moments, then appeared to come to a consensus.

She punched in the numbers they gave her without much confidence she would actually be connected to Beck, but to her surprise he answered.

"Broken Arrow," he said, with a brusqueness she should have expected, especially considering he probably didn't recognize her phone number.

Those two simple words in his deep, sexy voice seemed to shiver down her spine as if he'd trailed a finger down it.

"Beckett, this is Ella Baker. I was wondering...that

is, your sons were wondering, uh, are you coming to pick them up?"

Darn it, she *hated* being so tongue-tied around the man. She had all the poise and grace of a lumbering steer.

There was a long, awkward pause, then he swore. He quickly amended it. "Uh, shoot. I totally forgot about that. What time is rehearsal done?"

"About twenty minutes ago," she answered, letting a bit of tartness creep into her voice.

He sighed. "I've got the vet here looking at a sick horse. We're going to be another ten minutes or so, then I'll have to clean up a bit. Can you give me a half hour?"

He still couldn't seem to bring himself to ask for her help. Stubborn man. She glanced over at the boys, who were admiring the giant Christmas tree in the lodge. She wasn't sure she had the physical or mental capacity to keep them entertained and out of trouble for another half hour.

"I can give them a ride home, if you would like. It's an easy stop on my way back to the Baker's Dozen."

"Could you? That would be a big help. Thank you." The relief in his voice was palpable.

"You're welcome. Do you want me to drop them at the barn or the house?"

"The horse barn, if you don't mind. That's where I'm working."

She was suddenly having second thoughts, not sure she was ready to see him two days in a row.

"All right. We'll see you shortly, then."

"Thank you," he said again.

She managed to round up the boys in the nick of time, seconds before they were about to test how strong the garland over the mantel was by taking turns dangling from it.

How had Beck's house not burned down to the ground by now, with these two mischievous boys around?

"Why are you driving us home?" Colter asked when they had their seat belts on in her back seat. "Where's our dad?"

"He's taking care of a sick horse, he said. The vet's there with him and they lost track of time."

"That's Frisco. He was our mom's horse, but he's probably gonna die soon."

She wasn't sure how to reply to that, especially when he spoke in a matter-of-fact way. "I'm sorry."

"He's really old and too ornery for us to ride. He bites. Dad says he better not catch us near him," Trevor said.

She shivered, then hoped they couldn't see. She had to get over her fear of horses, darn it. After more than a year in horse and cattle country, she thought she would be past it—but then, twenty years hadn't made a difference, so why should the past year enact some miraculous change?

"You better do what he says."

"We don't want to ride that grumpy thing, anyway," Trevor said. "Why would we? We both have our own horses. Mine is named Oreo and Colt's is named Blackjack."

"Do you have a horse, Miss Baker?"

She remembered a sweet little roan mare she had adored more than anything in the world.

"I used to, when I was your age. Her name was Ruby. But I haven't been on a horse in a long, long time. We don't have any horses on the Baker's Dozen."

In one bold sweep, her dad had gotten rid of them all

twenty years ago, even though he had loved to ride, too. Thinking about it always made her sad.

"You could come ride our horses. We have like a million of them."

Familiar fear sidled up to her and said hello. "That's nice of you, Colter, but I don't know how to ride anymore. It's been a very long time since I've been in a saddle."

"We could teach you again," Trevor offered, with a sweet willingness that touched something deep inside. "I bet you'd pick it up again easy."

For a moment, she was very tempted by the offer but she would have to get past her phobia first. "That's very kind of you," she said, and left it at that. The boys didn't need to know about her issues.

"Hey, you know how to sing, right?" Colter said suddenly, changing the subject.

Considering she had one degree in music therapy and another in music education, she hoped so. "Yes. That is certainly something I do know how to do."

"And you play the guitar. You do it in school sometimes."

And the piano, violin and most other stringed instruments. "That's right."

"Could you teach us how to play a song?" Colter asked.

"And how to sing it, too?" Trevor said.

She glanced in her rearview mirror at their faces, earnestly eager. "Does either of you know how to play the guitar?"

"We both do, kind of," Colter said. "Uncle Dan taught us a couple chords last summer but then he said he wouldn't teach us anymore because we played too hard and broke all the strings on his guitar."

"Oh, dear."

These boys didn't do anything half-heartedly. She secretly hoped they would continue to be all-in as they grew up—with a little self-restraint when it was necessary, anyway.

"But we would never do that to your guitar, if you let us practice on it," he assured her with a grave solemnity that almost made her smile.

"We promise," his twin said. "We would be super careful."

She couldn't believe she would even entertain the idea for a moment, but she couldn't deny she was curious about the request. "What song are you trying to learn how to play and sing?"

"It's a good one. 'Christmas for the Cowboy.' Have you heard that one?"

"I'm not sure."

"It's about this cowboy and he has to work on Christmas Eve and ride his horse in the snow and stuff," Trevor informed her.

"He's real mad about it, and thinks it's not fair and he wants to be inside where it's warm, then the animals help him remember that Christmas is about peace on earth and stuff."

"And baby Jesus and wise men and shepherds," Trevor added.

"That sounds like a good one."

She combed through her memory bank but wasn't sure if she had ever heard it.

"It's our dad's favorite Christmas song in the whole wide world. He hums it all the time and keeps the CD in his pickup truck."

"Do you know who sings it?" she asked. It would be

much easier to track down the guitar chords if she could at least have that much info.

The boys named a country music group whose name she recognized. She wasn't very familiar with their body of work.

"So can you teach us?" Colter asked as they neared the turnoff for the Broken Arrow. "It has to be with the guitar, too."

"Please?" Trevor asked. "Pretty please with Skittles on top?"

Well, she did like Skittles. She hid a smile. "Why is this so important to you? Why do you want to learn the song so badly?"

As she glanced in the rearview mirror, she saw the boys exchange looks. She had noticed before they did that quite often, as if passing along some nonverbal, invisible, twin communication that only they understood.

"It's for our dad," Trevor finally said. "He works hard all the time and takes care of us and stuff and we never have a good present to give him at Christmas."

"Except things we make in school, and that's usually just dumb crap," Colter said. "Pictures and clay bowls and stuff."

Ella had a feeling the art teacher she shared a classroom with probably wouldn't appreciate that particularly blunt assessment.

"When we went to bed last night after the concert, we decided we should learn that song and play it for our dad because he loves it so much, but we don't know the right words. We always sing it wrong."

"Hey, maybe after we learn it, we could play and sing it in the Christmas program," Colter said.

"Yeah," Trevor said, "Like that guy and his wranglers last night."

She didn't know how to respond, afraid to give the boys false hope. She didn't even know what song they were talking about, let alone whether it was appropriate for a Christmas program designed for senior citizens.

"I'm afraid I'm not familiar with that song—" she began.

"You could learn it, couldn't you?" Colter said.

"It's probably not even too hard."

As she turned into the ranch, they passed a large pasture containing about a dozen horses. Two of them cantered over to the fence line, then raced along beside her SUV, their manes and tails flying out behind them.

She felt the familiar panic, but something else, a long-buried regret for what she had lost.

"If I can find the song and agree to teach you, I need something from the two of you in return."

"Let me guess. You want us to quit messing around at rehearsal." Colter said this in the same resigned tone someone might use after being told they faced an IRS audit.

"Absolutely. That's one of my conditions. You told me you could behave, but today wasn't a very good example of that. I need to be able to trust you to keep your word."

"Sorry, Miss Baker."

"We'll do better, we promise."

How many times had the boys uttered those very same words to one voice of authority or other? No doubt they always meant it, but something told her they would follow through this time. It touched her heart that they wanted to give this gift to their father, who had sacri-

ficed and struggled and refused to give up custody after
their mother died.

She wanted to help them give something back to
him—and she wanted something in return, something
that made her palms suddenly feel sweaty on the steering wheel.

"That is one of my conditions. And I'm very firm
about it."

She paused, sucked in a breath, then let it out in a rush
and spoke quickly before she could change her mind.

"I also have one more condition."

"What?" Trevor asked.

Her heart was pounding so hard, she could barely hear
herself think. This was foolish. Why did she think two
seven-year-old boys could help her overcome something
she had struggled with for twenty years?

"You said you could teach me how to ride horses
again. I would like that, very much. I told you it's been
a long time since I've been on a horse. I...miss it."

More than she had even dared acknowledge to herself.

Once, horses had been her passion. She had dreamed
about them, talked about them, drew pictures of them,
even during the months when she was living in Boston
during the ten months out of the year her mother had
custody of her. It used to drive Elizabeth crazy.

Everything had changed when she was eight.

"You really can't ride?" Trevor said. "You said that before but I didn't think you meant it. You're a grown-up."

These boys probably spent more time in the saddle
than out of it. She had seen them before as she was driving by the ranch, racing across the field and looking utterly carefree. Until now, Ella hadn't realized how very
much she had envied them.

"Not everyone is as lucky as you two," she said as she pulled up to the large red indoor horse barn and arena. "I learned how to ride when I was a child, but then I had a bad fall and it's been...hard for me ever since."

Hard was an understatement. What she didn't tell the boys was that she had a completely reasonable terror of horses.

She had been only a year older than the boys, on a visit here with her father. Her sweet little Ruby had been nursing an injury so she had insisted to her father she could handle one of the other geldings on a ride with him along their favorite trail. The horse had been jittery, though, and had ended up being spooked by a snake on the trail just as they were crossing a rocky slope.

Not only had she fallen from the horse, but she had also tumbled thirty feet down the mountainside.

After being airlifted to Idaho Falls, she had ended up in a medically induced coma, with a head injury, several broken vertebrae and a crushed leg. She had spent months in the hospital and rehab clinics. Even after extensive therapy, she still limped when she was tired.

Her injuries had marked the final death knell to the marriage her parents had tried for years to patch back together. They had been separated on and off most of her childhood before then. After her riding accident, her mother completely refused to send her to the ranch.

The custody battle had been epic. In the process, a great gulf had widened between her and her father, one that she was still trying to bridge, twenty years later.

If she could only learn to ride, conquer her fear, perhaps Curt Baker wouldn't continue to see her as a fragile doll who needed to be protected at all costs.

"I know the basics," she told the boys now. "I just need

some pointers. It's a fair trade, don't you think? I teach you a few chords on the guitar and you let me practice riding horses."

The boys exchanged looks, their foreheads furrowed as they considered her request. She caught some furtive whispers but couldn't hear what they said.

While she waited for them to decide, Ella wondered if she was crazy. She couldn't believe she was actually considering this. What could these boys teach her, really? She was about to tell them she had changed her mind about the riding lessons but would still teach them the song when Trevor spoke for both of them.

"Sure. We could do that. When do you want to practice? How about Saturday?"

"We can't!" Trevor said to his brother. "We have practice Saturday, remember?"

"Oh, yeah. But maybe in the afternoon, when we're done."

Why was she even considering throwing one more thing into her packed schedule? She couldn't do it. Ella wiped her sweaty palms on her skirt. "We can forget this. It was a silly idea."

"Why?" Trevor asked, his features confused. "We want you to teach us how to play and sing a song for our dad's Christmas present and you want to learn how to ride a horse better so you don't fall off. We can teach each other."

"It will be fun. You'll see. And maybe you could even buy one of our dad's horses after you learn how to ride again."

That was pushing things. Maybe she first ought to see if she could spend five minutes around horses without having a panic attack.

"So can you come Saturday afternoon?" Trevor asked.

"Our dad won't be home, so that would be good. Then he won't need to know why we're teaching you how to ride horses. Because otherwise, we'd have to tell him it's a trade. That would ruin the surprise."

"I...think I can come Saturday." Oh, she was crazy.

"Yay! This will be fun. You'll see."

She wasn't so sure. Before she could come up with an answer, the door to the barn opened and Beck came striding out with that loose-limbed, sexy walk she always tried—and failed—to ignore.

He had someone else with him. Ben Caldwell, she realized, the veterinarian in town whose wife, Caidy, had a magical singing voice. She barely noticed the other man, too busy trying not to stare at Beckett.

Her hands felt clammy again as she opened her car door, but this time she knew it wasn't horses making her nervous.

Chapter Four

"You know, it might be time to say goodbye."

Ben Caldwell spoke gently as he ran a calming hand down Frisco's neck. "He's tired, he's cranky, he can't see and he's half-lame. I can keep coming out here and you can keep on paying me, but eventually I'm going to run out of things I can do to help him feel better."

Beckett was aware of a familiar ache in his gut. He knew it would be soon but didn't like to think about it. "I know. Not yet, though."

The vet nodded his understanding but that didn't make Beck feel any less stupid. No doubt Dr. Caldwell wondered why he had such a soft spot for this horse that nobody had been able to ride for five years. Frisco had always been bad-tempered and high-spirited, but somehow Stephanie had loved him, anyway. Beck wasn't quite ready to say goodbye yet.

He shook the vet's hand. "Thanks, Ben. I appreciate you coming by."

"You got it."

Sal, one of Beck's border collies, waddled over to them, panting a welcome. The veterinarian scratched her under the chin and gently patted her side.

"She hasn't had those pups yet."

"Any day now. We're on puppy watch."

"You'll call me if she has any troubles, right?"

"You know it."

He had great respect for Ben. Though Beck hadn't been too sure about the city vet when the man moved to town a handful of years ago, Dr. Caldwell had proved himself over and over. He'd also married a friend of his, Caidy Bowman, who had gone to school with Beck.

They were finishing up with Frisco when he heard a vehicle pull up outside. Beck's heartbeat accelerated, much to his chagrin.

"You expecting somebody?" Ben asked.

"That would be Ella Baker. I, uh, forgot to pick the boys up from rehearsal at The Christmas Ranch and she was nice enough to bring them home for me."

"That Christmas program is all the buzz at my place, too," Ben said. "My kids can't wait."

Ben had been a widower with two children, a boy and a girl, when he moved to town. Beck sometimes had Ben's daughter babysit the twins in a pinch.

The two men walked outside and Beck was again aware of his pulse in his ears. This was so stupid, that he couldn't manage to stop staring at Ella as she climbed out of her SUV.

Ben sent him a sidelong look and Beck really hoped the man didn't notice his ridiculous reaction.

"I'll get out of your way," Ben said. "Think about what I said."

"I will. Thanks again."

Ella and the boys both waved at the veterinarian as they climbed out of her vehicle.

"Hey, Dad! Hey!" His boys rushed over to him, arms wide, and he hugged them, wondering if there would ever come a time in his life when they didn't feel like the best damn thing that had ever happened to him.

He doubted it. He couldn't even imagine how much poorer his life would be without Trevor and Colter. Whenever he was tempted to regret his ill-conceived marriage, he only had to hug his boys and remember that all the rest of the mess and ugliness had been worth it.

"Hey, guys. How was practice? Did you behave yourselves?"

"Um, sure," Colter said.

"Kind of," his brother hedged.

Which meant not at all. He winced.

"We're gonna do better," Colter assured him. "We promised Miss Baker. Me and Trevor thought maybe we could run around the building three times before we go inside to practice, to get our energy out."

"That sounds like a plan."

It was a strategy he sometimes employed when they struggled to focus on homework at night, taking them on a good walk around the ranch so they could focus better.

"I'm starving," Trevor said. "Can I have a cheese stick?"

"Me, too!" Colter said.

"Yeah. You know where they are."

The boys ran into the barn, heading for the fridge inside the office, where he kept a few snacks.

He turned to her. Like his father always said, better to eat crow when it was fresh. It tasted better hot and was much easier to swallow.

"How big of an apology do I owe you for the boys' behavior?"

To his surprise, she smiled, something she didn't do around him very often. For some reason, the woman didn't seem to like him very much.

"On a scale of one to ten?" she asked. "Probably a seven."

"I'm going to take that as a win."

Her smile widened. It made her whole face glow. With a few snowflakes falling in her hair and the slanted afternoon sun hitting her just right, the universe seemed to be making it impossible for him to look away.

"It's hard for two seven-year-old boys to be in school all day, then take a long bus ride, then have to sit and behave for another hour and a half," she said. "I understand that. They have energy to burn and need somewhere to put it. Today was hard because there was a lot of sitting around while we practiced songs. Things won't be as crazy for our next practice, I'm sure."

"It really does help if they can work out a little energy."

"We did elf jumping jacks. You're right, things were better after that."

She paused, her smile sliding away. He had the feeling she was uncomfortable about something. Or maybe he was the only uncomfortable one here.

"Do you need me to give the boys a ride to the rest of our practices?" she finally asked. "I can take them with me to The Christmas Ranch after school and bring them back here when practice is over."

Her generous offer startled him. The night before, he had wanted to ask her the same thing, but in the light of day, the request had seemed entirely too presumptuous.

"Are you sure that wouldn't be a problem?"

"You're right next door. It's only five minutes out of my way, to bring them up here to the house. I don't mind, really."

"That's very gracious of you. If you're sure it won't be an inconvenience, I would appreciate it."

"I don't mind. I should warn you, they might be a little later coming home than some of the other children, since I have to straighten up our rehearsal space after we're done. Perhaps they can help me put away chairs after practice."

"Absolutely. They're good boys and will work hard, as long as they have a little direction."

The wind was kicking up, blowing down out of the foothills with that peculiar smell of an approaching storm. She shivered a little and he felt bad for keeping her standing out here. He could have invited her inside the horse barn, at least.

"I really do appreciate it," he said, feeling as big and rough and awkward as he always did around her soft, graceful beauty. "To be honest, I wasn't sure how I would juggle everything this week. I'm supposed to be going out of town tomorrow until Monday to look at a couple of horses and I hate complicating the boys' schedule more than I have to for Uncle Dan and Jax."

"No problem."

"Thanks. I owe you one."

"You do," she answered firmly. "And here's how you can pay me back. We're signing up drivers for the night of the show to pick up some of the senior citizens who don't like driving in the snow. Add your name to the list and we can be even."

That would be no hardship for him. It would take up one evening of his life and he could fit a half-dozen senior citizens in his crew cab pickup.

"Sure. I can do that."

"Okay. Deal."

To his surprise, she thrust out her hand to seal the agreement, as if they were bartering cattle or signing a treaty. After a beat, he took it. Her fingers were cool, small, smooth, and he didn't want to let go. He was stunned by his urge to tug her against him and kiss that soft, sweet mouth.

He came to his senses just an instant before he might have acted on the impulse and released her fingers. He saw confusion cloud her gaze but something else, too. A little spark of awareness he instantly recognized.

"I need to, that is, I have to…my dad will be waiting for me."

"Give my best regards to Curt," he said.

The words were a mistake. He knew it as soon as he spoke them. Her mouth tightened and that little glimmer of awareness disappeared, crowded out by something that looked like resentment.

"I'll do that, though I'm sure he already knows he has your best regards," she said stiffly. "The feeling is mutual, I'm sure."

He frowned, again feeling awkward and not sure what he should say. Yes, he and her father got along well. He respected Curt, enjoyed the man's company, and was grateful he was in a position to help him. Why did that bother her?

Did she know Curt had offered to sell him the ranch?

He was hesitant to ask, for reasons he couldn't have defined.

"I should go. It's been a long day. I'll bring the boys back from practice tomorrow and take care of Saturday, too."

"Sounds good. I won't be here, but Jax and Dan will be."

She nodded and climbed into her SUV in her fancy leather boots and slim skirt.

He watched her drive away for much longer than he should have, wondering why he felt so awkward around her. Everyone in town seemed to like Ella. Though she had moved back only a year ago, she had somehow managed to fuse herself into the fabric of this small Idaho community.

He liked her, too. That was a big part of the problem. He couldn't be around her without wondering if her skin was as soft as it looked, her hair as silky, her mouth as delicious.

He had to get over this stupid attraction, but he had no idea how.

He was so busy watching after her taillights, he didn't notice the boys had come out until Trevor spoke.

"Hey, Dad. What are you lookin' at?" his son asked.

"Is it a wolf?" Colter vibrated with excitement at the idea. They had driven up to Yellowstone for the weekend a month ago and had seen four of them loping along the Lamar Valley road. Since then, the boys had been fascinated with the idea of wolves, especially after Beck explained the Pine Gulch area was part of the larger far-ranging territory of the various Yellowstone packs.

"Nope. No wolves," he said now. "I'm just enjoying the sight of our pretty ranch."

His sons stood beside him, gazing at the ranch along with him.

This was what should matter to him, passing on a legacy for these boys. He had worked his ass off to bring the Broken Arrow ranch back from the brink since his father died a decade ago. The ranch was thriving now, producing fine cattle and the best quarter-horse stock in the entire region.

He intended to do his best to protect that legacy for his boys and for his younger brother, so he could have something more than bills and barren acreage to give them after he was gone.

He would build on it, too, when he had the chance. Any smart man would take any opportunity to expand his holdings. Beck couldn't let anything stand in the way, especially not a pretty city girl who wore completely impractical boots and made him think things he knew he shouldn't.

Ella's pulse was still racing uncomfortably as she drove the short distance between his ranch and the Baker's Dozen.

Why, oh, why did Beck McKinley have to be so darned gorgeous? She didn't know how it was possible, but he seemed to get better looking every time she saw him.

This crush was becoming ridiculous. She felt like a giddy girl who had never talked to a man before. Completely untrue. She'd been engaged once, for heaven's sake, to a junior partner in her stepfather's law practice.

Okay, she had been engaged for a month. That counted, right?

On paper, Devin had been ideal. Handsome, earnest, ambitious. They enjoyed the same activities, listened to the same music, shared the same friends. She had known him since third grade and dated him all through college. Her mother and stepfather adored him and everyone said they made a perfect couple.

He proposed on her twenty-sixth birthday, with a ring that had been gorgeous and showy. Shortly afterward, they had started planning their wedding.

Well, her mother had started planning her wedding.

Ella's job in the process appeared to consist of leafing through bridal magazines and nodding her head when her mother made suggestion after suggestion about venues and catering companies and dress shops.

Three weeks into her engagement, she found out her father had Parkinson's. Not from Curt, of course. That would have been too straightforward. No, his longtime housekeeper, Alina, wife to his longtime foreman, Manny Guzman, called to let her know he had fallen again. That was a news flash to her, since she didn't know he had fallen before.

After some probing, she learned Curt had been diagnosed a year earlier and had kept it from her. Apparently he had balance issues and had fallen a few times before, requiring help from one of the hands to get back up.

This time, his fall had been more serious, resulting in a broken hip. She had taken leave from her job and immediately caught a flight to Idaho the next day, which hadn't made Devin very happy. After two weeks of him pleading with her to come back, she realized to her chagrin that she didn't want to go back—and worse, that she had barely given the man second thought.

She didn't love him. How could she possibly merge her life with someone she didn't love? It wasn't worth it, only to make her mother happy.

Ella had flown back to Boston, returned his ring and ended the engagement. He hadn't been heartbroken, which only seemed to reinforce her realization that theirs had been a relationship borne out of convenience and familiarity.

They would have been content together. She wanted to think so, anyway, but she wasn't sure they would have been truly happy.

Devin had never once made her insides feel as if a hundred butterflies were doing an Irish step dance. Not like...

She shied away from the thought. Yes, Beck was hot. Yes, she was attracted to him and he left her giddy and breathless.

So what?

She didn't *want* to be attracted to him. It was pathetic, really, especially when it was clear the man thought she was useless out here in ranching country.

Join the crowd, she wanted to tell him. He and her father ought to form a club.

Oh, wait. They already had formed a mutual admiration society that completely excluded her.

She sighed, frustrated all over again at her stubborn father, who couldn't see that she was capable of so much more than he believed.

A blue pickup truck was parked in front of the Baker's Dozen ranch house as Ella pulled up, and she made a face. She recognized the truck as belonging to Chris Soldado, the physical and occupational therapist who came to the house twice a month to work with her dad, both for his ongoing recovery from the broken hip and to help him retain as much use of his limbs as possible as his Parkinson's progressed.

He must be working after-hours. She grimaced at the prospect. His visits always left Curt sore and cranky. More sore and cranky than usual, anyway.

As she let herself in, she found Chris Soldado and her father in the great room. Her father was leaning heavily on his cane while Chris seemed to be putting equipment back into his bag. Chris was a great guy who had been coming a couple times a month for as long as she had been back in Pine Gulch. He was firm but compassionate with Curt and didn't let him get away with much.

"Hi, Chris," she said with a smile.

"Hey there, Ella," he said. He gave her a flirtatious smile in return. "I'm just on my way out. I was telling your dad, he needs to be doing these exercises on his own, every day. That's the best way to retain as much mobility as he can for as long as possible. Make sure of it, okay?"

She tried to nag, but it usually only ended up frustrating both of them. "I'll do that. Thanks."

"This will probably be my last visit for this year. I'll see you in January, Mr. Baker."

Her father made a face but nodded. He looked tired, his features lined with strain.

She let the therapist out, then returned back to her dad and kissed him on the cheek. He needed to shave, something she knew was difficult for him with the trembling of his hands. That was one more area where he didn't want her help.

Maybe she ought to ask Beck to help Curt shave, since he was so good at everything else.

She sighed. "How was your day?"

"I just had physical therapy and that was a high point."

Oh, she missed the kind, loving father of her childhood. Big, hale, hearty. Wonderful.

He was still wonderful, she reminded herself. She just had to work through the occasionally unpleasant bits to get there.

"How about yours?" he asked, which she appreciated. He didn't always think to ask. "You're late getting home, aren't you?"

"Yes. Remember, I told you I would be late for the next few weeks. We had our first practice for the Christmas pageant."

"Oh, right. It slipped my mind during the torture session. How did it go?"

"Good, for the most part. The McKinley twins caused a bit of trouble but nothing I couldn't handle."

"Those boys are rascals," Curt said, but she heard clear admiration in his voice. "Alina left shepherd's pie. She said we just had to bake it but after Chris showed up, I forgot to turn on the oven."

"I can do that. Let me help you to your chair."

"No. I'm fine. If I sit in that recliner, I'll just fall asleep like an old man. I'll come in the kitchen with you."

That was an unexpected gift, as well. She decided to savor the small victories as she led the way to the kitchen. She fussed until he sat on one of the kitchen chairs, then she poured him a glass of water before turning on the oven and pulling out the potato-topped casserole that had always been a favorite of her father.

"So tell me what those twins were up to today," he said. Curt always seemed to get a kick out of Beck's boys and their hijinks.

"Nothing too egregious."

While she made a salad and set the table, she told him

stories about the boys. He laughed heartily when she mentioned the bodily noises during "Away in a Manger" and about them trying to hang from the garland, and she was suddenly grateful beyond measure for those twins and their energy, and for providing this lighthearted moment she could share with the father she loved.

[faint mirror-image text bleeding through from previous page, illegible]

Chapter Five

"That was excellent. Really excellent," Ella said, praising the two little cowboys seated at a table in the classroom she shared with the part-time art teacher.

She had arranged for Trevor and Colter to stay after school for a half hour so they could rehearse the cowboy ballad they wanted to sing for their father. She would drive them out to The Christmas Ranch when they were finished.

This had been the most logical rehearsal spot, even if the walls were currently adorned with collage after collage of grinning Santas made out of dry macaroni and cotton-puff beards.

Fortunately, all those Santas checking to see whether they were naughty or nice didn't seem to bother Trevor and Colter McKinley.

"We sound good enough to be on the radio, huh?" Trevor said.

She envied their sheer confidence, even as it made her smile. "Definitely," she answered. "You picked up the words and melody of the chorus perfectly. Why don't we try the whole thing from the beginning? Straighten up in your seat, now. You'll sing your best if your lungs have room to expand and they can't do that when you're all hunched over."

The boys sat up straight and straightened their collars as if they were preparing to take the stage at the Vienna opera house. She smiled, completely charmed by them. If she wasn't careful, these two troublemakers would worm their way right into her heart.

"Okay. Hit it," Colter said.

"Please," his twin added conscientiously.

They had decided that because of time constraints, it would be better if she just accompanied them so they didn't have to learn the words to the song and the unfamiliar guitar chords at the same time. She played the music she had found, the first gentle notes of the Christmas song.

The boys sang the lines in unison, their voices clear and pure and quite lovely. Their voices blended perfectly. She could only imagine how good it would sound if they could learn a little harmony.

They could work on that. For now, she wanted to focus on making sure they knew the words and phrasing of the song.

"That sounded really great," she said, after they went through the song four more times in a row.

"Our dad's going to love it," Trevor declared.

"I'm sure you're right." She glanced at the clock. "We had better run or we'll be late for practice with the rest of the children. We can run through the song a few more times on the way."

They grabbed their coats and yanked on backpacks while she prepared to close up the classroom.

"We'll meet you by the office," Colter said. Before she could call them back, they headed out of the classroom. She locked the door and was about to follow after when the fifth-grade teacher from across the hall opened her own door.

"Was that really the McKinley twin terrors I heard in here?" Susan Black looked flabbergasted.

"Yes. They asked me to help them prepare a song they could perform as a gift to their father for Christmas."

The older woman shook her head. "How did you get them to sit still long enough to even learn a line? I think I may seriously have to think about retirement before those two hit fifth grade."

"They like to sing. Sometimes it's just a matter of finding the right switch."

"You've got the magic touch, I guess."

She had no idea why the boys were beginning to respond to her, she thought as she walked toward the office, but she wasn't about to jinx things by questioning it too much.

The boys were waiting impatiently for her and raced ahead when she opened the outside door. They found her SUV in the nearly empty parking lot immediately—no surprise, as she'd given them a ride just the day before.

"Thanks again for helping us," Trevor said when they were safely seat-belted in the back and she was on her way.

"It's my pleasure," she told them.

"Are you still coming tomorrow to ride horses?"

That panic shivered through her and she almost told them to forget about that part of the deal. Two things stopped her. They were proud little cowboys and she sensed they wouldn't appreciate being beholden to her for anything. And second, she knew she couldn't give in to her fear or it would control the rest of her life.

"Are you sure it's okay with your dad?" She couldn't quite keep the trepidation from her voice.

"He won't care and he's gonna be gone, anyway."

"Oh, right. He's looking at a couple of horses."

"Yep. We talked to our uncle Jax and he said he can help us saddle up the easiest horse on the ranch for you."

"That's Creampuff," Colter said. "She's a big softie."

"You'll like her," Trevor assured her. "Even though she likes to wander out when she gets the chance, Dad says he could put a kitten on her back and she'd never knock it off."

"Sounds perfect for me, then," Ella said, trying not to show her nervousness.

"Great. So just wear stuff you can ride in tomorrow. Boots and jeans. You know. Not teacher clothes."

Apparently they didn't approve of her favorite green wool sweater set and dressy dove-gray slacks.

"Got it. I'll see if I can find something a little more appropriate," she said.

"It will be fun. You'll see," Colter said.

She had serious reservations, but tried to swallow them down as they arrived at The Christmas Ranch for rehearsal.

First things first. She had to make it through two more practices before she could have time to worry about her upcoming horseback-riding lesson.

"We were good today, don't you think?"

After rehearsal on Saturday, Ella glanced in the rear-view mirror at the two boys sitting in her back seat.

"You really were." She had to hope they didn't hear the note of wonder in her voice. "And yesterday, too. You paid attention, you stayed in your seats, you didn't distract your neighbors. Good job, guys."

"Told you we could be. It wasn't even that hard. We just had to pretend we were dead mice."

"Dead mice who could still sing," Trevor added.

Ella tried to hide her smile. "Whatever you did, it worked perfectly. Let's see if we can do it again next week, through the rest of the rehearsals we have left until the show."

"We will be," Trevor said. "We promised you, and our dad says a man's word is his wand."

It took her a second to fit the pieces together. "I think he probably said bond. That means a commitment."

"Oh, yeah. That was it. A man's word is his bond."

That sounded like something Beckett McKinley would say to his sons.

He was a good father. The boys were high-strung, but their hearts were in the right place. They were working hard to prepare a Christmas gift for their father and that day she had also watched them show great kindness to Taft Bowman's stepdaughter, who had Down syndrome and some developmental delays. She was older than they were by a few years but they still seemed to have appointed themselves her champion.

She should tell Beckett what good young men he was raising. Something told her he didn't hear that very often.

She pushed away thoughts of the man, grateful at least that she wouldn't have to see him today. She was stressed enough about riding the horses. She didn't need to add any additional anxiety into the mix.

As she drove up the snow-packed road to the ranch

house, those same horses that had greeted them the first time she brought the boys home raced alongside her SUV, a beautiful but terrifying sight in the afternoon sunlight.

She wouldn't be riding one of those energetic creatures. She would be riding a horse named Creampuff. How scary could something named Creampuff really be?

Terrifying enough that she felt as if her heart was going to pound out of her chest. She let out a breath. Why was she putting herself through this, again? It wouldn't make any difference with Curt. Her father loved her but he couldn't see her as anything but fragile, delicate, someone to be protected at all costs.

She pushed away the thought. This wasn't for her father. She needed to ride again for *herself.* She needed to prove to herself she could do it, that she could overcome her fears and finally tackle this anxiety. The opportunity had presented itself through these twins and she couldn't afford to miss it.

"Where should I park?" she asked as she approached the buildings clustered around the ranch house. "Where do you think we will be having this lesson?"

"Uncle Jax said we could use the riding barn. He said he would have Creampuff all ready for you. But then Uncle Dan made us promise we'd stop at the house first to grab some lunch and put on our boots."

"That sounds like a good idea. I need to change my clothes, anyway."

Despite the boys' fashion advice, Ella had worn a skirt and sweater to the Saturday rehearsal, as if preparing for a day at school. It seemed silly in retrospect, but she hadn't wanted to appear in jeans. In her experience, she tended to command more respect with her students when she was a little dressed up.

Her riding clothes were packed into a small bag on the passenger seat beside her, but she hadn't given much practical thought to when and where she would actually change into them. She should have had the foresight to do it at The Christmas Ranch before they left.

They directed her where to park and she pulled her SUV into a driveway in back of the house. The boys led the way inside, straight to the kitchen.

They found Daniel McKinley, Beck's uncle, wearing an apron and loading dishes into the dishwasher.

"There you two are. Howdy, Miss Baker."

She smiled at him. As always, she was delighted by his old-fashioned, courteous nature and ready smile.

He was quite a charmer in his day, she had heard—a bachelor cowboy who cut a broad swath through the female population of the county. Now he was over seventy with a bad back and struggled almost as much as her father to get around these days.

"You ready for your riding lesson?" Dan asked, offering her a smile that still held plenty of charm.

Would she ever be? "Yes," she lied. "I can't wait."

"These boys will get you up on a horse, you wait and see. Best little cowboys I ever did see. They'll have you barrel racing in the rodeo by summer."

That was far beyond what she even wanted to attempt. She could only pray she would be able to stay in the saddle.

"I'm makin' sandwiches, if you want one," he offered. "Nothing grand, just grilled ham and cheese. It's one of the four things I know how to cook."

"What are the other three?" she asked, genuinely curious.

"Coffee, hot dogs and quesadillas. As long as I'm only

making them with cheese and salsa. Oh, I can do scrambled eggs, too, if you've got a hankering."

She had to smile, completely enchanted by him. "I'm great with a ham sandwich. Thanks so much for offering."

"It's no trouble. Just as easy to make four sandwiches as it is three, I suspect."

"I appreciate it, anyway. May I help you?"

"You can help me by sitting down and relaxing. Something tells me you don't do enough of that, Miz Baker."

True enough, especially the last month. She would have time to rest after the holidays.

"If it's all right with you, I would like to find somewhere to change into more appropriate clothing for a riding lesson."

"You can use Beck's bedroom. First door on the right."

She instantly wanted to protest. Was there really nowhere else in this big, beautiful log house for her to change, besides Beckett McKinley's bedroom? She didn't want to know where he slept, where he dressed, where he probably walked around in his briefs.

She let out a breath, aware that she would sound completely ridiculous if she raised a single irrational objection to his suggestion.

Nothing left but to accept with grace, she decided. "That sounds good. I'll change my clothes and then come help you with lunch."

He pointed her on her way, his leathery features split into a smile. Unlike her father, Dan McKinley still appeared to have a healthy appetite. He limped around the kitchen but other than that, his skin was firm and pink instead of the sallow tones her father sometimes had.

Curt had probably lost twenty pounds in the months

she had been back in Pine Gulch. He was still large-framed, but his clothing all sat loosely on him these days and he wore suspenders to keep up his pants.

It made her sad to see the comparison between the two men, though she reminded herself she couldn't change the course of her father's disease. She could only try to make his world as comfortable and accessible as possible.

She gripped her tote bag and hurried down the hall lined with beautiful western artwork, highlighted by tasteful inset lighting.

As she might have expected, judging by the rest of the house, Beck's bedroom was gorgeous, spacious and comfortable, with a river-rock fireplace in one corner and expansive windows that looked over both his ranch and her father's. It was dominated by a massive log bed, neatly made, with a masculine comforter in tones of dark blue and green.

The room smelled of him, of sagebrush and leather and rainy summer afternoons in the mountains.

She inhaled deeply and felt something visceral and raw spring to life inside her. Oh. She wanted to stand right here and just savor it.

That bed. Her imagination suddenly seemed entirely too vivid. A snowy night and the two of them tangled together under that soft blanket, with all those hard muscles hers alone to explore.

"Snap out of it," she ordered herself, just seconds before she would have pulled his pillow up to her face to inhale.

Good grief. She didn't come here to moon over Beck. She was here to conquer her fears and tackle something that terrified her.

Okay, he terrified her, too. But this was about horse-back riding.

With renewed determination, she quickly kicked off her dressy boots and slipped down her skirt, then pulled on her favorite weathered jeans.

Her Christmas sweater with the reindeer and sleigh had been fun for the kids during rehearsal for the program, but would be too bulky and uncomfortable under her coat while she was riding.

She started to pull it over her head but the textured heavy yarn that was part of the design tangled in one of the combs she'd used to pull her hair back. Shoot. If she tugged it too hard, she would rip the sweater and ruin it. She didn't want that. It was one of her favorites, a gift from a friend in Boston.

With her hands above her head and the sweater covering her face, she tried to extricate the design from her hair comb when suddenly she heard the door open.

Panic burst through her and she almost crossed her arms over her chest. At the last minute, she remembered she still had on the plain white T-shirt she wore underneath the sweater.

"Who's there?" she demanded, her face buried in sweater.

"Beck McKinley," a deep voice drawled. "I believe I should be the one asking questions, Miss Baker. It's my bedroom, after all, and to be perfectly honest, I can't begin to guess what you might be doing in it."

She closed her eyes, wishing she could disappear. She should have known. Who else would it be? Wasn't that just the way her luck went? The one person she didn't want to see would, of course, be the one who stumbled in on an embarrassing moment.

She would have far preferred his brother, Jax, who flirted with everyone and could be handled simply by flirting right back.

She ought to just yank down the sweater and rip it, but she couldn't quite bring herself to do that.

"I'm sorry. Your uncle told me I could use your room to change into riding clothes. Didn't he tell you?"

"I haven't talked to Dan since breakfast. I've been holed up in my office on the other side of the house all morning. Riding clothes, Ella?"

She did *not* want to have this conversation with him with her sweater tangled around her head. The only bright spot in this entire miserable predicament was that she was wearing a T-shirt underneath the sweater. She couldn't imagine how mortifying if he had walked in on her in only her bra.

"It's a long story. I can tell you, but would you help me with my sweater first?"

After a pregnant pause, he finally spoke. "Uh, what seems to be the trouble?"

His voice had an odd, strangled note to it. Was he laughing at her? Where she couldn't see him, she couldn't be quite sure. "It's stuck in my hair comb. I don't want to rip the sweater—or yank out my hair, for that matter."

He was silent, then she felt the air stir as he moved closer. The scent of him was stronger now, masculine and outdoorsy, and everything inside her sighed a welcome.

He stood close enough that she could feel the heat radiating from him. She caught her breath, torn between a completely prurient desire for the moment to last at least a little longer and a wild hope that the humiliation of being caught in this position would be over quickly.

"Hold still," he said. Was his voice deeper than usual?

She couldn't quite tell. She did know it sent tiny delicious shivers down her spine.

"You've really done a job here," he said after a moment.

"I know. I'm not quite sure how it tangled so badly."

She would have to breathe soon or she was likely to pass out. She forced herself to inhale one breath and then another until she felt a little less light-headed.

"Almost there," he said, his big hands in her hair, then a moment later she felt a tug and the sweater slipped all the way over her head.

"There you go."

"Thank you." She wanted to disappear, to dive under that great big log bed and hide away. Instead, she forced her mouth into a casual smile. "These Christmas sweaters can be dangerous. Who knew?"

She was blushing. She could feel her face heat and wondered if he noticed. This certainly counted among the most embarrassing moments of her life.

"Want to explain again what you're doing in my bedroom, tangled up in your clothes?" he asked.

She frowned at his deliberately risqué interpretation of something that had been innocent. Mostly.

There *had* been that secret moment when she had closed her eyes and imagined being here with him under that soft quilt, but he had no way of knowing that.

She folded up her sweater, wondering if she would ever be able to look the man in the eye again.

"It's a long story. Your sons offered to teach me how to ride horses."

"Trevor and Colter."

She finally gathered the courage to lift her gaze to his. "Do you have any other sons?"

"No. Two are enough, thanks. Why would Trevor and Colter offer to teach you how to ride horses?"

She suddenly didn't know how to answer that. He couldn't know the boys wanted to surprise him with a special song for Christmas, that they were bartering services. Telling him about it would completely ruin the surprise, and she wasn't about to do that to the boys, especially after they were trying so hard to uphold their side of the bargain.

"I guess they felt sorry for me when I told them I couldn't ride. I may have let slip at some point that I'm a little…nervous around horses and I would like to get over it."

He raised an eyebrow. "Let me get this straight. You're nervous around horses, but somehow you thought two seven-year-old boys could help you get over your fear?"

Okay, it sounded ridiculous when he said it like that. What had seemed like a good idea at the time now seemed nothing short of foolish.

"Why not? They're excellent riders and their enthusiasm is…contagious."

"Like chicken pox."

"Something like that." She forced a smile. "They aren't afraid to tell everyone what good riders they are. I figured it couldn't hurt to see if some of that enthusiasm might rub off on me."

It sounded silly in retrospect, but there was nothing she could do about that at this point. The deal had been struck and she didn't want to hurt the boys by pulling out of the arrangement now, when they were so excited to teach her.

Beck continued to watch her with a baffled look on

his features. What was he even doing there? She thought he was supposed to be out of town this weekend.

"If you would rather I didn't go riding with them, I understand. I should have asked you first. The boys and I talked about it yesterday after practice. They told me you wouldn't be here but that Dan said it was okay. I guess I assumed perhaps he would talk to you. I don't want to cause trouble, though. If you don't want me here, I can grab my Christmas sweater and go home."

She wouldn't blame the man if he threw her off his ranch. Without telling him about the deal she and the boys struck, she sounded completely irrational.

"No. It's fine. We have a couple of really gentle horses that are good for beginners."

She released the breath she hadn't realized she'd been holding. He didn't *sound* like he thought she was crazy.

"The boys promised me a horse named Creampuff. I like the sound of that name, if she lives up to it."

"That's just the horse I would have suggested. She's about as mellow as it gets."

"Sounds perfect. Thank you."

He tilted his head and studied her. "You can ride our sweet Creampuff on one condition."

"What's that?" she asked, suddenly wary at the look in his eyes.

"You let *me*, not the twins, give you riding lessons."

She instantly remembered standing close to him and the shivery little ache that had spread through her. The more time she spent with Beckett McKinley, the more chance she had of making a complete idiot of herself over him.

"That's completely not necessary," she said quickly. "I'm sure the boys and I will be fine."

"First lesson of horses, you can't be sure of anything. Even the most gentle horse can sometimes be unpredictable. I would hate for something to happen to you." He cleared his throat. "Just like I would hate for something to happen to *anyone* on my ranch, riding one of my horses."

Naturally, he wasn't worrying about her in particular. She told herself that little ache under her breastbone was a hunger pang, nothing more. It certainly wouldn't have been disappointment.

What exactly would riding lessons from Beckett McKinley entail? Did she want to find out?

"The boys were looking forward to teaching me." She tried one last time.

"They can still take the lead and give you some pointers. It will be a good experience for them, actually. I'm sure you've found that teachers often learn more than their students about a subject matter. It's good for them to think about the fundamentals of something that by now seems instinctive to them."

She would have to agree. Teaching someone else how to play a particular instrument always reminded her of the basics.

"They can take the lead but I would feel better if I could be there to keep an eye on things, just in case."

She told herself she didn't want his eyes—or anything else—on her. But what choice did she have? It was his ranch, his sons, his horses.

"I thought you were supposed to be out of town, buying horses."

She didn't want to tell him that she would never have agreed to come here for these lessons if she thought she would run into him. If she had known he would end up finding her half-dressed in his bedroom with a sweater tangled in her hair, she would have locked herself in her own bedroom at the Baker's Dozen.

"Plans changed. We found the horses we needed early on and agreed to a fair price with the owner, so we didn't need to stay for the entire sale. We came back last night."

No doubt that defined most of Beck's life. He made a decision early and then went for it. That was probably fine when it came to horses, but not so good when he made a snap decision about her and couldn't seem to see beyond it.

"You thought I was gone."

"The boys said something about it. I would never have come to your bedroom to change my clothes if I thought there was any chance you could be here to run into me."

"Were you hoping to avoid me?"

"Don't be silly," she snapped. "Why would I need to avoid you?"

He didn't answer, only raised an eyebrow.

Before she could think of a way to answer, she heard one of the twins from outside. It sounded like Trevor, but their voices were so similar, it was tough to tell them apart when she couldn't see them.

"Miss Ella? Is everything okay? Our sandwiches are all done but Uncle Dan says we have to wait for you so we can eat. He said that's the polite thing to do when you have guests."

He sounded so disgusted, she had to smile. "It is customary, yes."

"How much longer is it gonna take you to get dressed?"

He didn't say it outright, but the implication was clear. *What the Sam Hill is taking you so blasted long?*

"I'm ready now. I'm coming," she called, before turning back to Beck. "I'm sorry you were dragged into this when you probably had other things to do this afternoon. I'll make some excuse to the boys, tell them I changed my mind or something."

"Why would you go and do that, especially after we went to all the trouble to get you extricated from your Christmas sweater?"

The man had a point. Something told her she wouldn't be able to wriggle out of these lessons like she had eventually done with her sweater. She was stuck, so she might as well make the best of it.

Chapter Six

After she left, Beck released his breath, then inhaled deeply. The scent of her still filled his bedroom—peaches and cinnamon, a combination that made his mouth water.

How did Ella Baker manage to twist him into a dozen crazy knots every time he was with her? He felt as trussed up as a calf at a roping competition.

He closed his eyes, reliving how stunned he had been to walk into his own bedroom and discover her standing there, half-dressed, like all his illicit fantasies come true.

Okay, she hadn't really been half-dressed. She had been wearing a plain T-shirt, but he wasn't sure if she was aware it had ridden up with the sweater, revealing about three inches of bare, creamy abdomen.

At the sight of that little strip of skin, his stupid brain had taken him in all sorts of unruly directions. He had wanted to kiss that patch of skin, to slide off the rest of her clothes, to toss her down on his bed and spend the rest of the day tangled under the quilt with her.

Man, he had it bad.

He opened his eyes as the magnitude of what he had consented to do loomed suddenly as large as the Tetons outside his windows.

Riding lessons. How in the world was he supposed to give the woman riding lessons, when he couldn't stop thinking about all the inappropriate things he would much rather teach her instead?

And what on earth were his boys thinking, to invite her here without talking to him first? He sighed. Those two rascals had the funniest, most convoluted thought processes, especially when they had their minds set on a project. He supposed he should be happy they liked their music teacher enough to want to help her.

Wasn't that what the holidays were all about? Helping others? He didn't see how he could object, really.

She *did* have a phobia about horses. A fairly serious one. He had seen it for himself one day over the summer, when he had been repairing a fence line between the two ranches. Because it had been a lovely July morning, he'd chosen to ride Ace on a trail that connected the two ranches, to the spot that needed repair. He had been minding his own business, enjoying the splendor of the day, when Ella had suddenly jogged into sight on the trail ahead of him, listening to music through earbuds and wearing shorts that showed off her tanned legs.

She hadn't noticed him at first, probably because of the music. When she spotted him and Ace, she had jumped a mile and had scrambled onto a rock beside the trail to let him pass. He had stopped to greet her—the polite thing to do between neighbors—but she hadn't seemed at all in the mood to chat.

He thought it was because she didn't like him. Now he wondered if it had more to do with her aversion to horses.

He wasn't sure if he and the boys could do anything to help that kind of phobia, but he suddenly wanted to try. He would like to be able to give her this. It was a small thing, only a few hours out of his life, but if he could help her get over her fear of horses, he might feel a little less guilty about taking up Curt on his offer to buy the Baker's Dozen.

It only took a few moments for him to realize the task of helping Ella conquer her fear of horses might be slightly harder than he suspected.

"Nothing to be afraid of." He kept his voice calm, slow, just as he would do to a spooked mare. "Creampuff is as easy and gentle as her name. She's not going to hurt you, I promise. It's not in her nature."

"I'm not afraid," she said, which was an outright lie. Her body betrayed her. She trembled, muscles poised as if she was ready to bolt.

"Sure. I believe you," he said, his voice soothing.

Her nervousness temporarily lifted long enough for her to glare at him. "You don't have to patronize me," she said stiffly. "It must be obvious I'm terrified. I don't want to be, but I am."

"You don't have to be afraid, Miss Ella," Colter told her with an earnest look. "Creampuff is so lazy, she only moves every other Sunday. That's what Dad says, anyway."

"Good thing today is Saturday, then," she said, with a slight smile.

"Exactly," Trevor said. "Why don't you start by making friends with her? Dad keeps crab apples in the barn for her, since that's her favorite treat."

That was a good idea to break the ice between her and the horse, one he should have thought of himself. His boys were smart little caballeros.

"Colt, why don't you grab a couple? You remember how to open the box?"

"Yep." Colter headed over to the metal box containing the treat. "We had to put a latch on it after Creampuff here learned how to lift the lid and help herself."

"Did she?" Ella's voice was faint, as if coming from the other side of the barn.

"She would eat those until she's sick, unless we put a few obstacles in her way," Beck answered, still in that calming voice. "Here you are. Give her this, nice and slow."

He handed her a crab apple. "Put it on your palm, not your fingers." He probably shouldn't tell her that if she wasn't careful, Creampuff might munch on her fingers by mistake.

"There. She likes you," he said when the horse lipped the apple from her palm. He also didn't mention that Creampuff would take a crab apple from just about anybody or anything. She had no scruples when it came to her treats.

"How about another?" he asked. Without waiting for an answer, he handed her a second crab apple. She put it on her palm herself and actually smiled a little this time when Creampuff snatched it away before she could even thrust her hand out all the way.

"Now pet her," Trevor suggested. "She likes it when you scratch along her neck. Yep, like that."

"You must think I'm the world's biggest scaredy-cat."

His boys didn't say anything. Though no one could ever call them well-mannered, precisely, sometimes they could be surprisingly polite. This was one of those times. They looked at each other but chose to remain silent rather than agree with her.

"I don't think you're a scaredy-cat," Beck said quietly. "I think something terrible must have happened to you on a horse."

She sent him a swift look, and he could see the truth of his words reflected in the haunted shadows in her gaze. "How did you know? Did my father tell you?"

It didn't exactly take a crack detective to figure it out. She wasn't just nervous, she was petrified.

This hadn't been a good idea. He didn't like seeing her so upset.

"You don't have to do this, you know. There's no law that says you have to ride horses around here."

She was silent, petting the horse. He was happy to see her hands weren't trembling quite as much as they had earlier.

"You might not find it in any Pine Gulch city code," she said after a moment, "but it's one of those unwritten societal laws, understood by everyone who lives here. You have to know your way around horses if you want to truly fit in around here."

He opened his mouth to argue with her, then closed it again. There might be a kernel of truth to what she said, at least in some circles. He had a feeling Curt Baker saw things that way. He was an old-school rancher, through and through. Funny that Curt himself didn't ride, either. Beck had to wonder if that had something to do with whatever had happened to Ella.

"I've always figured most rules were made just so folks could figure out a creative way to break them. Really, Ella. Don't torture yourself. It's not worth it"

She gazed at him, eyes wide as if she didn't expect understanding from him. Her surprise made him squirm. What? He could be as sensitive as the next guy.

She looked at him, then at Creampuff. As he watched, determination flooded those blue eyes.

"I want to do this. I can't let my fear of something that happened when I was eight years old control the rest of my life," she said. "I've given it too much power already."

Eight years old. He tried to picture her, pigtailed and cute and blonde, with that little hint of freckles. What had frightened her so badly?

Whatever it was, he respected the hell out of her for her courage in confronting it.

"Okay, then." His voice came out more gruffly than usual. "Now that you've made friends with Creampuff here, I guess it's time to climb on. When you're ready, I'll give you a hand."

Her hands clenched into fists at her side then unclenched and she nodded. "I'm ready."

Filled with admiration—not to mention this blasted attraction he didn't want—he helped her hold on to the saddle horn and put her boot in the stirrup, then gave her a lift into the saddle.

She held tight to the horn. "I forgot how far off the ground I can feel on the back of a horse."

The twins had mounted by themselves and rode their horses closer to her. "It's great, isn't it?" Trevor said with a grin. "I feel about eight feet tall when I'm on Oreo."

She seemed to be close to hyperventilating. They

couldn't have that. He stepped closer and kept his voice low and calming.

"Just hold on to the reins. I've hooked a lead line here and I'm just going to walk you around the training arena a bit, until you feel more comfortable."

"You won't let go?" Her panic was palpable.

He gave her a reassuring smile. "I promise. You got this."

As he led her around the small arena where they held horse auctions and worked to train horses in bad weather, he kept talking in that slow voice about nothing, really. The year he constructed this building, the other barn that was built by his great-grandfather, the house his grand-father had added.

The boys could never have handled this level of fear. He was deeply grateful that his schedule had worked out so he could be here to help her through this.

"You're doing great," he said after about fifteen min-utes, when she seemed to have relaxed a little and her fea-tures no longer looked so pinched and pale. "You ready to take the reins on your own now?"

"Do I have to?" she asked ruefully. "I was just begin-ning to breathe again."

He tried to hide his smile. She had grit. He'd give her that. "You don't have to, but you'll never really get a feel for riding a horse until you're the one in command."

She released a heavy sigh. "I suppose you're right. Okay. You can let go."

He twisted the lead line onto the saddle horn and stood by her thigh. "Here are a few basics. Sit up tall, creating a nice, straight line from shoulders to hips. Don't hold the reins taut, just relax them in your hands, and use the least amount of pressure you can to get the horse to do what you want. It's all about pressure and release. The moment she starts doing what you want, going where you want, you let off the pressure."

He went over a few other basic commands but he could see Ella was starting to glaze over.

For all her complacency, Creampuff was a very well-trained horse. She tended to know what her rider wanted before the rider did.

"You got this," he repeated, then stood back to watch.

Ella sat atop the motionless horse for a long moment, then—just as he was about to step in and give Creampuff a verbal command—Ella gave the perfect amount of pressure with her knees into her sides to get her moving.

Though her movements were awkward and stiff, she had obviously been on a horse before. He was a fairly decent teacher but not *that* good that she could instantly pick it up. No, he had a feeling it was more a case of muscle memory. Ella held the reins in the best position and didn't yank them, but instead used slow, steady movements.

She had done this before. Even if it was a long time ago, something inside her remembered.

Colter and Trevor watched from the back of their horses. "You're doing great," Trevor called.

"Keep it up," his brother said. "Way to go, Miss Ella. You'll be riding the rodeo before you know it."

Ella's visible shudder at the suggestion might have made him smile under other circumstances, if he wasn't so worried about her.

"You *are* doing great," he called. "Now see if you can get her to go a little faster."

"Why on earth would I do that? I don't *want* her to go faster."

He tipped his hat back. "Okay. Take it slow and steady. Nothing wrong with that."

She kept going another twenty minutes, taking the horse around the arena several times, then practicing bringing her a stop again before urging her forward once more. By the time they were done and she rode to a stop in front of him, she looked exhausted but beautifully triumphant.

"You ready to call it a day?"

"Yes. I think so."

He reached up a hand to help her and as she slid off the horse and to the ground, he tried not to notice how wonderful her soft curves felt against him. He was quick to let go when her boots hit the dirt floor.

"How was it?" he asked.

"Not as difficult as I expected, actually." She looked surprised and rather pleased at that discovery. "You were right. Creampuff really is a sweetheart."

"She does live up to her name, doesn't she?" He gave the old horse an appreciative pat as the twins rode up and dismounted.

"You did super good," Colter said.

"Yeah," his brother agreed. "You hardly even bounced around in the saddle."

"I hate to admit it, but there is a certain part of me that would disagree with you right now," Ella said, rubbing the back pocket of her jeans.

The boys giggled while Beck did his best not to shift his gaze to that particular portion of her anatomy.

"Boys, can you take care of the horses? Miss Baker's, too."

The twins had been brushing down their horses since they were old enough to ride. They led the horses away and he turned to Ella, though he kept one eye on the boys, across the arena, as they scrambled to take off saddles and hackamores. They didn't need direct supervision but he still liked to monitor things in case they had trouble.

"That was some good, hard work. A lesson like that deserves a beer. Or at least a soda."

"I wouldn't mind some water," she said.

"I don't doubt it. Overcoming your fear is thirsty business."

In the harsh lights of the indoor arena, her color rose and she looked down.

"Hey. I meant that with upmost respect," he assured her. He led the way into the corner that functioned as the office out here. He reached into the fridge and pulled out a water bottle for her, a beer for him.

"You really did work hard. I could tell it wasn't easy for you."

She sighed and took a healthy swallow from the bottle. A few little droplets clung to her lips from the bottle's mouth and he had to fight the urge to press his own lips there.

"It's so stupid," she said, frustration simmering in her voice. "I don't know why I can't get past it."

"Want to tell me about it?"

She looked at the horses, then back at him with a helpless sort of look. "Not really. But I suppose you have the right to know, especially after all your help this afternoon."

"I don't know about that. But I'd like to hear, if you want to tell me."

She took another swallow and he had the feeling she was biding time as much as slaking her thirst. "You know I didn't grow up on the Baker's Dozen."

Considering he had lived next to Curt his whole life and only saw Ella a few memorable times over the years, until she moved back to Pine Gulch, he was aware of that fact. "I did. I gather your parents were divorced."

"Yes. Eventually. They were separated on and off through most of my early childhood. They would try to make it work for a month or two, usually for my sake, then things would go south and my mom would pack us up and move back to Boston."

"That must have been tough."

"Yes. I adored my father and I always loved coming out to the ranch, even when it was just for a short visit. My favorite times were the summers, when I could be here for weeks at a time. Back in Boston, I dreamed about horses all the time. In the pictures I've seen of my bedroom, there are dozens of pictures on the wall of horses I had either drawn myself or cut out of old ranch magazines I took back with me. I loved to ride. At least that's what they tell me."

That struck him as an odd way to phrase things, but she continued before he could ask what she meant.

"I was three the first time my dad put me on a horse. I don't have a memory of it. Or anything else before I was eight years old."

That seemed awfully late for a first memory.

"Eight? Why eight?"

She looked down at her water bottle with a faraway expression. When she looked back up at him, her expression was bleak.

"That's the year I died."

Chapter Seven

Died? What the hell was that supposed to mean? Shock tangled his tongue, but even if it hadn't, he would have had no idea how to respond.

"I know. That sounds ridiculous and melodramatic," she said, her expression rueful. "But it's the truth. I was dead for about five minutes before they could get my heart started again."

She spoke in a matter-of-fact way, but her hands trembled again, as they had when she first faced the horse arena.

"You were eight? What happened?"

She watched the boys as they competently brushed down the horses. "My mom and I were both here that summer. It was the last time my parents tried to reconcile, I guess, though they didn't tell me that was why we had come back to the ranch. They had been separated on and off most of my life, but neither of them could ever bring themselves to file for divorce. I don't know why but they couldn't seem to take that final step."

"Were you happy about it? About your parents trying to reconcile?"

"I wish I could tell you. Apparently I wanted nothing more than to live here permanently. According to my mom, all I talked about whenever we were in Boston was living here in Pine Gulch and having my own horse and riding whenever I wanted. I think she resented how much I loved the ranch, if you want the truth. She never did."

Yet one more thing he had in common with Curt Baker. The man had never come right out and said it, but Beck had guessed as much.

What was wrong with these Pine Gulch men who insisted on marrying completely inappropriate women who couldn't wait to leave?

"We had only been back about three weeks when I took out a new horse," Ella went on. "I was with my dad and we were just riding above the ranch, nothing too strenuous, but apparently a snake slithered across the trail and spooked the horse and I fell—not just off the horse but about twenty feet down a rocky slope. I ended up with multiple injuries."

His blood ran cold as he pictured it. "You stopped breathing, you said?"

"Yes. My father was right there and he managed to do CPR to eventually restart my heart. I was airlifted to the hospital in Idaho Falls, and then to the regional children's hospital in Salt Lake City."

"How long were you there?"

"Two months. Seven surgeries. I was in a medically induced coma for weeks while the swelling from the brain injury went down. When I came out of it, there was obvious damage. I didn't remember anything. Not just the accident, but everything that happened before. Total blank slate. I had to relearn how to walk, talk, use a fork. Everything. I still have no memory of what happened the first eight years of my life, only from pictures and what my parents have told me."

He shook his head, trying to imagine how tough that must have been, to lose eight years of her life. He glanced at the boys, who were just finishing up with Creampuff. She was only a little older than they were and had to relearn everything.

No wonder she had been terrified of horses! He wasn't sure he ever would have had the guts to get back on.

"I just have one question."

"What's that?"

His jaw clenched. "Why in *blazes* did you get back on a horse today, after everything you've been through? I would think any sane woman would try to stay as far away as possible from something that's caused so much suffering."

She looked pensive, her fingers curled around the water bottle. "Today wasn't about the horses, Beck. It was about me." She paused. "I keep thinking that if I learn how to ride again, I'll find some piece of me I lost when I was eight."

He couldn't believe Curt had never told him about Ella's accident. Maybe that explained why the man didn't have any horses on the Baker's Dozen. He knew some ranchers thought they were too much trouble and not worth the effort, preferring ATVs and utility vehicles to a good cattle horse. He had always assumed Curt was one of them.

"I guess your parents didn't get back together."

She gave a short laugh. "You could say that. My mother would have been happy if I never came back to Pine Gulch. She blamed my father, said Curt deliberately put me on a horse that wasn't appropriate for an eight-year-old girl with limited experience who wasn't the expert rider she thought she was. She filed for divorce while I was still in the hospital."

How had that impacted Ella? Did she blame herself for her parents' divorce? Did she wonder if they would have been able to finally piece things together, if not for her fall?

He couldn't help seeing her with new compassion and found himself impressed all over again at the courage it must have taken her today to climb up on Creampuff.

"For the first few years after the divorce, she made my dad fly out to Boston for visits, which he hated. They were awkward, tense episodes that weren't comfortable for either of us. When I got older, after the dust from their custody battle settled, I insisted on coming out as often as I could. My dad refused to let me get on a horse. To reduce temptation, he sold them all, even though it was something he always loved. That was a tough pill for me to swallow, but Curt said my mom wouldn't let me come back to the ranch if she found out I had gone riding again. He wasn't wrong, actually."

He couldn't imagine that kind of animosity. Beck's own parents had been happily married until his father's untimely death, even with his mom's rheumatoid arthritis, which limited what she could do around the ranch. His dad had been a loving caretaker as far back as Beck could remember, one of the things he respected most about him.

After his father died, Beck's mother had moved to

Florida to be closer to her sister. She was doing well there, though he missed her. She and the boys talked via Skype every Sunday evening.

"I can't believe I didn't know this about you," he finally said.

She made a wry face. "It's not like I go around introducing myself to people by telling them that I spent several weeks in a medically induced coma after falling off a horse."

"But my family lived next door to yours. I should have known. I would have been, what, eleven or twelve? That's old enough to be aware of what's going on in my own community."

On the other hand, Curt Baker had always been a little removed from the greater Pine Gulch society. Beck's parents may well have known and may have mentioned it to him, but since he didn't know Ella personally back then and she was several years younger—and a girl, to boot—he wasn't sure it would have had much impact on him.

"It doesn't matter," she said. "It was a long time ago. Almost twenty years. The doctors all said it was a miracle that I made it through without much lasting damage."

"Nothing?"

"My leg aches in bad weather and I still limp a bit when I'm tired. To be totally honest, I do have the occasional memory lapse. I call it a glitch. Every once in a while, I forget a word that's pretty basic."

"Everybody does that."

"That's what I tell myself. I'm lucky. It could have been much worse."

"It doesn't sound like nothing. It sounds like you've been through hell. Nobody would blame you for never getting on a horse again, Ella. Like I said, it's really not necessary out here. There are plenty of people in Pine Gulch who've never been on a horse yet somehow still manage to live good, productive lives."

She was quiet, her features pensive. "I hate being afraid," she finally said. "Especially of something I once loved."

He had to respect that. "I'm not sure you can force yourself to the other side of a perfectly justifiable fear, simply through willpower."

"Maybe not completely," she acknowledged. "I'm okay with that. Still, I'd like to see if I can regain a little of that passion I once had."

He wanted that for her, too. In that moment, Beck resolved to do whatever he could to help her. "In that case, you'd better come back tomorrow for a second lesson. One hour in a horse arena on the back of a narcoleptic nag like Creampuff isn't enough to inspire passion in anyone."

"I don't know about that. I enjoyed myself far more than I expected."

"Come back tomorrow. Let's see if you can enjoy it even more."

"I could do that." She considered. "It would actually be good timing. Some friends are taking my father to a cowboy poetry event in Idaho Falls and they're supposed to be gone most of the day."

"You're a grown woman, Ella. He can't stop you from riding now, even if he wanted to."

"I know. I usually make him a nice dinner on Sunday afternoons after church. Since he'll be gone, I won't have to do that—or explain why I'm leaving or where I'm going."

"Great. You can just come straight here after church,

then. You might as well stay for dinner. We'll probably grill steaks. It's just as easy to toss another one on the coals."

He wasn't sure why he extended the invitation. By her expression, it was clear she was as shocked as he was by it.

"I… Thank you. That would be nice. I'll bring a salad and rolls and some kind of dessert."

"You don't have to do that, but I'm sure the boys would enjoy it."

His side dishes usually consisted of baked potatoes or instant rice.

"Enjoy what?" Trevor asked. They had apparently finished with the horses, who were all fed and watered and turned out to pasture.

"Miss Baker is going to come for another riding lesson tomorrow. I invited her to have dinner with us, too."

"Yay!" Trevor exclaimed.

Colter, he noticed with sudden trepidation, was giving the two of them a speculative look that left Beck more than a little uncomfortable.

What was going through the kid's mind? Beck wasn't sure he wanted to know—any more than he wanted to examine his own thoughts, at least about Ella Baker.

She wasn't sure she should be doing this.

Even as she loaded food into her SUV in preparation for driving back to the Broken Arrow, Ella was filled with misgivings.

She still had no idea what had prompted Beck to issue this unexpected invitation to dinner and a second riding lesson. Maybe pity. He *had* invited her right after she spilled her entire pathetic story to the man, after all.

More puzzling than his invitation had been how quickly she accepted it, without really thinking things through.

She should have refused. As much as she might have wanted another lesson, another chance to recapture the joy she had once known while riding, she was beginning to think it might not be a good idea to spend more time with Beckett and his boys.

The lesson the day before had eroded her defenses, left her far too open and vulnerable to him. She rarely talked about her accident, even with close friends. It was a part of her, yes, but something that happened so long ago, it hardly seemed relevant to the woman she had become— except as it pertained to her lingering fear of horses.

Why had she confided in Beckett McKinley, of all people?

He had been so patient with her during the lesson and, dare she say, even kind. It was a side of him she wasn't used to seeing. She could admit, she found it wildly appealing.

She wished she could have been able to tell what had been running through his mind when she told him what had happened so long ago. No such luck. The man was still a mystery to her. Every time she thought she had him figured out, he did something to toss all her preconceptions out the window.

This invitation for dinner, for instance. It would have been kind enough to simply invite her over for the lesson. Why add dinner into the mix?

Maybe he just felt sorry for her. The poor, pathetic girl who had nearly died not far from here.

She sighed and climbed into the SUV. She didn't like that idea. But what else could it be?

Though she was tempted to call off the whole thing, she made herself drive through the lightly falling snow to the nearby ranch.

The snowflakes looked lovely as they twirled out of the sky against the pine trees that bordered the road. The perfect holiday scene—except this was her second winter in southern Idaho and she knew the winters here could be anything but idyllic.

Oh, she hoped the weather cooperated for the Christmas program the following week. The children had already worked so hard to learn the songs and would be putting in a full week of intense rehearsals. She hated to think of all their effort being wasted because bad weather kept people away.

That was a hazard of living here, she supposed. You just had to keep your fingers crossed and learn how to take what comes.

Her stomach knotted with nerves as she drove under the Broken Arrow arch, which also had their brand burned into it. She had seen the McKinley men only hours ago at church. Beck had looked big and tough and handsome in his bolo tie and western-cut suit and the boys had looked just as handsome in clean white shirts and similar bolo ties.

They had come in late, hair still wet and Trevor's shirt buttoned wrong, and had waved so enthusiastically at her as they took their seats that Celeste Delaney beside her had whispered a teasing comment about the McKinley twin terrors having a crush on her.

She hadn't responded, even though she wanted to tell Celeste they weren't terrors. They were sweet, good-hearted boys who happened to have a little more energy than most.

She wasn't sure how her feelings for the boys had shifted so abruptly after only a few encounters. A week ago, she would have been one of those rolling her eyes at their antics. Now she saw them through a new filter of affection and even tenderness.

Mostly, they needed a little more direction and restraint in their lives.

She pulled up to the ranch house, her pulse abnormally loud in her ears, aware it wasn't the horse riding that made her nervous this time, but the idea of spending an afternoon with Beck and his adorable sons.

It was too late to back out now, she told herself, as she headed up the porch steps and rang the doorbell. They were planning on her.

Colter answered before the doorbell even stopped echoing through the house.

"Hey, Miss Ella!" he exclaimed, giving her that irresistible gap-toothed grin. "Guess what? Our dog is having puppies, *right now.*"

"Is that right?"

"Yeah. She's down in the barn. Dad says we can go down to see her again after you get here."

Beck walked into the foyer in time to hear his son's announcement. He looked gorgeous and relaxed in jeans and a casual collared navy shirt that made his eyes gleam an even deeper blue.

"More excitement than you were probably expecting on a quiet Sunday afternoon."

As if she needed more excitement than the anticipation bubbling through her all morning at the idea of spending the afternoon with him and his boys.

"I would love to see the puppies, if you don't think the mother would mind."

"This is her fifth litter. At this point, I don't think she would care if the high school marching band came through during labor."

She couldn't hide her smile at that image. For a moment, something hot and glittery flashed in Beck's expression as he gazed down at her. Her resident butterfly friends danced harder in her stomach.

He seemed to have lost his cool politeness toward her and she didn't know whether to be relieved or terrified.

She was already ridiculously attracted to him, on a purely physical level. She would be in serious trouble if she actually *liked* him, too.

Something told her it was a little too late for caution now.

After a moment, he cleared his throat. "We can take a look on our way down to the horse barn."

"Sounds good. I have a salad that needs to go in the refrigerator and rolls that will need to continue rising. Mind if I put them in your kitchen first?"

"If it means fresh rolls, you can do anything you want."

Ella was quite certain he didn't mean the words in any suggestive way. That didn't stop her imagination from going a little wild for just a moment, until she reined it back with much more pressure than she would ever have used on Creampuff.

"This way," he said.

She followed him into his updated kitchen, with its stainless appliances and granite countertops.

The day before, when she'd eaten lunch here, she had observed that this was obviously a household of men. The kitchen wasn't messy, exactly, but it was more cluttered than she personally would have found comfortable. The sink had dishes left over from breakfast, and some kind of dried substance, likely from an overflowing pasta pot, covered one of the burners.

Just like the day before, she had a strong impulse to dig in and go to work cleaning things up, but she had to remind herself that wasn't her bailiwick. She was only there for dinner and another riding lesson.

"Sorry about the mess in here." Beck looked a little uncomfortable. "Until a few months ago, we had a nanny-slash-housekeeper, but she was having some health problems so had to take a break. My brother and uncle and I have been trading off household responsibilities until I can find someone new and I'm afraid none of us is very good at it."

The picture touched her, three men working together to take care of these twin boys. She remembered Faith telling her Beck had refused to give his in-laws custody, though the boys had only been toddlers.

Ella was aware of a small, soft warmth fluttering to life in her chest.

"It's a lovely home," she murmured. "I can tell the boys are very happy here."

He offered that rare smile again and for a moment, she felt as if that warmth was swirling between the two of them, urging them inexorably closer.

"I should put this in the refrigerator," she said quickly, holding out the bowl containing the green salad she had made.

"Let me make a little room." He moved a few things around, leaving her a space amongst a few leftover containers and a half-empty case of beer.

"Now I only need a warm spot for the rolls to rise. Any suggestions?"

"Judy, our old housekeeper, always used the laundry room."

"That works."

He led the way to a large combined mudroom and laundry room. There were two washers and dryers in the space and both were going, sending out humid heat that would be perfect for her wrap-covered rolls.

"Judy always used that shelf up there. It's a little high for you to reach, I can put them up there for you."

"Looks like a perfect spot. Thanks." She handed him the jelly-roll pan of dough balls. Their fingers touched as he took it from her and a shiver rippled over her.

She thought his gaze sharpened but she couldn't be sure. Oh, she hoped he didn't notice her unwilling reaction.

He took the pan but simply held it for a long moment as the tension seemed to thicken between them. He looked as if he had something he wanted to say and even opened his mouth, but the boys burst into the laundry room before he could.

Ella told herself she was relieved.

"Let's go! We want to see the puppies!" Colter said, voice brimming with excitement.

Beck finally looked away to focus on his sons. "We're coming. Grab your coats while you're in here."

The boys complied and Beck finally slid the pan of rolls onto the high shelf, where the warmth would help them rise more quickly.

"How long until they're ready to bake?"

"I pulled the dough out of the freezer, so it will need to thaw as well as rise. Probably about ninety minutes."

Her dad loved homemade rolls, but it was too much trouble to do very often for only the two of them, so she had started making a big batch every month and freezing the dough.

"That should be about perfect to give us time to see the puppies and ride for a while, if you're still up for it."

"I'm here, aren't I?" she said wryly. "I'm ready."

"Excellent. Let's go."

The twins led the way outside, chattering to each other about Christmas vacation and a school field trip during the upcoming week to The Christmas Ranch, where they both planned to visit Sparkle, the famous reindeer immortalized in books as well as onscreen in an animated movie.

She would have thought their daily rehearsals at the ranch were sufficient holiday cheer, but apparently not.

By default, she and Beckett fell behind the boys a little.

"How's your dad?" Beck said. "I haven't seen him for a few days."

She sighed with remembered frustration. Curt was having a hard time accepting his limitations. That morning, before he left for the cowboy poetry event, she had caught him trying to put up a stepladder to fix a lightbulb that had gone out in their great room. The man had poor balance on solid ground, forget about eight feet up in the air on a wobbly ladder.

"Stubborn as ever," she answered. "I'm beginning to think it must be something in the water up here."

He laughed, the sound rich and deep in the cold December air. "You might be right about that. I've got two boys drinking that same water and they could write the book on stubborn."

He definitely had his hands full with those twins. She

had a feeling things weren't going to get easier as they hit their preteen and teenage years.

"Anyway, your dad might be stubborn but he's a good man. After my dad died when I was still too young to know what the hell I was doing here on the ranch, Curt took me under his wing. I learned more from him those first few months than my whole twenty-three years before that."

She hadn't realized his father died when Beck was so young. Sympathy for him helped mute the sting of hearing her father had been willing to help a neighbor learn the ropes of ranching. Too bad he wouldn't do the same thing for his own daughter.

"What happened to your father?"

"One of those freak things. Doctors figured it was a brain aneurysm. He was out on a tractor, perfectly fine one minute, the next he was gone. I'd always planned to take over the Broken Arrow from him, since neither of my brothers was much interested in running the place."

"Jax works here, doesn't he?"

"Yeah, but it took him a while to figure out what he wanted to do. I'm still not convinced his heart's in it, but it's tough to tell with Jax. I always knew I wanted to run the ranch, I just didn't expect to do it so early."

"I'm sorry. That must have been tough on you."

"At first, but good neighbors like Curt stepped in to help me figure things out."

"I'm glad my dad was here for you," she said softly. "And now you're helping him in return."

Beck shrugged, looking embarrassed. "I'm not doing much. I'm glad I can help."

He stopped in front of a different barn than the larger, more modern facility where they had ridden the day before. "Here we are. Guys, remember what I told you. We can watch, if we do it quietly so we don't distract Sal while she's taking care of her puppies."

"We remember," Trevor said solemnly. The boys tiptoed into the barn—which wasn't particularly effective, since they were both wearing cowboy boots.

She followed, not sure what to expect. The barn was warmer than she might have thought, and smelled of straw and old wood and the earthy smells she associated with a ranch.

Beck led the way to a wooden stall about halfway back. She peered over the railing to where a mostly black border collie lay on her side on a blanket that had been spread over the straw.

She looked exhausted, poor thing, as her litter suckled for nourishment.

"They look like little rats," Trevor whispered.

"Beautiful little rats," his brother said loyally, which made Ella smile.

The puppies were small, eyes still closed. They made little whiny noises as they ate.

"Is that all of them, girl?" Beck asked in a low voice. "Looks like she might be done. How many do you count?"

"Seven," Colter said, moving his finger in the air to mark each one. "No, eight."

"Good job, Sal," Beck said softly. The tired mother gave a half-hearted tail wag before returning to care for her litter.

They all watched the little creatures with fascination for a few more moments. It was an unexpectedly intimate moment, standing there by the wooden stall beside Beck and his boys, almost like they were a family unit.

They most definitely weren't, she reminded herself. That sort of thinking could get her into all kinds of trouble.

"We should probably let her rest now," Beck said eventually.

"Will they all be okay out here?" Trevor asked. "It's cold outside."

"But warm in here. Sal and the puppies have everything they need here—warm, soft blankets, with plenty for Sal to eat and drink. My guess is, she'll probably want to sleep for a week after having eight puppies."

"What will you do with them all?" Ella asked.

"I'll probably keep a couple to train, then sell the others. Sal has champion bloodlines and the sire does, too. Those are going to be some excellent cow dogs."

He glanced down at her. "You ready to ride again?"

"I am," she admitted. "Believe it or not, I'm actually looking forward to it."

He gave her a full-on, high-octane smile that turned her insides to rich, gooey honey.

"That is an excellent sign, Miss Baker. Watch and see. We'll make a horsewoman out of you yet."

She didn't share his confidence—but as long as she no longer had panic attacks when she came within a hundred feet of a horse, she would consider these few days to be worth it.

Chapter Eight

An hour later, she managed to pull Creampuff to a stop squarely in front of the spot at the railing where Beck had stood for the last hour, offering advice and encouragement during the lesson.

"Good girl," she said, patting the horse's withers.

"Wait, was that an actual smile?" he teased. "If I didn't know better, I might think you're enjoying yourself."

"You might be right. I think I've almost stopped shaking. That's a good sign, isn't it?"

"An excellent one." He offered an encouraging smile. "On a day when it's not so cold, you should come out to take a trail ride above the house. It's slow going in the snow, but worth it for the views."

A few days earlier, the very idea would have sent her into a panic attack. Her accident had happened in those very foothills and while she didn't remember it, the specter of what had happened there still loomed large in her subconscious.

The fact that she could even consider such an outing was amazing progress. She shifted in the saddle, satisfaction bubbling through her. She had done it, survived another riding lesson, and had actually begun to enjoy the adventure.

Oh, she had missed this. She really did feel as if she was rediscovering a part of herself that had been buried under the rubble of her accident.

Trevor rode up on his big horse, so loose and comfortable that he seemed to be part of the horse. "Is it time for dinner yet? I'm starving."

"Me, too," his brother said, joining the group.

"I guess that's up to our guest," Beck said. "What do you say, Ella? Want to keep riding or would you like to stop for chow?"

"Let's eat, before you guys start chewing the leather reins."

The boys giggled with delight at her lame joke and warmth soaked through her. There was something so *joyful* about being able to make a child laugh. She had never realized that until going to work in music therapy.

"Chew the reins," Trevor said, shaking his head. "That would taste gross!"

"Yeah, steaks would be much better, all the way around," Beck said. "Why don't you boys take care of the horses and put them up while Miss Baker and I start dinner?"

She slid down without assistance. "I would like to help with the horses, actually. If I intend to start riding again, I need to relearn how to care for them."

His eyes warmed with approval. "Good point. It

should only take the four of us a few moments. Boys, let's show Miss Baker how it's done."

Beck couldn't remember the last time he had enjoyed an afternoon so much.

He was growing increasingly intrigued with Ella Baker, forced to completely reevaluate his preconceptions of her as just one more city girl who didn't belong.

She had far more grit than he ever would have believed a few days earlier. Most women who had gone through an ordeal like hers would have stayed as far away as possible from something that represented the trauma they had endured.

Not Ella.

When they had first come into the stables, he had seen how nervous she was. Her small, curvy frame had been trembling slightly as he helped her mount Creampuff, her features pale and set.

It had concerned him a little, especially after she seemed to have enjoyed it the day before. He supposed he should have anticipated her reaction. She had spent many years being afraid of horses, for legitimate reasons. He couldn't expect that to go away overnight, simply because she had an enjoyable experience on an easy mount.

He shouldn't have worried. Within a few moments, she had warmed to it again. After only a few moments, she had visibly relaxed, and by the end of the hour, she had been laughing.

Would she be afraid the next time? For her sake, he hoped she didn't have to fight that battle each time she wanted to ride a horse—though he had to admire the sheer guts she showed by putting herself through it. In his experience, few people demonstrated that kind of raw courage.

He liked her.

Entirely too much.

He frowned at the thought as he hung up the tack on the well-organized pegs. It was hard *not* to like her. She was kind to his sons, she had given up her life back east to come back and care for her father, and she had more courage than most people he'd ever met.

If he wasn't careful, he would do something really stupid, like fall hard for her.

He jerked his mind away from that dangerous possibility. He couldn't. She might be pretty and smart and courageous, but that didn't make her right for him. He would do well to remember she was a city girl. Like her own mother, like Stephanie. Ella was cultured, sophisticated, not the sort of woman who would be comfortable wearing jeans and boots and listening to old Johnny Cash songs.

The thought depressed him more than it should.

They could be friends, though. Nothing wrong with that. A guy couldn't have too many friends, right?

"Everybody ready to go get some food, now that we've all taken care of the horses?" he asked, forcing a note of cheerfulness he didn't feel into his voice.

"Me!" his twins said in unison. Ella smiled and the impact of it was like standing in the middle of a sunbeam.

"We should probably check on the puppies one more time before we head up to the house, if you don't mind," he said.

"Do you seriously think I would mind being able to see those cute puppies again?"

"Good point," he admitted.

The temperature had dropped several degrees by the time they walked outside toward the barn where he had set up Sal for her first few weeks postdelivery. His instincts, honed from years of working the land, warned him they would have snow before morning.

As they trudged through the snow already on the ground from previous storms, he went through his mental weather-preparedness checklist. It wasn't all that lengthy. From his father, he'd learned the important lesson that it was better to ready things well in advance. The Broken Arrow was always set up to deal with bad weather, which made it much easier for this particular ranch owner to sleep at night.

When he wasn't having completely inappropriate dreams about his lovely neighbor, anyway.

In contrast to the gathering storm, the old barn was warm and cozy, a refuge from the Idaho winter.

Sal and her puppies were all sleeping when they peered over the top railing of the stall. Despite Colter's and Trevor's careful effort to tiptoe in on their cowboy boots, Sal must have sensed them. She opened one eye but closed it quickly, busy with the task of keeping eight puppies fed and alive.

Without being asked, Trevor and Colter filled her water and added a bit more food to her bowl. They were such good boys. Yeah, they could be rambunctious at times, but beneath all that energy, they were turning into helpful, compassionate young men.

He couldn't have asked for more.

"She looks exhausted, poor thing," Ella said beside him, her expression soft and sympathetic.

"She's a good mom. She'll be okay after a little rest."

"Until she has eight wriggling puppies climbing all over her."

He grinned. "Shh. Don't say that too loudly or she might decide to hightail it out of here before we get to that point. I don't particularly fancy hand-feeding eight puppies."

"Would she do that?" Ella asked, plainly concerned.

"I'm teasing," he assured her. "Sal knows what to do."

They watched the puppies for a few more moments in silence before he ushered everyone back out into the cold.

"Race you," Trevor said to his brother and the two of them rushed away through the gathering darkness.

"I wish I had even a tiny portion of their energy," Ella said with a sigh.

"Right?"

She shook her head. "How do you keep up with them?"

"Who says I do? There have been more than a few nights when I fall asleep reading to them and only wake up when the book falls to the floor."

She smiled, probably thinking he was kidding. He only wished he were.

"They're good boys. You know that, right?"

He was touched that her thoughts so clearly echoed his own from a few moments earlier. "I do. Once in a while I forget. Like whenever I go to their parent-teacher conferences and hear the litany of classroom complaints. I have to remind myself I wasn't the most patient student, either, yet somehow I still managed to graduate from high school *and* college. My senior year, I was running the ranch, too, and taking night classes."

"It must be challenging on your own."

"Sometimes," he admitted. "There are days I feel like throwing in the parenting towel before we even finish breakfast. It's hard and frustrating and relentless. Each decision I make in the day has to focus on the boys' welfare first. Every other priority is a distant second."

"I can't even imagine." In the fading afternoon light, her features looked soft and so lovely, he had a hard time looking away.

"I'm not really alone, though. Until a few months ago, we had Judy to help us. She did all the heavy lifting when it came to the logistics of caring for the boys when they were smaller."

"You must miss her terribly."

"Definitely. She had been a huge part of our lives since the boys were small. Judy was just about the only mother figure they had. They don't seem to remember their mother much."

"How old were they when she…left?"

He hated thinking about Stephanie and all the mistakes he had made.

"Barely two," he said, his voice pitched low even though the boys had already made it inside.

"She had terrible clinical and postpartum depression as well as anxiety—made harder because, as it turns out, she hated living on a ranch. She missed her family, her friends, the excitement of her life back east."

Their marriage had been an epic mistake from the beginning. He thought they could make a go of things, though now that idea seemed laughable. Still, they had been wildly in love at first. After only a few fiery months, reality had begun to sink in that maybe they couldn't manage to reconcile their differences and then Stephanie found out she was pregnant.

She had cried and cried. He should have clued in to the challenges ahead when he saw her reaction. As for

Beck, he had been scared witless one moment, filled with jubilation the next. He had asked her to marry him and it had taken another three months of discussions—and the revelation through her first ultrasound that her pregnancy would provide a double blessing—before she agreed.

Things only went downhill from there, unfortunately. She had struggled fiercely with postpartum depression and hadn't really bonded with the twins. Even before she left to find help, he and the series of nannies he hired until they found Judy had been the ones getting up at night with them, making sure they were fed, providing the cuddles and the love their mother couldn't.

"That must have been tough," Ella said softly.

For both of them. Stephanie had been a mess emotionally and mentally and he had hated knowing he couldn't fix things for her.

"She stuck it out as long as she could, until both of us realized things weren't getting better. She needed help, more help than she could find here. Her parents are both doctors and had connections back east so they wanted her to get help there. It was always supposed to be temporary but the weeks turned into months and then a year. *Soon*, she kept telling me. Just another month and she would be ready to come back."

He sighed as the tough memories flooded back. "Eighteen months after she left, she died from a prescription-drug overdose. Doctors said it was probably accidental."

That *probably* always pissed him off. Even the smallest chance that Stephanie might have deliberately chosen to leave the two cutest kids on the planet just about broke his heart.

Something of his emotions must have shown on his

features. Ella made a small sound, her own expression deeply distressed.

"Oh, Beck. I'm so sorry."

"I am, too—for the boys' sake, anyway. They're doing okay, though. They ask about her once in a while, but not so much anymore. They don't remember her. They were only toddlers when she left. They ask after Judy far more often than they do their mother."

"I'm sorry," she said again.

"I don't know why I told you all that," he said. What was it about Ella that compelled him to share details of his life he usually preferred to keep to himself? There was something about her that drew him to her, something more than her pretty eyes and her soft, delicate features.

He liked her. Plain and simple. It had been a long time since he felt these soft, seductive feelings for a woman.

Not that he planned to do a damn thing about it— except spill all his dirty laundry, apparently.

"You're cold. I'm sorry I kept you out here so long."

"I'm not cold," she protested. "Only sad that any woman could deliberately choose to walk away from such amazing boys and—and you."

Was it his imagination or did she blush when she said that? His interest sharpened. Again, he was aware of the tug and pull of attraction between them.

He wanted desperately to kiss her. He ached with it, the hunger to pull her close and brush his lips across hers, gently at first and then, if she didn't push him away, with a little more intensity.

He caught his breath and inclined his head slightly. Her eyes went wide and she swallowed. He thought she might have even leaned toward him, but at the last moment, before he would have taken that chance, the back door opened.

"Hey, what are you still doing out here?" Trevor asked.

He couldn't very well tell his son he was just about to try to steal a kiss. Trevor didn't give him a chance to answer, anyway, before he went on.

"Hey, can Colter and me watch a Christmas show before dinner?" Trevor asked.

After mentally scrambling for a second, Beck did his best to shift back into father mode. It took great effort, especially when all he wanted to do was grab Ella close and explore that delicious-looking mouth until they were both breathless.

He cleared his throat. "You know the rule. The TV can come on when chores are done."

"They are. I just took the garbage out and Colt finished putting away the dishes in the dishwasher."

He couldn't ask for more than that. "Fine. One show. Fair warning, dinner shouldn't take long. You might have to stop the show in the middle, if the food is ready before the show is over."

"Okay." Trevor beamed, then hurried back inside to tell his brother the good news, leaving Beckett along with Ella and this awkwardness that seemed to have suddenly blossomed between them.

"Ella…"

She didn't quite meet his gaze. "Your boys are hungry. We should probably take care of that."

He was hungry, too, but the choice T-bones he had been marinating all afternoon wouldn't slake this particular appetite.

She was right, though. The boys needed to eat—and

he needed to do all he could to regain a little common sense when it came to Ella Baker.

Forty-five minutes later, nerves still shimmied through her from that intense moment on Beck's back step.

Had he really tried to kiss her?

She couldn't be completely sure but was about 95 percent certain. The vibe had certainly been there, crackling through the air between them.

She had done her best to ignore it through dinner, but couldn't seem to stop staring at his mouth at odd, random moments.

She caught herself at it again and jerked her gaze away quickly, setting her napkin beside her plate and leaning back in her chair.

"That was truly delicious," she said, trying for a casual tone. "I'm not exaggerating when I say that was probably the best steak I've ever had. What do you use for a marinade?"

"Nothing too complicated—soy sauce, honey, a little bit of ground black pepper and a splash of olive oil."

"Sometimes the simple things are the best. Thank you again for inviting me to dinner."

"I didn't do anything but grill some steaks and toss a couple of potatoes in the oven to bake. You provided everything else. I should be thanking *you*. Those rolls were little yeasty bites of heaven."

The description pleased her. Why was it so much more fun to cook when people appreciated the effort?

"We're done," Colter announced. "Can we go back and finish our show?"

"Yeah," Trevor chimed in. "The Abominable Snowman guy was just learning how to walk with one foot in front of the other. That's our favorite part."

Ella had to smile, since that had always been her own favorite part of that particular Christmas special.

"Clear your plates first. You can take our guest's, as well, if she's finished."

"I am, thank you."

"Do you want to watch the rest of the show with us?" Trevor asked.

Though the earnestness behind the request touched, Ella glanced at her watch. How had the entire day slipped away?

"Thank you, but it's later than I thought. I should go. I hate to eat and run, but I should probably be home before my father arrives back at the ranch. Sometimes he needs help getting out of his coat and boots."

By the understanding she glimpsed in his gaze, she understood that Beck knew as well as she did that the word *sometimes* was unnecessary. Curt might refuse to admit it, but he *always* needed help. His limitations were growing all the time, something that made her heart hurt whenever she thought about it.

"Let me hurry and wash the salad bowl and the pan you baked the rolls in, so you can take them home clean."

"Unnecessary. I have other dirty dishes at home I still need to wash. I can easily throw these in with them."

He looked as if he wanted to argue but held his tongue.

"Guys," he said instead to his sons, "can you tell Miss Baker thanks for joining us today?"

"Thanks, Miss Baker," they said in unison, something they did often. She wasn't sure they were even aware of it.

"I'm the one who must thank you for the wonderful

day. I'm so grateful to you for sharing your puppies with me and for helping me with my riding lessons again. I owe you. I mean it."

The boys nudged each other, hiding their matching grins that indicated they knew exactly what she meant, that she would in turn help them practice the song for their father before the show the following week.

"You're welcome," Trevor said.

"See you tomorrow. At practice," Colter added, with such a pointed, obvious look, it was a wonder Beckett didn't immediately catch on that something else was going on.

She followed Beck from the dining room to the kitchen. Despite her protests, he ended up washing the pan she had used for the rolls as well as the now-empty salad bowl.

She finally gave up arguing with him about it and picked up a dish towel instead. "While we're at it, we might as well finish cleaning your kitchen. I can spare a few more moments."

This time, he was the one who looked as if he wanted to argue, but after a moment, he shrugged.

She was right, it only took them a few moments. She found the domesticity of the scene dangerously seductive, the two of them working together in the kitchen while the sounds of the Christmas show filtered in from the television that was in a nearby room.

"It really was a great steak," she told him again.

"Thanks. I don't have many specialties in the kitchen, so I'm pretty proud of the few I can claim."

"With reason."

He tossed a spatula in the rinse water and she pulled it out to dry.

"One of the toughest things about us men being on our own now that Judy is gone is figuring out the food thing all the time. She used to leave food in the fridge for us to heat up, but now Jax and Dan and I have to take turns. I think the boys are getting a little tired of burgers and steaks, but that's mostly what I'm good at."

"I hear you. My problem is the opposite. I would like to cook other things, but my dad's a cattleman through and through. Red meat is about all he ever wants, though Manny Guzman's wife prepares meals for us a few times a week and she likes to slip in some chicken dishes here and there."

"You take good care of your father," he said, his voice slightly gruff.

She could feel her cheeks heat at the unexpected praise. "Whether he wants me to or not. He's constantly telling me he doesn't need my help, that I should go back to Boston. That's where my mother lives with her second husband."

"Why don't you?"

She wasn't sure she could articulate all the reasons. "I love my dad. He needs help, no matter what he says, and I'm in a position to offer that help. He doesn't have anyone else. Not really."

She shrugged. "Anyway, I like it here. The people are kind and my job is tremendously rewarding. It hasn't been a sacrifice."

He said nothing, just continued washing the last few dishes, then let the water out of the sink while she wiped down the countertops.

"That should do it," he said when she finished. "Thanks for your help. I've got to say, the kitchen looks better than it has in weeks. None of us enjoys the cleanup portion of the program. That's probably obvious."

"It wasn't bad," she assured him. "You know, even if you don't hire another full-time housekeeper, you could still have someone come in a couple times a week to straighten up for you."

"That would certainly help. Know of anyone looking for a job?"

"Not off the top of my head, but I can ask around." She glanced at the clock on the microwave. "And now I really do have to go. Dad expected he would be home in about a half hour from now. If he makes it home ahead of me, he's going to worry about where I am."

"I'll grab your coat."

He brought it in from the mudroom and helped her into it, which only seemed to heighten her awareness of the heat and that delicious outdoorsy scent that clung to him.

"Thanks again," she said, then reached for her dishes. He beat her to it, picking them up and heading for the door.

"What are you doing?"

"I'll walk you out. Even we Idaho cowboys learn a few manners from our mamas."

"I never said otherwise, did I?"

"No. You didn't," he said gruffly.

Who had? His troubled wife? The thought left her sad.

The storm hadn't started yet. Though it still smelled like impending snow, the clouds had even cleared a little, revealing a few glittery expanses of night sky.

"Oh," she exclaimed, craning her neck. "Look at all those stars. It always takes my breath away."

"Yeah, it's one of the best things about living out here, where we don't have much light pollution."

"A few times when I came here over the summers, my dad would wake me in the middle of the night so we could drive into the mountains to see the meteor shower."

"The Perseids. I do the same thing with the boys. Every August, we take a trail ride up into the hills above the ranch and spread our sleeping bags out under the stars to watch the show."

There was another image that charmed her, the picture of this big, tough cowboy taking his young twin sons camping to show them nature's fireworks show. "That sounds lovely."

"We've got another meteor shower this week. You should check it out."

"Thanks, but I think I'll pass on anything that involves sleeping out under the stars in December."

He smiled as they reached her SUV. She opened the rear door and he slid the pan and bowl inside, then stepped forward to open her door for her.

"Good night," she said. "Thank you again for a lovely afternoon."

"It was my pleasure. The boys loved having you out and…so did I."

His voice was low, intense. Shivers rippled down her spine and she couldn't resist meeting his gaze. All those glittery feelings of earlier seemed to ignite all over again, as if someone had just stirred a hearth full of embers inside her and sent a crackling shower of sparks flaring through her.

They gazed at each other for a long moment and then he uttered a long, heartfelt oath before he lowered his mouth to hers.

Chapter Nine

As his mouth descended and his arms enfolded her against him, Ella caught her breath at the heat and strength of him surrounding her. For a moment, she couldn't think straight and stood frozen in his arms while his mouth brushed over hers once, then twice.

As she blinked in shock, her brain trying to catch up to what was going on, the amazing reality of it seeped in.

She was kissing Beck McKinley—and it was so much better than she ever could have imagined. Still not quite believing this was real, she returned the kiss with all the hunger she had been fighting down for so very long.

She forgot about the boys inside, about the snow spiraling down around them, the cold metal of her SUV seeping through the back of her wool coat.

The only thing she could focus on was Beck—his delicious mouth on hers, the strength of his muscles under her exploring hands, the heat and wonder and sheer thrill of kissing him at last.

She wasn't sure how long he kissed her there in the cold December night—long enough, anyway, that when he pulled away, she felt disoriented, breathless, aware that her entire body pulsed with a low, delicious ache.

"I told myself I wasn't going to do that."

"I... Why?" His words jerked her out of that happy daze.

"Because I was afraid as soon as I kissed you once, I would only want to do it again and again. I was right."

"I wouldn't mind." Some part of her warned her that she probably shouldn't admit that, but the words spilled out before she could stop them.

He gazed down at her, his eyes flashing in the moonlight. He was so gorgeous, rough and masculine. How could any woman resist him?

"I like you, Ella. More than I should."

A thrill shot through her at his words, even though it was tempered by the reluctant way he said them. He liked her, but was obviously not crazy about that fact.

"I like you, too," she admitted. She didn't add that the more time she spent with him, the more she liked him.

Something bright flashed in his gaze and he kissed her again, this time with a fierce intensity that completely took her breath away.

After another moment, he sighed and pulled away, his forehead pressed to hers. "I have to stop, while I still can."

"You don't *have* to."

"It's freezing out here. That snow is going to start in about ten minutes and the temperature will drop more. I have a feeling it might be pretty traumatic for my boys to find us here after the spring thaw, still locked together."

With clear reluctance, he eased away. "That shouldn't have happened, Ella. You get that, right? I can't…start something with you."

Maybe he should have thought of that little fact before he kissed her until she forgot her own name, she thought tartly. After the heated embrace they had just shared, something had already started between them, like it or not.

Oh, this was going to get awkward quickly. She couldn't just ignore the man. They lived in the same community, were neighbors, for heaven's sake. He was at her father's ranch nearly every day for some reason or other.

How was she supposed to be able to look at him in the grocery store or the library or parent-teacher conferences without remembering this moment—the heat of his mouth on hers, the taste of him, minty and delicious.

"You should probably go. Your father will be home soon, if he isn't already."

"Right." Shaky and off balance, she managed to make her limbs cooperate long enough to climb into her driver's seat.

He stood for a moment, looking as if he wanted to say something else, but ultimately he only gave a little wave, closed the door, then stood back so she could drive away.

Her SUV had a key remote that started with a push button. She fumbled with it for several seconds, aware her hands shook and her thoughts were scattered. After an uncomfortably long moment, she somehow remembered she needed to press the brake at the same time she pushed the button before it could start. Finally she managed to combine all the steps and the engine roared to life.

As she drove away, she forced herself not to check the rearview mirror to see if he was still standing there. Her head spun with a jumble of emotions—shock, regret and, most of all, an aching hunger.

He was right. They shouldn't have done that. How on earth was she supposed to go back to treating him with polite distance, when all she would be able to remember was how magical it had felt to be in his arms?

Beck couldn't force himself to move for several moments, even after the taillights of Ella's SUV disappeared down the drive.

What the hell just happened? He felt as if a hurricane had just blown through his world, tossing everything comfortable and familiar into weird, convoluted positions.

Ella Baker.

What was he *thinking*, to kiss her like that?

He had been contemplating the idea of reentering the dating waters for the last year, had even dipped his toe in a bit and asked out a neighbor, Faith Nichols Dustin. That hadn't turned out so well—for him, anyway. Faith was now married to another rancher and friend, Chase Brannon.

He was happy for them. His heart had never really been involved, but he liked Faith and thought they had many things in common. They had both lost their spouses, were raising their children alone, ran successful ranch operations.

On paper, they would have made a good fit. It wasn't to be, though. Faith and Chase were obviously in love, and Beck was happy they'd been able to find joy together after all these years.

He envied them, really. The truth was, he was lonely, pure and simple. His life wasn't empty. Far from it. He had the boys and the ranch, his brother and his uncle, but he missed having a woman in his life. He missed soft skin and sweet smiles, the seductive scent of a woman's warm neck, the protective feeling of sleeping with someone he wanted to watch over in his arms.

He sighed. In the end, it didn't matter how lonely he was. He couldn't make another mistake like Stephanie. He had the boys to worry about now. If he ever became seriously involved with a woman again, he would have to pick someone he absolutely knew would stick—a woman who loved it here as much as he did, who could not only be *content* with the ranching life, but could also embrace it, hardships and all.

Too bad the one woman he had been drawn to in longer than he could remember was someone so completely inappropriate.

Ella Baker was delicate and lovely, yes. He could look at her all day long and never grow tired of it. She made him want to tuck her inside his coat and protect her from the cold, the wind and anything else that might want to hurt her.

She wasn't for him.

He needed a woman from this world, someone tough and hardy and resilient. Someone who wouldn't mind the wind or weather, the relentlessly long hours a rancher had to put in during calving and haying seasons, the self-reliance that was a vital, necessary part of this life.

He couldn't put his boys through losing someone else

they loved, simply because he was drawn to sweet, pretty, delicate types like Ella Baker.

He pressed a hand to his chest, to the sudden ache there. Just a little heartburn, he told himself. It certainly couldn't be something as useless and unwanted as yearning.

His boys were up to something, but damned if Beck could figure out what.

Despite his best and most subtle efforts to probe in the week following that Sunday dinner with Ella, they were being uncharacteristically closemouthed about things.

Still, it was obvious they had secrets. Seemed like they spent half their free time whispering to each other, then going suspiciously quiet whenever he happened to walk in.

He tried to give them a little latitude. It was Christmastime, when everybody seemed to turn into covert operatives, with secrets and hidden stashes of treasure. He had his own secrets right now.

He didn't like that Dan and Jax seemed to be in on the whole thing. More than once, he had seen the boys talking to them, only to shut things off again if Beck walked in.

Knowing something had been stirring at the Broken Arrow all week, he should have been prepared on Friday morning when the boys ganged up and ambushed him at breakfast.

"Dad, can we have Miss Ella over again tomorrow to ride Creampuff?" Trevor asked.

His skin seemed to catch fire just at the mention of her name. The ache in his chest that had been there since their kiss Sunday night seemed to intensify.

He had dreamed about her every single night, but hadn't seen her since then.

"She only rode here two times," Colter reminded him. "That's not enough."

"We promised we would teach her how to ride. If we're gonna do that, it has to be more than two times."

What sort of arrangement had they made with their music teacher? He still couldn't shake the suspicion that there was something fishy about the whole thing from the outset. He thought they were doing a nice thing to invite her out to ride, but he was beginning to wonder if there was something more to it, something he was missing.

What weren't they telling him?

"We thought maybe she could bring us home after practice tomorrow morning and then we can ride in the arena for a while, and then she could go see the new puppies with us," Colter said in what seemed like a deceptively casual tone.

Yes. They were definitely cooking up something.

"And maybe she could stay for dinner again," Trevor suggested blithely. Beck didn't miss the way Colter poked him with his elbow and gave him a shut-up sort of look.

"I don't know about dinner," he said slowly, "but she can certainly come out and ride again, if she wants to. You can invite her at practice. She might be busy, though. It wouldn't surprise me. Everyone seems to be, this time of year."

"We'll ask her," Trevor said. He cast a sidelong look at his brother, who nodded, another of their unspoken twin-talk kind of communications.

"You'll be here tomorrow, won't you?"

"I don't know. Like I said, it's a busy time of year. I'll have to see how my schedule plays out. I have to run into

Idaho Falls at some point this weekend to pick up a few things for Sal and the puppies." And for two certain little caballeros for Christmas, but he didn't tell them that.

"I can always run to Idaho Falls for you." Jax looked up from his coffee and his iPad long enough to make the offer.

"Yeah." Colter seized on that. "Maybe Uncle Jax can go to Idaho Falls for you. It would be better if you could be here when Miss Ella comes over."

"Why's that?" he asked with a frown.

The twins exchanged looks that were not at all subtle. He had seen that look before, too many times to count— usually just moments before they did something dangerous or destructive, like jump from the barn loft or try to take out ornaments on the Christmas tree with their little peashooters.

"Because you're, you know, a really good teacher and good with horses and stuff."

Colter's ready response didn't ease Beck's suspicions any.

"Uncle Jax is a good teacher, too, and he's even better than I am with horses." That wasn't always easy for him to admit, but it was true. His younger brother had an uncanny way with them. "Miss Baker will be okay."

Jax had been watching this exchange with unusual interest. Usually his brother kept to himself until at least his second cup of coffee. "Sure," he answered. "For the record, I'm happy to teach Ella Baker anything she would like to know."

Beck knew he had no right to the giant green tide of jealousy that washed over him at the thought of the sweet Ella in his brother's well-practiced hands.

"We're talking about horses, right?"

Jax gave him an innocent look that didn't fool Beck any more than the boys' had. His brother had the same uncanny way with women that he did with animals.

"Sure. That's what I was talking about. What else would be on my mind?"

Beck could only imagine. His brother was a notorious flirt whose favorite pastime, when he wasn't following the rodeo circuit or training his own horses, was hanging out with buckle bunnies who liked to admire his...trophies.

Come to think of it, he wasn't sure he wanted Jax within half a mile of Ella Baker.

"Maybe she can't even come over," Trevor said. "But we can ask her, right?"

He didn't miss the little thread of yearning in his son's voice. It made him wary and sad at the same time. Since Judy retired, they seemed a little more clingy than usual, probably hungry for a woman's softer arms and gentle ways.

"All you can do is ask. Find out if she's available and then we'll figure out the rest."

"Okay. Thanks, Dad."

"Finish your breakfast and load your dishes. You'd better hustle or you're going to miss the bus."

They shoveled in their eggs, then raced to brush teeth, grab homework and don coats and backpacks. Through it all, they continued to whisper, but he sent them on their way without making any progress at figuring out what secrets they were keeping from him.

Ella did her best to put the memory of that kiss behind her. It should have been easy. She was insanely busy as the calendar ticked inexorably toward Christmas.

In addition to the daily practices for the show at The Christmas Ranch, each of the grades at the elementary school was preparing a small performance for their parents—with plenty of music needed—and her middle school choir presented their annual holiday concert.

She also volunteered at the local senior citizen center in Pine Gulch and had agreed to lead carols for their holiday luncheon.

It was chaotic and hectic and...wonderful. She loved being part of the Pine Gulch community. She loved going to the grocery store and being stopped by at least two or three people who wanted to talk. She loved the way everyone waved as she drove past and gave genuine smiles, as if they were happy to see her.

Though she had good neighbors and friends in Boston, she had never known the same sense of community as she did here in Idaho.

Her life had changed drastically since she came to live with her father the previous year.

Occasionally, she missed her job there, her friends, the active social network and many cultural opportunities she found in Boston. She even missed her mother and stepfather and their lovely home in the Back Bay neighborhood.

She wouldn't go back. Her life here was rich and full and rewarding—even when she found her schedule packed with activities.

She hadn't seen Beck all week, but even her busy routine hadn't kept her from spending entirely too much time thinking about him and about that amazing kiss.

She wasn't sleeping well. Each night she fell into bed, completely exhausted, but her stupid brain seemed to want to replay every moment of that kiss, from the first brush of his mouth on hers to the strength of his muscles against her to the cold air swirling around them.

By the time Friday rolled around, she was completely drained. The show at The Christmas Ranch would be the following Tuesday, which meant only three more rehearsals—that afternoon, Saturday morning and Monday after school. With everything else going on, this would be her last chance to practice with Colter and Trevor for their special number.

Now, as they rehearsed one more time in her classroom, her fingers strummed the last chord of the song and she beamed at the boys.

"That time was perfect!" she exclaimed. "I can't believe how well you've picked up the harmony and you've memorized the words and everything. Your dad is going to love this so much. Everyone else will, too."

She wasn't exaggerating or giving false praise. Colter and Trevor actually sounded so good together, she would have loved to record it.

All her instincts told her that if she ever uploaded it to social media, the song would go viral instantly. Their voices blended perfectly and the twins had a natural harmony that brought out all the emotional punch of the song, the angst of a cowboy who has to spend the holiday alone in the cold elements instead of by a warm fire, surrounded by loved ones.

Beyond that, there was something utterly charming about these two redheaded little boys who looked like the troublemakers many thought they were, but when they opened their mouths, they sang like little cowboy angels.

On the night of the performance, she would have to make sure it was recorded. More than one parent had offered to film the entire show. She would have to be sure

Beck could obtain a copy, especially since he wouldn't be prepared to record it himself, considering the whole thing would be a total surprise.

"Thanks a lot for helping us," Trevor said.

"You're very welcome. I've enjoyed it. And you boys have been so good during the rehearsals. You've more than repaid me."

"No, we haven't," Colter argued. "We still need to take you horseback riding again. You only went two times and we practiced our song almost every day."

"Our dad said we could invite you to come over again tomorrow after practice, if you have time," his brother said.

"Yeah! You've got to come and see the puppies. They're growing *fast*."

"Their eyes are open now and they're not always sleeping every minute. They're so cute. You have to see them," Trevor said. "We got to hold one yesterday. Sal didn't like it much but Dad just petted her and talked to her so she didn't get too mad at us."

"I'm glad to hear that," Ella said, charmed despite herself by the image of Beck giving his boys a chance to hold the puppy.

Only a few weeks ago, she had thought him cold, emotionless. How had she managed to get things so very wrong?

He certainly didn't kiss like he was cold and emotionless. The memory made her ache.

"So do you want to come over after practice tomorrow afternoon?"

With everything on her docket, that was really her only free chunk of time all week to finish her own Christmas preparations, but this appeared to be a matter of honor to the boys. It was clear Trevor and Colter wanted to be sure they repaid her accordingly, after all her work helping them prepare the song.

Beyond that, she felt a little rush of anticipation at the prospect of riding again. She had begun recapturing something she thought had been lost forever and couldn't help being eager to continue on that journey.

"I have a busy day tomorrow, but I think I could make that work. I would love to visit Creampuff again and see Sal and her puppies."

"Yay!" Colter said.

"I'll plan on taking riding clothes again and we can practice after I take you home from rehearsal tomorrow."

"Maybe we can show you how to rope a calf," Colter said.

"I think I'll stick with trying to stay in the saddle," she said with a smile. "Are you sure this is okay with your father?"

Trevor's features fell a little. "He said we could ask you, but he might not be there."

"Yeah. He said he had some stuff to do tomorrow, so our uncle Jax said he could teach you anything you want to know."

"Dad didn't like that very much, though. He was kind of mad at Uncle Jax. He got a big, mean face, but Uncle Jax only laughed."

"Is that right?" she said faintly.

Jax McKinley was a flirt of the highest order. From the moment she moved to town, friends had warned her not to take him too seriously.

"Yeah. Uncle Jax is really good with horses. He even rides broncs in the rodeo and stuff."

"But our dad is even better," Colt assured her. "He's the best cowboy ever."

"And he's nice, too."

"Plus, he can cook good. He makes really good popcorn."

Don't forget that he can kiss like he was born knowing his way around a woman's mouth.

"I'll be grateful to anyone who might be there tomorrow to give me a lesson," she assured them. "Now, we'd better hurry or we'll be late to rehearsal."

As the boys grabbed backpacks and coats and she gathered her own things, she couldn't stop thinking about Beck. Big surprise. What would he think of the boys' special musical number? He would have to possess a heart of lead not to be touched by their effort on his behalf.

They were adorable kids. She would always be grateful she had been able to get to know them a little better these past few weeks.

She had completely changed her perspective about them, too. Somehow they had worked their charming little way into her heart when she wasn't looking.

The trick after the holidays would be figuring out how to extricate them all.

"I thought you were planning to be in Idaho Falls all day."

Beck fought the urge to rearrange that smirk on Jax's too-handsome face. His brother always seemed to know instinctively which buttons to push. Apparently Beck was more transparent than he thought.

"I took care of everything I had to do in town," he said. "It took less time than I expected. I knew what I wanted and where to get it, so there was no sense daw-dling, was there?"

"Words to live by, brother." Jax grinned, obviously taking his words to mean something entirely different from what Beck intended. "Too bad for me, I guess that means you can take over the riding lesson with our pretty little neighbor this afternoon. But I imagine you already knew that."

Beck frowned at his brother's teasing. "I don't know what you're talking about," he lied.

Jax only chuckled. "I guess since you're here, you can do the honors of saddling up all the horses for the lesson. I suddenly find myself with an afternoon free. Maybe I should run into town, do a little Christmas shopping."

"Sounds good." He wouldn't mind if his brother de-cided to stay away all afternoon.

He checked his watch. Practice was supposed to have ended about fifteen minutes ago, which meant Ella and the boys should be here shortly.

As unwelcome anticipation churned through him, Beckett tried to keep himself busy in the horse barn, readying the horses and the arena for their visitor. He was mostly unsuccessful, with little focus or direction, and was almost relieved when he finally heard a vehi-cle approach.

He set down the leather tack he had been organiz-ing and walked out to greet them, his heart pounding in his chest.

How had he forgotten how pretty she was? As she climbed out of her vehicle, winter sunlight glinted on her hair and her cheeks were rosy and sweet. She wore jeans, boots and a ranch coat open to reveal another Christmas sweater. Instantly, he remembered that moment in his room the week before, when she had appeared there like something out of a dream he hadn't dared remember.

"Hey, Dad," Trevor said, his features lighting up at the sight of them. "I thought you weren't gonna be here!"

"I took care of my business in Idaho Falls faster than I expected," he answered. They didn't need to know that he had practically bought out the entire toy aisle at the big-box store in his rush to get out of there quickly, before the Saturday rush.

"Great!" Colter said. "This way you can give this Ella her lesson."

The two exchanged delighted grins and an uncomfortable suspicion began to take root.

Something was up, all right, and he had a feeling he was beginning to know what that might be. The little troublemakers had romance on their minds. Somehow they must have got it in their heads that he and their music teacher might make a match of it.

Was Jax in on it? What about Dan? Was that the reason Jax was conveniently taking off and that Dan had made a point of saying he had plans today and couldn't help?

Were they all trying to throw him and Ella together?

His cheeks suddenly felt hot as he wondered if that was the whole reason the boys had come up with the idea for these riding lessons.

This wouldn't do. The idea was impossible. Completely out of the question. He didn't have the first idea how to break it to them.

They were children. They only saw a pretty woman who was kind to them, not all the many reasons why a relationship between Ella and Beck could never work.

He suddenly wished he'd stayed in Idaho Falls, so he

could head off this crazy idea before it had any more time to blossom.

Was it too late to drag Jax back to handle the lessons? He still didn't like the idea of his brother here with his flirty smiles and his admiring gaze. Beck would just have to tough it out.

Things would be easier, though, if they didn't stick around here in the intimate confines of the riding arena.

"What do you say we take a quick trail ride up above the house? You can only learn so much while you're riding around in a circle."

"Outside?" Her gaze shifted to the mountains then back to him, her big blue eyes widening.

She had been injured in those mountains, he remembered. He couldn't blame her for being nervous, yet he knew it was a fear she had to overcome if she would ever be able to truly rediscover the joy of riding horses again.

"You'll be okay. We'll keep you safe," he promised. "Do you have warm enough clothing for that?"

"Is anything ever warm enough for the winters around here?"

He had to smile. "Good point. There's no cold like trying to pull a stubborn calf at two in the morning when it's below zero, with a windchill that makes it even colder."

"Brrr."

He looked over her winter gear. "We should have some warmer gloves that will fit you and a snug hat. I would hate to be responsible for you coming down with frostbite."

"You make this whole outing sound so appealing."

Despite her dry tone, he could see the hint of panic in her eyes and in the slight trembling in her hands.

"Don't worry. We won't go far. I've got a fairly well-groomed trail that winds around above the house a little. We can be back in less than an hour. It will be fun, you'll see."

She still didn't look convinced.

"Trust me," he said. "You're never going to love riding a horse again until you let one take you somewhere worth going."

That seemed to resonate with her. She gazed at him, then at the mountains, then finally nodded.

Even if she wasn't for him, the woman had grit. He wanted to tell her so, right there. He wanted to kiss her smack on the lips and tell her she had more gumption than just about anybody he'd ever met.

He couldn't, of course, without giving the boys encouragement that their devious plan was working, so he only smiled and walked back to the barn to bring out the horses.

Chapter Ten

Ella refused to give in to the tendrils of panic coiling through her.

As the boys led out Creampuff and their two horses, saddled and ready to go, she drew in a deep, cleansing breath.

Beck was right. Riding around in an indoor space had been a great introduction for her, but it wasn't much different from a child atop a pony, going around in circles at the county fair. If she truly wanted to get past her fear, she had to take bigger steps, like riding outside, no matter how stressful.

Beck came out leading his own big horse and for a moment, she let herself enjoy the picture of a gorgeous cowboy and his horse in the clear December air.

"Need a boost?" Beck asked as he approached.

She wanted to tell him no, but the placid and friendly

Creampuff suddenly loomed huge and terrifying. "Yes. Thank you," she said.

He helped her into the saddle and gave her thigh a re-assuring squeeze that filled her with a complex mix of gratitude and awareness.

"You've got this, El. We'll be with you the whole time."

"Thanks," she mumbled through lips that felt thick and unwieldy.

Beckett mounted his own horse. Ella was again dis-tracted long enough from her worries to wish she didn't have to hold the reins in a death grip so she could pull out her phone and snap his photograph. Her friends back in Boston should have visual proof that she was actually friends with someone who should be featured in men's cologne advertisements.

The Great American Cowboy, at one with his horse and his surroundings.

"Trev, you go in front, then Colt, then Miss Baker," Beck ordered. "I'll bring up the rear. We're just heading up to the springs. You know the way, right, boys? Not too fast, okay? Just an easy walk this time."

"Okay, Dad," Trevor said.

The boys turned their horses and urged them around the ranch house. Creampuff followed the other horses without much direction necessary from Ella as they made their way around the ranch house and toward a narrow trail she could see leading into the foothills.

At first, she was too focused on remaining in the saddle to notice anything else. Gradually, she could feel her muscles begin to relax into the rhythm of the horse. Creampuff really was a gentle animal. She wasn't placid, but she didn't seem at all inclined to any sudden movements or abrupt starts. She responded almost instantly to any commands.

Ella drew in a deep breath scented with pine, snow, leather and horse. It truly was beautiful here. From their vantage point, she could see Beck's ranch, orderly and neat, joining her father's land. Beyond spread the town of Pine Gulch, with the silvery ribbon of the Cold Creek winding through the mountains.

In summer, this would be beautiful, she knew, covered in wildflowers and sagebrush. Now it was a vast, peaceful blanket of snow in every direction.

This was obviously a well-traveled trail and it appeared to have been groomed, as well.

Had he done that for her, so she would be able to take this ride?

Warmth seeped through her at the possibility and she hardly noticed the winter temperature.

Colter turned around in his saddle. "You're doing great," the boy said. "Isn't this fun?"

"Yes," she answered. "It's lovely up here."

Everything seemed more intense—the cold air against her skin, the musical jangle of the tack, the magnificent blue Idaho sky.

After about fifteen or twenty minutes, they reached a clearing where the trail ended at a large round black water tank.

Trevor's horse went straight to the water and the others followed suit.

"This looks like a well-used watering spot."

"Our cattle like to come up here, but if you stuck around long enough, you could also see elk and deer and the occasional mountain lion," Beck said.

"A mountain lion. Oh, my!"

"They're not real scary," Colter assured her. "They leave you alone if you leave them alone."

"We even saw a wolf up here once," Trevor claimed.

"A coyote, anyway," Beck amended.

"I still think it was a wolf, just like the ones we saw in Yellowstone."

"Want to stretch your legs a little before we ride home? We can show you the springs, if you want. There's a little waterfall there that's pretty this time of year, half-frozen."

"Sure."

This time she dismounted on her own and the boys tied the horses' reins to a post there. Beck waded through the snow to blaze a trail about twenty yards past the water tank to a small fenced-off area in the hillside that must be protecting the source of a natural springs from animal contamination. The springs rippled through the snow to a series of small waterfalls that sparkled in the sunlight.

"This is lovely," she murmured. "Do you come up here often?"

"I maintain it year-round. The springs provides most of our water supply on the ranch. We pipe it down from the source but leave some free-flowing. In the winter, this is as far as we can go without cross-country skis or snowshoes. The rest of the year, there's a beautiful back-country trail that will take you to Cold Creek Canyon. It's really a stunning hike or ride."

"Last year, we rode our horses over to see our friend Thomas."

"That sounds lovely."

What an idyllic place for these boys to grow up. Though they had lost their mother so young, they didn't seem to suffer for love and affection. She didn't envy them precisely—how could she, when they didn't have a mother? Still, she wished she could have grown up on the Baker's Dozen with her parents together, instead of having been constantly yanked in opposite directions.

They seemed so comfortable here, confident and happy and loved.

"You should see the wildflowers that grow up here," Beck said as they headed back to the horses. "There's something about the microclimate, I guess, but in the summer this whole hillside is spectacular, with flowers of every color. Lupine and columbine, evening primrose and firewheel. It's beautiful."

"Oh, I would love to see that." She could picture it vividly.

"You're welcome back, anytime," he said. "June is the best time for flowers."

"I'll keep that in mind."

It always amazed her when she went into the back-country around Pine Gulch that all this beauty was just a few moments away. It only took a little effort and exploration to find it.

"Can we go back now?" Colter asked. "I'm kind of cold."

"Yeah. Me, too," his brother said, with a furtive look at the two of them. "You don't have to come with us. You two can stay up here as long as you want. We're okay by ourselves."

Before their father could answer, the boys hopped back on their horses and headed down in the direction they'd come up.

She glanced at Beck, who was watching his sons with a look of consternation.

"Those two little rascals." He shook his head with

an expression that suggested he was both embarrassed and annoyed.

"What was that all about?"

"It's more than a little embarrassing," he admitted. "I think they're up to something. They've been acting oddly all week."

Oh, dear. She hoped the boys didn't reveal their surprise musical number before the performance in a few days.

"I'm sure it's nothing," she said. "Probably just, you know, typical Christmas secrets."

"That's what I thought at first, but not anymore. Today proved it." He was silent for a moment. "I think they're matchmaking."

She stared. "Matchmaking? Us?"

She felt hot suddenly, then cold. Did the boys know she was developing feelings for their father? Had she let something slip?

"I know, it's crazy. I don't have any definite proof, just a vibe I've picked up a time or two. I'm sorry about that."

Was he sorry because he was embarrassed or sorry that his boys might actually be crazy enough to think Ella and he could ever be a match?

"I… It's fine."

"If this keeps up, I'll talk to them. Make sure they know they're way off base."

"It's fine," she said again, though she felt a sharp pang in her heart at his words. "They are right about one thing, though. It is getting cold up here."

"Yeah. Guess we better head down."

"Thank you for showing me the waterfall, for making me ride up here, when I was afraid to try it. It is beautiful."

"You're welcome. Here. Let me help you mount up again."

She wanted to try herself, but her bad leg was aching from the ride and she wasn't sure she could manage it.

He gave her a boost up. This time, though, because of the stiffness in her leg, she faltered a little and his hands ended up on her rear instead of her waist.

Both of them seemed to freeze for just a moment and then he gave a nudge and she was in the saddle.

He cleared his throat. "I swear, I didn't mean to do that."

"I believe you. Don't worry. I guess it's a good thing the boys weren't here to see, right? They might get the wrong idea."

"True enough."

He looked as if he wanted to say something else but finally mounted his own horse. "You go first. I'll be right behind you. Creampuff knows the way."

She drew in a deep breath and headed down the mountainside.

A wise woman would have jumped back in her car and driven away from Beck McKinley and his cute twins the moment she rode back to the barn. Ella was discovering she wasn't very wise, at least not when it came to the McKinley men.

As soon as they arrived back at the horse barn, the twins came out, two adorable little cowboys. "We can put up Creampuff and Ace for you," Colter offered.

Beck looked surprised, then pleased. "That's very responsible of you, boys."

They beamed at the two of them. "While we do that,"

Trevor said, "you can take Miss Ella to see the puppies again."

"She has to see how much they've grown," his brother agreed.

"We'll wait until you're done with the horses, then we can all go see the puppies together."

"We've already seen them this morning, when we had to feed them," Colter reminded him. "And you said it's better if Sal doesn't have that many visitors at once. It stresses her. You said so."

"That's right. I did say that." Above their heads, Beck raised his eyebrows at Ella in a told-you-so kind of look.

"Go on, Dad. We promised Miss Baker she could see them."

"I guess I have my orders," he murmured to Ella. "Shall we?"

She didn't see a graceful way out of the situation, so she shrugged and followed him toward the older barn.

"What did I tell you?" Beck said as they headed inside from the cold December afternoon to the warm, cozy building.

"You might be right," she said.

"I'm sorry. I don't know what's come over them."

"You don't need to apologize. I think it's rather sweet. I'm flattered, if you want the truth, that they think I'm good enough for you."

You *obviously don't, but it's nice that your sons do.*

He gazed at her for a moment, before shaking his head. "They're rascals. I'll have a talk with them."

Though she fought the urge to tell him not to do that, at least until after Christmas, she knew he had to set them straight. Nothing would ever happen between her and Beck. He had made that abundantly clear.

They stood just inside the door of the barn. It was warm here and strangely intimate and she had to fight the urge to step forward and kiss away that rather embarrassed expression.

He was gazing at her mouth, she realized, and she saw awareness flickering there in his eyes.

He wanted to kiss her and she ached to let him.

No. That wouldn't do, especially if they wanted to convince the boys there was nothing between them.

She curled her hands into fists instead. "We'd better take a look at the puppies, since that's the reason we came in here."

After an awkward moment, he shrugged. "You're right. Absolutely right."

He turned and headed farther into the barn and she followed him to the stall that housed Sal and her new little brood.

Holding on to her suddenly grim mood was tough in the presence of the eight adorable little black-and-white puppies, who were now beginning to toddle around the stall. They appeared less rodentlike and more like cute puppies, furry and adorable, with paws and ears that seemed too big for their little bodies.

"The boys were right!" she exclaimed. "They've grown so much since I saw them last."

"You can hold one, if you'd like. Sal can be a bit territorial so I'll have to grab one and bring it out to you."

"I'm all right. I'll just watch this time."

"Come back in a few weeks and they'll be climbing all over. She'll be glad to let someone else entertain them for a moment."

"They're really beautiful, Beck."

He gazed down at her with a slight smile and she was

aware of the heat of him and the breadth of his shoulders. She felt a long, slow tug in her chest, as if invisible cords were pulling her closer to him.

"Thank you for sharing them with me—and for the rest of today. I'm glad you made me go on that trail, even though it scared me to death."

"I could tell."

She made a face. "Was I that obvious? I thought I was doing so well at concealing my panic attacks"

"There was nothing overt, just a few signs I picked up." He paused. "I hope you realize there's nothing wrong with being afraid, especially after your experience in childhood. Anyone would be. But not everyone would have the courage to try to overcome it."

"I don't think it's *wrong*, necessarily. Only *frustrating*. I don't want to be afraid."

"But you did it anyway. That's the important thing. You've got grit, El. Pure grit."

His words slid around and through her, warming her as clearly as if he'd bundled her in a soft, sweet-smelling quilt just off the clothesline. "I do believe that's the sweetest thing you've ever said to me."

He scratched his cheek, looking sheepish. "It must be the puppies. They bring out my gooey side."

"I like it," she confessed.

As he looked down at her, she again felt that tug in her chest, as if everything inside her wanted to pull her toward him. He must have felt it, too. She watched his expression shift, saw the heat spark to life there. His gaze slid to her mouth then back to meet her gaze and he swallowed hard.

Sunlight slanted in through a high window, making his gorgeous features glow, as if the universe was somehow telling her this was right. She had never been so aware of a man. He could carry her over his shoulders to one of the straw-covered stalls and she wouldn't utter a peep of protest.

The air around them seemed to hiss and snap with a sweet, fine-edged tension, and when he sighed and finally kissed her, it seemed as inevitable as a brilliant summer sunset.

Kissing him felt as familiar and *right* as being on a horse had earlier that afternoon. His mouth fit hers perfectly and he wrapped his arms around her as if he had been waiting for just this moment.

She returned his kiss eagerly, with all the pent-up longing of the previous week, when she had been tormented by heated memories.

Through the thrill and wonder of the kiss, as his mouth explored hers and his hands somehow found their way beneath her sweater to the bare skin of her lower back, she was aware of a tiny, ominous thread weaving through the moment.

It took several more long, delicious kisses before she could manage to identify the source of that little niggling worry, the grim truth she had been trying to ignore.

This was more than simple attraction.

She was falling in love with Beckett McKinley.

The realization seemed to knock the air right out of her lungs and she was suddenly more afraid than she'd been the first time she faced his horses.

He would hurt her. Badly. Oh, he wouldn't mean to— Beck was a good man, a kind one, as she had figured out over the last little while. But he had no real use for her beyond a few kisses. He had made that perfectly clear—

as far as Beck was concerned, she didn't belong here. She was no different from his late wife or her own mother.

Like her father, he couldn't see the truth of her, the part that loved afternoon thundershowers over the mountains or the sight of new crops breaking through the ground or a vast hillside covered in wildflowers.

One of the puppies made a little mewling whimper that perfectly echoed how she felt inside. Somehow it gave Ella the strength to slide her mouth away from his.

She caught her breath and tried to make light of the kiss, purely in self-defense. "Good thing your sons didn't come in just now. If they had seen us wrapped together there, they might have made the mistake of thinking we're both falling in exactly with their plans."

"Good thing," he murmured, looking dazed and aroused and gorgeous.

She had to get out of here, before she did something stupid, like yank him against her again and lose her heart the rest of the way. She drew a deep gulp of air into her lungs and forced a casual smile that she was fairly sure didn't fool him for a moment.

"I should, um, go. I've got a Christmas party tonight with some friends and still have to bake a dozen cookies for the exchange."

He said nothing for a long moment, then sighed. "Should we talk about that?"

She opted to deliberately misunderstand. "The cookies? I'm making my favorite white-chocolate cranberry recipe. There's really nothing to it. The secret is using a high-quality shortening and a little more flour, especially in this altitude."

"I'm sure you know I didn't mean we should talk about

the cookies—though those sound delicious. I meant the kiss."

He shoved his hands into the pockets of his coat, as if he was afraid if he didn't, he would reach for her again.

Or maybe his fingers were simply cold.

"There's nothing to say," she said with that fake smile that made her cheek muscles hurt. "The boys can play matchmaker all they like, but we both know it won't go anywhere. I'll just make a point not to visit any cute puppies alone with you again."

While she was at it, she would have to add walking together to her car to that list of no-no's, as well as helping her onto a horse and washing dishes side by side.

Come to think of it, maybe it would be better if they kept a nice, safe, ten-foot perimeter between them at all times.

"I really do have to go," she lied.

"I guess I'll see you next week at the Christmas show."

She nodded and hurried out before she did something else stupid.

Beck followed her out to be sure she made it safely to her vehicle. There were a few icy spots that worried him, but she hurried across the yard to her SUV and climbed inside without faltering or looking back, as if one of his cow dogs was nipping at her heels to drive her on.

He had screwed up. Plain and simple.

For nearly a week, he'd been telling himself all the reasons he couldn't kiss her again. What did he do the first moment they were really alone together? Yep. He kissed her. He hadn't been able to help himself. She had been so soft and sweet and lovely and all he could think about was tasting her mouth one more time.

The trouble was, he was not only fiercely attracted to her, but he also genuinely liked her.

He meant what he said to her. She had more grit than just about anybody he knew.

If she had the kind of raw courage necessary to ride again after an accident that nearly killed her, why was he so certain she didn't belong out there, that she would turn tail and run at the first sign of trouble?

She wasn't like Stephanie. That was clear enough. Yes, they had both been raised back east in big cities. They both came from wealthy, cultured backgrounds that seemed worlds away from this small Idaho town.

But Stephanie had been...*damaged*. He should have seen that from the start. She had managed to hide it fairly well at first, but when he looked back, he could clearly see all the warning signs he should have discerned much earlier. He hadn't *wanted* to see them. He had been busy growing the ranch, getting ready for the arrival of his sons, coping with a moody, temperamental wife.

If he had been more aware, maybe he could have found help for her earlier and headed off the debilitating depression that came later.

The truth was, he didn't trust himself these days. Things had gone so horribly wrong with Stephanie, and his sons had been the ones to suffer. He couldn't afford to mess up again.

If he didn't have the boys to consider—only himself— he might take the chance to see if these tender young feelings uncurling inside him for Ella Baker could grow into something sturdy and beautiful.

How could he take that risk, though?

If he pursued things between them and she ended up

leaving, too, like their mother—and like her own, for that matter—the boys would be shattered.

He couldn't do that to them.

He turned around and headed back to the barn, aware as he walked that Ella had the strength to confront her fears while he was letting his own completely chase him down and wear him out like one of the Yellowstone wolves on a wounded calf.

Chapter Eleven

If he could have avoided it, Beck would have stayed far away from the Baker ranch until he could manage to figure out a way to purge Ella out of his system.

He had a feeling he faced a long battle on that particular front.

Meanwhile, he couldn't avoid the place, especially not while he and Curt were still the copresidents of the local cattle growers association.

They had end-of-year paperwork to finish for the association. It had been on his desk for a week, but he had been putting it off. Finally, the day of the Christmas show the boys had been working so hard on, he knew he couldn't put it off any longer.

It was no coincidence that he tried to time his visit around noon, as he was certain Ella would be busy teaching music at the school and not here to torment him with visions of what could never be.

If that made him a yellow-bellied chicken, he would just have to live with it.

"Thanks for bringing this by," Curt said, gesturing to the folder of papers he needed to sign.

"No problem. I was out anyway," Beck assured him. "I'm heading over to Driggs to pick up the last thing for the boys' Christmas. I commissioned new saddles for each of them, since they're growing so fast and are too big for the ones they've been using."

"Watch those two. They'll be taller than you before you know it."

Since he was six-two and the boys were only seven years old, Beckett was pretty sure he was safe for a few more years on that front, unless they had an explosive growth spur.

"Need anything while I'm out?"

Curt shook his head and Beck couldn't help thinking his friend looked more frail every time he saw him.

"I can't think of anything," he said. "I did most of my shopping online this year, since it's hard for me to get around the crowded stores."

"Got it."

Curt gazed out the window, where a light snow had begun to fall in the last hour. "It's not coming down too much, but you'd still better hurry back from town. We've got a big storm heading this way."

"That's what I heard."

The weather forecast was predicting the storm might break records.

"It's not supposed to hit until tonight, but you never know. Better safe than sorry. I know you would hate to miss the show tonight at The Christmas Ranch."

"I'll be back in plenty of time. I'm only making one stop to the saddle maker's place."

"Good. Good." Curt reached for the big water bottle on the table beside him but his hands were trembling so badly today that it took him three tries to find the straw.

"How are you doing?" Beck asked. "Really doing?"

It seemed as if they always talked *around* Curt's condition and the challenge it presented, instead of talking *about* it. The older man frowned. For once, he didn't give his stock answer.

"I can't do a damn thing anymore," he said, frustration vying with self-pity in his voice and expression.

"I'm sorry," Beck said, though the words were hardly adequate.

"Parkinson's is the worst. I can barely sign my damn name on those papers. You saw me. If I could climb up on a horse right now, I would borrow one from you. He and I would ride up into the backcountry to die and you'd never see me again."

Man, it was hard to see such an independent, strong man laid low by this debilitating disease.

"That would be a waste of a good horse. Not to mention a good friend," he said quietly.

Curt sipped at his water again, then set it down on the desk in his ranch office. "Have you thought more about buying me out?"

There it was. The other thing he didn't know what to do about.

"Sure I've thought about it. I've run the numbers dozens of times. It's an amazing offer, Curt. I would love the chance to combine our two ranches and build the Baker-McKinley brand into one of the strongest in the world."

"You sound hesitant, though. Is it the asking price? We can negotiate a little."

He could handle the hefty price tag Curt was asking. It would mean leveraging his capital, but he'd had some great years and had money in the bank. What better use for it than taking advantage of the chance to double his usable acreage and water supply, not to mention keeping the Baker's Dozen land out of the hands of developers?

Like everywhere else in the West, this part of Idaho was experiencing a population boom, with people wanting to relocate here for the beautiful views, serenity and slower pace.

As developers built houses and newcomers moved in, they tended to crowd any agricultural operations farther and farther to the outskirts. It was the eternal paradox. People moved to an area because they loved the quiet way of life and what it represented, then immediately set out to change it.

"It's not the price," he said.

"Then what?" Curt persisted. "I'd like to seal this deal as soon as we can."

"What about Ella?" he asked, finally voicing the one concern that seemed to override all the others.

"What about her?"

"How does she feel about you selling the ranch to me?"

Curt flicked off the question with a dismissive gesture. It was obvious from his expression that he didn't consider that an obstacle at all. "She'll be fine with it. It's not like I'm *giving* it to you out of the goodness of my heart, right?"

True enough. He would pay a hefty sum, even slightly above market value.

"Ella stands to inherit my entire estate," Curt went on. "She's all I've got, so the whole kit and caboodle goes to her. Believe me, she's not stupid. She'll be better off having cold hard cash in the bank than being saddled with a cattle ranch she doesn't know the first thing to do with."

The words were barely out of the other man's mouth when Beck heard a gasp from the hallway outside the office.

With a sinking heart, he shifted his gaze and found Ella standing there, holding a tray that looked like it contained a bowl of soup and a sandwich for her father.

The tray wobbled in her hands and he thought for a moment she would drop it, but she righted it at the last moment. She didn't come inside, simply stood there looking devastated.

"Dad," she whispered.

Curt had the grace to look embarrassed. "How long have you been home?"

She ignored the question. "You're selling the ranch? To *Beck*?"

She said his name like it was a vile curse word and he flinched a little. None of this was his idea but he still felt guilty he had even discussed it with Curt.

"I offered it to him. We're still working out terms, but it makes the most sense for everyone."

She aimed a wounded look at Beck, which made him feel sandwiched between father and daughter. "You never said a word to me," she said to him.

He should have mentioned it. Now he wished he had, especially after the first time they kissed.

"Why didn't you tell me?"

Guilt pinched at him, harsh and mean. On its heels, though, was defensiveness. *He* had nothing to feel guilty about, other than not telling her Curt had approached him with an offer to sell. It hadn't been his idea or anything he had deliberately sought out. He had assumed her father had already told her about it.

Anyway, Curt was right. She would inherit the proceeds from the ranch and could live comfortably the rest of her life.

"It makes the most sense for everyone—" he began.

"Not for me! I love this ranch. I'd like to try running it, if my stubborn father would ever let me. I'm trying to learn everything I can. Why do you think I wanted the boys to teach me how to ride?"

"Ride what? I hope you're not talking about horses," Curt interjected, color suffusing his features.

"I am," Ella declared as she finally moved into the room and set down the lunch tray on the desk. "I've been to the Broken Arrow several times to go riding with Trevor and Colter."

"I can't believe you went horseback riding without telling me!"

"Really?" she snapped. "That's what you're taking out of this discussion? Considering you've all but sold my legacy out from under me without bothering to mention it, I don't think you've got much room to be angry about me riding a horse a few times."

"It's not your legacy until I'm gone," her father snapped back. "Until then, I've got every right to do what I want with *my* ranch."

The color that had started to rise on her features leached away and she seemed to sway. Beck half rose to catch her but earned only a scathing glare for his efforts.

"You certainly would never consider trusting me with it, would you?"

"You have no idea how hard this life is."

"Because you've shielded me from it my entire life!"

"For your own good!"

Now she was trembling, he saw, just as much as she had when facing down her fears and riding a horse.

"I'm twenty-seven years old, Dad. I'm not a broken little girl in a hospital bed. I'm not some fragile flower, either. I'm tough enough to handle running the Baker's Dozen. Why can't you see that?"

Curt's jaw clenched. "You have other talents, honey. You don't need to wear yourself out on this ranch."

"What if I want to? I love it here. You know I do."

"You love it *now*. Who's to say that won't change in a week or month or year from now? You have lived on the Baker's Dozen maybe a total of two years your entire life. I just don't want you to be saddled with more than you can handle."

"That's my decision to make, isn't it?"

"No," he said bluntly. "Beckett can take what I've built over my whole life—and what my father's built and his father—and make it even better. Can you say the same?"

She said nothing, only pressed her lips together. Her eyes looked haunted now, hollow with shadows.

Curt appeared oblivious to her reaction. He shrugged. "I wouldn't sell the ranch to Beck just to hurt you, honey. You know that, right?"

"But it *would* hurt me," she answered. "What hurts me more is that you will never even give me the chance to try."

She took a deep breath, as if fighting for control, then turned toward the door. "I can't do this right now. Not today. We can talk about it later. Right now, I have to go back to take my afternoon classes then focus on the children's Christmas show. I'll take the things I need for the show tonight. Don't expect me home between school and the performance."

She left without looking again at either of them, leaving behind an awkward, heavy silence.

Curt winced and picked up his water bottle again in hands that seemed to be shaking more than they had earlier. "I didn't want her finding out about our deal like that."

Beck frowned. "We don't have a deal. Not yet."

He was angry suddenly that Curt had dragged him into the middle of things and felt terrible for his part in hurting her. "If Ella wants to try running the ranch, Curt, I don't think I can stand in the way of that."

"She might think she wants it but she has no idea what it takes to keep this place going. She's never had to pull a calf when it's thirty below zero outside, or be up for forty-eight hours straight, trying to bring the hay in on time."

"So she can hire people to help her. You're not doing it on your own, either. Your foreman has stepped up to take on more and more of the load over the last few years. Why can't he do the same for her?"

"It's not the same. I know what I'm doing! I'm still involved in the day-to-day operations. What does Ella know about cattle? She can play four instruments and sings like a dream but she's not a rancher!"

"Not if you don't let her learn, Curt. Why are you trying so hard to protect her?"

"This ranch almost killed her once. I can't let it finish the job."

Curt blurted out the words, then looked as if he wished he could call them back.

Beck sat back, understanding dawning. He had suspected something like that after Ella told him about her accident.

"Your daughter inherited more from you than your eye color, Curtis Baker. She's tougher than you give her credit. You should have seen the grit she used to get back in the saddle, when it was obvious it scared her to death."

"I can't lose her," the man said, his voice low. "She's all I have."

"If you keep treating her like she's incompetent, you might not have much choice," he answered firmly. "You'll lose her anyway."

Ella sat in her SUV at the end of the driveway, trying to control the tears that burned her eyes.

No good deed goes unpunished, right? She thought it would be a nice thing to surprise her dad for lunch by bringing home a sandwich and some of his favorite take-out tomato bisque from the diner in town.

She never expected she would find Beck in her father's office, or walk in on the two of them negotiating away her future.

Her father had no faith in her.

She had suspected as much, but there was something heartbreaking and final about hearing it spoken so bluntly.

She'll be better off having cold hard cash in the bank than being saddled with a cattle ranch she doesn't know the first thing to do with.

Since coming to live here, she had done her best to learn the ropes. When she wasn't teaching music, she had helped with the roundup, she had driven the tractor, she had gone out with Manny to fix fences.

It wasn't enough. It would never be enough. Curtis Baker could never see her as anything more than a weak, frightened girl.

Did she know everything about running a ranch? No. But she was willing to learn. Why wouldn't her father let her try?

She brushed away a tear that fell, despite her best efforts.

She was stuck here. Her father needed her help. She couldn't just abandon him. But how could she face living here day after day with the knowledge that the ranch she loved—the ranch that felt like a huge part of her—would someday belong to someone else?

To Beck?

The pain intensified, bringing along the bitter taste of betrayal. Damn him. Why hadn't he bothered to mention that Curt had approached him about buying the ranch?

That hurt almost as much as her father's disregard for her feelings.

She let out a breath and swiped at another tear. Just as she dropped her hand, a knock on the window of her vehicle made her jump halfway out of her seat.

She turned to find Beck, big and rugged and gorgeous, standing out in the gently falling snow.

She thought about putting her SUV in gear and spraying him with mud as she peeled out, but that would be childish.

Wouldn't it?

He gestured for her to roll down her window. After a moment, she did but only about three inches. Cold air rushed in, heavy with the impending storm.

"I don't have time to talk to you," she snapped. "I have a class in twenty minutes."

"The school is only a ten-minute drive from here. That means we still have ten minutes."

She set her jaw. Did he think she could just run into her classroom and miraculously be in a mental space to take on thirty-three fourth graders who had been dreaming of sugarplums for weeks?

"What do you want?" she said. Even as she spoke, she was aware she sounded like one of those fourth graders having a verbal altercation with a schoolmate.

"I'm sorry I didn't tell you your father had offered to sell me the ranch. I guess I assumed you and Curt had already talked about it. I thought maybe that was the reason you're sometimes a little…cool to me."

Had she been cool to him? She was remembering a few specific encounters when the temperature had been the exact opposite of cool.

"He never said a word to me. But why would he? As he made it abundantly clear in there, he doesn't need to tell me anything."

Beck sighed. "He should have. Told you, I mean. That's what I just said to him. More than that, I think he should give you a chance to run the Baker's Dozen along with him for a few years, then both of you can decide if you want to sell."

"That's a lovely idea. He would never consider it."

"Have you talked to him about it?"

"Of course! Dozens of times. My father sees what he wants to see. Like I said in there, to him, I'll always be that broken girl in a hospital bed."

"He loves you and worries about you. Speaking as a father, it would be hell to see your child hurt and spend all these years afraid it was your fault."

Curt had sold all his horses after her accident, though he had always loved to ride.

She sighed. "I can't worry about this today," she said. "In a few hours, I'm in charge of a show that involves dozens of children, twenty songs and an audience of three hundred people. I don't have time to stress about my stubborn father right now."

Tomorrow she would. Tomorrow her heart would probably break in jagged little pieces. She would compartmentalize that for now and worry about it after the show. The children had worked too hard for their music director to fall apart because her father had no faith in her.

"I'm sorry," he said again.

"I'm sure you are. Not sorry enough that you would refuse to buy the ranch, though, are you?"

A muscle worked in his jaw but he didn't answer. His silence told her everything she needed to know.

"That's what I thought. I have to go. Goodbye, Beckett."

She put her SUV in gear and pulled out into the driveway, her heart aching with regret and sadness and the tantalizing dream of what might have been.

Chapter Twelve

"Okay, kids. This is it. Our audience is starting to arrive. You've practiced so hard, each one of you. I hope you know how proud of you I am. Each number sounds wonderful and I know you've all put in so much effort to memorize your parts and the words to the music. This show is going to be amazing! Let's make some people happy!"

The children cheered with nervous energy and she smiled reassuringly at them all, though she could feel emotion building in her throat.

This was her second year directing the Christmas show and it might just be her last. If her father sold the ranch to Beckett, she wasn't sure she could stay in Pine Gulch, as much as she loved it here. It would be too difficult to watch.

She snared her thoughts before they could wander

further down that path. Tonight wasn't about sadness and regret, but about the joy and wonder and magic of Christmas. For the children's sake, she needed to focus on the show right now. She would have time to process the pain and disappointment of the day later, when this program was behind her.

"Our guests are arriving now but they will need to eat dinner first. That gives us about thirty minutes before our show. Everyone follow the older girls into the office. We have a special treat in store for you. Celeste Delaney is going to read to you from the newest, still-unpublished Sparkle the Reindeer book!"

An electric buzz crackled through the crowd at that announcement. She knew the children would be excited about the prospect of a new Sparkle book, as everyone adored the charming stories.

When she was certain the children were settled comfortably, Ella returned to the large reception room in the lodge to check on the rapidly filling tables. She greeted a few friends and made small talk as she assessed the crowd.

"We crammed in three more tables, so fifty more people can squeeze in." Hope Santiago came to stand beside her and watch people jostling for space. "I hated to turn people away last year. I hope we've got enough room this year."

It still might be tight, judging by the crowds still coming in.

"How's the weather?" she asked. It wasn't a casual question.

Hope shrugged. "It's snowing a bit but it's not too bad, yet. I still enlisted everybody with four-wheel drive to pick up some of the senior citizens who don't like to drive in the snow. I was hoping we wouldn't have to do that again this year but Mother Nature didn't cooperate. Thanks for signing up Beck, by the way. He's out there now, bringing in his last shuttle group."

So much for trying not to think about the man. She couldn't seem to escape him.

"The show is amazing, El," Hope said, her expression earnest. "You've outdone yourself this year. Every number is perfect. Honestly, I don't know what we would do without you."

She wasn't yet ready to tell her friend The Christmas Ranch might have to do just that next year.

Instead, she forced a smile and prepared to go back and check on the children. To her shock, she came face-to-face with her father, who was just coming in from outside.

What was he doing there? Curtis hadn't said a word to her earlier about attending the show.

An instant later, Beck came in behind him, helping a woman whose name she didn't know navigate the crowd with a walker.

Beck must have given her father a ride. Big surprise. The two of them were no doubt plotting their ranching world domination.

That wasn't really fair, she acknowledged, a little ashamed of herself. Her father and Beck had been friends and neighbors a long time.

Beck looked up from helping the woman and caught sight of her. Something flashed in his gaze, something intense and unreadable.

She let out a breath. Despite her hurt over that scene in her father's office that afternoon, she couldn't help a little shiver of anticipation.

He was going to love the special number his twins had prepared for him out of sheer love. She had no doubt it would touch everyone at the performance—especially Beck.

In a small way, she felt as if the gift was coming from her, as well.

She turned away just as Hope hurried over to her. "We've got a little problem. Somehow two of the angels showed up without their wings. There's no time for someone to fetch them. I know we had extras. Do you remember where we put them?"

"Absolutely. I can picture the box in the storage room perfectly. I'll grab them." She hurried away, forcing herself again to focus on the show and not on her impending heartbreak.

"Oh, Ella. This show has been nothing short of magnificent this year," Celeste whispered backstage as a trio of girls, including her stepdaughter, Olivia, bowed to thunderous applause out on stage. "We could stop there and it would be absolutely perfect. Well done!"

She smiled at her friend. She had to agree. So far the show had gone off without a hitch.

"Is it time for us to go out for 'Silent Night'?" one of the older girls asked.

"In a moment. We have one more special number."

None of the other volunteers or the children in the program had heard Colter and Trevor's song yet, as she and the twins had practiced in secret. Only Hope knew about it, since Ella had to work out the lighting and sound with her and Rafe.

"After we're done, I need you girls to lead the younger

children out, then we'll sing the final number. Boys, are you ready?"

Trevor and Colter both nodded, though their features were pale in the dim light backstage. She had a feeling they would look nervous under any light conditions, as if only now realizing the magnitude of what they had signed up for that long-ago day when they had approached her about singing in the show.

She picked up her guitar from the stand and walked out ahead of the boys, who looked absolutely adorable in matching white shirts with bolo ties and Christmas-patterned vests that Hope had sewn for them. They wore matching cowboy hats and boots and giant belt buckles that were just about as big as their faces.

Oh, she hoped Rafe was videoing this.

Ella sat on a stool as the boys took to the microphone. The crowd quieted, all the restless stirring and rustling fading away.

She had performed enough times to know when she had an audience's attention. With the spotlights on her, it was tough to see Beckett's reaction, but she thought she saw his eyes widen. He would no doubt be completely shocked to see his sons up here onstage, since he had no idea they were performing a duet.

Ella didn't want this number to be about her, but she felt compelled to take the microphone before the boys began.

"It is my great pleasure to introduce to you Colter and Trevor McKinley. They're seven years old. And yes, you guessed it, they're twins."

This earned a ripple of laughter, since that was more than obvious to anyone without cataracts.

Ella waited for the reaction to fade away before

she went on. "A few weeks ago, Trevor and Colter approached me with a rather unusual request. They wanted to perform a special song at this Christmas show as a gift to someone they love very much. They asked me to help them prepare, so it would be perfect. Since then, they have been practicing several times a week with me after school, trying to learn the harmony, the pitch, the dynamics."

She smiled at the boys. "They have worked very hard, which I see as a testament to the value of this gift, which is intended for one person—their father, Beckett."

Though she was a little afraid to look at him, her gaze seemed to unerringly go in his direction. In the brief instant their gazes met, she saw complete shock on his features as people around him smiled and patted him on the back.

"This is his favorite Christmas song, apparently," she went on, "and I have it on good authority he sings it to himself when no one is around."

She didn't look at him now, but she was quite certain he would be embarrassed at that snippet of information. Too bad for him.

"While Trevor and Colter prepared this song especially for their father," she continued, "this is one of those rare and wonderful gifts that benefits more than its recipient. We all are lucky enough to be able to enjoy it. Boys."

She leaned back and softly strummed the opening chords on her guitar. For just a moment, the boys stood frozen in the spotlight, missing their cue by about a half second, but Trevor nudged his brother and a moment later, their sweet young voices blended perfectly as they sang the slow, pensive opening bars.

The crowd seemed hypnotized while the boys sang about spending Christmas Eve in the saddle, about feeling alone and unloved, about finding the true meaning of Christmas while helping the animals.

They had never sung the song so beautifully or with such stirring emotion. When they finished, even Ella—who had heard them sing it dozens upon dozens of times—had to wipe away a tear.

After the last note faded, the crowd erupted into thunderous applause.

"You did great," she murmured over the noise of the crowd. The boys beamed and hugged her, which made more tears slip out.

"Thank you for playing your guitar and teaching us the song," Trevor said solemnly over the noise of the crowd.

Oh, she would miss these sweet boys. She wasn't sure how her heart would bear it.

"You're very welcome," she said. "Now, go find your places for the final song."

The boys rushed to their designated spots as the other children surged onto the stage—angels and shepherds, candy canes and cowboys and ballet dancers in tutus. It was a strange mishmash of costumes, but somehow it all worked perfectly together.

Olivia, who had a pure, magical voice and performed professionally, took the guitar from Ella as they had arranged, and stepped forward to strum a chord. She sang the first line of the song, then the other children joined her to sing "Silent Night" with a soft harmony that rose to fill the St. Nicholas Lodge with sweet, melodious notes.

On the last verse, the senior citizens were encouraged to sing along, which they did with stirring joy.

When the last note died away and the audience again erupted in applause, Hope went to the microphone, wiping away a few of her own tears.

"If you're all not overflowing with Christmas spirit now, I'm afraid there's no hope for you," she declared stoutly, which earned appreciative laughter.

"Wasn't that a spectacular show?" Hope asked.

She had to wait for the audience to quiet before she could speak again. "So many people had a hand in bringing this to you. The fabulous caterer, Jenna McRaven, the high school students who volunteered to serve the meal to you, those who provided the transportation."

She paused and smiled at Ella. "I would especially like to thank the one person without whom none of this would have happened tonight. Our director, organizer, producer and general talent-wrangler, Miss Ella Baker."

The crowd applauded her and she managed a smile. These were her friends and neighbors. They had embraced her, welcomed her in their midst. How would she be able to say goodbye to them?

"Now, I do have a rather grave announcement," Hope went on. Her tone was serious enough that the crowd quieted again and fixed attention on her. "While we were here enjoying this fantastic dinner and truly memorable entertainment, Mother Nature decided to let loose on our little corner of paradise outside with a vengeance. I guess she was mad she wasn't invited to the show so decided to put on her own. As much as I know we all love to visit with each other, I'm afraid that's not a good idea tonight. There will be other chances. We're going to cut things short now and encourage you all to head for home as soon as you can, before conditions get even worse— though if all else fails, we can hitch up the reindeer and sleigh to carry you home. Safe travels to you all, friends. Good night and merry Christmas."

The audience applauded one last time and gave the children a standing ovation, then people began to gather up their coats and bags and stream toward the door.

For the next several moments, Ella tried to hug as many of the children as she could and thank them for their hard work. Through it all, she noticed The Christmas Ranch staff quietly ushering people out.

"I'm sensing urgency here," she said when her path intersected with Hope's through the crowd. "Is it really that bad?"

Hope's eyes were shadowed. "I've never seen a storm come on so quickly," she admitted. "We've already got a foot of new snow and the wind out there is howling like crazy. If the crowd wasn't so noisy in here, you would hear it rattling the windows. I want people to hurry home, but I don't want to incite a panic. It's going to take some time to get everyone out of here."

"I can take more than one group." Somehow, Beckett had appeared at her side without warning and she jumped. She told herself it was only surprise, but she suspected it was more nerves. She was dying to ask how he enjoyed the song, but the urgency of the storm evacuation took precedence.

"Thanks, Beckett. I knew there was a reason I adored you." Hope smiled at him so widely that Ella might have felt a twinge of jealousy if she didn't know Hope adored her husband, Rafe.

"I'll have to factor in taking the boys, too. I'll drop them off in the first batch, then come back for a second trip."

"I can take my father home, so you don't have to do

that," Ella said, though she was still so angry with her father, she didn't know if she could be in the same vehicle with him. "If you want, I can also drop the boys off at the Broken Arrow, as it's on our way home. That should free up a couple more spots in your truck for people who need rides home."

He looked torn. "That's true, but I would feel better if you could head straight home, instead of having to detour to our place."

"We'll be fine," she said. She couldn't believe the storm was really that bad. "I have four-wheel drive and new snow tires. I'm not worried."

One of The Christmas Ranch workers came up to ask Hope a question and she walked away to deal with the situation. When they were gone, Beck turned to her, his expression solemn.

"El, I… Thank you for helping the boys with that song. I've never been so touched. It means more than I can ever say."

Warmth seeped through her at the intensity in his voice. "They did all the hard work. I only guided them a little," she said. "Anyway, we made a fair trade. They agreed to give me riding lessons if I would help them learn the song."

Surprise flickered in his eyes. "That's the reason you've been coming out to ride?"

"The opportunity was too good to pass up. I wanted to ride again for a long time. They wanted to learn the song. This seemed the perfect arrangement."

It *had* been perfect, until she made the mistake of falling hard for the boys—and for their father.

"Well, thank you. Every time I hear that song now, I'll remember them…and you."

Before she could answer, Rafe Santiago came over looking harried. "It's crazy out there. Several people have decided to leave their vehicles here and come back for them when the storm passes, so we've got even more to take home. Do you think you could take home Martha Valentine and Ann and Max Watts? They all live on the same street near the park."

"Absolutely." He turned to her. "Are you sure you don't mind taking the boys home? That would help."

"No problem. I'll get them home safely," she promised.

"Thanks."

He gave her one more smile then turned to take care of his responsibilities.

That was just the kind of guy he was. When something needed doing, he would just tip his hat back and go to work.

It was one of the many reasons she loved him.

She couldn't stand here mooning over him when she had her own responsibilities, people who needed her. After one last look at him helping the frail Martha Valentine into her coat with a gentleness that brought tears to her eyes, she turned away to gather up her own charges.

The storm was worse than she had imagined.

The moment they stepped out of the St. Nicholas Lodge, snow blew at them from every direction and the wind nearly toppled them over. Everyone was huddling inside their winter coats as they made their way through the deepening drifts to the parking lot.

"Boys, grab hold of me and my father so you don't blow away." She had to raise her voice to be heard over the whining wind. She wasn't really worried about that, but

needed their help more to support her father—something
she couldn't tell him.

Fortunately, her vehicle was parked close to the entry
and it only took them a few moments.

She opened the driver's side first so she could start
the engine to warm up the heater and defrost, then hurried around to help her father inside. Her SUV passenger
seat was just a little too high for him and Curt didn't have
enough strength to pull himself into it alone.

"Thanks," he muttered when she gave him a boost,
clearly embarrassed about needing help.

By the time he was settled and the twins were buck-
led into the back seat, Ella was frozen through from that
icy wind—and she still had to brush the snow from the
windows so she could see to drive.

Finally, they were on their way. She took off at a pon-
derous pace, her shoulders taut and her hands gripping
the steering wheel. She could hardly see through the
blinding snow that blew across the windshield much
faster than her wipers could handle.

Her father looked out the window at the relentless
snow while the boys, oblivious to the storm outside or
the tension inside, chattered to each other about the show
and the approaching holidays.

"We had about ten people tell us our song was the best
one," Trevor said proudly.

"You did a great job," she said, tightening her fingers
on the wheel as a particularly strong gust of wind shook
the vehicle and sent snow flying into the windshield.

Usually she didn't mind driving in a storm, but this
was coming down so fast. Coupled with the wind and
blowing snow, it made visibility basically zero.

"Can we listen to the radio?" Colter asked.

"I need to concentrate right now. Can you just hum to yourselves?"

"We can sing our song again," the boys offered.

"I'd like that," Curt said, to her surprise.

While her eyes were glued to the road, she was vaguely aware from her peripheral vision that he had half turned in his seat to face the twins. "I always loved that song. You boys *were* the best thing on the show," he told them.

She couldn't spare a look in the rearview mirror right now. If she did, she was sure the twins would be grinning.

"We'll have to do it without the guitar," Trevor warned.

"That's okay. You can sing without it." Her father turned to her and spoke with a guarded tone. "That won't be too stressful for you while you're driving, will it?"

She shook her head and the boys started singing the song she had heard them practice so many times before. There was something special about this time, in the warm shelter of her vehicle while the storm raged outside.

"That was wonderful," her father said when they finished, his voice gruff. "I'm sure your dad loved it."

"He did," Trevor said. "He came and found us after and gave us big hugs and said he was so proud of us and had never been so touched."

"He said it was the best gift anybody ever gave him," Colter added. "He said it made him cry and that there's nothing wrong with a guy crying when something makes him too happy to hold it in! Can you believe that?"

She didn't answer as she felt emotion bubble up in her chest.

"It's a good song," her father said gruffly.

"Want us to sing another one? We can do 'Jingle Bells' or 'Rudolph' or 'Away in a Manger.'"

"Sure. We'll have our own private Christmas show," Curt said.

The boys launched into song and she was grateful to her father for distracting them so she could focus on driving.

She could usually make it between The Christmas Ranch and the Broken Arrow in about ten minutes, but she was creeping along at a snail's pace because of the weather conditions.

"Almost there," she finally said after about a half hour. "Your turnoff should be just ahead."

At least she was fairly certain. It was hard to be sure with the poor visibility and the heavy snow making everything look alien and *wrong* somehow.

She turned her signal on, though she couldn't see any lights in either direction, when suddenly her own headlights caught something big and dark on the middle of the road just ahead of them.

It was an animal of some kind. A cow or horse or moose. She couldn't be sure and it really wouldn't matter when two thousand pounds of animal came through the windshield.

Reflexively, she slammed the brakes. She wasn't going fast at all but the road was slick, coated in a thick layer of ice, and the tires couldn't seem to catch. The vehicle fishtailed dangerously and she fought to regain control.

She tried to turn the wheel frantically, with no success. It was a terrible feeling, to be behind the wheel of a vehicle she had absolutely no control over.

"Hang on," she called.

The boys screamed and her father swore as the vehicle

went down a small embankment and into a snowbank about ten feet down.

Her heartbeat raced like she had just finished an Olympic sprint and her stomach twirled in an awful imitation of her wheels spinning out of control.

"Is everybody okay?" she asked.

"Yeah," her dad said gruffly. "Gave me a hell of a start."

"We're okay," Trevor said.

She turned around to reassure herself but all she could see in the darkness were their wide eyes.

"Are we stuck?" Colter asked.

She tightened her shaking fingers on the steering wheel. "I don't know. I haven't tried to get us out yet. You're sure you're both all right?"

"Yeah. It was like the Tilt-A-Whirl at the county fair."

Now she remembered why she had always hated that ride.

"Well, that was fun. Let's get everybody home."

Ella put the vehicle in Reverse and accelerated but the wheels just spun. The snow was too deep here for them to find purchase. She pulled forward a little, then tried to reverse again. She thought she made a little progress but, again, the SUV couldn't pass a certain point.

She went through the same process several times until her father finally stopped her. "You're only making things worse," he said. "Face it. With that incline, this thing doesn't have the horsepower, at least not in Reverse. We're going to need somebody to pull us out."

The boys had fallen silent in the back and she could tell they were beginning to grasp the seriousness of the situation.

It could be hours before someone came by. As the snow piled up, their tracks would quickly be wiped away.

She could still call for help. She could tell Beck how to find them. She reached for her purse and fumbled for her cell phone, scrolling through until she found his number.

She tried to connect but the call didn't go through that time, or the second time she tried.

"What's wrong?" her father asked.

"Why don't I have any service?" she wailed.

"Must be in one of the dead zones around here."

Naturally. It was just her luck to get stuck in one of the few places where she couldn't call for help. "What about yours, Dad?"

"I didn't bring it."

"Why on earth not?"

He didn't answer for a long moment, then shrugged. "What's the point? You know I can't work that damn thing very well."

He could barely hold it in his trembling hands. Hitting the numbers was even harder. She had tried to coach him through speech-to-text methods but he couldn't quite master it.

It wouldn't make much difference. They had the same carrier. If she didn't have service, he likely wouldn't, either.

That gave her very few options.

"In that case, I don't see a choice," she said after a moment of considering them. "I better head to the Broken Arrow for help. Jax and Dan are there. Somebody should be able to pull us out with the one of the ranch tractors."

"You can't wander around in that storm. Just wait here. Beck will be home soon."

"Yes, but all the people he was taking home live south

of here, which means he'll likely be coming to the ranch from the other direction. He won't even pass this way."

"When he sees the boys haven't made it home, don't you think he'll come looking for us?"

"Probably." That did make sense and provided some comfort to the worry and grave sense of responsibility she was feeling for the others in her vehicle. "The problem is, he might be shuttling multiple groups of people home. I have no idea how long he'll be at it, and to be honest, I don't feel good about waiting here, Dad. The snow keeps piling up and the temperature is dropping. I need to get you and the twins home where it's safe. The fastest way to do that is to walk to the ranch house. It can't be far. I can be there and back with help in no time."

"I don't like it."

What else was new? She could write a book about the things her father didn't like about her, apparently.

"I'm sorry, but right now I have bigger things to worry about than your opinion of me," she said, more sharply than she intended.

Curt opened his mouth, then closed it again. Good. She didn't have time to argue with him.

"I need you to stay here with the boys and watch over them. I have a full tank of gas. I'll make sure there's no snow obstructing the exhaust, so no worries about carbon monoxide building up inside. You should be fine to keep the engine running and the heater on."

"We can come with you," Colter said.

She had no doubt that the boys would be able to keep up with her. Her father, on the other hand, would not, and she didn't want to leave him here alone.

Torn, she gazed at all three of them. She didn't want to go out into that storm but she didn't dare take her chances of Beck miraculously just stumbling onto them. From the road above, they would be impossible to spot once the snow obscured their tracks, especially with that blowing wind and poor visibility.

This was serious, she realized. This country could be unforgiving and harsh and she would have to draw on all her reserves of strength to help them get through this.

"I need you boys to stay here where it's warm. Do what my dad says, okay? I'll be back shortly."

"Here. Take my coat. It's heavier than yours," Curt said gruffly.

"Mine is plenty warm. You might need yours. I will take the flashlight in the glove box, though."

She reached across him to get it out, grateful she had changed the batteries to fresh ones a few weeks earlier.

"In the back, there's a bag filled with bottled water, some granola bars and a couple of emergency blankets. You're probably not going to need them, but you should know about them, just in case."

"You're prepared," her father said, surprise in his voice.

"I have a father who taught me well about the harshness of Idaho winters."

She wanted to tell him she could learn all sorts of things, if only he were willing to teach her, but this wasn't the time to rehash that argument.

"Sounds like a smart man," he said after a moment.

"About some things, anyway," she said tartly.

Focused on the job at hand, she wrapped her scarf around her face and buttoned up her coat. "I'm going to give you my phone. You don't have cell service here but if I'm not back in a timely manner, you can try climbing up the incline and see if you have better service up there. Give me half an hour to get help first, though. I would rather you didn't leave the vehicle."

After a tense moment, her father finally nodded. "Be careful. I've only got the one daughter, and I'm fairly fond of her."

His words made tears thicken in her throat. Why did he have to be so stubborn?

"I'll be careful. You, too. See you in a little bit." She paused. "I love you, Dad."

She climbed out of the vehicle and whatever he said in response was snatched away by the howling wind that bit through her clothing and stung her face like a thousand knives.

She slipped several times as she tried to make it up the slight hill. Her boots were lined and warm but they weren't meant for heavy-duty hiking, more for walking through the snowy streets of Boston.

By the time she made it back to the road, she was already out of breath and perspiring inside her coat. She stood for a moment to catch her bearings. Everything was disorienting. White upon white upon white.

Fear was heavy on her shoulders. This was serious, she thought again. She had heard horror stories of people being lost in blizzards, their frozen corpses only found months later. Perhaps she would have been better off staying in the car.

But even now, knowing it was just below her, she could hardly see her SUV. Someone with no idea what had happened to them would never find it.

She headed off in the direction of the ranch house, tucking her chin in against the wind, praying she didn't miss his driveway and struggling step by step through the deepening snow.

It was much harder going than she had imagined, but she remained solely focused on doing what she had to, to save her father and the twins.

Shouldn't she have found the ranch road by now?

Panic began to flutter through her. She had to be close, but where was it? She couldn't even see the roadway anymore. She was almost certain she was still on it, but what if she wasn't? What if she had somehow taken a wrong turn and was somehow heading in the wrong direction? She would die out here—and her father and the twins would eventually run out of gas and would freeze to death, too.

What had she done? She should never have trusted her instincts. She should have stayed in the SUV with Curt and the twins. Had she doomed them all?

The panic ratcheted up and she tried frantically to see if she could find a light, a landmark, anything. All she could see was white.

Dear God, she prayed. *Please help me.*

The only answer was the constant whine of the wind churning the snow around her.

She had to keep moving. This had to be the way. There. Was that a light? She peered through the darkness to a spot set back from the road about the correct distance to be the Broken Arrow ranch house.

Was that the log arch over his driveway? She thought so but couldn't quite be sure. Instinct had her moving in that direction, when suddenly a dark shape again loomed out of the darkness.

Ella's instinctive scream tangled in her throat as the dark shape trotted closer. In her flashlight's glow, she suddenly recognized the calm, familiar features of an old friend.

She had never been so very grateful to see another living soul.

"Creampuff! What are you doing out here?" Ella exclaimed. At her voice, the horse ambled closer.

She must have somehow gotten out. She remembered the boys telling her the horse could be an escape artist. Why on earth would she have chosen this particular moment to get out?

Was Creampuff the thing she had almost hit on the road, the shape that had frightened her into hitting the brakes and sliding off the road?

Ella didn't like the consequences, but she was very grateful she hadn't hit the horse.

"You shouldn't be out here," she said to the horse. "It's dangerous."

Creampuff whickered and nudged at her. She seemed happy to see Ella, too.

She suddenly had an idea. It was completely impractical, but if it worked, it might be the answer to her current dilemma.

The storm was so disorienting, she was worried that she would end up miles from her destination. What were the chances that the horse could get her to Beckett's ranch house?

It was worth a try. Better than wandering aimlessly out here on her own. The only trick would be mounting up without a saddle, stirrups or reins—especially when she could barely manage it when she had all those necessary items.

The horse would lead her back to the barn on the Broken Arrow. Somehow she knew it.

If she wanted to save her father and the twins, she had to try.

Chapter Thirteen

"What the hell do you mean, they're not here? They left forty-five minutes before I did!"

Beckett stared at his brother, fear settling like jagged shards of ice in his gut.

"I don't know what to tell you. Nobody is here but Dan and me. We haven't seen a soul. Maybe she took them to her ranch house instead."

Wouldn't she have called him if her plans had changed? He couldn't believe she would simply abscond with his children with no word.

Those ice shards twisted. "Something's wrong."

"You don't know that," Jax said, his tone placating.

"I do. Something's wrong. They should have been here half an hour ago. They're in trouble."

Jax started to look concerned. "Before you run off, why don't you try to call them?"

Good idea. "You call the Baker's Dozen. I'll try their cell phones."

He dialed Curt's first and it went immediately to voice mail. He left a short message, telling the man to call him when he heard the message, then tried Ella's. It rang twice and he thought it would be connected but it shortly went to voice mail, too.

"No answer at the ranch," Jax said. He was beginning to look concerned, as well.

Beck had just spent an hour driving through these terrible conditions. He knew how bad it was out there—just as he knew Ella and her father had left with the boys well before he could load his first group of senior citizens into his vehicle to take them home.

Something was wrong. He knew it in his bones.

He hung up the phone after leaving her a terse message, as well, then faced his brother.

"I'm going to look for them. Call me if they show up."

Jax was smart enough to know when to not argue. He nodded. "What do you need me to do?"

"Stay in touch. For now, that's all."

He rushed out the door, doing his best to ignore the panic. He knew what could happen under these conditions. A few years ago, a rancher up north of them had gotten lost in a blizzard like this and ended up freezing to death just a few feet from his own back door.

The storm hadn't abated a whit in the few minutes he'd been inside. It whistled down through the mountains like a wild banshee. This was going to be one hell of a white Christmas. No doubt about it. He wouldn't be surprised if they ended up with at least two or three feet out of one storm, with much deeper drifts in spots from that wind.

He headed down the long, winding driveway, his heart in his throat and a prayer on his lips.

He had just started down the driveway when his headlights flashed on something dark and massive heading straight for him. If he had been going any faster, he would have inevitably hit it. As it was, he had to tap his brakes, even in four-wheel-drive low, to come to a stop.

It was a horse, he realized as he muscled the truck to a stop and his eyes adjusted to the shifting light conditions.

A horse carrying a rider!

What in the world? Who would be crazy enough to go riding on a night like tonight?

He yanked open his door and stepped out of his truck, boots crunching in calf-high snow, even though Jax had already cleared the driveway once that night.

"Beck! Oh, Beck. I'm so happy to see you!"

"Ella!" he exclaimed.

She jumped off of the horse and slipped to the ground and an instant later, she was in his arms. He didn't know if he had surged forward or if she had rushed to him, but he held her tightly as she trembled violently in the cold.

"What's happened?" he demanded. "Where are the boys?"

Her voice trembled. "I—I slid into a ditch back on the r-road. I don't know how far b-back. I thought it was closer b-but it seemed like f-forever that I w-walked."

"Why were you walking in the first place? Why didn't you call me to come find you?"

"I t-tried. I didn't have cell service. We're off the road, out of sight. E-even if someone t-tried to find us, they wouldn't be able to. I—I knew I had to f-find help, but I think I must have been lost or missed the road or something. I was panicking but I—I prayed and suddenly Creampuff appeared."

She shivered out a sob that made his arms tighten around her. For just a moment, she rested her cheek against him and he wanted to stay keep her safe and warm in his arms forever.

"It f-felt like some kind of m-miracle."

She was a miracle. She was amazing. If she hadn't faced her fear of horses, she might be wandering out there still. Somehow she had found the strength to climb on a horse without tack or saddle and made her way here, to him.

What would he have done if Creampuff hadn't found her, if she was still wandering around out there, lost in the storm?

He couldn't bear to think about it. If anything had happened to her, it would shatter him. His arms tightened as the feelings he had been fighting for weeks burst to the surface.

He shoved them back down, knowing this wasn't the time or the place to deal with them.

"You're frozen. Let's get you up to the house."

"No! I—I have to show you where to find my dad and the boys. You'll never see my car from the road."

She was so certain of that, he had to accept she was right. "At least hop inside the truck while I put Creampuff in the barn. Jax can take care of her. She deserves extra oats after tonight."

He helped her inside his cab—something he should have done the moment she hopped off that horse, he realized with self-disgust. The heater was blasting and he found the emergency blanket behind the seat and tucked it around her.

"We have to hurry."

"We will. This will only take a moment, I promise."

He closed the door and called his brother as he led the heroic Creampuff toward the barn, thirty yards away.

"Need my help?"

"Maybe. Not yet. Take care of Creampuff for me and give her all the crab apples she wants right now. I'll stay in touch."

He hurried back out to his truck through the storm, trying not to think about how very close they had come to a tragedy he couldn't bear to think about.

Ella had never been so cold, despite the blanket and the blessed warmth pouring full-blast from the heater of Beck's pickup. Occasional shivers still racked her body and Beck continued casting worried looks her way.

"How much farther?" he asked.

She peered out the window at the landscape that seemed familiar but not familiar. Everything was white, blurred by blowing snow.

She recognized that fence line there, and the curve ahead, and knew they had to be close but she could see no sign of her SUV.

"There!" she suddenly exclaimed. "Down there, just ahead. See the glow of my taillights?"

He tapped his brakes and brought the truck to a stop. "Wow. You were right. There are no tracks left on the road and it's well out of view from up here. If you hadn't pointed it out, I would have missed it."

"The engine is still running. I had a full tank of gas so they should have had enough for a few more hours."

He opened his door and frowned when she opened

hers, too. "Ella, stay here. You're still half-frozen. I'll get them."

She shook her head. "Dad's going to need help getting up that little slope. It might take both of us."

Her father had grown so frail this past year that she suspected Beck could carry the other man up the slope over his shoulder in a fireman's carry without even having to catch his breath, but after a moment he nodded.

"I'm sorry you'll have to go out in the cold again."

"Only temporarily. I'll be okay."

She opened her door before he could argue further and climbed out, then headed down the slight slope to her snow-covered SUV.

The door opened before she could reach it and her father stuck his head out.

"Ella? Is that you?" he called, peering into the snowy darkness.

"Yes."

"Oh, thank heavens. I've been worried sick," he exclaimed.

With good reason, she acknowledged. She could have died out there—and there was a very good chance her father and the boys might have, too, before help could arrive.

"I brought Beck."

"I knew you could do it."

"How are the boys?" she asked as she reached the vehicle, with Beck right behind her.

"See for yourself," her father said. "They're sound asleep."

Sure enough, the boys were cuddled together under one of her emergency blankets.

Colter was the first one to open his eyes. He blinked

at her sleepily, then his gaze caught his father, just behind her.

"Hey, Dad!" Colter smiled. "I think I fell asleep."

"Looks like it. We'll get you to the truck and then home in no time."

"Okay." He yawned, then shook his brother awake. Trevor looked just as happy to see both of them. Neither boy seemed the worse for wear after their ordeal.

"Boys, let's get you back to the truck. It's probably better if I carry you, since your cowboy boots aren't the best for snow. Ella, why don't you stay here where it's warm for a few moments?"

She wanted to offer to take one of the boys and then come back down to help her father, but she wasn't sure she would have the strength to make that trip twice more.

"Me first," Trevor said.

Beck scooped him up onto his back and Ella slid into his warm spot as they headed up the slope. In seconds, the still-blowing snow obscured their shapes from view.

"You guys did okay?" she asked Colter.

He nodded. "You were gone a long time."

"I know. I'm sorry. I had some complications."

"We sang just about every song we knew, then Mr. Baker told us stories about Christmas when he was a kid."

He started reciting a few of the stories, one she remembered her father telling her and another that seemed new. Maybe Curt had told it to her once, but it had been lost along with everything else the summer she was eight.

It seemed like forever but had probably been only two or three minutes when Beck opened the door. "Okay, kid. You're next."

He repeated the process with Colter, leaving her alone with her father.

"You sure you're okay?" Curt said, his voice gruff.

"I got lost. You were right. I probably should have stayed with you until the help arrived."

"That's funny. I was about to say *you* were right. Nobody would have found us until morning, when it would have been too late."

She was spared from having to imagine all the grim possibilities when Beck opened the door.

"Turn off your engine and bring along the key."

"What about my SUV?"

"Jax and I can come down and pull it out after I get you home."

She nodded and did as he said, hoping he would be able to find it again without the gleam of the taillights to light the way.

"I wish I could give you a piggyback ride, too," Beck said to her father.

"I'll be fine. I just need a little support."

In the end, Beck all but carried her father, anyway. She was deeply grateful for his solid strength but also for the gentle way he tried to spare her father's pride as he helped him into the truck's passenger seat. Once he was settled, Ella slipped into the back seat of the crew cab pickup with the boys and Beck headed for the Baker's Dozen, driving with slow care.

Just before he reached their turnoff, she heard her phone's ringtone distantly. It took her a moment to remember it was in her father's pocket. He fumbled with it but finally managed to pull it out. Before he could hand it over, Curt checked out the display with the caller ID.

"It's Manny. Wonder why he's calling you?"

"Maybe because you usually leave your cell phone at home," she replied, reaching over the seat for her phone.

"Do you know where your padre is?" the foreman asked as soon as she answered. "Is he with you?"

"Yes. We've had a rough evening but should be home soon. Beck is bringing us."

"He can't. Turn around."

"Turn around? Why?"

"You can't get through. One of the big pines along the driveway blew over in the wind and there's no way around it. It's a good thing nobody was driving under it when it fell."

"What's going on?" Beck asked, coming to a slow stop just before the turn.

"The driveway is blocked. We won't be able to get through."

Could this evening get any worse? First she ran off the road, now they were stranded away from home.

"Okay. No problem," Beck answered. "You can just come back to the Broken Arrow with us. I'll feel better about that, anyway."

"Will you be okay for tonight?" Manny asked.

"I suppose," she answered, though she dreaded the prospect. "What about you?" she asked the foreman. "You're stuck on the ranch."

"We're fine. We have plenty of food and so far the electricity is still on. I can take care of everything up here, as long as I know the two of you are safe and have a place to sleep."

"Thanks, Manny. Be safe."

"Same to you."

She hung up. "I guess we're spending the night at the Broken Arrow, if that's okay with you."

"Just fine."

He turned the pickup around slowly and began inching back to his own ranch.

"Dad, what about your prescriptions?" Ella asked, as the thought suddenly occurred to her.

"I took my evening pills before I went to the show, since I wasn't sure what time we'd be back. I'll be fine."

"You're staying at our house?" Trevor asked, excitement in his voice.

"You can have our beds," Colter offered. "Only someone will have to sleep on the top bunk."

"We have plenty of space," Beckett assured them. "We don't have to kick anybody out of bed. We've got a couple spare bedrooms and a comfortable sofa in the family room. You're more than welcome, and in the morning we can head over with chainsaws and clear a path."

"Thank you," she murmured. She really didn't want to spend the night at his house, but unless she wanted to take another merciless trudge through that storm, she didn't see that they had any choice.

"Are you sure you're okay, Dad? Is there anything else I can get you?"

An hour later, she stood in a comfortable guest room with a leather recliner, a wide bed and a flat-screen TV. Her father was already stretched out on the bed with a remote and a glass of water. He wore his own shirt and a pair of pajama bottoms borrowed from Beck's uncle.

She wore another pair, but they were about six sizes too big, baggy and long.

"I don't think so. I haven't been this tired in a long time. I'm probably going to crash the minute the news is over."

If not before. Curt had become good at dozing off while the television still played.

"All right. Good night." She leaned in to kiss his stubbly cheek. As she turned to go, she was surprised when Curt reached his trembling fingers out to touch her arm.

"I didn't say this earlier, but...I was proud of you tonight."

Her father's unexpected words sent a soft warmth seeping through her. "Thank you. I'm happy you enjoyed the program, but it was the children who did all the work."

"I'm not talking about the show, though that was excellent, too. I meant later. When you went to find help. You risked your life for me and those twins of Beckett's. I was never more proud to call you my daughter."

He gave her arm a squeeze and she looked down, wanting to wrap his liver-spotted, trembling fingers in hers and tuck them against her cheek.

"I can do all sorts of things, if you only give me the chance," she said softly.

His hand stiffened and he pulled it away. "You're talking about running the ranch again."

Stupid. She wanted to kick herself. Why bring up a point of contention and ruin what had been a rare, lovely, peaceful moment between them?

"Yes. I am talking about running the ranch. I want to. Why won't you even give me the chance?"

To her chagrin, her voice wobbled on the last word. Exhaustion, she told herself. Still, she couldn't seem to hold back the torrent of emotions. "No matter what I do, you can't see me as anything but the silly girl who fell off a horse."

"You were in a coma for weeks. You nearly died."

"But I didn't! I survived."

"More than that," he said gruffly. "You thrived, especially after your mother took you away from here."

She stared, speechless at his words. "Is that what you think?" she asked, when she could trust her voice. "That I only thrived because Mom took me back to Boston? I grieved every day I was away. I love it here, Dad. I came back, didn't I?"

"To care for a feeble old man. Not because you belong here."

"The ranch is part of me, no matter what you say."

"So is Boston! You have a life there. I can't ask you to give up everything that's important to you. You love music—the opera, the symphony. Not J. D. Wyatt and his Warbling Wranglers. You belong to a different world."

"Yes, I love those things you mentioned. But I also love J.D. and George Jones and Emmylou Harris. The music you and I listened to together. Why can't I have both? Why do I have to choose?"

He appeared struck by this, his brow furrowed as he considered her words. She didn't know what might be different this time, when they had had similar arguments before, but something she said seemed to be trickling through his stubbornness.

"Honey, you don't know anything about running the ranch." She might have been imagining it, but his voice sounded a little less certain.

"You can teach me, Dad. I've been telling you that for months. There's no better time than now. I want to learn from you, while you're still here to teach me. This is my heritage, half of what makes me who I am. I don't understand why you can't see that."

He appeared struck by her words and she decided to

quit while she was ahead. Perhaps she had given him something to think about—but why should this time make the difference when all those other times hadn't?

"I don't want to fight with you, Dad. It's been a long day. Can we agree to focus on the holidays and talk about this again after Christmas?"

"That sounds like a good idea." Her father paused. "I love you, you know. No matter what else you think. I love you and I've always been proud of you."

Tears welled up in her throat at this hard, stubborn man she had considered her hero all of her life. "I love you, too, Dad. Get some rest."

Beck slipped into his own room across the hall as he heard her last words and realized she would be coming out at any moment. He didn't want her to leave her father's guest room and find him standing outside the door.

He hadn't meant to eavesdrop, had only been there to check on his guests and see if they needed anything. The slightly raised voices had drawn his attention and he stopped, not wanting to walk in on an argument between Ella and her father.

This is my heritage, half of what makes me who I am. I don't understand why you can't see that.

Her words seemed to howl through his mind like that wind, resonating with truth.

He couldn't buy the ranch out from under her.

Beck leaned against his bedpost as the assurance settled deep in his chest. On paper, purchasing the Baker's Dozen was the smart play. He needed to expand his own operations and grow the Broken Arrow and it made perfect sense to merge the two ranches.

A month ago, he would have jumped at the chance

without a second thought, assuming Ella had no interest in ranching and would be happy to take the money and run back to Boston.

He knew better now. He knew her hopes and her dreams and her yearnings. He had seen her face when they went on that ride into the backcountry as she looked at her family's land from the foothills. He had watched her tackle her own fear of horses in order to prove her own mettle. He had seen the courage she showed during a blizzard, her willingness to put her own comfort and safety at risk to help those she loved.

Her heart would break if Curt sold the ranch out from under her.

Beck couldn't do that to her.

He loved her too much.

The truth seemed to blow through him with all the impact of that storm rattling the windows of his room, crashing over him as if he were standing directly under the big pine that had fallen on the Baker's Dozen.

He loved Ella Baker.

He loved her sweetness, her grace, the gentle care she took with his sons. He loved her sense of humor and her grit and the soft, sexy noises she made when he kissed her.

He loved her.

What in heaven's name was he supposed to do about that now?

He assumed the normal course of action in this sort of situation would be to tell the woman in question about his feelings and see if she might share them—or at least see if she didn't reject them outright.

This wasn't a typical situation.

He thought of the precious gift she had helped his

boys give him that day, the song that always touched him about a cowboy being alone on Christmas. He didn't want to be alone, like that cowboy. He wanted sweetness and warmth and a woman's smile, just for him.

He wanted Ella.

Did he have the courage to try again? His marriage had left him uncertain about his own instincts, completely aware of all the ways he had screwed up.

He couldn't afford to make a disastrous mistake like that again, but something told him with sweet certainty that allowing himself to love Ella could never be anything but perfect.

She filled his life with joy and wonder, reminded him of everything good and right in his world.

His boys loved her, too. They had thrived under her loving care, in a way he hadn't seen them do with anyone else. Somehow, she had managed to reach them, to sand away a few of their rough edges.

They needed that in their lives. *He* did, too.

Could he find the strength and courage to overlook all the ugliness of his past to build a brighter future with Ella?

As he stood in his bedroom with the storm raging outside, he wasn't sure he knew the answer to that.

He still hadn't figured it out an hour later as he finally settled the boys for the night and closed the door to their room, confident they were finally asleep.

The combined excitement of their stellar performance at the Christmas show, being trapped in a snowbank during the blizzard and then having their favorite teacher staying in their house seemed to have made sleep elusive, but exhaustion at last had claimed them.

It was late, past midnight, but they could sleep in the next day. He had already received an alert that school would be canceled tomorrow because of the storm, still raging throughout the region. It hadn't surprised him. Nobody would be able to get through on the roads out there until at least noon or later.

He needed to sleep, too. The next day was bound to be a busy one and would start early.

Like his sons, though, he felt too wired to sleep. He had a feeling that if he tried to climb into bed now, he would only toss and turn.

His thoughts were in tumult and he still didn't know what to do about Ella and his feelings for her. Meantime, he decided to grab a drink of water and maybe one of those cookies a neighbor brought over earlier, then head into his ranch office to catch up on paperwork.

He was heading through the great room toward the kitchen when he spotted someone sitting in the darkness, just out of reach of the glow emanating from the Christmas tree and the dying embers of the fire burning in the hearth.

His gaze sharpened when he realized it was Ella. He had almost missed her.

Had she fallen asleep out here? Her day had been more strenuous than anyone's, between orchestrating that amazing performance earlier, then rescuing her father and the boys.

What was she doing out here? Was she all right?"

Her face was in shadows but he thought he glimpsed the streak of tears on her cheeks, reflecting the colored Christmas lights. As he moved closer, she must have sensed his presence. She looked up then quickly away but not before he was able to confirm his suspicion.

She was crying.

"Oh. You startled me." She swiped her cheeks and kept her face averted, obviously trying to hide them from him. He was torn between wanting to respect her obvious desire for privacy and being unable to bear the thought of her hurting.

Finally he sat beside her on the sofa. "El. What is it? What's wrong?"

"Nothing. I'm fine. It's just…been a long day."

"You need to be in bed. Why are you sitting out here by yourself?" *Crying*, he added silently.

She sighed. "Do you ever have those times when it feels like your mind is spinning so fast you can't keep up with it?"

"All the time. If it's not the ranch I'm worrying about, it's the boys or Jax or Uncle Dan."

Or her father, he wanted to add, but didn't want to upset her more. Most likely, that conversation with Curt was the reason for these tears.

He couldn't bear them, especially when he had the ability to dry them right here, right now.

"Ella, I don't—"

"Beck, I have to—"

They started to speak at the same time, then both faltered. After an awkward little moment, she gestured to him. "It's your house. You first."

He wanted to argue, but couldn't see any point. Better to tell her what was on his mind as quickly as he could.

"You should know, I've decided to tell your father I won't be purchasing the Baker's Dozen."

Her eyes looked huge in the multicolored light from the tree as she stared at him. "You *what*?"

"It was early days in the discussions between us.

Whatever you heard today when he and I were talking, nothing has been signed. There's no breach of contract or anything. So I'm officially backing out. I won't buy it."

"But...I don't understand. I thought you needed the watering rights and the pasture land to expand your operations."

"I do. I will, someday, but I'll figure something out when the need is more critical."

"Why?"

He needed to expand the Broken Arrow, but he couldn't do it in good conscience by buying her father's land out from under her.

"You should be running your family's ranch, Ella."

She made a disbelieving sound and though he feared it might be a mistake, he reached for her hand. "You are perfectly capable. You've got exactly all the traits it takes to make a go of things out here. You're tough, spunky and bold. You're willing to learn and you're not afraid to ask for help when you need it. You've shown all those things, again and again. Your father knows it, too—it's just taking him longer than it should to admit it."

Her fingers trembled in his as if she were still cold, and he wanted to wrap her in his arms until her shivering ceased.

"I don't understand," she finally said.

"What's to understand? I'm withdrawing my tentative agreement to purchase the property. It's yours. Curt can show you how to run it, just like he helped me figure things out here after my father died. If he doesn't, *I* will show you the ropes and find other local ranchers to do the same. Wade Dalton. Chase and Faith Brannon. Justin Hartford. You have good neighbors who will want nothing more than to see you succeed."

In the light of the Christmas tree, he saw something bright and joyful flash across her expression—hope and an eagerness to prove herself. For one beautiful instant, she looked exactly what she was, strong and capable of anything.

That's why he was doubly shocked after a moment when she pulled her hand away from his and rose as if to put space between them.

"I don't think I can do that."

"Why not? There's not a single doubt in my mind you'll make a go of it, with or without your father's help."

She gave him one quick look, her lips pressed together and her chin quivering, then she shook her head.

"I...can't. I'm not staying here. I've made up my mind to return to Boston right after Christmas."

Shock tangled his thoughts and his words. Had he misheard her? Not an hour ago, she had pleaded with her father to give her a chance at running the Baker's Dozen and now she was turning tail and taking off? What in Hades had happened?

"Why would you do that? I just told you that I won't be making an offer on the ranch—and I'll make sure nobody else around here does, either. There won't be much I can do about things if Curt decides to sell to an outsider, but I don't think that's what your dad wants, anyway."

As he watched, another tear dripped down her cheek, iridescent in the Christmas tree lights.

"I can't do it," she whispered.

"Are you kidding me? You can do any damn thing you put your mind to. You tamed the twin terrors, didn't you?"

He meant his words as a joke. It seemed to fall flat and she hitched in a breath that sounded more like a sob.

"That's why I…can't stay. Because of the boys and—and you."

Another tear dripped. He couldn't bear this. What had he done to offend her so grievously that she couldn't even stand to stay in the same county with him? He would fix it, whatever it was.

He rose. "I'm sorry. You're going to have to forgive me for being a big, dumb cowboy, but I don't know what the heck you're talking about."

She didn't answer him for several moments, the only sound the relentless wind and the click of branches from the red-twigged dogwoods outside the window.

Finally she swallowed. "I have come to…care deeply for—for Trevor and Colter. I don't see how I could continue to live here, always stuck on the edges of your, er, *their* lives. Just the nice neighbor who once taught them how to sing a song for their dad. I don't want that. I—I want more."

He couldn't catch his breath, suddenly. She was talking about the boys, right? Or did she mean something else? "Ella."

She didn't meet his gaze. "I'm sorry. Forget I said anything. I shouldn't have. It's late and I'm tired and not thinking straight. I'll go to bed now."

She tried to slip past him but he couldn't let her. Not yet. He blocked her path, never more grateful for his size than he was in that moment. "Stop. What are you saying?"

"It doesn't matter."

He tipped up her chin, until she had no choice but to look at him, his strong, amazing Ella. "I think it matters more than anything else in my world right now."

Her mouth wobbled a little again, then tightened with belligerence. "Do you want me to completely humiliate myself? Why not? I've already made a complete fool of myself. Fine. I'll say it. I'm in love with you. Are you happy now?"

She hadn't finished the words before he kissed her fiercely, pouring out all the emotions he had been fighting for weeks. Months, he realized. He had fallen for her when she first came back to Pine Gulch to stay with her father, he just hadn't been able to admit it to himself until now.

He kissed her until they were both breathing hard and the room was beginning to spin and he wasn't sure he would ever be able to bring himself to move from this spot.

"Does that answer your question?" he finally asked against her mouth. Joy continued to pulse through him, bright and shining and as beautiful as any Christmas tree. "*Happy* doesn't begin to cover how I feel to know the woman I love with all my heart shares a little of my feelings."

She stared at him, shock warring with the arousal in her eyes. "You love me? That's impossible."

"Need another demonstration?" He kissed her again, this time with a sweet, aching tenderness he felt from the depths of his soul. He lowered them to the sofa and held her on his lap, teasing and touching and tasting.

"I guess that wasn't really an answer, was it?" he murmured, after another long moment. "Kisses are wonderful, don't get me wrong, but any guy who's attracted to you—which would have to be every sane guy with a pulse—could give you those."

She swallowed, her hands tangled in his hair and her lips swollen from his mouth. "That's right." Her voice sounded thready, low, and made him ache all over again.

"You'll have to be more persuasive than that if you expect me to believe you want me and not my father's ranch."

He tightened his arms around her, loving this playful side of her. As he gazed at her eyes reflecting the lights of the Christmas tree, he thought that he had never loved the holidays so very much as he did right now, with his own Christmas miracle in his arms.

"I stand by what I said before. I don't want the Baker's Dozen, and I'll be sure to tell Curt that as soon as I get the chance. We can go wake him up, if you want."

"You really think I would be stupid enough to want to wake my father up right now? I'm a little busy here," she said, pressing her mouth to his jawline in a way that made his breath catch and everything inside him want to slide over her to show her just what her teasing did to him.

He gazed into her eyes, hoping she could see he meant his words. "Curt will come to his senses. I'll make sure of it. As far as I'm concerned, that ranch is yours, to do with as you see fit. If you want to sell all the cattle and start raising alpacas, that's your business."

Beck decided he wouldn't mind spending the rest of his life trying to make that soft, sweet smile appear again.

"I do love alpacas," she murmured. "They're so much cuter than cattle—and think of all the adorable Christmas sweaters I could make out of their wool."

"I can picture it now. And to show you what a great guy I am, I would even let you take those sweaters off in my bedroom, if you wanted."

She laughed. "Wow. That's very generous of you."

This was what he had missed—what he had never really known. This laughter and tenderness, this binding of his heart to hers. It seemed perfect and easy and absolutely right.

He kissed her once more, wishing they could stay here all night wrapped together by the fire and the Christmas tree while the storm raged outside.

"I meant what I said earlier," she said a long time later. "I love you and I love the boys. I wasn't expecting it, but you McKinley men are pretty hard to resist."

"We do our best," he drawled.

His sons would be over the moon to know their not-so-subtle matchmaking had paid off. He hoped that didn't set a dangerous precedent. Maybe he should warn Jax he had better watch out, or they might turn their attention to him next.

On second thought, Jax was a big boy. He could fend for himself.

He gazed down at her, unable to believe she was really here in his arms. He would never need another Christmas gift as long as he lived. This moment, this night, this woman were beyond his wildest dreams.

He turned serious, compelled to tell her a small portion of what was in his heart. "I love you, Ella. I hope you know that. I wasn't expecting it, either, but nothing has ever felt so right. I love your strength and your courage. I love how sweet you are with my sons. I love that you sacrificed to come back to Pine Gulch and take care of your father, though he's given you nothing but grief in return."

He kissed her again, his heart overflowing with joy and wonder and gratitude. "Most of all, I love that whenever you're near me, I could swear I hear music."

She gave that slow, tender smile he was quickly coming to crave, wrapped her arms around him and let the song carry both of them away.

Epilogue

"**I** don't know how you did it, but somehow that show was even bigger and better than last year's," Ella's father said as Beck drove away from The Christmas Ranch after her third successful Christmas show in a row.

"You'd better dial it back a bit, babe," her husband said, with that teasing smile she adored. "Everybody's got such high expectations now, you're going to find yourself having to throw a Broadway-quality production in order to meet them."

"I still think last year's show was better," Trevor said from the back seat. "This year Colt and me didn't even get to sing a duet together."

"No, but you played your guitar while all your friends sang 'We Three Kings,'" she answered. "You guys brought down the house, kiddo."

"We were awesome, weren't we?" he said, with that complete lack of humility that always made her smile.

"Hey, Grandpa Curt, what was your favorite part this year?" Colt asked.

Ella knew it always tickled her dad when the boys called him Grandpa Curt, as they had taken to doing since her and Beck's wedding over the summer.

They still usually called her Ella, but had recently asked if she would mind if they called her Mom once in a while. She still teared up every time they did.

As she listened to the twins chatter away to her father, Ella leaned back in the seat and closed her eyes, a wave of fatigue washing over her. The adrenaline rush of finishing a performance was always exhausting, but this seemed to be hitting her harder than usual.

She knew why. After two weeks of achy breasts, mild nausea in the mornings and this unusual fatigue, she'd taken a drugstore test that morning that confirmed her suspicions.

She still hadn't told Beck yet. She was trying to figure out exactly how. Maybe she would wait until Christmas Eve and tell him during their own private celebrations after everyone was in bed and the house was quiet.

Or maybe she would do it tonight. She didn't know how to contain this joy that bubbled through her.

However she told him, she knew Beck would be as happy as she was about adding to their family.

As he drove them toward home, he reached for her hand and brought it to his mouth. He was a big, tough rancher, but every once in a while he did these sweet, spontaneous gestures that completely swept her off her feet.

"You've had quite a day."

She smiled, eyes still closed. "Quite a year, actually."

"It has been amazing, hasn't it?"

Amazing was an understatement. A year ago, she never would have believed her life could be filled with this much joy.

Somehow they were making it work. Shortly after the New Year, her father had finally come to his senses—persuaded in large part by Beck, she knew—and started giving her more and more responsibility at the Baker's Dozen. As of now, she and Curt were comanaging the ranch. She envisioned a day when she and Beck would merge the two operations, as her father intended, but for now the system worked.

She still taught at the elementary school but had surrendered her middle school choir to another teacher.

She even had a small but growing herd of alpacas. The first breeding pair had been Beck's surprise wedding gift to her and she had added three more since then, plus the new offspring of the first pair. She adored them all and had become obsessed with learning all she could about alpaca husbandry.

"Hey, remember last year, when we had that big storm?" Colter said.

"Yeah, and we slid into the ditch and had to wait while you went for help?" Trevor added.

Her journey through the storm had become something of a family legend. Creampuff had earned crab apples for life because of her heroic rescue. Ella still rode her often, as well as the younger, more energetic mare she and Beck had picked out.

"There's the spot, right there," Curt said.

Though it had been a harrowing experience, Ella always smiled when she passed this spot. It had been such a pivotal moment in her life, she would have liked to put a little commemorative plaque on a nearby tree.

A short time later, they pulled up to the ranch house of the Baker's Dozen.

"Can we go see the cria while we're here?" Colter asked.

Cria was the official word for an alpaca baby and her new one was the most adorable thing in the world.

Her father complained the animals were a waste of space, but she couldn't count the number of times she'd caught him sitting by their paddock, just watching them play.

"Sure. Check their water for me while you're there, okay?"

The boys raced off through the cold night to the barn, where the alpaca sheltered in cold weather.

"Let's get you inside," Beck said to her father.

As he helped her father out of the truck, her heart seemed to sigh inside her chest. Every time she saw him offer this kind of patient, gentle care for her father, she fell in love all over again.

Curt's health issues had been the one gray cloud in what had otherwise been a year overflowing with happiness. He was trying a new medicine, though, and so far it seemed to be slowing the progression of his Parkinson's and even reducing some of his trembling.

She knew it was a temporary improvement, but she would take whatever bright spot she could.

The lights were on in the house, which meant Manny and Alina had made it home before them. The ranch foreman and his wife had moved into the big house shortly after Ella's marriage, along with Alina's older brother, Frank. Between the three of them, they took amazing care of Curt and he seemed to enjoy their company.

At some point, she anticipated that her father would

end up moving into the Broken Arrow ranch house with them. He spent much of his time there, anyway, and having him closer would make it easier for her to keep an eye on him. For now, he treasured whatever small portion of independence he still had, and she tried to facilitate that as much as she could.

Now, she saw the Christmas lights were on inside and the Baker's Dozen ranch house was warm and welcoming.

"I'd better go make sure the boys don't try to ruin their good shoes," Beck said after he helped Curt inside.

"I can help you into your room, Dad," she said.

For the next few moments, she was busy easing his swollen feet out of the boots he insisted on wearing and taking off his coat.

"Manny or Frank can help me with the rest," he said.

"All right. I'm glad you came with us, Dad."

"So am I. It really was a great show."

She smiled. "Thanks. I'll be by first thing in the morning to meet with the vet."

Her father tilted his head and gave her a considering look. "You know you're not going to be able to juggle everything when you have that grandbaby of mine, don't you?"

She stared. "How did you know?"

His eyes widened for just a moment, then his expression shifted to a smirk. "You make a poor poker player, honey. That was just a lucky guess—or maybe wishful thinking on my part—but you just confirmed it."

"Don't say anything to Beck," she pleaded. "I haven't told him yet."

"I won't say a word," he promised, then paused. "You picked a good man, Ella."

She smiled. "You don't have to tell me that, Dad. I'll see you in the morning. And don't forget, we have the McRavens' annual party tomorrow night, remember?"

"You ask me, this town has too many damn parties," her father grumbled, though she knew he enjoyed every one of them.

"Good night. Love you."

When she returned to the living room, Beck and the boys had all come back inside and sat in the glow of the Christmas tree they had all decorated here a few Sundays ago. The twins were telling him a story about one of their friends and he nodded solemnly, his gorgeous, masculine features intense as he listened.

As she watched the three of them, her heart couldn't contain all the joy.

Her life was everything she might have wished for and so much more. She had a husband she adored and two stepsons who filled her world with laughter and Legos and tight hugs. She had music and horses, her father, her friends and now this new little life growing inside her.

This was the season of miracles and she would always be grateful for her own—and it had all started with a song.

* * * * *

*If you loved this book, be sure to catch up with the
Nichols sisters, Hope, Celeste and Faith, in the latest
heartwarming holiday stories in*
THE COWBOYS OF COLD CREEK *series:*

THE HOLIDAY GIFT
(Faith's story)

A COLD CREEK CHRISTMAS STORY
(Celeste's story)

THE CHRISTMAS RANCH
(Hope's story)

*Available now wherever Mills & Boon Cherish
books and ebooks are sold!*

MILLS & BOON®

Cherish™

EXPERIENCE THE ULTIMATE RUSH OF FALLING IN LOVE

A sneak peek at next month's titles...

In stores from 16th November 2017:

- **Married Till Christmas** – Christine Rimmer *and*
  Christmas Bride for the Boss – Kate Hardy
- **The Maverick's Midnight Proposal** – Brenda Harlen
  and **The Magnate's Holiday Proposal** –
  Rebecca Winters

In stores from 30th November 2017:

- **Yuletide Baby Bargain** – Allison Leigh *and*
  The Billionaire's Christmas Baby – Marion Lennox
- **Christmastime Courtship** – Marie Ferrarella *and*
  Snowed in with the Reluctant Tycoon – Nina Singh

Just can't wait?
Buy our books online before they hit the shops!
www.millsandboon.co.uk

Also available as eBooks.

MILLS & BOON®

EXCLUSIVE EXTRACT

With just days until Christmas, gorgeous but bewildered billionaire Max Grayland needs hotel maid Sunny Raye's help caring for his baby sister Phoebe. She agrees – only if they spend Christmas with her family!

Read on for a sneak preview of
THE BILLIONAIRE'S CHRISTMAS BABY

'Miss Raye, would you be prepared to stay on over Christmas?'

Oh, for heaven's sake...

To miss Christmas... Who were they kidding?

'No,' she said blankly. 'My family's waiting.'

'But Mr Grayland's stranded in an unknown country, staying in a hotel for Christmas with a baby he didn't know existed until yesterday.' The manager's voice was urbane, persuasive, doing what he did best. 'You must see how hard that will be for him.'

'I imagine it will be,' she muttered and clung to her chocolates. And to her Christmas. 'But it's...'

Max broke in. 'But if there's anything that could persuade you... I'll double what the hotel will pay you. Multiply it by ten if you like.'

Multiply by ten... If it wasn't Christmas...

But it was Christmas. Gran and Pa were waiting. She had no choice.

But other factors were starting to niggle now. Behind Max, she could see tiny Phoebe lying in her too-big cot. She'd pushed herself out of her swaddle and was waving her tiny hands in desperation. Her face was red with screaming.

She was so tiny. She needed to be hugged, cradled, told all was right with her world. Despite herself, Sunny's heart twisted.

But to forgo Christmas? *No way.*

'I can't,' she told him, still hugging her chocolates. But then she met Max's gaze. This man was in charge of his world but he looked…desperate. The pressure in her head was suddenly overwhelming.

And she made a decision. What she was about to say was ridiculous, crazy, but the sight of those tiny waving arms, that red, desperate face was doing something to her she didn't understand and the words were out practically before she knew she'd utter them.

'Here's my only suggestion,' she told them. 'If you really do want my help… My Gran and Pa live in a big old house in the outer suburbs. It's nothing fancy; in fact it's pretty much falling down. It might be dilapidated but it's huge. So no, Mr Grayland, I won't spend Christmas here with you, but if you're desperate, if you truly think you can't manage Phoebe alone, then you're welcome to join us until you can make other arrangements. You can stay here and take care of Phoebe yourself, you can make other arrangements or you can come home with me. Take it or leave it.'

Don't miss
THE BILLIONAIRE'S CHRISTMAS BABY
by Marion Lennox

Available December 2017
www.millsandboon.co.uk

Copyright ©2017 Marion Lennox

Join Britain's BIGGEST Romance Book Club

- **EXCLUSIVE offers every month**
- **FREE delivery direct to your door**
- **NEVER MISS a title**

50% OFF your first parcel

Call Customer Services
0844 844 1358*

or visit
millsandboon.co.uk/bookclub

*This call will cost you 7 pence per minute plus your phone company's price per minute access charge.

BKCB4